GHOST IN THE MACHINE

POLICE SCOTLAND
BOOK 2

ED JAMES

For Kitty.

DAY 1

Wednesday
27th July

1

Where was he?

Caroline was still waiting in the bar where they'd arranged to meet. She checked her watch — he was twenty minutes late.

It felt like hours.

She shouldn't have got there half an hour early. She took another sip from her cocktail, staring into the ice.

The music playing on the bar's stereo switched song. She recognised it, something about making him magnificent tonight. She looked over at the barmaid and pointed up at the speakers. 'What's this?'

The barmaid checked a CD case. 'Sleeper. *Atomic*.'

Caroline nodded. 'Thanks.'

Taking a deep breath, she hoped Martin would be magnificent. She rummaged around in her handbag and found her mobile. She opened the Schoolbook app and found her train of messages with him, re-reading the instructions again, just like she had four times on her laptop at home.

No, there it was — meet in the bar of the Jackson Hotel at half seven.

She went into Martin's profile, looking at the baby-blue eyes in the photo, the wide smile, the perfect teeth. Almost too good to be true.

The only messages on his profile were hers — she wondered if she looked like some mad stalker woman.

She scanned around the room again for anyone even vaguely resembling Martin's profile shot. Nobody came close.

Caroline looked over at the barmaid. 'I'm supposed to be meeting someone.' She held up her mobile. 'Has he been in?'

The barmaid inspected Martin's profile for a few seconds before shaking her head and returning the phone. 'Don't recognise him. He's pretty, though.' She wiped the counter with a cloth then pointed at Caroline's mobile. 'Did you meet him on Schoolbook?'

'If you can call it meeting.'

'Happens a lot these days, I suppose.'

'We'd been talking about films on a message board.'

The barmaid moved off to fuss over the coffee machine.

Caroline took another sip and looked back at the message chain stretching back almost two months, the flirtatious subtext getting ever stronger towards the inevitability of their meeting.

She'd not felt that level of connection with anyone for a long time. It felt like he knew everything about her.

Her heart was thudding in her chest. She took another sip to steady her nerves.

The CD switched track again and she started humming along. She made eye contact with the barmaid. 'What's this one?'

The barmaid looked at the box again, her eyes squinting. 'New Order, *Temptation*.'

Caroline frowned, thinking she knew the album. 'What CD it?'

The barmaid held up the box. '*Trainspotting* soundtrack. It's just what was here. Got some decent tunes on it, though.'

'That's my favourite film. It's what we were chatting about on Schoolbook.' Caroline looked down at her glass again and bit her lip. 'Rob bought me that.'

'Who's he?'

'My ex-husband. He's a wanker.'

The barmaid snorted. 'Don't get me started on mine.' She moved off to serve another customer.

Caroline stabbed at her phone, tempted to delete Rob from her friends list there and then. She should never have accepted his invite in the first place, but she'd been trying to be *friends* for Jack's sake.

She noticed her fists were clenched. She let them go, taking another drink, hoping nobody noticed.

She looked across the bar area, seeing herself in the mirror. She sighed, reflecting on how little had outwardly changed in her — she'd lost weight after having Jack and didn't look much older than her thirty-two years. The divorce had added dark rings around her eyes she just couldn't get rid of.

Her mobile lit up — a text from Amy. *'Jack's just gone to sleep. No more phone calls. A x'*

Caroline swallowed hard, feeling guilty at being out and leaving her son with a friend.

The music changed again. Anger burned through her as she thought of Rob moving on, leaving her with Jack. Not that she resented him it was just—

Caroline put the phone back on the bar.

It buzzed almost immediately — a text from Steve Allen, one of her oldest friends. *'Just on my way to Parkhead, wanted to wish you good luck for tonight. Not that you'll need it.'*

She texted back. *'I don't think I will. You might.'*

She tapped send and the phone rang, an unknown number. Her hands shook as she put it to her ear.

'Caroline, hi, it's Martin.'

His voice was familiar, almost reassuring. She loved Northern Irish accents.

'Hi.' Her voice was a nervous croak. She cleared her throat. 'Hi, Martin.'

'I'm really sorry, but I'm running late. I've just got back from the office, had a last minute meeting thrown at me and I'm only getting ready now. And I left my personal mobile in my hotel room like an idiot.'

Caroline wasn't sure what to make of it. 'That's okay.'

'Tell you what, I'm just about ready now so why don't you come meet me at my room and we'll go on from there?'

'Sure.'

'It's just at the back of the ground floor. Room twenty.'

The phone clicked dead.

Her heart was racing again. She was finally going to meet him. *In person.*

She wondered about meeting him in his room but they'd talked so often on Schoolbook it felt like they'd known each other for years.

She grinned at the barmaid as she got up, leaving the ice at the bottom of her glass. She walked through reception, a brass plate on the wall indicating room 20 was along a wood-panelled corridor.

When she got there, the door was ajar.

She called into the room. No answer.

She frowned and looked back along the corridor, her heart racing.

She took a deep breath and knocked on the door. It opened further.

'Come in.'

She entered.

The door slammed behind her. A hand clasped over her mouth. 'Hello, Caroline.'

As she twisted around, she saw his face. Her eyes bulged.

A rope bit into her neck.

A fist slammed into her skull.

DAY 2

*Friday
29th July*

2

D etective Constable Scott Cullen stood on Leith Walk, staring up the road at the police station. He held an Airwave handset and glared at Keith Miller, the Acting DC who had been shadowing him for the last month. 'You've done it again, haven't you?'

Miller shrugged. 'Done what?'

'Arsed it up.' Cullen shook his head. 'We've been staking that flat for a week. Kenny Falconer killed someone. You let him get away.'

Miller sniffed. 'You were in the shop. He must have seen you.'

'I wasn't the one pissing about on his phone when Falconer did a runner.'

The Airwave crackled to life. 'PC Angela Caldwell for DC Cullen. Over.'

Cullen glared at Miller as he put the device to his mouth. 'This is Cullen. Over.'

'I've just spotted Falconer at the entrance to Pilrig Park.'

Cullen started running, turning right into Pilrig Street. 'On our way.' He jogged down the pavement, heading for the park at the end, a large patch of grass between side streets.

Cullen called into his Airwave again. 'Give me an update. Over.'

His reply was a burst of feedback from Angela, still out of sight a couple of hundred metres ahead of them in the park.

Cullen was breathing hard. 'Have you got him?'

'He's still here. You don't need to worry. Just apprehending him now.'

Angela screamed.

Cullen quickened his pace. 'What's happened? Are you okay?'

'Little bastard's hit me and made a run for it!' Another blast of static. 'Shite.'

Cullen entered the park and spotted Angela, doubled over in pain.

Miller quickly overtook Cullen, his long legs giving him an advantage. He changed direction to follow a figure in a hooded top closing on the football pitch, the goalposts still down for the summer.

Cullen stopped alongside her. 'Are you okay?'

'I'll be fine,' said Angela. 'He got me right in the guts. Go on, get after him.'

Cullen darted after Miller, now being led towards the road through the park.

Miller caught up with Falconer just as they entered a thin wood and Cullen quickly lost sight of them.

Cullen tentatively entered the patch of trees and heard a shout. 'Here!'

He slowed to a walking pace. Through the branches, Miller stood with his hands out in front of him, baton extended. Falconer had a knife out, his hand and Miller's eyes doing a synchronised dance. He kept lunging towards him, thrusting the knife closer.

This was all Cullen needed — as well as running operation disasterzone, he was now risking the death of a fellow officer. It wasn't going to happen. He circled round and came at them from the road side, hoping the steady stream of mid-morning traffic would mask his approach.

Falconer was shouting. 'Think you can catch me, you pig scum? I'll gut you.'

Miller had his hands held high. 'I'm not trying to start anything here, Kenny. Put the knife down on the ground and we can all have a chat about it.'

'This knife is going in you, pal, and then I'm getting out of here.' Falconer slashed forward, causing Miller to dodge backwards. 'Stay still, would you?'

Miller backed off a little, letting Falconer approach him.

Cullen came up behind Falconer, readying himself to grab hold.

Miller's eyes darted from the knife to Cullen.

Falconer spun round and lashed out, catching his knife in the bark of a tree.

There was a moment of silence as they stared at each other — Cullen with his baton still retracted and Falconer with his knife stuck.

Falconer tugged at it. Cullen extended his baton and lashed out. Falconer dodged at the last minute, much faster than Cullen had expected, and lurched forward, slashing the knife at Cullen, missing by inches. Miller jumped in but caught an elbow in the face from Falconer, sending him sprawling on the ground.

'Pig scumbag.' Falconer lashed out at Cullen with the knife, each slash getting closer and closer.

Cullen moved quickly forward, flicking out with his baton, cracking Falconer's wrist and making them both drop their weapons. Cullen kicked the knife towards Miller, lying prone on the ground. Falconer moved his knees up quickly, almost battering Cullen in the groin. He grabbed Cullen by the hair and tried to punch him. Cullen yanked Falconer backwards, pulling him down. He rolled over, putting Falconer in a hold he'd learned long ago in his training days. Breathing hard, he reached behind his back for his handcuffs.

Falconer elbowed Cullen in the stomach and pushed him over, kicking him in the side — twice — before running off.

Cullen tried to get up but couldn't.

Falconer dashed into the middle of the road — cars screeched to a halt.

Cullen thought about giving chase but decided assessing Miller's condition was his highest priority. He jogged over, Miller still lying on his back, staring up and making a lot of noise.

'Are you okay?' said Cullen.

'I'll live,' said Miller. 'Did you catch him?'

'He got away.'

'Shite,' said Miller. 'I took a kicking for nothing. Next time that happens, go after him, right?'

Angela appeared beside them. 'That's gratitude.'

'Tell me about it,' said Cullen. 'Did you see where he went?'

'Rosebank cemetery, I think,' said Angela. 'There's like a hundred ways out of there.'

Cullen closed his eyes. If he could have run after Falconer, he would. 'I'm going to get such a doing.'

This wasn't going to look good on his record.

3

Cullen yawned as he walked down the corridor in Leith Walk police station, heading back to his desk, trying to ease out the lactic acid in his legs. It was Friday lunchtime at the end of four straight day shifts and he was knackered, and not just from the incident in Pilrig Park. He carried his lunch — a BLT clutched in one hand, a coffee in the other, steam wafting out of the hole in the lid.

Detective Sergeant Sharon McNeill was walking alongside. She stopped, looked around at him and laughed.

Cullen frowned. 'What?'

'You haven't listened to a word,' she said, with a grin.

'Sorry,' said Cullen. 'I'm starving. I've not eaten since six this morning and I've had too much excitement for one day.'

McNeill was tall, early thirties, her dark hair loosely tied back in a ponytail. She was maybe carrying a few extra pounds, but if Cullen could ever be described as being selective enough to have a type, she was it. She wore a charcoal trouser suit and a cream blouse, open at the neck. 'Yeah, well, at least you're not in tomorrow.' She led on.

'What was it you said anyway?'

McNeill's eyes darted over at him. 'I asked if you had any plans for your days off.'

'Avoiding detective inspectors.'

McNeill grinned. 'Other than that?'

'Just out drinking with my flatmates tonight,' said Cullen. 'If the pain in my side eases any, that is.'

'Messy one?'

Cullen smiled. 'Hope so.'

She stopped outside their office space, a small portion of the third floor. Egg mayonnaise roll in one hand, tea beaker in the other, McNeill struggled to push the door. Cullen had learnt the hard way not to offer his assistance. Eventually, she barged it open.

Cullen's four-man team occupied a bank of desks by the window. Leith Walk station had opened the previous summer and now housed the bulk of Edinburgh's CID, though there was still a presence in Torphichen Street and St Leonards stations.

Cullen and McNeill both reported to Detective Inspector Brian Bain, who sat at his desk poring through a file, an open can of Red Bull in front of him. He was early forties, tall and thin with a neat moustache and grey hair shaved almost to the bone. He wore a black suit and white shirt with a red tie hanging loose from the collar. He glanced up, made eye contact and looked back down again.

Cullen sat at the desk across from Bain and logged in to his computer.

Bain made eye contact again. His face grew into a rictus of a smile. 'Need to get an appraisal done on you, Cullen.'

Cullen had been working for Bain for the last three months since receiving his full DC tenure. He wouldn't exactly describe it as having lucked out — far from it. 'Let me know where and when.'

'Less of the cheek,' said Bain. 'It's your responsibility to arrange time with me.'

Cullen was determined not to rise to the bait. 'Fine.'

Bain had already given Cullen the requisite doing for the morning's disaster. Falconer was finally apprehended just off Broughton Street, a mile or so from the incident, and it looked like he might finally be going away.

Not that Bain saw any of it in a good light — Cullen had bollocksed it up. He'd been shouted at in a meeting room for a good forty minutes, becoming numb to it after twenty. If it wasn't for the fact Cullen had been pestering Bain for three months to lead some investigations, he'd be able to let it go. As it was, the failure stung — he'd not get another chance for months, if at all.

Bain threw a file across the partition onto Cullen's desk. 'Anyway, here you go. Get reading that. You and Butch are digging this one up. Don't buggering it up.'

Butch was Bain's less than affectionate nickname for McNeill, now sitting at the desk to Cullen's right. Ignoring him, she took a bite of her roll, daintily covering her mouth with her hand as she chewed, staring into space.

Cullen bit his tongue. 'I'll get on it.'

Bain got to his feet and stretched out. 'Right, I'm off for a shite.' He crumpled the can. 'That stuff goes straight through me.'

Cullen started eating his own roll, sifting through the file as he chewed. It was a cold case still open from the previous November, the trail long since frozen over, though Cullen couldn't see why the Cold Case Unit had pushed it back to active CID. By the time he finished his lunch, he had no new insights the previous investigating team hadn't found. Standard protocol would involve re-interviewing victims, relatives and witnesses — weeks of work.

There was a sound from across the partition and Cullen looked up. At Bain's desk stood Detective Chief Inspector Jim Turnbull, Bain's boss, clutching a sheet of paper. He was the hairiest man Cullen had ever seen — thick tufts sprouting from everywhere — the top of his collar, between the buttons on his shirt, down his neck.

'Jim, how can I help?' said McNeill with a warm smile.

'Sharon, always a pleasure.' Turnbull nodded at Bain's desk. 'I was looking for DI Bain, but I see he's not around.' His voice was deep and syrupy, the accent Borders, most likely Melrose.

McNeill grimaced. 'He's off to the toilet.'

Turnbull grinned. 'Ah, I see. I take it he drilled down to a sufficient level of granularity in terms of what he would be producing?'

McNeill just raised an eyebrow.

Turnbull bellowed with laughter.

Bain approached, drying his hands on his trousers. 'Boss.'

'At least you washed your hands for once,' said Turnbull.

'Always do,' said Bain. 'Now, what can I do you for?'

'Just had Queen Charlotte Street on the phone,' said Turnbull. 'They've got a MisPer case, wondered if we could have a look at it.'

Bain exhaled. 'We're pretty much flat out here, sir.'

McNeill shook her head in disbelief at Bain, out of sight of Turnbull. 'Lying bastard,' she said, just loud enough for Cullen to hear.

Cullen leaned over. 'Why's he lying?'

'His stats are looking good at the moment,' she said, 'doesn't want anything else to lower his average like your trip to Pilrig Park did this morning.'

Turnbull sat on the edge of Bain's desk, both turned away from Cullen and McNeill, continuing their chat with lowered voices.

Miller, the fourth member of their team, wandered over and sat at the desk next to Bain, across from McNeill. He was tall and skinny with it, his spiky dark hair as long as was permitted for a police officer. He always looked uncomfortable in a suit, as if it wore him rather than the other way round. 'You been for a roll yet?'

McNeill shushed Miller and leaned closer to Turnbull and Bain, her finger pretending to scan through the lines of the report in front of her.

Turnbull stood up and turned around, causing McNeill to pretend she was reaching for the phone. Cullen could hear them clearly now.

'I understand what you're saying, Brian, but this is of the utmost importance. We've got to build bridges with our uniformed brethren, you know that. We can't just cherry-pick the low-hanging fruit all the time or storm in and demand resource as we see fit. It cuts both ways.'

'I'll see what we can do,' said Bain.

Turnbull handed the sheet of paper to Bain then play-punched his shoulder. 'Thanks, Brian. I've already assigned the case to you.' He checked his watch, nodded at Bain and set off towards the stairwell.

Miller sprang from his seat like a greyhound out of the traps, intercepting Turnbull by the door.

Bain glared at them and muttered something under his breath. He turned around and logged in to his computer, tapping furiously at the keys. He lifted the mouse up and slammed it on the desk a couple of times. He glared at the sheet of paper, now face up on his desk.

Miller wandered back over, smiling to himself.

'What were you up to?' said Bain.

'Nothing. Just asking Jim there about getting my DC role made permanent.'

Bain glowered. 'All that shite's supposed to go through me.'

'You weren't doing anything about it,' said Miller.

'You're a cheeky wee bastard.' Bain grinned then turned his glare to McNeill. 'Right, Butch, you probably overheard anyway but we've been given a case. Seems like tedium. I want the Sundance Kid here on it to help with his development, so you're on your own with that cold case.'

Cullen closed his eyes in frustration — *Sundance Kid* again. He hated the nickname.

Bain handed him the sheet. 'Young woman from Leith has been missing since Wednesday night. Name of Caroline Adamson.'

'You know what they say about women from Leith,' said Miller, looking for a laugh.

Bain glared at him. 'Miller, this is serious. CID wouldn't be getting called out if it was some scrubber disappearing after a night out, all right?'

'Sorry, Gaffer.' Miller's eyes looked anywhere but at Bain.

'It's got the address of her pal who called it in.' Bain looked straight at Cullen. 'There's a uniform round there now.' He nodded at Miller. 'Take Monkey Boy here with you. And try and keep him away from superior officers.'

'Is this anything to do with what happened in Pilrig Park?' said Cullen.

'It might or it might not,' said Bain. 'Far as I'm concerned, what goes on in Pilrig Park stays in Pilrig Park.'

4

Cullen turned the pool car off Leith Walk onto Dalmeny Street, taking a left at the end and driving down Sloan Street, a generic block of tenements between Leith Walk and Easter Road. They struck lucky — a car pulled off from outside number ten, allowing Cullen to park in the space. They could just as easily have walked down from the station — it was less than half a mile — but it was standard policy to drive.

'Used to live round the corner from here,' said Miller.

'Very interesting,' said Cullen.

He picked up his notes off the back seat and opened the MisPer report. It told him very little. Someone in Queen Charlotte had done some legwork already, checking the hospitals and crossing off the few dead bodies that had turned up across Scotland and the north of England since Wednesday. He checked the MisPer's description — five foot four, thin, dark hair and brown eyes.

The address they'd been sent round to was the home of an Amy Cousens.

'Come on,' said Cullen, 'let's go.'

'What's the story with you and Sharon?' said Miller as they walked down the street.

Cullen reddened. 'Story?'

'You're following her round like a little lost puppy,' said Miller. 'Slipping her a length, are you?'

'No.'

Miller laughed. 'Aye, aye. I've touched a nerve there.'

Cullen had clocked early on that Miller didn't exactly have a positive attitude to women. He wasn't Mr Sensitive himself, but Miller seemed like a caveman. He'd decided ignoring him would be the best policy.

Like so many tenements in the city, the front door intercom had been vandalised, the stairwell open to the street. They climbed the stairs to the third floor and chapped on the flat door.

A bald-headed PC answered, looking like he should have retired years ago. He came out onto the landing, pulling the door to behind him and grunted an introduction. 'PC Willie McAllister. Who are you then?'

Cullen got out his warrant card and introduced himself and Miller. 'Care to bring us up to speed?'

'Her pal disappeared,' said McAllister. 'Didn't show up to collect her wee boy yesterday. The lassie through there gave Queen Charlotte station a buzz this morning. Someone came over, did a report, that's all I know. Our Inspector was a bit suspicious about it, so he called you lot in.'

'I've read the file,' said Cullen. 'Dredged up anything else since?'

'Nothing so far. You'd better speak to the lassie herself.' McAllister pulled his Airwave out of his jacket pocket. 'I'd better get off and do some proper police work, let you boys go in and chat her up.' He headed down the stair, a slight limp in his stride.

'Old bastard,' said Miller.

Cullen gently knocked on the door as they entered. The flat was small, sparsely furnished and reasonably tidy. It was like every one bedroom flat in Edinburgh Cullen had been in over the years.

'Amy Cousens?'

The young woman sitting in an armchair in the living room was staring into space, her fingers drumming. She glanced at him then got to her feet. 'That's me.'

Cullen figured she was quite pretty. She was in her late twenties, good figure and with blonde hair most likely out of a bottle.

A small boy lay on the floor in the bay window, playing with some Doctor Who dolls, seemingly oblivious to the two strangers in the room. Cullen assumed it was Caroline Adamson's young son — he didn't remember the boy's name from the file. He was next to useless with children, figuring the kid could be anything from two to five years old.

Cullen sat on the tattered leather sofa, with Miller at the far end.

Amy returned to the armchair, her hands twitching against the fabric, her foot tapping. 'Can I get you some tea? I've just made a pot.'

Cullen couldn't quite place her accent, West Coast somewhere, though less harsh than Glasgow. 'I'm fine, thanks.' He smiled.

'I've just had one,' said Miller.

Cullen pulled his notebook from his coat pocket and turned to a fresh page. 'I need to ask you some questions about Caroline Adamson. I'll apologise in advance if I go over anything you've already covered with another officer, but it's important I get a full account from you.'

She sighed. 'Fine.'

'You reported Ms Adamson missing,' said Cullen. 'Do you have any idea where she might be?'

Amy rolled her eyes. 'That's why I phoned the police.'

Cullen smiled, trying to disarm her. 'Can you tell me where she was going when she disappeared?'

Amy took a deep breath. 'She was out on a date with some guy. It was somewhere up the Bridges, near the Uni. Don't know where exactly. She just said it was on the Southside.'

'Was it a bar or a restaurant?'

'I don't know.'

'Okay. What do you know about the person she was meeting?'

Amy rubbed her eyes. 'Not much to tell. She met him online. I don't even know his name. Caz could be like that. I think she's been chatting to him every day on the internet. It's been a few weeks at least.'

'I see. Do you know what site they met on? A dating site, maybe?'

'Schoolbook.'

Cullen knew it — he had a profile on the site and had just down-loaded the app for his mobile. He was constantly bombarded with friend requests from people at school, which he generally accepted then ignored. 'When did you start worrying about Caroline?'

Amy glanced at the small boy on the floor and bit her lip. 'She dropped Jack off here from nursery after work on Wednesday. Caz was supposed to pick him up yesterday afternoon. I don't work Thursdays so I was keeping him.'

Cullen nodded. He drew a timeline in his notebook, running from Wednesday to now — Friday lunchtime — marking Thursday afternoon for the arranged collection. 'So she's been gone almost two days?'

'Aye.'

'When was the last time you actually heard from her?' said Cullen.

'I got a text at about seven on Wednesday asking how Jack was.'

Cullen added it to the timeline. 'What did the text message say?'

'I let her know he was asleep,' said Amy, 'but she didn't reply. She'd been on the phone a few times before that. I think it was nerves.'

'Was it unusual she didn't reply?'

'She likes to text, I suppose,' said Amy, 'and she likes to get the last word in. But I can go weeks without hearing from her.'

'Okay.' Cullen sifted through his notes. 'I assume you've tried to get hold of her on her mobile since then?'

'Yeah, I called loads of times, but it just rang through to voice-mail.' Amy sat forward on her chair. 'I left messages, sent a million texts. It's just not like her. She would always answer, just in case anything had happened to Jack.'

'Could she have gone back to this man's flat after their date?'

Amy looked up at the ceiling. 'Well, I suppose so, aye, but she should still have had her phone on.' Her hand shook as she picked up her cup, tea spilling down the sides.

Jack wandered over to Amy, his steps slow and unsteady — even Cullen now realised he couldn't be any more than two.

'If she had gone back to his flat,' said Amy, 'that was two nights ago. She would've at least phoned me yesterday to see how Jack was, and to tell me she wasn't coming to pick him up.'

'Have you tried her flat?'

'Aye, I've got a key,' said Amy. 'I was round there yesterday. I didn't want to barge in, in case they'd, you know, gone back there, so I just knocked. I went round again this morning. I let myself in, but she hasn't been back as far as I could tell.'

'And that's when you reported her missing?'

'Aye.'

Cullen jotted some notes down — so far, he'd only confirmed what he already knew, though this mystery man was already digging at his synapses. 'Have you contacted anyone who might know where she is? Any family?'

'I phoned her parents, but they hadn't heard from her.'

'Any brothers or sisters?'

'Caz is an only child,' said Amy.

'Where do her parents live?'

'Carnoustie, near Dundee.'

Cullen knew it well — he was from Dalhousie in Angus, a small fishing town up the coast, the other side of Arbroath. The local football teams, Carnoustie Panmure and Dalhousie Trawlers, had a fierce rivalry in the Juniors league. If you asked anyone in Dalhousie, they'd tell you their golf course was the equal of their more famous close neighbour.

Amy gave him contact details for Caroline's parents.

'How about Jack's father?' said Cullen.

Amy scowled. 'Rob?' She looked away, her fingers gripping the armchair tight. 'They divorced last year. They'd been together since they were at school, went to uni together, got married, had this wee fella then that scumbag had an affair with this girl he worked with, some tart called Kim. It tore Caroline in two.'

'What's his name?'

'Rob Thomson.' Amy stared at the floor for a moment — Cullen let her take some time. 'He's a nasty piece of work.'

'Do you think he could have anything to do with her disappearance?'

Amy hesitated for a moment. 'I wouldn't know.'

'Do you have an address or phone number for him?'

'Aye, Caz gave me some for when I had Jack.' Amy sifted through her mobile and he noted them down.

Cullen clocked Miller ogling Amy as she leaned forward to replace the phone, his tongue practically hanging out of his mouth.

'Could Caroline have run away?' said Cullen. 'Maybe with this guy she was meeting?'

Amy stared into space for a few seconds. 'I doubt it. Jack's her life. She adores him.'

It seemed unlikely to Cullen — in his experience, most young mothers had at least some level of resentment towards their children, mixed with varying levels of maternal love. 'She never expressed any frustration or irritation with her son?'

'Not once, not ever.' Amy shook her head, emphatically. 'Caroline was very open about that sort of thing. She loved Jack. My other pals that have kids moan about them, but Caroline never did. I mean, she'd say if he'd been a nightmare that morning or whatever, but it never seemed to bother her.'

'Are there any friends or colleagues who might know where Caroline is?'

Amy bit her lip. 'You could maybe try Steve Allen. He was at school with her and Rob. Think he lives in Glasgow now. He's a really good pal of hers. He might have heard from her, I suppose. I tried but I couldn't get hold of him.' She gave him a mobile number.

'Anyone else?'

Amy rubbed her nose for a few seconds. 'There's maybe Debi Curtis. We both worked with Caroline a few years ago. I hardly see her now, but Caroline's still pretty close to her.'

Cullen noted her number down. 'Where does Caroline work?'

'The University. In the Linguistics Department. She's a senior secretary.'

Cullen noted the contact details. He reckoned he'd got all the information he could out of her. He needed to speak to Rob Thomson. 'Is there any family Jack can stay with?'

Amy nodded. 'I spoke to her folks. He'll be fine with me until Caz shows up. If she's not turned up by the weekend, they'll come and get him.'

'What about her ex-husband?'

'What about him?'

'Have you spoken to Mr Thomson?' said Cullen.

'He didn't answer my call.'

Cullen stood up, not sure whether to believe her or not. 'You mentioned you had a key to Caroline's flat. Could I have a look around?'

5

The summer wind howled down the street as Cullen and Miller stood outside, having driven round in silence even though it would have been quicker walking. Caroline's top floor flat was on Smith's Place, a cul de sac just off Leith Walk full of ornate Victorian buildings now subdivided into flats.

'Oh, man.' Miller gave a lewd cackle. 'That Amy would get it.' He ground his hips for emphasis.

Cullen opened the front door of the building. 'You're a dirty bastard.'

'Who gives a shit?' said Miller. 'She's a tidy little piece.'

'You might want to think about acting a bit more professionally.'

'Eh?'

'You just sat there looking her up and down,' said Cullen. 'Don't make me tell Bain about it.'

'You wouldn't dare.'

'Wouldn't I?' Cullen led them inside. 'What do you make of the story, then?'

'Don't know, man,' said Miller, as they begun the climb. 'Something seems a bit fishy.'

'Were you actually paying attention?' said Cullen, as they reached the top floor.

'I was a bit, aye.'

'How much is a bit?'

'Well, you know,' said Miller. 'Her pal went missing, hasn't turned up.'

Cullen held up the brass key. 'I'm going to have a look around. I want you to give Rob Thomson and Steve Allen a call, see if we can set some time up with them.'

'Right.' Miller frowned and looked away.

Cullen sighed. 'Tell me you copied the numbers down.'

'I thought you were.'

Cullen doubted Miller would ever get past the Acting DC stage to being a full detective, but the mystery remained as to how he'd even got there in the first place. He showed Miller the numbers in his own notebook. 'There.'

'Aye, cheers.' Miller took Cullen's notebook and started copying.

Cullen pulled on a pair of rubber gloves and opened the front door. All of the rooms in the flat faced into the street. It was dark inside, despite it being midday at the end of July. They entered the open plan living room and kitchen, which seemed perfectly ordinary, nothing particularly amiss.

Miller sat on the sofa and started fiddling with his mobile.

Cullen checked the calendar stuck to the fridge — the only allusion to going on a date was a note to take Jack to Amy's.

He left Miller and went into the first room, obviously Jack's bedroom. It was small yet crammed with toys. Cullen wondered if they were presents from the guilty father.

Caroline's bedroom was almost as big as the living room. On the dressing table sat an empty wine glass and a half-empty bottle of Chardonnay, the top screwed back on. He took a look through the wardrobe, stuffed with clothes and shoes. The chest of drawers by the bed was full of underwear and cosmetics. Under the bed were two new-looking suitcases, both empty.

It looked like she hadn't run away.

In the middle of the double bed sat a sleeping Apple laptop, not a new model. Cullen took a few seconds before deciding to wake it up. It was logged into Schoolbook. He sat on the bed and looked closer — there was a stream of messages between Caroline and someone called Martin Webb. He scanned through the message chain — this was definitely the guy she was meeting.

He felt slightly guilty about reading through the personal messages, thinking how he would feel if someone did the same to him.

From the profile picture alongside every message, Cullen could tell Martin Webb was a pretty boy — the guy was either good-looking or had spent a lot of money on getting a photo professionally taken. His own profile photo had three days of stubble and he'd been hung-over when one of his flatmates snapped it.

Cullen clicked to Martin's profile — if he could find him then maybe he could find Caroline. The icon in the middle of the screen spun round for a couple of seconds then took him to the login screen. The password field stayed blank, no asterisks auto-populated. He clicked on the back button, but it returned to the home page.

He swore, angry with himself and pissed off at her bloody laptop.

He got up and tried to think if there was anything else he could glean from the flat, coming up short. He went back to the living room, Miller still on the sofa, mobile in his hand, looking out of the window. He chucked Cullen's notebook back over.

Cullen pocketed it. 'Anything?'

'No answer from either of them.'

'How many of Rob Thomson's numbers did you try?'

'House and mobile.'

'Not the office?' said Cullen.

'Just away to, then you came back.' Miller smirked. 'Finished sniffing her dirty knickers?'

Cullen laughed despite himself. He got his phone out and called Steve Allen's number. It was engaged. He tried Rob Thomson's numbers, all going through to voicemail.

'Believe me now?' said Miller.

'Aye, I suppose so.'

'Nice phone, though, Scotty,' said Miller. 'iPhone 4, right?'

Cullen shrugged. 'It's just a phone.'

'Aye, right. It's more than a phone.' Miller rubbed his hands together. 'Anyway, I called that Debi bird. She works at the History Department at the Uni. She can see us this afternoon.'

'Good. We can speak to Caroline's work colleagues while we're up there. Maybe you're not such a useless bastard, Miller.'

'I am if you listen to Bain.'

Cullen grinned. 'For once, he might have a point.'

6

Cullen parked the car on the double yellow line across from Appleton Tower, one of two high rises built by Edinburgh University in the late sixties, architecturally at odds with the surrounding buildings. The Linguistics Department was in a townhouse round the corner on George Square, one of the few old buildings still standing.

'Just here, isn't it?' said Miller.

'Aye.'

Cullen knew the area well from his student days but right now he didn't recognise it. Bristo Square — usual haunt of skateboarders and teenagers — was now cordoned off ahead of the impending Festival, the square becoming a number of different venues centred around the Student Union. For one month of the year, the centre of the city twisted into a parallel twenty-four hour version of itself. Cullen imagined London festivalgoers returning for a November weekend, surprised to be turned away from student unions.

A new office building stood across from Appleton Tower, looking like a stretched-out sibling of Leith Walk station. When Cullen was a student it had been a car park and he'd once fallen headlong across the gravel on a drunken night in his first year, slicing his arm open. He was so drunk he didn't even notice until he was barred entry to the Student Union.

'Seems like a different place now,' said Cullen, as they got out of the car.

'You went to uni?'

Cullen nodded. 'English Literature.'

Miller snorted with laughter. 'Isn't that a poof's subject?'

Cullen didn't answer.

'Did you finish?' said Miller.

'Dropped out after third year. Got an Ordinary Degree.'

'That when you joined the force?'

'No,' said Cullen. 'I worked in a shitty office for a couple of years while I got myself fit.'

'It's a bastard,' said Miller. 'I hate running but you've got to keep it up.'

'What about you?'

'Wasn't smart enough to go to uni.' Miller smirked. 'I worked in an office for a couple of years after school. Old man got us the job. *Hated* it.'

'Why?'

Miller's expression was the most serious Cullen had ever seen on him. 'Put it this way, Bain seems all right compared to some of the wankers I worked for.'

Cullen laughed as he pressed the buzzer. 'Tell me about it.'

'How do you want to play this?' said Miller as they waited.

'You speak to the office staff, I'll speak to the boss. There will be academics in the department, but I suspect they won't know much about Caroline so we'd best avoid them. Then we'll go and see Debi Curtis.'

'Aye, fine, sounds good,' said Miller, as though he'd suggested it.

They were buzzed up to the office. A middle-aged woman stood at the top of the stairs, hand on her hip, glasses on a chain round her neck, looking every inch the sort of battleaxe Cullen had been shit-scared of as a student.

She held out her hand. 'Margaret Armstrong.'

Cullen shook it, then flashed his warrant card and introduced himself. 'This is Acting DC Miller.'

'Can I ask what this is about?' Armstrong smiled politely, her forehead betraying a frown.

'We're investigating the reported disappearance of Caroline

Adamson,' said Cullen. 'We believe she works here. Is that correct?'

Armstrong's lined face creased further. 'Oh.'

'I wanted to ask you a few questions about Caroline,' said Cullen, 'to see if there were any leads we could perhaps investigate.'

'Certainly.' She was still frowning.

'Could I speak to some of your staff?' said Miller.

Armstrong looked him up and down. 'Very well.' She pointed towards a closed door with a concerned look on her face. 'The girls are in there.'

Miller thanked her and entered the room.

Armstrong led Cullen along the corridor in the opposite direction into a plush first-floor room overlooking George Square, the view of the gardens marred by the abomination of the library and lecture theatres. She sat at her desk and put her glasses on, before taking a drink from a cup. 'Can I get you a tea or coffee?'

'No, I'm fine, thanks.' Cullen got out his notebook. 'I take it Caroline hasn't turned up for work?'

Armstrong grimaced. 'No, I'm afraid not.'

'Has she called in sick?' said Cullen.

Armstrong shook her head. 'No, she hasn't.'

'Has this sort of thing happened before?'

'Absolutely not.' Armstrong took another drink. 'There were times when young Jack — that's her son — when he wouldn't be well, but she would always have called in by the time I got here. And I'm *always* in early, I can assure you.'

Cullen didn't doubt it. 'How would you describe your relationship with Caroline?'

'Professional.'

'I see.' Cullen imagined Armstrong didn't have many close friends. 'So you weren't friends as well as colleagues?'

Armstrong folded her arms. 'I don't fraternise with my staff. Caroline was on good terms with my girls. Of course, there were the girls we had before Kelly and Lesley. Amy and Debi. All three of them used to go out for a glass of wine of a Friday night. I just let them get on with it.'

Cullen smiled. 'Amy Cousens called this in and we plan to see Debi Curtis next.'

'Very well.'

'Do the current girls go out with her for a drink, do you know?'

Armstrong gave a slight shrug. 'I don't think so. Not with young Jack on the scene these days. Caroline always rushed home at five on the dot to see him.'

'Would any of the academic staff know anything about Caroline?'

Armstrong shook her head. 'We operate a strict though informal demarcation between the administration staff and the academic staff in this office. It helps to keep it working efficiently and effectively.'

'I see. So none of them would be particularly acquainted with Ms Adamson?'

'Aside from asking her to photocopy lecture notes or re-arrange seminars,' said Armstrong, 'there would be very little direct interaction. All of the work comes through myself.'

'I know you and Ms Adamson had a strictly professional relationship,' said Cullen, 'but how had she seemed over the last few weeks?'

Armstrong furrowed her brow and paused for a moment. 'I would say that, on reflection, Caroline had seemed a tad distant, but then she was often like that. Having a young son has been quite a strain on her, what with her being on her own.'

'Did Caroline talk about her ex-husband often?' said Cullen.

'Seldom.' Armstrong's expression seemed to warn him not to plough too far down that furrow.

Cullen ignored the perceived warning. 'And when she did?'

Armstrong's nostrils flared slightly. 'Never in good terms. She took a couple of weeks leave to get her affairs in order when the divorce was going through.' Her expression got sourer. 'Terrible business.'

'And did anything untoward happen at the time?'

'Not that I knew of.'

Cullen smiled. 'Okay, one last question then. Did she mention anything about having a new man in her life?'

'Nothing at all, I'm afraid.'

Cullen had exhausted all avenues of questioning. 'Thanks for your help, Mrs Armstrong.' He got to his feet and handed her a card. 'If you hear from Caroline, please get in touch.'

7

Miller was waiting for Cullen in the corridor. They didn't speak until they were outside.

'I'm totally starving, man,' said Miller. 'You'd been for your rolls when I got back. Can I go get a sandwich now?'

'There's a decent place round the corner.' Cullen led him past Appleton Tower and on to Potterrow. 'Did you manage to get anything?'

'Only thing those pair were worried about was her weight,' said Miller. 'She'd been getting quite thin. Typical birds.'

'Did they know why?'

Miller shrugged. 'New man on the scene. Wanted to look her best.'

Cullen could well imagine. 'Anything else?'

'They were both pretty fit.' Miller laughed. 'Glad you weren't in there, both of them would be pregnant by now.'

Cullen shook his head. 'I don't know where you get that from.'

'You're a proper swordsman, aren't you?'

'Eh?'

'There was that bird at the Christmas party, wasn't there?' said Miller. 'And there's DS McNeill.'

'There's nothing going on between me and DS McNeill.' Cullen gestured at the sandwich shop. 'Don't be ages.'

Miller went inside with a smile on his face.

Cullen glanced up at the sky, the dark grey clouds belying the fact it was the middle of summer — if Miller was inside too long, they might get caught in the rain. He leaned against the wall and called Steve Allen. He pushed the phone between his shoulder and neck and listened to the ringing tone.

Allen answered, sounding flustered.

Cullen introduced himself. 'I believe you're acquainted with a Caroline Adamson.'

'That's right.'

Cullen found it hard to make out his voice over the noise of the wind at the other end of the line.

'I'm trying to ascertain her whereabouts,' said Cullen. 'When was the last time you heard from her?'

'Can I ask why?'

'She's gone missing,' said Cullen. 'One of her friends has reported it to us.'

'Oh sweet Jesus.'

'I need to track Ms Adamson's movements,' said Cullen. 'It could be you were the last person to speak to her before she disappeared.'

'Okay, okay,' said Allen. 'Give me a second.' There was a pause. 'I think I texted her on my way to the Celtic match. About seven, I suppose.'

'And Ms Adamson replied?'

'Yes. I'd wished her luck on her date and she said I needed more luck than she did what with going to see Celtic.'

Cullen noted it down — she had been jovial enough on Wednesday night, then. 'Was this the last time you heard from her?'

'Yes, it was. I texted her back but she didn't reply.'

'And was this unusual?'

'Now you mention it,' said Allen, 'she does usually reply to texts quite quickly.'

Cullen noted it down — that was the second unanswered text message. 'And before that, when was the last time you'd spoken to her?'

'The previous evening,' said Allen. 'We sometimes have a chat on a Tuesday night to see how things are going. I think we spoke for about half an hour.'

'And how did she seem?'

'Nervous, I suppose,' said Allen, after another brief pause. 'Excited, maybe. She was going out on a date the next night, after all. I mean, she barely spoke about Jack at all on the call, only about five minutes, which is a record with Caroline, believe me.'

'We're keen to get in touch with the man she was out with,' said Cullen. 'Do you know anything about him, any way we could get in touch with him?'

'Not really, no,' said Allen. 'I just knew he was from Edinburgh. She met him on the internet, I think.'

Miller appeared from the shop, putting his mouth round a massive baguette.

Cullen looked away. 'Mr Allen, can you think of anyone I should get in touch with about Caroline? Someone who might know her whereabouts?'

'Look, how serious is this?'

'We're concerned for her safety,' said Cullen. 'She left her son with a friend and hasn't been to pick him up, or been heard from since Wednesday night.'

'Jesus Christ.' Allen didn't speak for a few seconds. 'This is off the record, but if anything happened to Caroline the first person I'd be talking to would be Rob.'

'Her ex-husband?'

'Yes, him,' said Allen. 'Look, I'm afraid I've got to go. Give me a call if you need anything.'

Cullen took down a couple of other contact numbers for him and ended the call. He pocketed his phone and notebook.

'Who was that?' said Miller through a mouthful of mashed up chicken and white bread.

'Steve Allen.'

'Good work getting through to him.'

Cullen nodded at the roll. 'What did you get?'

'Cajun chicken,' said Miller. 'Pretty decent, likes.'

'Come on, let's get going,' said Cullen. 'When you've finished chewing, could you call Control and see if Rob Thomson's got a record?'

Miller did a mock salute. 'Yes, boss.'

Walking a few steps ahead of Miller, Cullen dialled Thomson's number. It rang and rang. He didn't want to get into a conversation with him on the phone — he would much rather speak face to face and get the measure of the man. It went through to voicemail and he left a message. He hung up then turned to Miller. 'You got anything yet?'

'Nothing at all,' said Miller. 'Squeaky clean.'

They headed towards the History Department and Debi Curtis.

DEBI CURTIS' office was old and in dire need of repair. The white paint covering the furniture was chipped and the cabinets had seen better days — the late seventies, thought Cullen. They sat across the desk from her.

'I haven't seen Caroline for about a month,' said Debi. 'I'm studying for an MBA just now and work was really busy towards the end of the academic year.'

Cullen placed her accent as being somewhere near London and she was one of the smallest women he had ever met — easily a couple of inches under five foot. Her dark hair curled around her ears giving her an elfin look. She wore thick, chunky glasses embossed in gold with a three-letter acronym Cullen didn't know.

'Were you good friends?' said Cullen.

'We were, yes,' said Debi. 'We worked together at Linguistics just after I graduated. We used to go out on a Friday night and chat about stuff, you know. Me, Caroline and Amy.'

'When was this?'

'That'll be 2005 to June 2008,' said Debi. 'I got this job then, it's much more senior. I'm on a fast track to management.'

'And do you still email or text her at all?'

'A few messages on Schoolbook, that's pretty much it.'

'Did she mention anything about a new man in her life?'

'Just that she had one,' said Debi. 'Nothing more. It was funny — I've got one as well.'

'Okay.' Cullen was keen to move away from her love life. 'Can you tell me anything about her marriage and divorce?'

'I tried to stay out of it,' said Debi, slowly. 'We weren't working together any more and I was friends with both Rob and Caroline, so I wanted to remain impartial.' She sighed. 'I haven't seen Rob in a long time, though. He can hold a grudge, believe me. Caroline had a hell of a time with him. I mean she's no wallflower herself, but he was a right Jack the Lad.'

This hooked Cullen. 'What do you mean by that?'

'There was all that stuff with Kim. I don't really want to go into it now. I'm happy to talk to you if you need a statement but it's not something I want to discuss.'

Cullen was sorely tempted to progress it further.

'And you haven't heard from her since Wednesday?' said Miller.

'No,' said Debi. 'It would be at least a week before that, maybe ten days. I mean, I could check.'

Miller handed her a card. 'If you could. Is there anyone else we should speak to who might have heard from her?'

Debi shrugged. 'Just Amy or Rob.'

'Okay, thanks.' Cullen looked over at Miller. 'Anything else from you?'

'No, that's more than enough to be going on with for now.'

They got up and went to the door.

'If there's anything you want to add, just give either of us a call,' said Cullen.

He led them back out to George Square, an old guy with grey dreadlocks cycling past as they stepped onto the cobbles.

'She was a right minger,' said Miller.

Cullen raised an eyebrow — he wanted to wind Miller up. 'I don't know. She had a nice nerdy look about her.'

Miller laughed. 'See, you are a dirty bastard.'

Cullen took out his phone and called Rob Thomson again. Same result — voicemail. He took a deep breath.

'We're going to see Rob Thomson.'

8

Cullen waited in the Alba Bank reception area, checking his watch for the umpteenth time, itching closer to calling Thomson's mobile again.

The businessman on the sofa opposite had clearly overheard Cullen's conversation with the receptionist and seemed wary. After a flurry of phone calls, she had managed to track Thomson down. Cullen had sensed reluctance, but the mention of the word 'police' was enough.

Miller was reading the sports pages of *The Edinburgh Argus*, muttering to himself. 'We'll get relegated at this rate and the season's not even started.' He folded the newspaper and tossed it onto the coffee table. 'Aw, man.' He snorted, rubbed his nose then looked over at Cullen. 'Turnbull needs to get his act together.'

Cullen frowned at him. 'In what way?'

'Getting me made a proper DC. I'm not waiting around forever.'

'Do you think you're ready for it?'

'Do you think I'm not?'

Cullen smiled. 'Bain's got a point. You are a cocky wee bastard.'

Miller screwed his face up then looked away. 'The gaffer's got it in for me.'

'You think?'

'Aye.' Miller sighed. 'He doesn't like us. No idea what I've done. Have to keep going to Turnbull to get stuff sorted out.'

'That might be what pisses Bain off.'

Miller turned to another paper.

Cullen picked up a leaflet from the stack on the table, which told him everything he already knew about the company. Alba Bank was Scotland's third biggest bank, the only one not to over-reach itself before the credit crunch hit. Cullen's flatmate, Tom, worked for them, which meant he knew a few tales the leaflets didn't mention.

Cullen put it back and looked around the reception area. The building itself was impressive, an ultra-modern construction in steel and glass, replacing the previous eyesore atop the St James Centre. The Alba pyramid pierced the skyline directly above where Cullen and Miller sat and was visible all across the city centre. It made Cullen feel like he was living in the future.

'DC Cullen?'

Cullen looked up at Rob Thomson and was immediately surprised by the size of him. He was a lot bigger than Cullen imagined from Amy's description — tall and muscular, shaven head and could have been anything from twenty-five to thirty-five. He wore a pinstripe suit, a fake tan and a fake smile.

Thomson introduced himself. Cullen shook his hand then introduced Miller, who nodded before wiping his nose.

'Can we do this in my office?' said Thomson.

'Fine,' said Cullen.

Thomson emitted a long sigh as he signed them in, before leading them down the left-most corridor, strutting around like he owned the place. They passed tables full of people mid-meeting, Cullen thinking the place was more like a Parisian terrace than an office. It was drowning in light, flooding down from the glass of the pyramid. Thomson stopped at a security door just by a café and swiped with his badge before proceeding down another long corridor, an open plan area visible through the glass wall.

Miller practically ricked his neck looking around at the girls dressed like they were heading to a club rather than work.

At the end of the corridor Thomson led them into an office with his name on the door, plus his job title 'Programme Manager, IT Services'.

The room was lavishly decorated with expensive designer furniture and lighting. There was a single internal window, which looked back to the corridor, and the walls were filled with artworks and a framed Rangers shirt.

'Have a seat.' Thomson sat at the desk, which was cluttered with empty coffee cups and bottles of mineral water. He took a Blackberry from his jacket pocket, setting it beside his laptop. He leant back and crossed his legs.

Cullen and Miller sat in the two armchairs facing the desk.

'You're a difficult man to get hold of.' Cullen pointed to the Blackberry. 'I've called you a few times.'

'I'm a busy man, Constable. I've got a project implementing at the weekend. It's been non-stop all day.' Thomson picked up the Blackberry and started fiddling with it. 'How can I help?'

'I need you to answer a few questions about your ex-wife, Caroline Adamson. We're trying to trace her current location.'

Thomson frowned. 'Has something happened to her?'

'She's been reported missing,' said Cullen.

Thomson leaned forward. 'Is Jack okay?'

'Your son's with a friend of Ms Adamson's, Amy Cousens. I believe she's tried calling you.'

Thomson sat back in his chair. 'I don't have the time to listen to all my voicemails.' His eyes darted back to Cullen. 'Hang on — is she saying I've abducted Caroline?'

'Have you?'

Thomson laughed nervously. 'Would I say so if I had?'

'This is a serious investigation.' Cullen sat forward in his chair. 'I can't stress strongly enough the magnitude of the situation. It's your duty to divulge any information that could help us track down your ex-wife.'

'I'd say if I knew where she was,' said Thomson, 'but I've not heard from her in weeks. And that's the truth.'

Cullen stabbed his pen into his notebook. 'Where were you on Wednesday evening?'

'What's Wednesday got to do with anything?'

'That's when Caroline disappeared.'

Thomson ran his hand across the stubble on his head. 'I was in work till eight.'

'Is there anyone who can corroborate that?'

'I left with Kim.'

Cullen recalled Amy Cousens mentioning Thomson had an affair with a Kim. 'Can I have her full name?'

Thomson dropped his Blackberry on the desk. 'It's Kimberley Milne.'

'Can I ask what you did after you left for the evening?'

'We went for a pizza down Leith Walk,' said Thomson. 'Very nice it was indeed.'

'And do you have a receipt for this meal?'

'I only keep work receipts,' said Thomson.

'I see,' said Cullen. 'And this Kim Milne is a colleague?'

'She was. She's my partner now. They separated us when we got together.'

'Was Kim Milne the cause of your marriage breaking up?'

Thomson sat forward in his chair. 'What's that got to do with anything?'

'I'm trying to put together a picture of your ex-wife's life,' said Cullen. 'It might help to track her down before some harm comes to her. She's already been missing since Wednesday evening, so time is of the essence. Any assistance you can give us would be appreciated.'

Thomson rubbed his head again. 'Okay. I started seeing Kim before me and Caroline divorced, that's true.'

'And you worked together?'

'That's right.' Thomson nodded. 'I had to come clean to the powers that be and we got split up at work. Kim's in a different division now. I'm in IT, she's in Corporate Banking.'

'How would you describe your relationship with your ex-wife?'

Thomson leaned back in his chair. 'Cordial.' He looked away. 'I pick my wee boy up every second Saturday. I see Caroline when I pick him up and drop him off. That's it. Supposed to be picking him up tomorrow, in fact.' He picked up the bottle of water from his desk and took a drink. 'I've had absolutely nothing to do with Caroline's life since before our divorce.'

'And you didn't think it suspicious she didn't get in touch regarding arrangements for tomorrow?'

Thomson just shrugged.

Cullen was becoming irritated by the man. 'Mr Thomson, I'm sure you'll appreciate Ms Adamson has disappeared in suspicious circumstances and we're keen to track down anyone who might wish to cause her harm.'

Thomson's face flushed red. 'Now wait a minute here.' He stabbed his finger at Cullen. 'If you think I did anything, you should be arresting me.'

'Is that an admission of guilt?'

'No, it's bloody not.' Thomson checked his watch. 'I need you to leave. I've got a meeting I have to dial into.'

'Is there anybody you could imagine would wish to cause your ex-wife harm in any way?' said Cullen.

'No.' Thomson reached over to unlock his laptop.

'Is there anyone else who might be able to assist us?' said Cullen.

Thomson thought about it as he logged in to his laptop. 'Amy or Debi,' he said, after a pause. 'Maybe Steve Allen. Her parents.'

Cullen got to his feet. 'Thank you for your time.'

Thomson looked relieved. 'If there's anything else, just let me know.'

Cullen put his card on Thomson's desk. 'Just one thing. We'll need to get in touch with Ms Milne to get a statement to cover your whereabouts on Wednesday evening. Can you give us her details?'

The colour drained from Thomson's face.

9

Cullen pulled in on East London Street. He pointed up. 'Nice flat.'

Miller nodded. 'Bit snooty here.'

'This is too good for you, Keith. This is the second rung of the property ladder for Edinburgh's professional classes.'

'Quite happy with Easter Road, thank you very much.' Miller undid his seatbelt. 'Bit of a prick that boy.'

'Not the nicest, was he?' Cullen didn't get a good feeling from Rob Thomson and his sheer arrogance, but he was trying not to let it prejudice him. 'Can you take the statement here? I'll ask the questions, but I want you to write everything down and read it back to her and get it signed.'

'Aye, primary school stuff,' said Miller. 'I'm not as useless as Bain makes out.'

They got out of the car and crossed the road, Cullen getting them buzzed up to the second floor flat.

Kim Milne met them in the stairwell.

Cullen clocked Miller checking her out — long blonde hair, short skirt and orange skin.

Cullen introduced them. 'Your partner, Rob Thomson, told us you'd be working from home today. We need to ask you some questions in relation to the apparent disappearance of his ex-wife.'

Kim put a hand to her mouth. 'Oh my God.' She bit her lip. 'I'd better see Jenny out.'

They went inside the expensively decorated flat — dark wooden furniture, cream walls, stripped floors — leading them into the kitchen.

A carbon copy of Kim stood there, slightly different face and wearing thick-rimmed glasses.

'I need to help the police,' said Kim to Jenny.

'I'm happy to stay if you need me,' said Jenny.

Cullen didn't want to leave anything to chance. 'Can I take your name?'

'Jenny Scott.'

'Jenny's going travelling to Thailand,' said Kim. 'We were out last night and she left her purse in the restaurant. Luckily, I'd picked it up thinking it was mine.'

'Was Mr Thomson with you?' said Cullen.

Kim exchanged a look with Jenny. 'No, it was a girl's night out.'

'I see.' Cullen handed Jenny one of his cards. 'Can I take a mobile number in case I need to contact you again?'

Jenny shared a look with Kim. 'I'm leaving for Thailand tonight.'

'I'd still like to make sure I can get in contact with you,' said Cullen. 'I don't want to overlook anything in this case.'

Jenny relented and he scribbled her number in his notebook. She looked at Kim. 'I'll be off, then.'

'I'll just show her out,' said Kim.

They left the room and Cullen could hear the front door opening.

'Wish I could work from home when I had a hangover,' said Miller.

'You'd never be in the station, though.'

Miller laughed. 'You can talk.' He pointed towards the door. 'Tasty bit of skirt. You were pretty swift there, getting her mate's phone number.'

Cullen smiled reluctantly. 'That's in case this alibi falls apart and I need to retrace both of Kim and Rob's steps.'

Miller saluted. 'You're the boss.'

Cullen looked around the kitchen. It was in dire need of modernisation, totally at odds with the other bits of the flat they'd seen. It had some tired melamine door fronts and a laminated wood worktop curling up at the edges. The counter was festooned with gadgets and a range of high-end pots and pans hung from the ceiling.

A laptop sat on the kitchen table, the screen open at School-book, an iPhone and a Blackberry next to it. There were two coffee mugs on the table.

The front door closed and Kim returned. 'Sorry about that. Can I get you a coffee?'

'We're fine.' Cullen pointed at the laptop. 'I see you're working hard here.'

Kim laughed. 'Aye, I'm addicted to Schoolbook. I'm on it all the time, on my phone, on my laptop.'

'I'm on there too,' said Cullen.

They sat around the table, Kim at one end, Miller and Cullen at the other.

'As I mentioned, we're investigating the disappearance of your partner's ex-wife,' said Cullen.

Kim rubbed her hands together slowly. 'How can I help?'

'Caroline went missing at some time on Wednesday evening,' said Cullen. 'It would appear she went on a date with a man and didn't return to her flat or collect her son.'

'Christ.'

'Can you detail your and Mr Thomson's movements on Wednesday evening?' said Cullen.

Kim's eyes widened. 'You don't think Rob had anything to do with it, do you?'

'I'm sure you want to help eliminate Rob from any possible suspicion,' said Cullen.

'Is he under suspicion?'

'At the moment, there's nothing to be suspected of,' said Cullen. 'As far as we know, no crime has been committed. However, we have to make sure any investigations we undertake now are appropriate and we don't disappear down any rabbit holes. So, can you confirm your activities on Wednesday evening?'

'We were both in work late.'

'And you work at Alba Bank?'

'Aye, that's right. I'm in Corporate, he's in IT.' Kim bunched her hair up and placed it over one shoulder. 'We went for dinner to that Italian on Leith Walk, Vittoria or Victoria, whatever it's called, then we went home. Rob paid, so I don't have a receipt or anything.'

'What did you do when you got back here?'

'I think we watched some telly then went to bed.'

Cullen scribbled it down — Thomson's alibi checked out but neither of them had a receipt for the meal. That was a task for Miller. 'Can I ask about your relationship with Mr Thomson?'

'You can ask, but I'm not really happy talking about it.'

'I understand that,' said Cullen, 'but can I remind you we're dealing with a disappearance and we need to check all avenues.'

'Okay.' Kim bit her lip again. 'Rob and I got together at a night out when we were working in Dublin. We'd just finished migrating some old mortgage systems to new ones.' She picked up the other coffee mug and set it alongside hers. 'We tried to keep it under wraps for a bit cos of Rob's family. But Caroline found a text from me on Rob's Blackberry. She went mental.'

'When was this?'

'This was in March last year. They got divorced last August, but Rob had moved in with me in April, I think. I had a flat in Polwarth at the time. We bought this place in September. Rob earns a decent amount of money, which helped.' She pointed around the room. 'It was in a bit of a state at the time, but we're slowly getting there.'

'Thank you.' Cullen finished jotting the information down, having already managed to form a loose timeline. 'Were you close to Caroline at all?'

Kim looked out of the window. 'We used to go out together occasionally, Rob, Caroline, me and my boyfriend at the time. That obviously stopped after Rob and I got together.'

'And how do you get on with Jack?'

'I'm not the maternal type,' said Kim. 'Not yet anyway. It's good for Rob to see him, I suppose, but it's not like I get all broody or anything. Far from it. And I don't resent him seeing his boy.'

'And do you spend time with them on Rob's days?'

'I just let them get on with it, to be honest,' said Kim. 'I prefer to go shopping, maybe meet them for a bite to eat later on.'

'Okay,' said Cullen. 'I think that's all for now.'

He got Miller to read out her statement.

10

Cullen was already driving by the time Miller got his seatbelt on.

'Can't believe how much you were flirting with her there,' said Miller.

'I wasn't.'

'You were.'

Cullen tried to distract Miller. 'How do you think that went?'

'Went all right, I suppose. Feels like a bit of a waste of time, though.'

'Even though it might feel like we're just going through the motions,' said Cullen, 'we need to cover absolutely everything. Last thing we want is Bain going mental cos we forgot to ask her about the alibi, or some lawyer tearing the case to shreds cos of something we did or, more likely, didn't do.'

Cullen knew he'd have to give Bain chapter and verse when they got back to the station, so he wanted Miller to get some much-needed practice at note taking. Plus, he needed to spend some time looking for Martin Webb and not having to answer Bain's questions. 'Can you write up the notes? If you want to be a proper DC then your note taking has to be perfect. It can be brutal, especially if you're in court.'

Miller looked irritated. 'How do you mean? You're not exactly Gene Hunt, are you? How long have you been a DC?'

'Three months,' said Cullen. 'Had six months as Acting before that, and two previous six month detachments.'

Miller looked out of the window. 'Aye, fair enough, then.'

Cullen crossed the roundabout at London Road and continued down Leith Walk. Two blocks further and the main entrance of Leith Walk station welcomed them in, nestled between tenements on one side and McDonald Road library on the other, eight wide storeys of glass and stone facing.

Leith Walk was a long stretch lined with tenements and shops, which had been attempting to gentrify itself for the past fifteen years or so, struggling to match the New Town at the Edinburgh end or the upmarket Shore in Leith. Style bars were wedged in amongst charity shops and bookies, an old gym had turned into a designer light shop stuck next to a KFC clone.

Cullen flashed his warrant card to the security guard in the booth then drove down to the basement garage, where he dumped the pool car.

Miller slammed the car door far too hard. 'Still can't get over how swanky it is in this place.'

Cullen nodded agreement — he'd previously only known crumbling local stations and cheaply-built replacements in West Lothian, plus the already dated St Leonards, built in the mid-nineties. Leith Walk had only opened in the summer, providing much needed permanent office space for CID and other investigatory teams, including the city's mortuary, previously sited in the Cowgate.

'I was in Fettes for six months,' said Miller as they started climbing the stairs at the back of the building. 'That's a total shitehole. You'd expect it to be gleaming what with all the brass in there, as well. No idea where they got the money for this place.'

'Doubt it'd get built now.'

'How's that?'

'Government cuts and all that,' said Cullen.

Bain and McNeill were at their desks, each staring at computers.

Bain shot a glance up at Cullen. 'Well, if it isn't Tweedledum and Tweedledumber. Found her yet, Sundance?'

'Not yet,' said Cullen.

'Been keeping Monkey Boy out of trouble, though, I hope,' said Bain.

Cullen shrugged. 'We've been making progress.'

'Oh aye?'

'Do you want a timeline?' said Cullen.

'Suits me,' said Bain.

They all moved to the meeting table just behind Bain's desk.

Cullen shook his jacket off, chucking it onto his desk chair. He got out his notebook and flicked to the relevant pages. 'Caroline Adamson dropped her son, Jack, off with her friend Amy Cousens at the back of six on Wednesday night.'

He paused, looking around at blank faces, none blanker than Miller's. 'She was going on a date with a man she met on the internet. None of the friends I've spoken to know the name of this guy. I found her laptop at her flat and ascertained the name of the man she was meeting, a Martin Webb.'

'I hope you weren't messing about with her computer, Sundance,' said Bain.

'Hardly.' Cullen blushed slightly as he recalled losing the screen it was on. 'Bloody thing timed out on me. She was meeting this guy somewhere on the Southside.'

'Where exactly?' said McNeill.

'No idea.' Cullen shook his head. 'We've spoken to Amy Cousens, a school friend called Steve Allen and a former work colleague called Debi Curtis. None of them knew where she was going. Spoke to her ex-husband, but he's not seen her in a while.'

He turned the page of his notebook. 'She sent a couple of text messages in the hour between seven and eight, one to Amy and one to Steve. Both replied to her, but they didn't get anything back. Both stated this is unusual for her.'

'Does it look like she's run away?' said McNeill.

Cullen sat back in the chair. 'I doubt it. I had a good look through her flat. Her wardrobe and chest of drawers were absolutely rammed with clothes and her suitcases were still under the bed. Plus, it just doesn't fit. According to her friends, Caroline lived for her son. She wouldn't just leave him like that.'

'Wasn't pissed off with him or anything?' said Bain. 'Didn't think he'd ruined her life?'

'Quite the opposite, I gather,' said Cullen.

'Go on, then,' said Bain.

Cullen turned the page. 'Next is the following afternoon when Caroline was supposed to pick Jack up from Amy Cousens.'

'When was this?' said Bain.

'They hadn't set a time, just early afternoon,' said Cullen. 'That's when Amy started getting worried. She tried calling her a few times, went round to her flat, but there was no sign of her.'

'And so she called Queen Charlotte Street this morning?' said Bain.

Cullen nodded. 'Yes.'

Bain scratched the top of his head, face scrunched up. 'Right, Sundance, tell us about this ex-husband?'

'Rob Thomson,' said Cullen. 'They divorced in a bit of a hurry. He had an affair with someone at work.'

'And you boys spoke to him?' said Bain.

'Aye, we did.' Cullen nodded at Miller. 'He has an alibi for Wednesday night — his girlfriend, Kim Milne. She's the cause of the divorce, by the way. Keith's got a statement from her to write up.'

Bain nodded. 'Good work. Well, obviously he's got a motive. He wants his son back or revenge for something in their divorce — too much money, maybe.'

'Neither of them got a receipt for the alibi, though,' said Cullen. 'Might be something, might be nothing. They both worked to the back of eight that night then went for a meal at an Italian just down the road.'

'You think she could be lying for him?' said Bain.

Cullen thought it through. 'Wouldn't rule it out, but I wouldn't build a case around it either.'

'Did this Kim lassie have anything to do with Caroline?' said Bain.

'They used to double date as couples before the divorce,' said Cullen. 'She didn't appear to have anything against her.'

'And she doesn't want to grab this Jack laddie off Caroline?' said Bain.

'Don't think so,' said Cullen. 'According to her she isn't interested in kids.'

'Aye, according to her.' Bain scowled at Miller. 'Monkey Boy, can you go and visit this Italian, see if they had the pair of them in?'

'Come on, gaffer.'

'Shut it and do it, Miller.' Bain's voice was almost a snarl. He looked at Cullen. 'Is that all you've got?'

'For now. I was going to look for this Martin Webb guy next.'

'Has anyone spoken to her parents yet?' said Bain.

'Amy Cousens did,' said Cullen.

Bain stroked his moustache. 'Probably don't want to overly concern them just now.'

'What do you want us to do then?' said Cullen.

Bain looked at McNeill. 'Butch, can you continue the sterling progress you're making with our cold case there?' He had a quick look through the file on Caroline. 'Looks like plod have already called round the hospitals and so on, but it won't harm to do it again. Miller, once you've finished with the Italian, I want you on that. And typing up that lassie's statement, too.'

'Right,' said Miller.

Bain smacked his hand off the table. 'Miller, you're an Acting DC. You do whatever I say unless you want to go back to wearing a woolly suit rather than the cheap nylon one you've got on.'

11

Cullen slumped back in his chair, unsure what to do next. The rest of the team were away from their desks. He decided he could get his timeline nailed while he waited for inspiration — he didn't want to be pulled up for his note taking after the pep talk he'd given Miller.

McNeill appeared with a coffee for them both.

He thanked her as he opened the lid. 'You got a minute?'

'Sure.' She pulled her desk chair over to face him.

He rubbed his hand over his face. 'I'm struggling to find Martin Webb.'

'This is the guy she was on a date with, right?'

He nodded.

'Where have you looked?'

'I've checked all the databases we've got access to, *twice*,' said Cullen. 'I've phoned three directory enquiries numbers. So far I've found seventeen matches for the name within the UK.'

'And?'

Cullen counted them off on his fingers. 'Four OAPs, two guys in their fifties, seven guys in their forties, a teenager, two children and a severely disabled man in his thirties.'

'Couldn't our man be one of the old men or the guys in their forties or fifties?'

'Well, that's just it. This guy is in his thirties at the very most and looks pretty healthy.' Cullen tapped on the monitor. 'This is his profile on Schoolbook.'

McNeill wolf-whistled. 'He's a looker, all right.'

'Aye, well.'

She raised an eyebrow. 'Could it be Martin with a 'y'?'

Cullen tapped the screen. 'Martin with an 'i'. But anyway, I've searched for that, not a single one.'

She leaned back in her chair and folded her arms. 'Have you tried phoning Schoolbook?'

'Aye.' He checked his notebook. 'Spoke to a Gregor Aitchison. They've actually got an office in Livingston.'

'And who's he?'

'Said he was a manager, but he didn't give a clear title. He said we'd need a warrant for any information on their servers.'

McNeill nodded slowly. 'Doesn't mean we can't head over there and see what we can force out of him.'

12

C ullen parked outside the Schoolbook building. 'Here we are.'

McNeill looked up from her notebook.

The Schoolbook office was a corrugated iron warehouse, painted purple over the rust, the *Schoolbook.co.uk* logo etched in light blue. The building was totally dwarfed by the BSkyB campus next door, one of the biggest employers in West Lothian.

McNeill followed Cullen across the car park, her heels clicking on the tarmac. The clouds were dark grey again, a sign the day hadn't finished with its rain.

The front door was unlocked and there was no obvious reception area inside. They walked past rows and rows of computers, walls piled high with servers — racks of desktops with no monitors, all with banks of flashing lights. It reminded Cullen of a mailroom he worked in as a student, but filled with computers rather than post boxes. They came to an open office area full of twenty-something men with loud t-shirts and headphones on, all tapping at laptops. One walked along the far end of the room with a PC under each arm. Nobody looked around at them.

Cullen asked the guy at the nearest desk for Gregor Aitchison. He pointed to the far corner at a fat man with a beard, wearing combat trousers and a violent orange t-shirt. They crossed the room and he lumbered to his feet as they approached.

Cullen showed his warrant card. McNeill had agreed he should lead, as she wasn't formally assigned to the case. 'Gregor Aitchison?'

'Aye. What do you want?'

'We spoke on the phone,' said Cullen. 'About a missing person.'

Aitchison stared at the floor. 'I told you. You need a warrant.'

'All we're looking for is a little bit of information that may help us contact one of your users,' said Cullen.

Aitchison closed his eyes for a few seconds. 'Fine. I'll see if there's anything I can do. There's a limit to what I can give out, mind.'

'Sure.'

Aitchison's desk was covered in rubbish. He grabbed a handful from a big bag of cheese Doritos.

Cullen and McNeill found some unoccupied chairs and sat down.

Cullen moved a half-eaten ham and mushroom Pot Noodle onto the floor. 'You might want to think about some sort of security here. We just walked right in.'

Aitchison raised his eyebrows. 'I'll get that looked at.'

Cullen didn't imagine he would. 'As I said on the phone earlier, the missing person we're looking for is a user of Schoolbook. We have reason to believe she met someone on your site and arranged to meet up with him, a man called Martin Webb. We believe she went on a date with him on Wednesday, which is when she was last heard from.'

Aitchison finished chewing and rubbed his orange-stained fingers against his trousers. 'What's this woman's user name then?'

'Caroline Adamson.'

Aitchison navigated to Caroline's profile and retrieved a list of what looked like her friends. He wiped his hands on his trousers again and ran his finger down the screen, leaving a cheesy smudge. 'You're right. He's a friend of hers.'

'Can you check for any activity in the account since Wednesday?'

'Sure.' Aitchison went into another window and tapped some keys. 'Got something. Somebody tried to access her account today.'

Cullen's heart fluttered. 'What?'

'About twelve thirty-five,' said Aitchison.

'It was me,' said Cullen.

McNeill frowned. 'You were trying to log into her account?'

'It was already logged in,' said Cullen, 'I was trying to look at his profile.'

Aitchison took another handful of Doritos. 'Database agrees with you. Says she was still logged in from Wednesday night. Account was sitting dormant till you got chucked out.'

'Doesn't it time out?' said Cullen.

'It's not that smart yet,' said Aitchison. 'Only chucks you out when you try to do something. Next release, maybe.'

'Has there been anything else?'

'There's a fair amount of messages between these two accounts,' said Aitchison. 'Hundreds, goes back months.'

McNeill raised her eyebrows. 'Did you say *hundreds*?'

'Aye,' said Aitchison. 'At least a hundred and fifty each.'

'Can you give us a copy of the messages and any information about Martin Webb?' said Cullen.

Aitchison looked round at him. 'Look, pal, it's not me who sets the rules, okay? I told you on the phone, if you've not got a warrant, then I can't give you anything. If I got caught doing this, my knackers would swing. And anyway I'd need a DBA for what you're after.'

'A what?'

Aitchison rolled his eyes. 'A database administrator. I'd have to get one of them allocated to this if you wanted access to the tables or any extracts done. It all costs, you know. We run a pretty tight ship here. We're not like an American start-up.'

Cullen thought about mentioning the lax security at the front door again, but he let it pass. 'Can you print them out?'

'On what?' said Aitchison. 'We don't have a printer here.'

'You're kidding me.'

'No.' Aitchison sniffed and took a drink from the bottle. 'Nobody uses them for anything other than photos these days.'

'What about personal details?' said Cullen. 'Email addresses, house address, phone number?'

'I'll see what I can do,' said Aitchison, 'but, if anyone asks, I didn't give you it, right?'

Cullen nodded at him. 'Your secret's safe with us.'

Aitchison looked through screens of data, frowning. 'There's no postal address.' He tapped away again. 'Got an email address, mind. Big_Martin_Webb@intarwubs.com.'

'Shite,' said Cullen. 'That's obviously made up.'

Aitchison narrowed his brow. 'No it's not, pal. We've got a ton of users on there. I've got an account myself.'

Cullen was dumbfounded. 'Intarwubs?'

'Aye, it's magic,' said Aitchison. 'Funny videos and that. Pisses all over YouTube. There's talk of us buying the site outright.'

Cullen scribbled the email address in his notebook, still not believing it was valid.

'What else can you tell us about him from your database?' said McNeill.

Aitchison sighed. 'Look, I've pushed it really wide here giving you that. Any more and it's got to be a warrant.'

McNeill closed her eyes. 'Can you access the messages they've exchanged?'

'I can,' said Aitchison.

She leaned in close to him 'Could you?'

'I could.'

'For us?'

Aitchison looked at her, his mouth practically hanging open. 'No, I can't. It's got to be a warrant.'

~

MᴄNᴇɪʟʟ ᴅʀᴏᴠᴇ, taking the back way along the A71. As they crossed the City Bypass it was nose to tail, Friday early leavers contending badly with the relentless rain.

'Do you think we'll get a warrant for Schoolbook?' said Cullen.

'It's all up to Bain, really,' said McNeill. 'We need a RIPSA request.'

Cullen nodded — Regulation of Investigatory Powers (Scotland) Act. 'I've used that before, but only to get texts or numbers off a mobile, not to extract chunks of a private database.'

'Aye, same here,' said McNeill. 'The form needs the authorisation of a superior officer — Bain would do, but it'll probably get referred up the way. Who knows where it'll end up.'

'You tried flirting the information out of that poor guy, didn't you?' said Cullen.

'Aye, fat lot of good it did us.' McNeill smirked. 'Are you jealous?'

Cullen felt himself redden.

13

'That's not the issue right now,' said McNeill. 'Scott needs a RIPSA. Can he get it?'

'Let me think about it,' said Bain.

They had been at it hammer and tongs since they got back to the station. McNeill was becoming increasingly aggressive, with Bain digging his heels in more. Cullen kept catching people looking over, people who obviously knew Bain's reputation and just laughed it off.

'You've had more than enough time to think about it,' said McNeill.

'I can't hear myself think with you nipping my head all the time.' Bain glared at her for a few moments. 'Listen, Butch, I do need to have a proper think about this. It's political. Besides, I put Cullen on this one — you shouldn't even have been out there.'

'Scott asked me for support,' said McNeill. 'I'm a DS, he's a DC, he needed my support so I gave it.'

Bain looked at Cullen. 'This true?'

'Aye.'

'Fair enough,' said Bain.

McNeill pushed a form across the table. 'We just need this authorised and then we'll stop nipping your head.'

Bain grabbed it from her and read it. He tapped the tabletop for a few seconds. 'I need to speak to DCI Turnbull about this.'

'Why can't you just authorise it?' McNeill's voice rose as she spoke. 'Why do you need to speak to Turnbull? This information might help us find a missing person.'

'Calm it, Butch,' said Bain. 'There was a memo came out about this a couple of months ago. We need to be very careful with what we're doing with these powers.' He sniffed. 'The press can be real arseholes when it comes to us nicking people's mobiles and hacking into their emails. It's all this shite about privacy these days, nothing about us catching murderers or anything.'

McNeill grimaced. 'Can you go and speak to Jim, or do you want me to?'

Bain's nostrils flared as he got to his feet. 'Right. I'll go and see if I can catch him.' He marched off with the form.

McNeill pinched the bridge of her nose. 'Why does everything have to be such a bloody ordeal with him?'

'Cos he's a prick?'

'You're right.' McNeill looked around her desk. 'Back to that cold case, then. I need to see James Anderson in Scene of Crime. If I'm not back in ten minutes, send a search party.' She got up and trudged off.

Cullen opened up intarwubs.com. It was full of techy jokes and cartoons, with links to a few sites that looked like FHM but even less classy. He eventually found a contact number for a company called Infinite Communications. A quick Google showed the company ran several similar sites — yummymummy.com, chiefex-ec.com and premiershipbanter.com. Opportunists, he thought.

Cullen dialled the number and, after a few transfers, was put through to someone who could assist. 'I'm trying to find out who set up an email address on your site.'

'I understand you're with the police?'

Cullen gave his warrant number.

'And it's for the user big underscore martin underscore webb at intarwubs? I'll see what I can do then get back to you, is that okay?'

'How long?' said Cullen.

'I'm not sure. There are a few procedures I need to go through before I can give the information out, but it shouldn't be too long.'

'I'll wait.' Cullen sat listening to hold music, tinny and slightly out of tune. After three minutes of waiting, his mobile rang in his jacket pocket. He put the other phone on the desk and answered the mobile.

'DC Cullen?' A woman's voice. 'This is Debi Curtis, we met earlier?'

Cullen was unsure why she was calling. 'How can I help?'

'I was just checking my Schoolbook account. Just called to say I hadn't heard from Caroline for three weeks. I think I said a week when we met earlier. Sorry.'

'That's okay.' Cullen struggled to understand why she was calling about that.

'She was chatting about Jack in the message,' said Debi. 'She did say she'd got a new man on the scene. Oh and I think she'd had a row with Rob about Jack.'

Cullen sat forward. 'What did she say?'

'He'd cancelled picking Jack up at the last minute. Caroline said it was the second time in a couple of months.'

'And did you reply?'

There was a pause. 'No, I didn't. It was still sitting unread until I checked. Haven't had the time, I'm afraid.'

'Can I ask when you last contacted Mr Thomson?' said Cullen.

'Not for a good six months. I went out for drinks with him and Kim. I think it was her birthday. I didn't really have anything to say to her, but I still get on with Rob. He occasionally makes a comment about some of my posts on Schoolbook, but if you're asking about personal messages, then there's nothing.'

'Okay. If you do hear from Caroline, please give me a call.'

He put the mobile on the desk and picked up the other handset, still the same hold music. He wondered if the argument with Rob was anything important.

McNeill came back to her desk with a bigger scowl than the one she'd left with.

'No need for the search party, then?' said Cullen.

'No,' said McNeill. 'Actually, our Scene of Crime Unit might need them to help search for a clue.'

Cullen laughed.

The voice came back on the line. 'DC Cullen?'

'Have you got anything for me?'

'Why yes, I have. The account was set up three months ago.'

He read out the details Martin Webb had provided — age twenty-nine, full name Martin David Webb, place of birth Belfast. 'And there's a CV as well.'

Cullen was perplexed. 'A CV?'

Cullen could almost hear him smiling down the phone line. 'Our site's heavily used by technology professionals for networking.'

Cullen wondered why technology professionals would be posting public information about themselves on a site covered in glamour models. 'Can you send it through?' He gave his email address.

'No problem.' There were a few clicks and taps. 'That should be in your inbox now.'

'Is there any other information you can give?' said Cullen.

'Nope, I'm afraid that's it.'

'Okay, thanks for your help.' Cullen ended the call and opened up his email program. There was one from a generic address at Intarwubs dot com, sitting at the head of the usual long list of memos. He clicked on the attachment — the machine took an age to open it.

McNeill looked over his shoulder. 'What's that?'

'Martin Webb's CV,' said Cullen as he read the document. 'Holy shit — there's an address.'

14

Cullen struggled to find a parking space on Arden Street. Cars were double parked on the street, so Cullen joined them.

McNeill scrawled *'On Police Business'* on an old envelope and placed it on the dashboard.

They got out and looked up and down the road. They were parked outside number thirty-four, which was a stair door. The main door flats either side displayed no numbers.

Cullen pointed to the right. 'They start low at the Warrender Park Road end.' He then nodded at the main door on the left. 'This must be thirty-six.'

McNeill raised an eyebrow. 'Well deduced.'

He grinned as he rang the bell.

The door opened slightly and a woman's head appeared in the gap. 'Hello?' Her accent was American.

He showed his warrant card and introduced them.

She opened the door fully. An extremely fluffy ginger cat swarmed around her thin ankles. 'Anne Smythe.'

'Ms Smythe,' said Cullen, 'we're looking for Martin Webb.'

Smythe frowned. 'Martin Webb?'

'Yes,' said Cullen. 'This is the address he gave on a CV.'

'There's no Martin Webb here,' said Smythe. 'Just myself and my husband.'

'What about any old post you get?' said McNeill.

'We've been here for ten years,' said Smythe. 'I'm afraid I don't recognise that name at all.'

McNeill furrowed her brow. 'This is thirty-six Arden Street, isn't it?'

Anne Smythe smiled. 'No, this is number thirty-eight.'

'Thirty-eight?' said McNeill. 'Where's thirty-six then?'

Smythe laughed. 'There is no thirty-six Arden Street.'

15

Cullen and McNeill were sitting at a meeting table just beside their desks giving Bain and Miller a progress update, with Miller picking his nose and looking bored.

Bain had been busy in their absence — a press release was in the process of going out.

'Just another dead end case, then,' said Bain. 'Woman disappears, end of story. Christ knows we've got enough of them.'

'There's a couple of things irritating me about this Martin Webb guy,' said Cullen.

'Go on,' said Bain.

'First,' said Cullen, 'the address he gave on his CV on the Intarwubs site is fake.'

'How's it fake?' said Bain.

'It doesn't exist,' said Cullen. 'There's no thirty-six Arden Street. It goes thirty-two, thirty-four, thirty-eight.'

Bain looked at McNeill for confirmation. 'Is that right?'

McNeill nodded.

'Bloody hell,' said Bain. 'This bloody city.'

'Also,' said Cullen, 'I just had a look through his CV in more detail. None of the companies he's listed on there actually exist. I checked with Companies House and on a few search engines.'

Bain scowled. 'So, he didn't give a wrong address, he gave a bogus one and he's got a fake employment history as well.'

'Suspicious or what?' said Cullen.

'What are you planning to do about it?' said Bain.

'I need you to authorise that RIPSA request so we can get access to his Schoolbook account,' said Cullen.

'It's in hand,' said Bain.

Cullen sat back and folded his arms. 'Did you speak to Turnbull?'

Bain avoided Cullen's gaze. 'No idea where he was this afternoon. I'll get him in the morning. Might be more pliable by then.'

'There's a big gaping hole in this case,' said Cullen. 'Caroline Adamson goes on a date with some guy then disappears. Turns out we can find very little about him and what we do has been made up.'

'Look,' said Bain, 'for all we know Caroline could be setting all this up herself so she can escape her life. Wouldn't be the first time.'

Cullen slouched back in his chair. 'I'm not going to get this RIPSA form authorised, am I?'

'I didn't say that,' said Bain.

'Why are you being so difficult about it?' said McNeill.

'As I said earlier, the RIPSA powers are sensitive,' said Bain. 'I need Jim Turnbull to be okay with it.'

'But you haven't asked him yet,' said McNeill.

'Just drop it Butch, all right?' said Bain. 'I'm not convinced we need it. It's a big step.'

Cullen sat back and folded his arms. 'Has nothing we've said gone in? We can't find the guy she was on a date with, she still hasn't turned up after two days. This is highly irregular behaviour for her.'

'Aye well, there are other avenues we haven't exhausted yet,' said Bain. 'This husband seems the most likely.'

'You think?' said Cullen.

Bain nodded. 'I'd say so. He's got a pretty clear motive. Messy divorce, maintenance payments, maybe she's just a nightmare. He might be trying to put the frighteners on her by abducting her.'

'Seems a bit extreme,' said Cullen.

'Nothing's ever too extreme in my experience,' said Bain. 'Now, is there anything more we can do with him?'

'Aside from putting a tail on him to see if he leads us to a secret underground lair where he's keeping her,' said Cullen, 'then no.'

Bain narrowed his eyes and looked down his nose at Cullen. 'Less of the lip.' He looked over at Miller. 'Did the Italian corroborate this boy's alibi?'

Miller looked up and wiped his hand on the underside of the table. 'The boy couldn't say either way. It was busy that night. Lots of couples in.'

'Are you happy with that?' said Cullen.

'We'll see,' said Bain. 'Let's not lose too much sleep over this, Sundance. She'll probably turn up tomorrow. It'll be some misunderstanding and then we can all go back to the cold cases until someone sticks a knife in someone.' He got up and groaned as he stretched out. 'Right, who's up for a pint?'

Miller immediately got to his feet. 'Aye, count me in.'

Cullen folded his arms. 'Don't we need to find Caroline?'

Bain leaned over the table and got in Cullen's face. 'Sundance, will you relax? There's bugger all we can do for now. We've got the press release going out tonight. Jim should authorise the RIPSA form tomorrow.'

Cullen sighed. 'I'm not in tomorrow.'

'Well, you can come in on your day off, then,' said Bain.

'If we want to find her, we need to keep moving,' said Cullen. 'Unless someone else is taking this over it'll just get left till I'm back in on Monday.'

Bain checked his watch. 'Cullen, it's half six on a Friday and we're bloody quiet. That sounds a lot like pub time to me. Come on, I want to get out of here before the Friday night crowd start murdering each other and giving me something to do. Are you up for a pint?'

Cullen was pissed off — he couldn't escape the feeling Caroline was out there somewhere and he should be doing something to help. 'I'm not sure.'

'Sundance, I'll be in tomorrow,' said Bain. 'I'll make sure this is kept ticking over. Come on, just the one.'

Cullen hesitated for a moment. He looked at McNeill. 'Are you going?'

'I am.'

'Aye, go on then. I've got to meet some mates later, so I'll not stay that long.'

'Aye, right.' Bain put his suit jacket on. 'Need one last dump. Something's the matter with my bloody innards. I'll see you lot downstairs.'

'Could do with a slash,' said Miller.

They both headed off.

McNeill looked around at Cullen, shaking her head. 'He's some guy.'

Cullen tapped his pen on the tabletop. 'I'm not happy with this. Caroline's still missing and we still haven't found out who this Martin Webb guy is.'

She put on a weary look. 'This is Bain's case to screw up.'

'Aye, right,' said Cullen. 'Do you think he'll be carrying the can when this goes tits up?'

'The ball's in his court now,' said McNeill. 'If he says there's nothing more to do, there *is* nothing more to do.'

'What's his agenda here? Why haven't we got the RIPSA approved? We're missing out on something, I just know it.'

McNeill gave a deep sigh. 'Bain's obviously had his arse kicked a few times for that sort of thing. He's just covering himself.'

Cullen's blood was close to boiling. 'But why? I don't get it.'

'Put it this way, if he approves the RIPSA and we tear off to Schoolbook and get a load of data from them, and she turns up tomorrow morning, he'll look like an idiot.'

'He looks like one anyway,' said Cullen. 'Besides, that's a very big if. We're losing hours here, maybe days.'

'Come on.' McNeill got to her feet. 'We'd best get over the road.'

16

They went to the Elm, an old-fashioned pub just across from the station. It was at the Leith end of Elm Row, at least a block away from the actual trees — Cullen didn't know if they were elms or not. There was a horseshoe bar in the middle of the pub, with tables and chairs scattered haphazardly throughout the big room. The walls were covered with hundreds of mirrors advertising long-dead breweries.

DI Paul Wilkinson, Bain's peer, was playing pool in the back room with a couple of his officers. McNeill was at the other end of the bar, deep in what appeared to be a personal conversation with Chantal Jain, one of Wilkinson's DCs. Cullen reckoned he should sit with Bain and Miller, but he would much rather be with McNeill.

Bain set the tray down and distributed the three pints — Tennent's for Miller and himself, Stella for Cullen.

'Cheers.' Cullen took the first sip from his pint.

Bain grunted.

'Celtic at home for you boys next weekend,' said Miller. 'Tough first game of the season.'

Cullen had started a chat about football with Miller while Bain was at the bar, before quickly realising it was a big mistake — he'd let slip he was an Aberdeen fan. Miller was a Hibs season ticket holder and lived on Easter Road, just round the corner from their ground.

'No doubt we'll get turned over as ever,' said Cullen.

Bain said nothing, but eyed Cullen suspiciously.

'Fancy going to Hibs-Barca on Wednesday, then?' said Miller.

'Maybe.' Cullen had seen the match advertised in the papers — Hibs were playing Barcelona in a pre-season friendly, despite the Scottish football season already being underway.

'Could get you a ticket,' said Miller. 'My brother knows people.'

'Didn't know you had a brother,' said Bain.

Miller looked at his pint. 'He's not the sort of punter I want you knowing about.'

'Younger or older?' said Bain.

'Younger,' said Miller. 'Just turned twenty-one.'

'What's he do?'

Miller laughed. 'Sod all. He's a dirty little dole bastard.'

Bain snorted with laughter.

'He's a bit of a ned,' said Miller. 'Been in bother a few times.'

'What sort of bother?' said Bain.

'Nothing too bad. Never in trouble with us lot.'

'I thought your old boy was on decent money?' said Bain.

'Aye, he is,' said Miller, 'but we never seen him much when we were growing up. He was always busy with work.'

Cullen reappraised Miller, having previously taken him for just another Leith ned. He now saw him fit another profile entirely. At his school, some of the kids with the wealthiest parents — rich from the Aberdeen oil — tried the least hard and ended up mucking about and joining gangs in Arbroath or Dundee, generally up to no good. Spoilt kid syndrome.

'Derek had trials with Hibs and Rangers a couple of years ago,' said Miller. 'Stupid bastard got pissed the night before both of them. He was good enough to make it as a professional. He's a casual now.'

Bain shook his head. 'Hibs casuals. By the way, I'm not exactly happy with him getting you free tickets for games. That'll no doubt blow up in my face.'

'I'll watch my step,' said Miller.

Bain took a long drink of his pint. 'So you're an Aberdeen fan then, Sundance?'

'Aye,' said Cullen, cautiously.

'I hate Aberdeen.'

Cullen tried to smile. 'I take it you're a Rangers fan?'

Bain grunted.

The rivalry between Aberdeen and Rangers stemmed back to before Cullen was even born. In the eighties, Aberdeen were one of the best teams in Europe — let alone Scotland — under Alex Ferguson but their fortunes had declined greatly since.

Cullen tried to engage Bain. 'You go to Ibrox much?'

'Every game when I lived through there,' said Bain. 'Chance would be a fine thing these days.'

'You fancy coming along to the Barca game then, Gaffer?' said Miller.

Bain glared at him. 'I'd rather lose a bollock than stand in a stadium full of smack-head Hibs fans with a ticket your brother's nicked off somebody.'

'Suit yourself.'

They sat in silence for a bit, drinking. Cullen caught McNeill's eye over Bain's shoulder.

Bain looked at Cullen. 'I was on the phone to some boy in Bathgate earlier. You came over from F Troop, didn't you?'

'Aye.' Cullen knew F Troop meant F Division — West Lothian. He only recently found out it was a reference to an old American TV series about a bunch of idiot soldiers in the American civil war. 'I was in uniform there for six years. Livingston, Broxburn and Bathgate. Then I was an Acting DC at St Leonards.'

Bain sat back, his arms folded. 'St Leonards, eh?'

'I was in DI Ally Davenport's team,' said Cullen.

Bain nodded. 'Never heard of him.' He put his glass back down. 'How do you think you're getting on?'

Cullen had been in Bain's team for just over three months and had yet to have anything resembling a formal one-to-one, despite Bain's continual references to it.

'Well, it's early days.' Cullen took a sip of his pint trying to buy time. 'I've had a lot of autonomy and we got a result with the last case. It's why I wanted to join CID.'

Bain sneered. 'You're an idealist, then?'

'As opposed to what?'

'A realist,' said Bain. 'There are generally two types of detective.

There's your idealist, and then there's your realist. The idealist feels like they're born to be this great detective, the realist just gets there by *being* one.'

'So which type are you, then?'

Bain's eyes flickered with menace. 'I'll let you decide that.'

Cullen kept his mouth shut.

Bain smirked. 'Definitely an idealist.' He picked up his glass and finished it, then slammed it on the table. 'Whose round is it?'

Cullen glanced at his pint, at least half full. 'I'll get them in. Tennent's again?'

They both nodded.

'All right boys?'

Cullen swung round. DI Paul Wilkinson, his shirt untucked, his trousers stained, looking a total mess.

'All right, Wilko.' Bain raised his glass. 'Did you win?'

Wilkinson was the other DI who reported to DCI Turnbull. 'Too right I did,' he said in his Yorkshire accent, his ruddy face almost glowing. 'Those bastards were trying to use some Jock rules — two shots carry, bollocks like that.'

'I'm just off to the bar,' said Cullen, 'can I get you a drink?'

'Stella.'

Cullen went to the bar and ordered. He checked his watch — he could really do with pissing off soon. He needed to go back to the station and change before he met his flatmates. He had half a mind to just leave and get an early pint on his own somewhere else, especially now Wilkinson had joined them.

'Having a good time there?'

McNeill.

Cullen shrugged. 'Not exactly. You've managed to get out of it pretty easily.'

'Chantal's just broken up with her boyfriend. Needs to get a lot off her chest.'

'A likely tale.'

The barmaid gave Cullen his change.

McNeill ordered two glasses of rosé. 'How's it going with the stag party?'

Cullen shrugged. 'I could think of a million places I'd rather be.'

'I'd invite you over but I wouldn't want to break my own cover,' said McNeill.

Cullen smiled. 'Catch you later.' He picked up the tray of pints and headed back to the table full of idiots.

17

Cullen walked along Rose Street, finding his flatmates outside the Slippery Chopper. Johnny and Tom sat at an outside table with Johnny's girlfriend, Dawn, an array of empty glasses in front of them. The sun was out, in total contrast to the rest of the day.

Tom raised his empty glass. Cullen nodded and Tom went inside.

Cullen nodded at the glasses. 'Been here a while I see.'

'It's a nice night, like.' Johnny was skinny and almost as short as Dawn. 'You been out with work?'

'Sadly,' said Cullen. 'Just an hour of bollocks and three pints.'

Dawn laughed. 'Your boss still giving you hassle?'

'Not just me,' said Cullen.

Tom returned clutching two pints in his giant hands. 'Here you are.' He handed Cullen a Stella and sat his bulk down.

Cullen took a big drink. 'Cheers.'

'Should be a good night tonight,' said Tom.

'Yeah, should be good.' In truth, Cullen's head was still with Caroline Adamson and her disappearance. Sitting with Bain, Miller and Wilkinson had only heightened his sense of frustration.

'How's your new t-shirt?' said Tom.

'I like it.' Cullen had changed out of his suit back at the station.

He opened his jacket to show it to the others, a DJ scratching a record, wearing a policeman's helmet, *On the Beat* emblazoned in large letters.

Dawn laughed and looked over at Tom. 'How's that going?'

Tom looked bashful. 'Going all right. Those t-shirts pretty much keep me in beer money.'

'And you drink like a fish,' said Cullen.

Dawn laughed. 'How's your flat-hunting going?'

Cullen took another drink. 'Can't say it's really going anywhere.'

'Don't see why you want to move out,' said Tom.

'Not all of us are lucky enough to inherit money from our gran and get a staff mortgage at Alba Bank,' said Cullen.

'My flat's tripled in value since I bought it,' said Tom.

'Precisely,' said Cullen.

'Fancy going for a look on Sunday?' said Dawn. 'We're going.'

'Maybe.' Cullen didn't know if he could be arsed with flat hunting. 'You getting any joy?'

'None at all,' said Dawn. 'The market's totally dead.'

'It's depressing.' Cullen drank some more. 'Who are we meeting tonight?'

'Becky,' said Dawn. 'It's her birthday.'

Cullen got worried. 'Katie's not going to be there, is she?'

'I don't know.' Dawn shared a look with Johnny.

Katie was the reason Cullen moved in to Tom's flat four years previously. He'd gone out with her all the way through university but they started to drift apart after he joined the police and eventually split up, mostly at her insistence.

Cullen sunk the last of his pint and stood up. 'I'm off to the bar.'

He went inside, deciding the last thing he needed tonight was to see Katie.

∽

HOURS later in the Liquid Room, Cullen waited at the counter while the staff flirted with each other. He looked across the bar and locked eyes with Katie. She came over. He looked away.

'Hi Scott,' she said, all friendly.

'Katie.' Cullen looked at the barmaid, willing her to hurry up getting his drinks.

Katie moved over beside him. 'We've just got here,' she said, struggling to be heard over the music. 'I can't see Becky anywhere. Do you know where she is?'

'They were over on the dance floor.'

'It's nice to see you, Scott.'

Cullen just shrugged.

'I like your t-shirt.' She ran her hand through her hair, seeming nervous.

He looked away.

She came right up to him and spoke into his ear. 'Look, Scott, there's no need to be so hostile, okay?'

'Yeah, whatever.'

The barmaid handed him his drink in a plastic cup, and a bottle of water. By the time he'd paid, Katie was getting served.

As Cullen moved away from the bar, Katie turned and looked at him. 'I'm sorry about what happened between us. Can't we be friends?'

'I don't think we can.' Cullen walked away from the bar, looking for somewhere to sit and be alone.

Finding a seat at a table near the back of the room, he downed the water in one. His mouth was drying up — the dancing had made him sweat, the sweating had made him almost sober.

He was tired, feeling battered by the workload. He'd done the months as an ADC, on top of the years as a PC, but it hadn't prepared him for the long, relentless shifts he was now facing. He was thrown into it, drowning in exhaustion but at the same time expected to be at the top of his game. It was supposed to be nine to five.

He looked over at the dance floor, clutching his vodka and watching the crowd dancing. Johnny had Dawn straddling him. Beside them, Tom had his fist in the air, pumping to the beat. Cullen could see Becky dancing with a group of people he didn't recognise.

One of the girls was pretty, short dark hair held back off her face with a hair clip, wearing a tight silver kimono.

He spotted Katie heading over to join the group, holding hands with a short guy, his hand casually placed on her bottom.

Cullen turned away and sipped at the vodka.

'How's it going?'

He looked up. Dawn.

'Okay,' said Cullen.

'It's not, is it?' She sat next to him.

Cullen looked away. 'Not really.' He crunched some ice. 'Katie's here.'

'She's moved on, you know?'

Cullen nodded. 'I know. She tried to ram it in my face earlier.'

'Maybe it's time for you to find a girl and settle down.'

'Yeah, right,' said Cullen. 'My job and the hours I work aren't exactly giving me much opportunity for finding the right one.'

'At least you know you want to.'

Cullen laughed. 'True.' He took a deep breath. 'I need a new start, Dawn. I'm almost thirty and here I am in some shitty night-club with the same old people from university.'

'Are you bored of us?'

'It's not that. I just need to move on, as you say.'

'Cheer up, you bugger,' she said.

'Look, the music is shit tonight and I'm nowhere near drunk enough,' said Cullen.

'You need a Jaegerbomb.'

18

Cullen linked his arm with Dawn's as they walked up South Bridge, heading away from the centre, in the middle of a group of people he didn't recognise, trying to get a taxi to a house party somewhere. He had no idea where Tom and Johnny were. The guy Katie had her arms around earlier shouted something, then ran off laughing.

Two taxis pulled up and they got into one. Tom and Johnny appeared from somewhere and joined them.

Katie's boyfriend climbed in as well. He called an address out to the driver. 'Party at ours.'

'You're going out with Katie, aren't you?' said Cullen after a while.

The guy held out his hand. 'Steven. And we're not just going out, mate. We're engaged.'

Cullen ignored the hand. He looked at Dawn, looked at Johnny, looked at Tom. They all looked away.

Why had nobody told him?

~

Cullen stood at the kitchen sink in Katie and Steven's flat on Grange Loan, drinking from a can of Red Stripe he'd taken from the fridge. Shit French house music spewed out of the speakers.

Tom was standing by the sofa in front of Cullen, playing the ten-pin bowling game on the Wii. The big lummox had almost smashed into the TV twice already. Johnny sat on another sofa, Dawn sprawled all over him.

Katie and Steven stood by the door, laughing with kimono girl and another couple.

Cullen burped and tasted Red Bull and Jaegermeister. He took a swig of beer and looked out of the window. There was a good view across the back of the tenements, the communal lawn lit up by lights in the flats exactly like all of the others he'd ever been in. This was turning out just like so many other nights, except without a drunken fumble with some random girl.

He looked back into the room. Kimono girl was reaching into the fridge for a drink. She looked up at him and smiled. Cullen raised his can, and returned the smile.

'Hiya, I'm Alison.'

Cullen recalled someone saying they shared the flat with a girl called Alison who worked with Steven. 'Scott.'

'Ah, so *you're* Scott.'

'What's that supposed to mean?'

'Let's just say Katie's mentioned you once or twice,' said Alison.

'She has, has she? I sincerely hope she's not been honest.'

Alison laughed. 'So, I hear you're a policeman, then?'

'I am.' Cullen took another slug of beer.

She raised an eyebrow. 'I love a man in uniform,' she said, licking her lips.

Cullen laughed — she was even more pissed than he was. That was an awful line. 'Yeah, well, I'm a detective so I don't actually wear a uniform any more. Just a suit.'

'Oh, didn't know that,' said Alison. 'So you, what, catch murderers, is that right?'

'Supposedly.'

'Are you on a case just now?'

'Yeah, supposed to be,' said Cullen. 'I'm off tomorrow so I won't be catching anyone.'

She leaned against the counter, supported by her arms. Cullen caught Katie scowling at him from across the room.

'So you're like *Taggart* then?' said Alison.

'The reality of it is very different from TV,' said Cullen. 'Long hours, frustration, dealing with a boss who wants to kill you.'

'It's very glamorous on the telly.'

'It's not like that in reality,' said Cullen. 'Crawling around murder scenes in a big white suit, chasing loose ends, dealing with wankers. I almost got stabbed this morning. That's the reality. And don't get me started on the books. Half of them have a DCI or a bloody ACC running round investigating crimes. All they really do is massage statistics and give crime prevention seminars. It's a joke. It's people like me who do all the work and get none of the thanks.' He took a swig from his can, looking her up and down just as she did the same. He moved closer, Katie was looking over at them, even more disapproving than before.

Bollocks to it. He leaned over and kissed her.

CULLEN OPENED his eyes and stared at the ceiling.

Where was he?

What was that noise?

His mobile.

He struggled out of the bed, almost tripping up, his head throbbing. He rummaged around in the pile of clothes, dug under the t-shirt, under the silver kimono, fumbled with his jeans, reached in the wrong pocket, then the correct one, all the while his head battered away. The clock on the bedside cabinet said ten thirty — he hadn't a clue when he'd got to sleep.

He answered the phone without checking the display.

'Sundance?'

Bain.

'What is it?'

'You better get your arse over here.' Bain sounded agitated. 'We've found Caroline Adamson.'

Cullen sat back. 'How is she?'

'She's dead.'

DAY 3

Saturday
30th July

19

Bain's 'here' was the Jackson Hotel on Minto Street. Cullen had been in the function room as a student in full Highland dress — kilt, sporran, jacket, the lot — and he'd hated it. The night itself was a disaster, mainly due to a row he had with Katie.

Cullen walked from Alison's flat, just over a mile away, feeling guilty for leaving her asleep in bed. He'd left his mobile number, but it didn't stop him feeling shallow.

Katie had really wound him up — he hadn't expected her engagement and she'd just flaunted it, her paws all over that guy. So, he'd slept with her flatmate in retaliation. Smart move.

Christ, was he tired. He checked his watch as he entered the hotel — just before eleven.

He followed the signs down the corridor towards the room where they'd found Caroline's body, number 20 on the ground floor. The place was rammed with Scene of Crime Officers, dressed in their white overalls, looking to Cullen like they were almost finished their examination.

He vaguely recognised a short man with a goatee and slicked back hair heading into the room, as he put on his own set of overalls and signed into the crime scene.

He spotted Bain and McNeill standing in the hallway outside the room, looking out of the window to the car park at the back,

Bain's hand stroking his moustache. An officer wearing overalls and holding a clipboard stood beside them.

Cullen caught his own reflection in a mirror hanging on the wall in the corridor — he looked even worse than he felt and that was like he'd died twice over.

He approached them. 'Sir.'

'Sundance, I've told you before — just call me Brian.' Bain turned round. His eyes just about popped out on stalks. 'Jesus Christ, Cullen, what the hell have you been up to?'

'I was out clubbing.'

'You should have bloody said, Sundance.'

McNeill looked at his t-shirt and laughed.

'What happened here?' said Cullen.

'Cleaner found her,' said Bain.

McNeill picked up the thread. 'There was a *'Do Not Disturb'* sign on the door since Wednesday night. She came in this morning to clean. They've got a policy of disturbing after two days.' She paused. 'She got lucky today, though.'

'Aye, some jokers from your old patch came sniffing around,' said Bain, alluding to St Leonards. 'One of them recognised Caroline from the photograph in the press release we sent out last night. We've just completed a handover from them.'

'Jesus,' said Cullen. 'Have the parents been told?'

Bain scowled at him. 'I do know how to run a murder investigation, Cullen. Yes, they have. A local teuchter plod is on their way round to the house as we speak.'

'Where's the body?' said Cullen. 'Can I have a look?'

'In there.' Bain nodded into the room. 'Jimmy Deeley's just about ready to take her up to the morgue after we've finished. The SOCO boys are done with her now.'

'What's the cause of death?' said Cullen.

'Don't know yet,' said Bain. 'There was a shitload of blood in there, though. Looks like a stabbing.'

Cullen finished putting on the overall and a pair of disposable plastic shoe covers, and Bain led them both through.

James Deeley, the city's Chief Pathologist, stood with his back to them, his bulk blocking the doorway into the bedroom, talking into a digital recorder as the temporary spotlights gleamed off his bald head. He turned around and nodded acknowledgement to Cullen. They knew each other from St Leonards.

'Got a time yet, Jimmy?' said Bain.

'I'd say between eleven pm on Wednesday and seven am on Thursday,' said Deeley. 'She's been dead for at least a couple of days, but she's clean as a bloody whistle.'

Cullen thought he noticed an air of disappointment in Deeley's voice.

'Have you or Anderson found anything yet?' said Bain.

'We haven't managed to find any forensic traces here,' said Deeley, 'but we may be able to get something back at the lab.'

'Thanks for that. I'll take it up with the SOCOs.' Bain pointed into the room. 'Now, talk to me. What's happened here?'

'It looks like she was tortured for a good few hours before she died,' said Deeley.

Bain looked at McNeill. 'And nobody heard anything?'

'No,' she said, shaking her head.

'Go on, Jimmy.'

Deeley cleared his throat. 'Cause of death is strangulation. Some sort of rope. Hopefully we can get some fibres from the wound that Forensics can do something with.'

From the way they talked to each other, Cullen guessed they were either old friends or old adversaries, but he couldn't decide which.

'Anything else?' said Bain.

'There's a huge gash on her throat caused by a large knife.' Deeley's expression darkened. 'It didn't kill her, though. It looks like a serrated blade.'

'Was there anything sexual here?'

Deeley shrugged. 'Too early to say for sure, but it doesn't look that way. What I would say is this is definitely a deliberate killing, not some sex game gone wrong or anything like that.'

'No signs of rape then?' said Bain.

Deeley rolled his eyes. 'As I say, I'll know for certain once I've done the post mortem, but I don't think so.'

Bain scratched at his scalp. 'Cheers.'

'I'll get out of your way for now,' said Deeley. 'Let me know when you've finished and I'll get one of the boys to remove her.

Don't be too long, mind — I need to get that PM done, cos some bloody DI wants to know if she's been raped.'

Bain grinned at Deeley as he made his way past, allowing them into the room.

Cullen stopped and looked at Caroline's body. She lay on the bed, arms and legs spread, her skin pale, as if all the blood had drained from her, the white sheets now almost completely dyed dark red. Her mouth was covered with gaffer tape. The only colour on the upper surface of her body was a set of crimson, raw-looking marks all over her throat, beneath a long ragged cut, looking like someone had crudely hacked at her rather than doing a neat butchery job.

Cullen's stomach lurched. He raced through into the bathroom, just catching his vomit in the pan. Three heaves and it was over.

A voice behind him swore.

Cullen slowly turned around, a dribble of sick still on his chin.

A SOCO stood over him, the one with the goatee. 'I've not finished examining the bog yet.'

20

C ullen finished his second mug of canteen tea just before noon, starting to feel a little more human, but he was still exhausted. He had changed back into his suit in the locker room and put on the same crumpled shirt he'd worn the previous day, only slightly sweat stained.

Cullen, Bain and McNeill stood in front of a whiteboard, Bain running through the file Cullen had collated, trying to summarise the case so far. He looked stressed, but still he spoke calmly and clearly in measured tones. He'd already got through at least half of a litre bottle of Red Bull clone, enough to stop anyone else's heart, Cullen figured. Or start it.

DS Holdsworth was called in from a day off to set up the Incident Room - a large custom space at the opposite side of the building, facing north towards the Forth. The giant plasma screen mounted on the wall showed the standard Lothian & Borders screensaver. The opposite wall was covered with large prints of the photos taken at the crime scene, interspersed with some of Caroline alive, including the one used in the press release plastered all over that morning's papers.

Officers were being dragged in from the day shift — Cullen had already seen McAllister hovering around. Wilkinson and his team were now formally allocated to the case and were interviewing guests at the hotel, trying to track down anyone who was there on Wednesday night.

Miller was assigned to putting the case into HOLMES — the Home Office Large Major Enquiry System. He'd done the training course while still in uniform — Cullen was grateful to have avoided the dubious pleasure so far. No doubt Miller would mention his HOLMES certification to Turnbull in his quest for full detective status.

'The post mortem's in an hour, so I want to get this out of the way quickly,' said Bain. 'Sharon, I want you there with me.'

'Fine.'

'How are you getting on with the RIPSA form?' said Cullen.

Bain evaded his gaze.

'I thought I didn't need to come in today and you'd progress it?' said Cullen.

'Well, I never got round to it, did I?' said Bain. 'I was in at seven then I got called out to that hotel.'

'Yeah, but what time was that?' said Cullen. 'You called me at half ten.'

Bain glared at him. 'Constable, drop it.'

Cullen took his gravelly voice as a warning, which he decided to ignore. 'Come on.'

'Sundance,' said Bain, 'you've just decorated a crime scene with the contents of your guts and you turned up for work half-cut.'

'Today's supposed to be my day off.'

'Okay, okay, okay.' Bain shut his eyes and stroked his moustache. 'What was this RIPSA request about again?'

Cullen took a deep breath. 'To get access to Schoolbook.'

'Right.' Bain checked his watch. 'Turnbull's in this afternoon, I'll have a word with him then.'

'Can't you authorise it now?' said McNeill.

'No.' Bain fixed a glare on her. 'It needs to go through Jim.'

Cullen shook his head in disbelief.

'Can't you get anything off them without a warrant or RIPSA?' said Bain.

'They were pretty hard line about it yesterday,' said Cullen. 'They gave us what they could.'

'What about playing the daft laddie? Or the big, scary police-man?' Bain laughed at his own joke.

'I thought you were worried about how this would look to the press?' said Cullen. 'Breaking through red tape wouldn't exactly look good.'

'As I say, I'll speak to Jim this afternoon and that's the end of the matter.' Bain took another swig of energy drink. 'Let's think about suspects.' He wrote 'Rob Thomson' on the whiteboard. 'What do we know about him?'

'He's the victim's ex-husband,' said McNeill.

Cullen felt his stomach lurch again, realising Caroline was no longer a missing person — she was now officially a murder victim.

'And there's no history of violence between them?' said Bain.

'Not that we can find,' said Cullen. 'Miller checked his record — nothing came up when we asked her friends.'

Bain looked thoughtful for a moment. He drew in a line connecting Rob's and Caroline's names. 'They've got a wee boy, right?'

'Jack,' said Cullen.

'What's Thomson's relationship with his son like?' said Bain.

Cullen smiled. 'He's not going to climb up a crane dressed as Spiderman to get access rights, put it that way.'

McNeill laughed.

'Very good, Sundance, but this is a murder now, so try and cut the humour a bit, okay?'

'Fine.' Cullen was starting to see which buttons to press with Bain.

'How often does he see him?' said McNeill.

'Once a fortnight,' said Cullen. 'Debi Curtis said they'd recently had a row about it.'

'Climbing a crane time?' said Bain.

'Thought there was no joking allowed?' said Cullen.

'Only from me,' said Bain. 'Was Rob arguing about more access?'

'I got the impression it was about Thomson cancelling at the last minute,' said Cullen. 'It happened a few times.'

'If that's true then we can rule out him killing her to get access to his son,' said Bain.

Cullen thought it over. 'Probably. He acts like a single guy, if you know what I mean. He's got a younger girlfriend, and neither of them seems to be into the whole family thing.'

'Is he getting stung for a big wad?' said Bain.

'I don't know,' said Cullen.

'We can look into that,' said Bain. 'Sharon?'

'Okay.' She scribbled it in her notebook.

'Even though he's got an alibi, he's our number one suspect here.' Bain wrote 'Martin Webb' and 'AN Other' on the board. He tapped 'AN Other'. 'I've put that up just to cover all bases. We might be dealing with a random attack, but that'll come out in the wash, I guess.' He put the cap back on the pen. 'So, Martin Webb. Amy Cousens reckons Caroline was meeting this guy for a date?'

'Corroborated by Steve Allen,' said Cullen. 'I spoke to him on the phone yesterday. He lives in Glasgow. I think they were at school together, but they were still close. She'd told both Steve and Amy about a date but neither of them knew Martin Webb's name.'

'Right.' Bain's eyes were focused on the board.

'There were a few postings by Caroline on Schoolbook about meeting him,' said McNeill. 'Stuff like *'Off on date tonight'*. Nothing too explicit.'

'I still don't get what Schoolbook actually is when it's at home,' said Bain.

Cullen threw his pen on the table — he'd been over this several times already. 'It's like Google+ or Facebook. Have you seen that *Social Network* film?'

'Like I get time to go to the bloody pictures,' said Bain.

'But you get the general idea?' said Cullen.

'Right, I've had the training.' Bain sniffed. 'So people go on it and find their friends?'

'And meet people,' said Cullen.

'Then what?' said Bain.

'They chat,' said Cullen. 'You can find people you were at school with. It's like an online pub.'

McNeill piped up, a wry smile on her face. 'Not such a good analogy. The Inspector doesn't go to the pub to meet people, he goes to sit with his cronies and make bad jokes about me.'

Bain laughed and looked at Cullen. 'Who's been grassing?'

McNeill grinned but Cullen knew she was just putting a front on it.

'So Caroline met Martin Webb on this website,' said Cullen.

'Do we know for definite it's where they met?' said McNeill.

Cullen thought it through for a few seconds. 'Her friends said she met him online.'

'Could she have known him offline?' said McNeill. 'Could she have met him elsewhere on the internet, some dating site or a chat room?'

Cullen shrugged. 'Could have done. I do get the impression it was Schoolbook, though.'

Bain looked thoughtful for a few moments.

Cullen butted in. 'The RIPSA would help.'

'Aye, whatever.' Bain glared at him. 'Cullen, I thought you said you'd looked for Martin Webb?'

'I have,' said Cullen. 'I didn't find him, though.'

McNeill looked at Cullen. 'You've struggled to find him in the real world. It could be someone posing as Martin Webb.'

Cullen nodded. 'He's not in any of our databases. There's nothing to match his profile picture. I put this stuff in the file — there are matches for the name, but they don't fit the profile.'

Bain pinched his nose as he stared at the whiteboard. He scribbled 'Assumed Name?' under Martin Webb then clipped the lid back on the pen. 'Right, so AN Other. This could just be a random crime, nothing related to Martin Webb or her ex. Is that likely?'

'Don't know,' said Cullen.

'We can't discount it,' said McNeill.

'We shouldn't discount it, no.' Bain took another drink. 'But at the moment, we've got a hell of a lot of other stuff to think about before we're that desperate. So this Schoolbook, when you add someone as a friend can you see who's friends with who?'

'Yes,' said McNeill.

Bain was looking at Cullen. He could almost see the gears grinding behind his eyes. 'I need someone to look through her list of friends on that website.'

'Me?'

'Aye,' Bain had an evil grin on his face. 'Go through all of her friends and try to find something to go on. Speak to them, ask questions. Usual drill.'

'Fine.' Cullen felt deflated — from pretty much leading the

investigation, he was now running a stupid little errand. 'When do you need it by?'

'Yesterday would've been useful,' said Bain.

Cullen tried to think back to how many friends Caroline had. There were pages and pages of them, at least forty. He wouldn't surface for weeks. 'A couple of bodies might help.'

'I can spare Caldwell and McAllister till the new press release goes out,' said Bain. 'They're yours today.'

Cullen scowled. 'McAllister? Jesus.' He sighed. 'I need detectives for this.'

'Remember you're the detective, Sundance,' said Bain. 'Get the uniform to do the donkey work.'

21

Half an hour later, Cullen sat with Angela and McAllister in a corner of the Incident Room, briefing them on the search through Caroline's friends. He had printed off their Schoolbook profiles and allocated them between them, keeping a smaller list for himself.

Cullen prepared a list of questions to ask: confirm they were friends with Caroline; when they'd last heard from her; ask if anyone would want to harm her; finally, tell them she'd been murdered and see if the shock jogged any memories.

He explained the process they were to go through, though McAllister struggled with the concept. They were to find contact details for everyone on the list they'd been given and then phone them — some had mobile numbers on the profile, some didn't. They had access to enough search engines to be able to find details for them all, unless there were other enigmas like Martin Webb on there.

Angela had been asking sensible questions and had stayed alert, while Willie McAllister had slouched and fiddled with his cigarette papers, continually glaring at Cullen.

'Is everything clear now?' said Cullen.

McAllister was still frowning. 'I'm still struggling to get how would they be friends with her on this site, but not know her.'

'I take it you've never used a social network, Willie?' said Angela, like she was speaking to a small child.

McAllister squinted at her. 'Do I look like I'm on Schoolbook?'

'All you need to know is there are people on there who've become Caroline's friend without knowing her,' said Cullen.

'How?' said McAllister.

'There are message forums on there,' said Angela. 'If you're talking about, say, a film or a record, then you might chat to someone and they might add you as a friend.'

McAllister scowled. 'That's a bit weird.'

'Just accept it,' said Angela.

'Fair enough.' McAllister dropped his roll-ups, then slowly reached down to pick them up.

Angela rolled her eyes.

'Anything else?' said Cullen.

McAllister stopped playing around, then held his hands up. 'What's the point in all of this? From what I see, we've been roped in to do your work for you.'

Cullen glared at him. 'I've been asked to do this by the Senior Investigating Officer. Yourself and PC Caldwell have been allocated to help me. There are forty-three potential leads sitting there. Would you be able to look at yourself in the mirror if the murderer got away with it because we didn't look through the list properly? If anyone can shed any light on this Martin Webb, it does the case good.'

McAllister glanced at his cigarette. 'Fair enough.'

Cullen knew then he was going to have to double-check McAllister's list himself.

22

Angela stood by Cullen's desk. 'Can I get you a coffee?'

He looked up at her — his head was still throbbing. She was possibly the tallest woman he had ever met — well over six foot and not a beanpole, either. He found it strange having to look up to a woman — he didn't have to with many people.

'I'm just away up to the canteen,' she said, as if to elaborate.

Cullen decided a coffee might help. 'Aye, go on, then.' He reached into his pocket and handed her a fiver. 'Get us a ham sandwich as well.'

She smiled. 'Last time I ask you.'

'How are you getting on?'

Angela raised her eyebrows. 'Not too bad. Made a few calls, got nothing so far.'

'Good opportunity for overtime.' They'd been at it almost two hours, but it felt like days. 'Where's McAllister, by the way?'

'He's been out for a fag every two minutes,' said Angela, 'and he never stops complaining.'

'I'll have to do something about that,' said Cullen.

After she left, Cullen picked up her sheet and scanned through it. She'd made some solid progress, though there were a couple of clarifications he wanted. He was already dreading having to write it all up, but at least her notes were decent.

He went over and picked up McAllister's sheet, sitting back down and looking through it. As far as Cullen could see, he'd completed just one call compared with Angela's six and the notes he'd made were poor. Perhaps he'd made more calls but hadn't got through or found contact details — Cullen simply couldn't tell from the notes.

He leaned back in his chair. He was going to have to replace McAllister — it was his neck on the line for this.

McNeill sat without greeting him, her face white.

'You okay?' said Cullen.

'Just been at the post mortem,' said McNeill. 'Time of death looks like eleven thirty on Wednesday night, plus or minus an hour. She'd been strangled and stabbed.'

'Any DNA?'

'None at all.'

'None?' said Cullen. 'Shite.'

'Aye.' McNeill took a drink from the bottle of water on her desk.

'What about that rope burn?' said Cullen. 'Did they get anything from it?'

'Aye, they did,' said McNeill, 'but it's not exactly going to help. How many blue ropes get sold in Edinburgh every single day?' She sighed. 'How's your stuff going?'

'Getting there. Nothing earth-shattering so far.'

'It's important stuff, I guess.' She seemed distracted.

'Did you get anywhere with her bank records?' said Cullen.

'Nowhere so far but then it is a Saturday. No doubt Bain will have a go at me for that as well.' She tightened the cap on the bottle and set it aside. 'The card used to book the hotel room was reported stolen on Wednesday morning. Dead end.'

'Bollocks.'

She nodded over his shoulder. 'Here comes trouble.'

Cullen turned to see Bain approaching, practically shouting into his mobile.

He slumped into his seat, ignoring them. 'Paul, Paul, Paul, you'll have to take that up with Jim when he gets in. You're reporting to me, all right? Now get the other guests found.' He paused. 'Aye, whoever you need.' Another pause. 'No, not McNeill or Cullen. You can have Miller. Okay, there's another couple coming in from St Leonards, I'll get them up to you. Bye.' He snapped his phone shut. 'Arsehole.' He looked at Cullen and McNeill. 'Have either of you seen Miller?'

'Not all day,' said Cullen.

'Me neither,' said McNeill.

'Got a lead,' said Bain. 'Wilko's turned up some CCTV footage at the hotel. I wish I could spare either of you two. In lieu of a safe pair of hands, I'll have to get Monkey Boy on it. I've got to lead the press conference at three. Christ.'

'Got my RIPSA approved yet?' said Cullen.

Bain shot him a glare. 'I'm seeing Jim in ten minutes, no doubt after Wilko's finished moaning about me.' He picked up his bottle of energy drink. 'Get back to your phone calls, Cullen.'

∼

CULLEN FINISHED a call with a man who seemed at best a vague acquaintance of Caroline's. He slammed the phone down.

Another half hour and nothing to show for it. He looked through his friends and saw no one else from Caroline's list. Another dead end.

McNeill grabbed his shoulder. 'Come on, Scott. We've got our RIPSA approved.'

23

They pulled into the car park at Schoolbook's office in McNeill's yellow Fiat Punto. Cullen would much rather they'd gone in a squad car as he wouldn't have had to put up with her music on the way over — he had discovered there was no volume setting too quiet for Lady Gaga.

Cullen looked across the Livingston skyline. Even if it meant having to work with Bain, he was glad he wasn't based there any more. 'How do you want to play this?'

'We need to get an extract of their database,' she said. 'Charlie Kidd's supposed to be heading over, but I can't see his Mini.'

Kidd was the Technical Support Unit analyst assigned to Turnbull and his teams. As far as Cullen knew, they'd only ever used him for scouring through suspects' laptops and mobiles.

'He wants a dump of the database to do whatever it is they do in Technical Support, right?' said Cullen.

'Other than drink Dr Pepper and eat cheese Doritos.'

Cullen laughed. 'So we can get IP addresses, messages, absolutely anything else Martin Webb has left on there.'

'Quite the closet geek, aren't you?'

'Did a course on this stuff earlier in the year,' said Cullen. 'Part of my Acting DC tenure. It's going to become a much bigger part of our jobs.'

A Mini Cooper pulled up in the next space, a vintage model — early eighties by the number plate.

'There he is,' said McNeill.

'That's him?' said Cullen. 'When you said a Mini, I thought you meant the new ones.'

She laughed.

They got out and headed over. Kidd got out of the driver's side. He was a skinny guy in his late thirties with bad skin, his thinning hair tied tightly in a ponytail, shaved up to ear level.

As they shook hands, Cullen did a double take — Kidd was wearing one of Tom's t-shirts — *Isn't it 2000 already? Where's my jetpack?*

'I was on my day off,' said Kidd, in a rough Dundee accent.

'You're not alone,' said Cullen.

McNeill led them inside.

Gregor Aitchison was sitting just inside the front door waiting for them, his leg jigging up and down. He'd clearly done something about letting the police in unsupervised the previous day. Cullen introduced Kidd.

'Got a DBA waiting at my desk,' said Aitchison. 'He'll help you with your extract.'

Heads glanced up at them as he led them through the open plan office, looking away just as quickly. At Aitchison's desk sat a big man in jeans and a loose-fitting jumper. He got to his feet — he was taller and more muscular than he'd initially appeared.

'Duncan Wilson.' His stare seemed to bore through Cullen. He grinned at them, revealing yellow teeth. 'How can I help?'

'I'm sure Mr Aitchison has briefed you on DC Cullen's visit yesterday?' said McNeill.

Wilson raised an eyebrow. 'Indeed. Gregor was just giving me the background. It seems strange.'

'Well, as you'll be aware, the disappearance has turned into a murder investigation.' McNeill brandished the RIPSA form. 'We want to speak to whoever's using the name Martin Webb on your website. We now have authority to obtain a copy of your database.'

Wilson frowned at Aitchison. 'Are you happy with this?'

'Aye, I've spoken to the boss.'

Wilson raised his eyebrows. 'Are you really sure?'

Aitchison looked away from them.

Wilson moved close to Aitchison, seeming to loom over him. 'Legal told us we shouldn't.' He looked at Cullen and McNeill. 'There's no way we can just hand this over, warrant or not. As well as the data, we would be handing over our intellectual property, our code and database structures. Our competitors would kill for some of the tricks in there.'

McNeill rolled her eyes in despair. 'Just read the form.'

Aitchison made a show of reading the document. 'Okay.' He handed it to Wilson, who scanned through it.

'Gregor, you really should check with Clive,' said Wilson.

Aitchison looked twitchy, obviously uncomfortable with the stance he was forced to take. Cullen wondered if it was the fact he had to take a stance at all.

'Look, we're a law-abiding company and we're more than happy to assist your search,' said Aitchison. 'But I can't pass this database on to the police. Our lawyer says I don't have to. This document only gives you access to the records pertaining to Martin Webb.'

McNeill folded her arms. 'If that's all you're prepared to deliver, then I'll see what the Procurator Fiscal has to say about the remainder.'

Aitchison was perspiring. 'I'll have to run this by the boss. He's based at our Head Office in Croydon.' He picked up his big Samsung mobile and wandered off out of earshot.

Kidd tried to start a conversation with Wilson. 'Didn't know Schoolbook was based in Croydon.'

'I didn't know myself until I started,' said Wilson. 'I'm just a contractor. Self-employed. Pays the bills, but I don't take my work home with me, if you know what I mean.'

'What is this place?' said Kidd.

'Data centre,' said Wilson. 'The entire database is stored in these buildings. There's a back-up on some servers in the states and on some Alba Bank servers as well.'

Cullen raised an eyebrow. 'Alba Bank?'

'Aye,' said Wilson. 'They're rock solid.'

'Why Livingston, though?' said Kidd.

Wilson shrugged. 'Proximity to Alba Bank? Their data centre's just down the road in an unmarked building. Also, they can hire decent people on cheap rates compared with London.' He grinned. 'The joke is the reason they're up here is they don't need to cool the servers because it's so cold outside.'

Cullen knew from bitter experience how cold West Lothian could be.

Aitchison reappeared, the armpit area of his t-shirt dark with sweat. He tapped his mobile against the side of his head, his eyes closed.

'Well?' said McNeill.

Aitchison reopened his eyes. 'Duncan, can you get an extract of the record for Martin Webb, please?'

Wilson scowled. 'How much of it?'

'All tables.' Aitchison sighed. 'Full history.'

'Are you one hundred per cent sure?' said Wilson.

'Just do it,' said Aitchison.

Wilson tilted his head then started tapping at the workstation.

'That's all you're going to get with that document,' said Aitchison.

'We'll accept the records for that account for now,' said McNeill, 'but we'll be back to get the rest.'

'Fine,' said Aitchison.

Kidd leaned over the back of Wilson's chair. 'What are you up to?'

'What we agreed.'

Kidd turned to McNeill. 'This isn't right. His SQL statement's all over the place.'

McNeill scowled. 'Do we need to have a conversation about obstruction?'

Aitchison closed his eyes and took a deep breath. 'I've been told I can't give away any intellectual content relating to our database structures or data model, so the files you'll get will just be the raw data.'

Kidd's eyes bulged. 'You're kidding me.'

'What does that mean?' said Cullen.

'Imagine a spreadsheet full of data with no column headings,' said Kidd.

'So you'll be flying blind?'

Kidd nodded.

'You're just after messages and IP addresses,' said Wilson. 'I can show you that.'

'It's not just that,' said Kidd. 'I need to look at everything to check for patterns. This boy has been elusive and anything on your database could help us find him. You'd be surprised at what I need to look at.'

Wilson shrugged. 'I'm not sure your RIPSA covers all of that.'

'It does,' said Kidd. 'If you don't give us everything, then we're not much further forward.'

McNeill looked at Wilson and Aitchison. 'Is that right?'

Eventually, Aitchison nodded.

'This is a murder investigation,' she said. 'If I want to, I could have this entire place shut down. There's nothing we can do without that information.'

Aitchison sat blinking. He reached for his mobile again.

'No, you don't.' McNeill grabbed the phone out of his hands. 'You're giving us headings and anything else Mr Kidd here needs to unpick this.'

Aitchison slumped back in his chair. 'Fine. Duncan will note the relevant fields and tables.'

'And I need primary keys, joins and all that,' said Kidd.

Cullen thought it sounded good but he had no idea what Kidd was talking about — he hoped Wilson and Aitchison did.

'Fine, fine,' said Aitchison.

Kidd reached into his pocket, retrieving a Lothian & Borders branded memory stick. 'Put it on here.' He looked at McNeill. 'We're going to have to set up an extranet socket to get the full database though.'

'That's for the lawyers to agree,' said Aitchison. 'As I've said, we're a law-abiding company.'

Kidd pointed at Aitchison's screen. 'If you're so law abiding, how come you've got ten torrents running?'

Aitchison blushed. 'They're all legal.'

24

McAllister got up and kicked the chair back under the desk. He glared at Cullen, a look of fury in his eyes, then marched off towards the exit without saying anything.

Cullen called after him. 'Get back here.'

McAllister stood in the doorway and laughed at Cullen. 'No way, pal. I'll see you the morn's morn.' He turned around and left the Incident Room.

The room was half empty, with most officers either on phone calls or out of the station on one of the many investigations Bain was running. Cullen breathed a sigh of relief — hardly anyone had witnessed the exchange, only Angela had really been paying attention. He sat in his chair and leaned back, his heart thudding from the confrontation.

'McAllister's an arse,' said Angela from across the desk.

Cullen rubbed the back of his neck. 'I know that, but I'm the one who'll look bad.'

'No, you won't. Just speak to Bain, get him reallocated.'

'Yeah, I would if I thought it would do any good.' Cullen put his pen on the desk and rubbed his eyes. 'What time are you in till tonight?'

'I'm on the back shift. Ten.'

Cullen picked up McAllister's sheet and scanned it. 'Jesus

Christ. It's worse than I thought. He's only done *two*. What's he been doing all day?'

Angela sighed. 'Smoking and drinking coffee. I worked with him on the beat a few years ago. He's the laziest person I've ever met.'

'How do these people not get found out?'

'Here.' She took the sheet off him. 'We'll split the remainder. I've finished mine.'

'Already?'

'Aye, but I must have had the easy list, and I didn't have to go over to Schoolbook. Not that it got us anywhere, mind.' She pointed to her laptop. 'Six of them had emailed Caroline about films from the discussion boards, three of them hadn't seen her since school and the other five were acquaintances from university who hadn't seen her since 2002. I've just been typing the notes up. How are you getting on?'

Cullen looked through his own list. 'I've done nine.'

'Well, I'll take eight off Willie's list. You take the other four.'

'Make it nine and five,' said Cullen. 'I don't trust he's done the first two correctly.'

She smiled. 'Race you.'

'What does the winner get?'

'Not to write the report up?'

Cullen laughed. 'You're on.'

'Enough flirting, you pair.'

Bain stood behind them, hands on his hips.

'We weren't—'

'Leave it, Cullen.' Bain crossed the Incident Room to his desk and sat down, cracking open a can of energy drink.

Cullen followed him over, pulling up the chair next to him. 'There's something I need to speak to you about.'

Bain huffed. 'Cullen, if you love me, I've told you — when we're off duty.'

'This is serious.'

Bain put his feet up on the desk and took a long look at Cullen. 'Right, go on then. Fire away.'

'It's McAllister. His attitude's bad. He's only completed two calls all day, which we reckon we'll have to redo. Caldwell's finished her list already. He's dead weight.'

Bain yawned. 'He's resource, unfortunately.' He took another sip. 'You struggling to manage him?'

Cullen paused, realising he shouldn't have taken this to Bain. Any problem would inevitably be seen as a result of Cullen's inadequacies. 'He's unmanageable.'

Bain eyed him, seemed to make a judgment. 'I'll see what I can do. The door-to-door might be more his thing.' He winked at Cullen. 'This managing people thing is a learning curve, Sundance.'

Cullen was fed up with being patronised. 'I suppose it must be.'

Bain drained the can then crushed it. 'How did it go with that RIPSA form? Am I going to get a doing for it?'

'We sort of got what we wanted.'

'Sort of doesn't sound good,' said Bain.

'We were after the full data set, but they just gave us the Martin Webb stuff.'

'Do we need the rest of it?'

'It could prove useful,' said Cullen.

'Could and useful aren't good enough,' said Bain. 'We're trying to get personal data about members of the public. We've got to have a very good reason for that.'

'Well, I'll leave it for you to arrange getting the rest of it,' said Cullen.

Bain smiled broadly, a twinkle in his eye. 'Sneaky little bastard, aren't you?'

Cullen tried to laugh along, to see if that made him stop.

'Speaking of sneaky wee bastards,' said Bain, 'where the hell is Miller?'

'Thought you had him looking through the CCTV footage from the hotel after the HOLMES stuff?'

'Aye, but he can't be taking that long, can he?' said Bain.

'Why do you need him?' said Cullen. 'Surely if there's anything on there, he'll find you.'

'Aye, maybe.' Bain smacked his hand on a brown envelope lying on his desk. 'Got Caroline Adamson's mobile records from the Forensic Investigation boys. I wanted Miller to look through it. Maybe that way he'll keep out of Turnbull's way.'

'How's it going up at the hotel?'

'Wilko's making an arse of it as usual.' Bain shook his head. 'Chantal and Irvine have interviewed everyone who was there that night and they've turned up absolutely nothing. Now they're trying to find everyone who's stayed there over the last week. Needle in a bloody haystack.' He exhaled. 'Have to wait and see what happens when the press release goes out.'

'Well, if you don't need me,' said Cullen, 'I'll go back to flirting with PC Caldwell.'

25

Cullen walked through the Technical Support Unit office on the fifth floor of the station. While the building had only been open a matter of months, the tech guys had already made the place look like a pigsty, their desks covered in junk — soft drink bottles, bags of crisps and tortilla chips, fast food containers, nothing natural or nutritious in sight, not that coppers were much better. The window blinds were all closed despite it being the middle of summer, making Cullen feel like he was in the mortuary.

Kidd's desk was an IT paradise — two big flat panel displays, four desktop units and a wealth of dark grey boxes, all with various unobvious interfaces tangled together by a nest of cables covering the entire top. He was ploughing through a screen of data, which looked like gibberish.

Cullen gave up waiting for Kidd to notice him. 'Have you finished extracting the data yet?'

Kidd jumped off his seat. 'Christ, Cullen, you gave us a fright.'

'Sorry.'

Kidd started playing with his ponytail. 'What was it you wanted?'

'How are you getting on with the extract?' said Cullen.

Kidd pointed at the screen of gibberish on the right-hand panel. 'Here's the raw data.'

Cullen could make out certain text fields and dates, things like that, but it was mostly full of odd characters.

Kidd pointed to the screen on the left. 'And here it is all tidied up.'

A big table showed information on Martin Webb. Kidd scrolled down the page, showing messages between Webb and Caroline Adamson.

'This looks great,' said Cullen. 'Can you print it out?'

'It's already spooling,' said Kidd.

'Cheers,' said Cullen. 'Did you get an IP address or anything out of it?'

'That's my next task,' said Kidd. 'Shouldn't take too long, really.'

'Good. Is there anything else we can do?'

'Aye.' Kidd pointed to the image of Martin Webb on his profile. 'I was thinking earlier, you can see why she'd go on a date with this punter.'

'How?'

'Well, I'm not gay,' said Kidd, 'but he looks like a model.'

Cullen looked at the image and saw his point. 'Aye, he does.'

'Want me to run a search for him?' said Kidd. 'That's something I can actually do. We've got access to image banks all the law enforcement agencies pay for. They mostly use it for anti-terrorist stuff, but I think this would be a good excuse as any. Google are going to introduce a public one soon.'

'What does it do?'

'Searches every image on the internet, looking for a match,' said Kidd.

'So we can see where else Martin Webb has used this image?' said Cullen. 'And maybe who he actually is?'

'Aye,' said Kidd. 'Are you with me?'

Cullen thought about it for a moment. 'Right, do it.' He collected the printout and headed back downstairs.

CULLEN'S EYES WERE STINGING — he'd had his contacts in for over thirty-six hours. The words on the pages were starting to dance before him. He either needed sleep or more coffee.

The bulk of the messages he'd read were between Caroline Adamson and Martin Webb. They mostly tallied with the story Cullen had collated so far, as vague as it was. He found some potentially useful nuggets, though they were mostly about Caroline. There were messages between her and a few of her other friends, such as Steve Allen. Cullen realised the extract they'd received was obviously not fully secure, as it contained other users' messages, but he wasn't in a hurry to tell Schoolbook.

He scribbled a note in the margin to follow up on Martin being in town on business at the time and therefore wasn't an Edinburgh resident. It was likely another tale he had spun Caroline, but it was something that should be checked out — if they became really desperate, every business in Edinburgh could be trawled for employees visiting the city.

Cullen checked the next message, between Caroline and Debi Curtis. Caroline said she had to slam the phone down on Rob Thomson, going into detail about the number of times he had failed to show up to take his son as agreed. She complained about how much it cost her. Cullen initially thought she meant having Jack, but it quickly became apparent she didn't resent her son. She did resent her ex-husband not meeting his responsibilities, stopping her from going out and having a social life.

The next alarmed him — it was from Debi Curtis. He checked his notebook — she'd said she hadn't replied to the message from Caroline. He read it again and almost fell off his seat — the message was between Debi Curtis and Martin Webb.

His pulse started racing as he scanned through it.

'Hey Martin! That was really funny what you said on Caroline's message board. I think exactly the same thing about that film — really tedious. I can't believe she likes it. Have you seen Superbad? *It's much better. Debi x'*

Cullen realised Debi was introducing herself to Martin, similar to the way Martin had introduced himself to Caroline — using a conversation on a forum.

Cullen flicked through the remaining sheets — in amongst the messages between Caroline and Martin was a rich seam between Debi and Martin. He turned to the last few sheets and check the final one — it was from Martin to Debi, sent that morning.

'Hey Debi. See you there. X'

He looked at the previous message. Debi gave Martin Webb her home address. They were meeting at half six.

Cullen's hand shook as he checked his watch — it was just before seven.

26

Bain acted quickly, resisting bringing an Armed Response Unit in, telling Cullen he preferred to take those around him, those he could trust. Or as near to trust as Bain got, Cullen thought.

Those he trusted include Cullen and McNeill alongside Angela and two other uniforms. They stood outside Debi Curtis' flat on Bryson Road, a low-end street in the west side of Edinburgh between Gorgie and Fountain Park. The flats on this stretch were all brick, unusual for the city.

'Remember, we're to be subtle here, okay?' Bain looked around the officers. 'Cullen, Caldwell, I want you in the flat with me. The rest of you cover the exits — two at the back, two on the street. Let's go.'

The stairwell door was propped open with a flower pot. Debi Curtis' flat was on the first floor. The carpeted stairs were straight with a landing at each half turn, not the curving stairwells Cullen was used to. There were a few neglected pot plants in the space between the two flat doors.

Bain marched up to Debi's door and knocked. 'Ms Curtis, this is the police. Please open the door.'

He waited a few seconds. Nothing.

'Right, Cullen,' said Bain. 'Break it down.'

Cullen had done this a few times before in his uniform days in

Livingston. The trick was to lead with the shoulder. It took him three clear attempts before it gave way, the lock splintering open, the door still on the hinges.

Bain burst past as Cullen clutched his shoulder.

A scream came from the room immediately to the right.

Cullen ran into the room. Debi Curtis lay on the bed, naked and covered in her own blood. 'Help me.' Her throat was lacerated.

There was a crash from behind. Cullen spun round.

Angela clutched her head and crouched. 'Ah, you bastard.' A cereal bowl lay broken on the floor at her feet.

The flat door slammed shut.

'I've got it.' Cullen ran for the door, fumbling with the door handle and pulling. It didn't give, the splintered door lock still stuck on the snib. He twisted the catch and tore the door open.

There was a noise from below, a door banging. He leapt down the stairs three at a time.

A uniformed officer lay prostrate on the floor, clutching his head.

McNeill appeared in the stairwell from the front. 'What's going on?'

'Bastard smacked my head off the wall.' The uniform pointed to the door behind him. 'He went that way.'

Bain came running down the stairs. 'Get after him!'

'Come on,' said Cullen to McNeill.

The rear door led to a car park. Cullen saw a pair of legs disappear over the wall at the back. He clocked a Volvo estate backed up against the wall. He ran for the car, jumped onto the bonnet, over the car roof and clambered onto the wall. There was a sharp drop to another car park below.

As he set himself for the jump, he spotted the figure running away between the houses. A big, stocky man, not a million miles from Rob Thomson's build.

Cullen jumped onto the pavement, his ankle almost snapping as he landed. Limping, he followed the path between the houses onto Angle Park Terrace beyond.

The road ran left to right just across from Ardmillan Place. He looked up and down but couldn't spot his target anywhere.

He turned around as McNeill and Bain closed on him. He

gestured for them to go left and right, and for him to head across the road.

He stepped into the traffic waving his warrant card. Cars reluctantly stopped. He staggered on across the street then around the bend opposite, coming out opposite the cemetery.

There was no sign of his quarry.

27

'I can't believe it,' said Bain. 'I cannot believe it.'

They were back at the station, Bain, Cullen and McNeill having left SOCOs crawling all over the crime scene in Debi's flat. Debi was rushed to the Royal Infirmary at Little France, the paramedics suggesting she had very little chance of pulling through.

'We had him,' said Bain.

Cullen piped up. 'He got away and he assaulted two officers in the process.'

'We still should have had him.' Bain stroked his moustache. 'How good a look did you get of him?'

'Not much better than you,' said Cullen. 'Big guy, shaved head.'

Bain raised an eyebrow. 'That fits Rob Thomson, doesn't it?'

Cullen nodded slowly. 'Aye, it does, but I couldn't reliably identify him from a line up, put it that way.'

'For Christ's sake,' said Bain.

'How's Caldwell?' said McNeill.

'She's okay,' said Cullen. 'Just bruised.'

'Did she see anything?' said Bain.

'Nothing,' said Cullen. 'Came at her from behind.'

'What about the plod at the back door?' said Bain.

'Nothing either,' said McNeill. 'He was off to the side, looking up at the flat.'

'Couldn't make some of this shite up.' Bain took a deep breath. 'I could do with speaking to Caldwell, see if I can jog anything in her memory.'

'I sent her home,' said Cullen. 'Doubt we can keep her from coming in tomorrow, though.'

'She's a decent copper,' said Bain. 'Much better than Miller. Any idea where he's got to this time? Could have used the lanky bastard tonight.'

McNeill shrugged. 'Not sure. I haven't seen him for a while.'

'What do you want us to do now?' said Cullen.

'I want you to keep on checking through Caroline's friends and acquaintances,' said Bain, 'try to see what else you can find.'

'What about Debi?' said Cullen. 'These attacks are related.'

'I know that,' said Bain. 'I want Irvine on it. I don't want you spread too thin, all right? Slow and methodical, okay?'

'Fair enough,' said Cullen.

～

CULLEN SPENT another ten minutes looking at the messages before realising his brain had stopped taking anything in. He grabbed his jacket and headed down the back stairwell to the garage, his car still there from the previous day. He had planned to come in and collect it that afternoon.

'I got those tickets, Scotty.'

Cullen turned round. Miller. 'Where have you been all day? Bain's been looking for you.'

'Been doing some HOLMES stuff for Wilko,' said Miller. 'Stupid arse can't use it. Wait till I tell the gaffer.'

Cullen shook his head in amusement. 'Bain reckoned you were looking at CCTV.'

'Shows how much he pays attention.'

Cullen laughed. 'What tickets are you on about?'

'The Hibs game on Wednesday,' said Miller.

Cullen had forgotten. 'Oh, right, aye. How much am I due you?'

'Nothing,' said Miller. 'My brother and his mate couldn't make it, so I got the pair for nowt.'

'Thanks.' Cullen yawned. 'Right, I'm off home. Catch you tomorrow.'

'No bother, Scotty.' Miller headed off towards his own car.

The prospect of sitting in the Hibs end as Barcelona thumped them didn't fill Cullen with anticipation. Still, when else would he get to see Messi or David Villa in the flesh?

Cullen got into his car and fiddled about with his iPod, cueing up some German techno Tom had given him. He needed to chill out. He thought about what to get for tea — he'd hardly eaten anything all day. Curry.

His phone rang — he looked at the display but didn't recognise the number.

'Hi, is that Scott?' It was a girl's voice, vaguely familiar.

'Yes it is.'

'Hi, Scott, it's Alison.'

It took a moment for Cullen to remember who Alison was. Kimono girl. The one he'd shared bodily fluids with that morning. *Shite.*

'How are you doing?' he said, trying to recover from his pause.

'I'm okay. I was just wondering if you fancied meeting up for a drink sometime? I mean you disappeared so quickly this morning and, well...'

'That would be good. I'm really sorry about that. It's the nature of my job, I'm afraid. I've got to be available twenty-four seven.'

'I understand,' said Alison. 'When are you free?'

'How about Monday night?' Cullen half hoped the case would still be too busy then, giving him a good excuse to get out of the date.

'Sounds good. There's this great bar on Hanover Street, *Number 99.* Can we say seven?'

'I'll see you there.'

'Great,' she said, then hung up.

Cullen saved her number to his phone then put it back in his pocket.

With everything that happened, he just hadn't thought about their one night stand and whether there would be any other nights.

∾

Cullen struggled up the stairs, still limping from the chase. He had a curry carryout bag in his hand. Opening the door, he was serenaded by Tom and Johnny singing *Sex Bomb*. Johnny got up and pranced around like Tom Jones.

'Piss off,' said Cullen, only half-joking.

Dawn looked hurt.

Johnny frowned. 'We're just arsing about, mate.'

Cullen slumped at the table with his head in his hands. 'Yeah, I know. Sorry. I've just been at work all bloody day.'

'Oh,' said Dawn.

'We thought you'd been boning that girl in the kimono all day,' said Johnny.

Dawn punched him on the arm.

'No.' Cullen looked up. 'I got a call from my DI at the back of ten, had to go to a crime scene.'

'Jesus,' said Johnny.

'So are you seeing her again?' said Tom.

'Yeah. Monday night.'

'Wow, it's serious,' said Dawn.

Cullen shrugged. 'We'll see. I barely spoke to her for ten minutes.'

Tom shook his head. 'You're such a shagger.'

Cullen yawned. 'Look, I've only had about two hours sleep and I've got to be in for a briefing at seven tomorrow, so I'm eating my curry then going to bed.'

DAY 4

*Sunday
31st July*

28

Sunday morning, seven on the dot and Bain stood at the front of the Incident Room, clutching a mug of coffee. He took a sip, winced at the taste then looked around the room at the forty-odd police officers before him. The majority were uniform and Cullen only recognised Angela and McAllister. A couple of the other faces Cullen recalled from the previous evening, including the guy who got clobbered at Debi's flat. McNeill nodded at him as he found a place to stand.

Cullen hadn't slept the full night, managing about four hours after his head hit the pillow then tossing and turning for the remainder. The killer escaping his clutches continuously ran through his mind, at times appearing to be Rob Thomson, at others someone else. He never clearly saw his face.

At the front, Bain closed his eyes, called everyone to attention and took a deep breath while the room quietened.

'Caroline Adamson.' He paused before pointing at the plasma screen showing a picture of Caroline taken from above, lying on the bed — naked, bruised, damaged. *Dead*. 'You've all seen the photographs and read the briefing packs. You should all know her story, but I'll go through it anyway.'

He looked over at Cullen, held his gaze. Cullen folded his arms, determined not to look away. Bain glanced at the screen.

He went on to brief them on Caroline's background — Rob, Jack, Amy, her parents, Margaret Armstrong, briefly mentioning Martin Webb then going over the searches at the hotel. Cullen zoned out — nothing new.

Bain put his mug on the desk and looked around the room again. 'Caroline's body was found in the early hours of Saturday morning at the Jackson Hotel on Minto Street. She'd been dead since Wednesday night and had suffered significant injuries. The post mortem was performed yesterday. Jimmy Deeley couldn't find anything that could help us identify the killer, the body having been thoroughly cleaned. The cause of death was a large knife cut to the throat. In addition, there were signs of prolonged strangulation using a rope, probably over a number of hours. It looks as if Caroline suffered a great deal during the last few hours of her life.'

He took another deep breath before switching the plasma screen to a picture of Debi Curtis in a hospital bed, tubes coming from her mouth. 'Deborah Curtis was one of Caroline's closest friends, known as Debi. Yesterday evening we discovered she had also been in contact with Martin Webb and they'd arranged to meet at her flat in Gorgie last night. When we arrived, the attacker was still in the flat. We were distracted by cries from the bedroom, where Ms Curtis was still alive. The attacker fled the building and we gave chase, but he lost us in the surrounding streets. Ms Curtis was taken to the Infirmary.'

He took another drink of the coffee.

'She died during the night.'

Cullen felt as if the wind was being ripped from his lungs. He thought he'd saved her. Why hadn't Bain told him when he arrived? He thought back to when Miller and he had spoken to her at her office — he felt guilty for commenting on her looks. He could be such a dick.

Bain took another sip of coffee then put the mug down. 'Scene of Crime are going over her flat as we speak. Given the killer was still there when we arrived and subsequently fled, there's a significant chance he's left some forensic evidence. The post mortem is this afternoon.' He nodded at James Anderson, the SOCO whose toilet Cullen had decorated. 'Mr Anderson, can you give an overview of your investigation?'

It was unusual in Cullen's experience for any of the SOCO team to be involved in a CID briefing, but there he was.

'Both bodies were strangled,' said Anderson. 'We believe it was with the same piece of rope or the same type, at least. On Caroline's body, we found a few threads of a blue rope in the burn marks on her throat. We found similar threads on Debi, but more of them.'

Cullen looked round at McNeill, who looked to be as surprised as he was.

Anderson cleared his throat. 'I can only assume it's because we caught him in the act, he didn't have time to clear up after himself this time. We'll be running exhaustive forensic tests on the rope fibres. I doubt we'll get anything, but we've already got some officers going round hardware shops in the city to see if they've sold this type of rope to anyone we know. We haven't found any traces from the killer — hairs, fingerprints, semen, nothing like that so far.'

'Thanks.' Bain tapped a key on a laptop, making a set of bullet points appear on the screen behind him. 'Here are the actions. DI Wilkinson will assist me in co-ordinating the investigation. You should all note I am the Senior Investigating Officer and all formal requests go through me.'

Cullen noticed Wilkinson raise his eyebrows at this.

'DS McNeill will lead the investigation into Caroline Adamson's death, DS Irvine will lead on Debi Curtis.'

Cullen looked round at McNeill again. She nodded at him.

'Our current prime suspect is Rob Thomson, Caroline's ex-husband. I intend to formally interview him at some point today. The divorce was fairly acrimonious, so there's an obvious motive there. He also knew Debi through Caroline according to the intel gathered by DC Cullen.'

Cullen frowned — he didn't like information he had gathered being touted as criminal intelligence.

'Rob Thomson has an alibi for Caroline Adamson's killing which I strongly suspect to be false. DC Cullen will provide a detailed statement at some point today on who he saw escaping last night.'

Bain paused. Nobody knew whether to move off or to stay.

He started speaking again, slowly. 'We're looking for a man who's killed a young mother and left a young boy without a mother. We strongly believe this same man also murdered another young woman in cold blood, one with a promising career. I want a result. I know you all do too. Let's get it.'

29

Cullen pointed to the car stereo. 'What the hell is this?' He had tolerated more than enough of it.

'Texas,' said McNeill. 'The Best Of.'

'I'd hate to hear the worst of.'

They were in McNeill's car, on their way to Carnoustie. They'd drawn the short straw in the actions lottery, Bain having allocated them to interview Caroline's parents. Despite the additional officers Bain had acquired overnight, none were coming Cullen's way for the search through Caroline's list, leaving Angela to continue calling through the friends on her own.

'Are Texas not cool enough for you?' she said.

Cullen shrugged. 'I'm hardly Captain Metrosexual.'

'Aren't you?' She glanced over at him, an eyebrow flicking up. 'You with your nice tight suit, short haircut, DJ culture t-shirts. I bet you moisturise.'

Cullen rolled his eyes. 'Could you at least turn it down?'

She fiddled around with the buttons on the steering wheel and the music stopped.

Cullen knew the route well from seemingly endless bus journeys home to Dalhousie when he was a student. 'We're about half an hour away.'

She glanced over. 'You're from round these parts, aren't you?'

'Yeah. Dalhousie.'

'Never heard of it,' said McNeill.

Cullen laughed. 'Not a lot of people have. It's not far from Carnoustie, actually. It's between Arbroath and Montrose. It's like Carnoustie without the golf, but with a harbour.'

'I've been to Carnoustie.'

'When?' said Cullen.

'The Open in 1999. I was working on the bar in the big tent. Earned a packet. Three of us slept on one of our mate's brother's floors in Dundee. He was in Canada all summer, I think.'

'Was this at uni?'

'Indeed,' she said. 'I was at Aberdeen.'

'I went down for the day with my dad,' said Cullen. 'The train was packed. I'm not much of a golfer but it was a good laugh. We went for a few pints in a pub by the station.'

'The Station.'

'Eh?'

'That's what that pub's called.'

'Right.' Cullen watched the green fields of Perthshire as they ploughed on down the road.

'Thirty-three,' she said.

'Eh?'

'You're working out my age, aren't you? I was between third and fourth year at uni.'

'Older lady.'

She ignored it. 'You went to uni too, didn't you?'

'Aye. Never fully graduated, though.'

'I got a First,' said McNeill. 'Fat lot of good it did me.'

'What in?'

'Criminology, would you believe,' said McNeill.

'Are you from Aberdeen?' said Cullen. 'You don't have the accent.'

'No, Edinburgh,' said McNeill. 'I'm a Trinity girl.'

'That's a posh way of saying Newhaven.'

She laughed. 'Yeah, well, it's probably closer to the truth.'

They drove on in silence, the dull greyness of Dundee appearing over the crest of the hill, doused in rain even in the middle of summer.

'You've been a bit quiet,' she said.

'It's hard to talk when my ears are still bleeding from that CD you were inflicting on me,' said Cullen.

'Okay, but beside that, it took you over an hour to get me to turn it down.'

Cullen exhaled. 'Didn't get much sleep last night. I can't believe that guy got away.'

They passed the city's small airport on the right.

'Were you ever based up here in Tayside police?'

'No,' said Cullen. 'I went to Edinburgh Uni and just stayed on after I dropped out. I worked for an insurance company down Dundas Street for a year and a half before I joined the police.'

'Why did you leave?' said McNeill.

Cullen thought of Miller's comments the previous day. 'Put it this way, even Bain's all right compared to some of the wankers you get in those companies.'

'I'll bear that in mind next time I think of jacking it in,' said McNeill.

Cullen looked at her in surprise — she wasn't smiling. 'How long have you worked for him?'

'Three years coming up,' said McNeill. 'He worked some big cases in the late nineties as a DS in Strathclyde then got a transfer through to Edinburgh as a DI.'

'He's not exactly an inspiration, is he?' said Cullen. 'Classic divide and conquer behaviour.'

'So you didn't buy his whole Al Pacino thing, then?'

'Huh?'

'You've seen that film *Any Given Sunday*?' said McNeill.

'Don't think so.'

'Al Pacino plays the coach of this American Football team,' said McNeill. 'At the end of the film, his team are losing at half time or whatever, usual nonsense. He gives this big inspirational speech.' She paused. 'That's Bain's favourite film ever. He played it to us at a team away day a couple of years ago. Our stats were shite for a couple of months running, so he took us out to get pissed and motivated. That was his big effort.'

Cullen watched the train station on the left as they drew up to a set of traffic lights. 'So he sees himself as this great inspirational figure?'

'Oh totally,' said McNeill. 'He's maybe not that bad at it. He's had enough training.'

Cullen didn't respond. He leaned back in his seat thinking about what she'd said. After a while, they passed a giant gas storage cylinder on the left as they pushed on heading for Broughty Ferry. 'So Bain likes his films?'

'He does, aye,' said McNeill. 'Why do you ask?'

'Well, he calls me after an American film festival.'

Once her laughing subsided, she tried to explain. 'The Sundance film festival was founded by Robert Redford, you rube.'

'What's a rube?'

'It's a redneck or something,' said McNeill. 'Homer says it in *The Simpsons*.'

Cullen laughed. 'So who's Robert Redford?'

She grinned. 'Oh, Scott, you're so young. He's an actor, played the Sundance Kid in *Butch Cassidy and the Sundance Kid*. I think Paul Newman played Butch Cassidy.'

Cullen vaguely knew the name.

She grimaced. 'It's Bain making yet another joke at my expense. He's called me Butch Cassidy for a while.'

'You're not exactly butch.'

She looked around at him, an impish grin on her face. 'Why, Mr Cullen, are you coming on to me?'

They drove the rest of the way in embarrassed silence. Cullen eventually broke it by navigating them through the maze of the housing estate Caroline's parents — Joan and David Adamson — lived in, a modern development at the far end of Carnoustie. A white van was parked outside with *'David Adamson Repairs'* stencilled on the side.

Cullen and McNeill sat on the sofa facing a giant television. David Adamson, a thin grey man, sat on a reclining armchair, his wife perched on the matching cream leather footstool in front. Bain had arranged for a Family Support Officer to come round and break the news to them the previous day, staying with them all afternoon until David Adamson forced him out in the early evening for some privacy. Both parents' eyes were now bloodshot.

Cullen and McNeill had sat and listened — probing, questioning, reassuring, commiserating — but no new information or contacts came out. In truth, they had nothing more to go on than

Cullen had already gained from Amy Cousens. Aside from the fact their daughter was dead, Caroline's parents were mostly concerned about what was going to happen to their grandson, but McNeill told them it was entirely out of their jurisdiction.

After more than an hour there was nothing more to be discussed. Joan Adamson suggested putting on another pot of coffee. McNeill made their apologies and Joan took the tray through to the kitchen.

David Adamson led them into the hall and, with his hand on the door latch, leaned towards them. He spoke quietly, obviously to save his wife from hearing. He hadn't said much in the living room, merely concurring with his wife's pronouncements and answers.

'Please find the bastard who killed my lassie.' Adamson's voice was soft but struggled to contain the emotion.

McNeill tilted her head slightly. 'We're trying our hardest.' She rested her hand on his sleeve. 'Our best officers are on this case.'

Cullen leaned closer. 'I didn't want to ask in front of your wife, but do you have any suspicions about your daughter's ex-husband?'

'Rob?' Adamson paused for a few seconds. 'Maybe.' His eyes welled up. 'Listen. I've no idea who it bloody was, whether it was my ex-son-in-law, or whoever, I just want you to find him, okay?'

McNeill held his gaze throughout. 'We will, Mr Adamson, believe me we will.'

Adamson looked into their eyes for a few seconds, his own filling with moisture. 'Just make sure you do, for my grandson's sake and for my poor wife's sake. She's on medication. Christ knows what this is going to do to her.'

30

On the way back, they'd dissected the meeting with Caroline's parents, hunting for clues, leads, anything, but came up with nothing. David Adamson's words still rang in Cullen's ears — he thought of Jack Adamson playing with his Doctor Who dolls, oblivious to what was happening. Surely by now he would be aware his mother wasn't coming back, even if he didn't understand why.

They got back to the Incident Room in the early afternoon. The place was a hive of activity — DS Holdsworth was running around with a clipboard, his face redder than ever.

Bain lurked at a laptop at the end of the room, scratching the back of his head. He looked up as they approached. 'How did it go?'

'As I expected,' said McNeill. 'The only thing I got out of it was a form to claim back half a tank of petrol.'

'Keep an eye on your expenses, you're not an MP.' Bain checked his watch. 'Took your time.'

'Bad traffic on Ferry Road,' said McNeill. 'Sunday shoppers heading to Ocean Terminal.'

'Anything to nail Rob Thomson with?' said Bain.

'Were you expecting anything?' said McNeill.

Bain grunted. 'Not really.'

'Have you got anything to charge him with yet?' said McNeill.

Bain looked away. 'Not yet.'

'What's been happening here?' said Cullen.

Bain sat at his desk. 'Nothing much, to be honest. Jim Turnbull's gone to see the Procurator Fiscal to talk strategy.' He picked up a bottle full of foul-looking pink gunk. 'Pepto-Bismol. Hopefully it'll nuke my insides.' He measured out a capful and downed it.

'What do you want us to do now then?' said Cullen.

Bain swallowed a few times then cleared his throat. 'Butch, I want you to go over all of the interviews we've done so far, see if there's anything jumps out at you. Probably have to re-interview everyone Sundance here met on Friday — just keep away from Rob Thomson for now.'

McNeill nodded.

'And me?' said Cullen.

'Two things,' said Bain. 'First, you'll need to get back to those phone calls. Caldwell can't be seen to be doing them all.'

'I need more people,' said Cullen.

Bain poured out another capful and swallowed it, a pained expression on his face. 'I'll see if there's any slack.'

'And the other thing?' said Cullen.

Bain picked up an envelope — Cullen had last seen it on Miller's desk. 'Monkey Boy hasn't even looked through Caroline's phone records yet. I want you to do it. Highest priority.'

'Why me?' said Cullen.

Bain shrugged. 'Safe pair of hands I suppose. I've not seen the useless bastard all morning. Need to see what on earth Wilko's been doing with him.'

31

C ullen sat at his desk in the Incident Room, next to Angela with her headset on. She rolled her eyes and wound her finger through the air, as if the motion would make the call finish.

Cullen tore open the envelope, retrieving three sheets of A4 comprising Caroline's call record for the last month. He checked through the numbers, both inbound and outbound, and started cross-referencing them against those he'd taken for Amy Cousens, Steve Allen, Debi Curtis, Rob Thomson and the rest. He quickly eliminated at least three quarters of the list, leaving him with eighteen unknown. He typed those into the national database and looked through the results. They were mostly plausible names and numbers — her parents, work, Steve Allen's landline, Rob Thomson's work Blackberry. He'd have to add them to the list of calls he and Angela were working through — hopefully he'd get some uniform to call through the list and verify it all.

The eighteenth number, from an incoming call, didn't show up.

Cullen picked up his desk phone and dialled it.

A sparkly female voice answered. 'We're sorry, but this GoMobile number is unavailable. Please try again later.'

The line went dead, no voicemail.

GoMobile was the network Cullen was on. He quickly found

the customer service number and dialled it. While he waited he looked at the call record again. The call was made at 7.38pm on the night she was abducted. It tied in with the timing of the unanswered text messages from Steve Allen and Amy Cousens and might shed some light on her last few minutes of freedom.

He was passed through a number of lines, accompanied by Boyzone's greatest hits, before finally getting through to the legal department.

'DC Cullen? You're wanting to trace a mobile number on our network, is that right?'

'Yes, it's in connection with a murder case,' said Cullen.

'I'm afraid we're unable to provide information like that without a formal request being provided.'

Cullen took a note of her name and contact details, in the unlikely event Bain could be bothered to give him another RIPSA. He completed and printed another form, ready for Bain to sign. Or not.

Looking up, he saw Bain sauntering over from the entrance carrying a brown paper bag, drinking from a can of Red Bull Cola.

'How's it going?' Bain sat at his desk. He opened up a windowed sandwich bag, tomato ketchup smeared all over the inside, and tucked into the bacon roll within. He ate noisily, his lips slapping with every chew.

Cullen passed him the form. 'I need you to sign another RIPSA.'

'Good for you, Sundance,' said Bain, through a mouthful, the pinks of the bacon and his tongue indistinguishable.

'I found a mobile number I need to investigate,' said Cullen. 'The network needs a formal request.'

'I'll think about it.' Bain went back to his roll.

'Just sign the bloody form,' said Cullen.

Bain stopped chewing and put the roll down. 'Cullen, don't you *ever* speak to me like that again, okay?'

Cullen flared his nostrils. 'With all due respect, I've got a lead and it may give us some useful information.'

'How likely is it?'

'I won't know till I get what I need.'

Bain shook his head slowly. 'All right.' He snatched the form and signed it. 'Now get this out of your bloody system and don't go pushing anybody too far, okay?'

'Thank you.' Cullen grabbed the form back. 'By the way, did Miller ever finish reviewing the CCTV from the hotel?'

Bain let out a slow sigh. 'Waste of time. There's only CCTV in the reception area. We just got a few glimpses of Caroline heading to that room.'

'What about when our killer left?' said Cullen.

'No idea. Can't trace him. There are thirty rooms on that bit of the hotel. He just sauntered out the front door without us spotting him.'

'What about the front desk?' said Cullen. 'Couldn't they give a description?'

'Sundance, get back in your box,' said Bain. 'We've got one, but it's so vague it's unusable.' He picked up his roll again. 'Will you get out of my face? I'm trying to eat my roll here and I've got another bloody press conference I need to prepare for.'

Cullen picked up his phone again and called GoMobile back, getting put through to their fraud department. He faxed the RIPSA form through before being put on hold yet again while they checked it.

Some guy called Ian Archibald came on the line, based at their call centre in Inverness. Cullen dreaded having to make a trip in person — GoMobile's offices were either there or in Bradford.

'Well, the records don't show much,' said Archibald. 'The phone came with a twenty pound credit, of which thirty-nine pence has been used. Last of the big spenders.'

'How many calls were made?' said Cullen.

'Just the one, actually. I can give you the number if you want.'

'When was the call?' said Cullen.

'Seven thirty-nine pm on Wednesday.'

'You said thirty-nine pence *has* been used,' said Cullen. 'Is the phone still active?'

'Hang on.' Archibald breathed through his mouth for a few seconds. 'Aye, it's still active.'

'When was it last used?' said Cullen.

Archibald sounded bored. 'Wednesday.'

'Is that as in used to make a call,' said Cullen, 'or the thing being on?'

'Both.'

'So it's not been *on* since Wednesday?' said Cullen.

'That's right,' said Archibald.

'I want to know where the call was made from.'

'Good luck.'

Cullen frowned. 'Don't you store the GPS information of the calls?'

Archibald laughed. 'No, pal. This is the most basic model we sell — I'm surprised we still do, to be honest.'

'So you can't tell me where the calls were made?' said Cullen.

'Not with this phone.'

'If we knew where the call was made,' said Cullen, 'we might be able to build a picture of who was using the phone.'

'I see. We've done a bit of that in the past. You'll need to check on the cell sites to get anything meaningful.'

'And what's a cell site when it's at home?' said Cullen.

Archibald sighed. 'When you use your phone, it connects to the nearest mobile mast or cell site, which is connected to our network. That's logged with the call.'

'And can you run a cell site search for me, then?'

Archibald sniffed. 'You'd have to get your Phone Squad or whatever they're called to do it. We only give them access to the data.'

'Fine,' said Cullen. 'Do you have any information about how the phone was bought?'

Archibald whistled through his teeth. 'Let me have a wee look.' The keyboard sounds were audible down the telephone line. 'Here we are. Sold to Tesco. Part of a batch.'

'Any idea where it went after that?'

Archibald laughed. 'Hardly. You'll need to take that up directly with Tesco.' He read out a consignment number and a depot contact.

Cullen rubbed his forehead. 'Is there anything else you can tell us?'

'Not really. There's precious little here. No texts, one call and that's your lot.'

'What about personal details?' said Cullen. 'Home address, bank account, that sort of thing?'

Archibald snorted. 'It's Pay As You Go, we don't get an address or anything like that.'

'So anyone could buy a phone and you don't know who's using your network?' said Cullen.

Archibald spoke in a monotone. 'That's the case.'

'Can you email that information through?'

Archibald exhaled down the line for a few seconds. 'Will do.'

Cullen gave his Lothian & Borders email address. 'Thanks for your help. Hopefully it can help us track down the killer.'

He ended the call and slouched in his seat, trying to think through what he could do next. He knew the phone was bought in Tesco. It might lead somewhere.

Bain had his head down, scribbling on a notepad.

'Brian,' said Cullen.

Bain looked up. 'Come on, Sundance, I've got this press conference coming up.'

'I know. I've got a lead from this phone number, wanted to walk you through it.'

Bain exhaled through his nose. 'Right, fire away, Sherlock.'

'Caroline's mobile received a call from an unknown number at seven thirty-nine on the night she was killed.'

'This is your latest wild goose chase, right?'

Cullen shrugged. 'Maybe not so wild.'

'So she got a call from this number and the next thing we know she's dead in that hotel?' said Bain. 'What do you know about the phone?'

'Cheap Pay As You Go, bought from Tesco,' said Cullen. 'Can I chase it up?'

Bain nodded slowly. 'Go for it. Let me know if you get anywhere. This guy has to have made a mistake somewhere.'

'The other thing is we need a cell site search for that call,' said Cullen.

Bain shrugged. 'Go for it.' He went back to the notepad.

Cullen fished out the envelope with Caroline's call records. The Forensic Investigation Unit had provided the extract. Cullen found a number.

'Phone Squad. Tommy Smith.'

'Tommy, it's DC Cullen at Leith Walk. I'm looking through that set of phone records you got for Caroline Adamson. Couple of things. First, have you had a look at the phone?'

'Aye,' said Smith, 'Jimmy Anderson handed it into us to look through.'

'Did you find anything?'

'Not a sausage,' said Smith. 'Not even a wee willy winkie.'

'Right,' said Cullen. 'Can you run a cell site search on one of the numbers off the list?'

'Aye, I suppose I could.'

Cullen gave him the number.

'Might take a while,' said Smith, 'there are a few hoops I have to jump through.'

'If the hoops are to do with the network,' said Cullen, 'then we've got RIPSA approval.'

'How do you think I managed to have a look at her phone?' said Smith. 'DI Wilkinson approved it.'

Cullen sighed — nothing was joined up on this case. 'Give me a shout if you get any bother from them.'

'Will do, buddy,' said Smith, 'will do.'

'How long will it take?'

'About a day,' said Smith, 'maybe two.'

Cullen leaned back in his chair. 'Could you get it done any quicker?' He rubbed his temple. 'This is a high priority case now.'

'They all are,' said Smith. 'I'll see what I can do, buddy.'

'Give me a call tomorrow with your progress.'

Cullen slammed the phone down then dialled the Tesco depot number Archibald had given him. After the expected redirecting and lengthy periods on hold, they eventually managed to trace the mobile phone shipment to a store in Edinburgh.

He sat up in his seat, looked over at Angela.

'I'm so desperate for a coffee,' she said.

'Better hope you can hold out,' said Cullen.

'Why?'

'We're going shopping.'

32

'The traffic's always this bad on a Sunday,' said Angela. 'Usually have to battle through it on my way home from a day shift.'

They were driving out to the Tesco at Hermiston Gait, their route was more like a car park than a road at three on a Sunday afternoon. They were trudging through Corstorphine, a large characterless expanse on the west side of Edinburgh.

'You live out here, right?' said Cullen.

'Aye, Clermiston, right at the top of the hill. It's not exactly great, but it's a house in Edinburgh. Where do you stay?'

'Portobello,' said Cullen. 'Shared flat.'

'Don't you want your own place?'

Cullen sighed. 'Been saving for a deposit for two years, but the amount I need to save keeps going up. If it's not house prices, it's the percentage I need to put in.'

'We've had our house for five years now, think it's doubled in value in that time,' said Angela.

'All right for some.'

'Well, the prices have been going down for a while.'

'Aye, but the deposits have been going up,' said Cullen. 'Last year, I needed a five per cent deposit, this year it's *fifteen*.'

They finally got over the roundabout, past the purple PC World building, a giant Tesco to their left — roughly a mile from their target — continually in a state of extension. Cullen pressed the accelerator down and headed west.

'You can get some good deals out in Livingston,' she said.

'You couldn't *pay* me to live out there,' said Cullen. 'Used to be in F Division.'

'Where were you based?'

'Livingston, Broxburn then Bathgate,' said Cullen.

'Ooh, lovely,' said Angela. 'The Wild West.'

'Aye.'

'Did you enjoy it?'

'Yes and no,' said Cullen. 'I liked being in the police, but I didn't like the people I dealt with.'

They passed the Marriott, heading on to the Gogar round-about, the multi-level construction currently being rebuilt to let the new tram system flow above, the works undoubtedly the cause of their hold-up.

'You enjoy being a detective?' she said.

Cullen pulled to a halt at the roundabout. 'Aye, it's much better than the beat. It's what I wanted to do.'

'How long were you on the beat?'

'Six years,' said Cullen.

'That's a long time.'

'Tell me about it.'

'And six months as an Acting DC?' said Angela.

'Aye, St Leonards.' Cullen pulled away, turning left onto the City Bypass. 'Why all the questions?'

'Oh, no reason,' said Angela.

Cullen nodded at her and smiled. 'You're thinking of applying for CID, aren't you?'

She looked away. 'Maybe.'

'You'd make a decent detective, you know.'

'You think?' said Angela.

'If Keith Miller can get through,' said Cullen, 'anybody can.'

She laughed. 'He doesn't seem like the sharpest tool in the box.'

'Indeed.' Cullen pulled off at Hermiston Gait before navigating through a series of roundabouts, eventually finding a free space in front of the supermarket.

'Why did it take you so long to apply to be a detective?' she said. 'Miller's only been in the force two and a half years.'

'I applied loads of times,' said Cullen. 'I was seconded a few times to murder cases early on, just like you are now, and really enjoyed it. I applied for CID about six times but I got knocked back because of my sickness record.'

'How?'

'I had three bloody colds in six months,' said Cullen, 'which triggered absence management. I passed my sergeant's exams, too, but kept getting knocked back because of it.'

'That's rough.'

'Bain was saying something about me being an idealist the other night,' said Cullen. 'I suppose I must be. Nobody would do this job otherwise.'

As they walked over to the store, Cullen could see people looking at her uniform. He thought the biggest advantage from the number of uniforms seconded to the investigation was it provided a visibility his suit didn't.

At the customer service counter, Cullen showed his warrant card to the young girl, her face plastered with cheap make-up. 'I need to speak to a Sam Weston.' The name was on the invoice for the mobile phone consignment.

The receptionist looked nervously at Angela then picked up the phone, calling for Sam Weston, her mouth moving slightly ahead of the projected sound. 'Should be here any second.' She looked past them at the next customers in the queue.

Cullen and Angela moved off to the side, waiting in silence.

A stocky man in a suit approached them. He held out his hand to Cullen, his smile revealing gleaming white teeth. 'Sam Weston.'

Cullen knew the type — Management Trainees. He had dealt with a fair few of them in West Lothian, mainly thefts from the Asda in Livingston. Get a degree from a former polytechnic some-where down south, work your arse off in a series of roles super-vising shelf stackers then, with luck, get your own store to manage with the company car, pension scheme, health insurance and all the other benefits. Cullen wasn't the sort to chase money.

Cullen introduced them. Weston nodded at Angela. 'Do you have anywhere we can go to talk?'

Weston grinned again, though he looked nervously at both of

them. 'Sure. Let's go to my office.' He led them past the fruit and
veg section then through the big doors at the back of the store.
They followed him up a set of stairs.

Cullen had worked in the Tesco in Dalhousie when he was at
school, though it was nothing like the scale of this place.

Weston showed them into a tiny office, basically a computer on
a desk with a chair. He brought over two more seats, squeezing
them into the tiny room and struggling to shut the door behind
them. 'Now, how can I help?'

'We're investigating the murder of a woman named Caroline
Adamson,' said Cullen.

'Ah yes,' said Weston, 'I heard about that on the news just then.
Awful business.'

'We're looking for a mobile phone which was used to call the
victim shortly before she disappeared.' Cullen leafed through his
notebook and clicked his pen. 'We have managed to trace the
mobile to a batch delivered by the GoMobile network to your
store.'

'I see,' said Weston.

'We were wondering if you could help us identify who bought
the phone,' said Cullen.

'Do you have a serial number?'

Cullen handed him one of the prints. 'This is from the
supplier. Your central stock system said it came here.'

Weston logged on to the PC on his desk. He swivelled the
monitor around to let Cullen and Angela watch as he navigated
through a sophisticated stock control system. He pointed on the
screen. 'There's the delivery. I'll see if I can trace the unit through
to a transaction. The system's updated hourly, so we know exactly
which units are on the shelf at any one time.' He tapped away.
'There. Arrived on the twenty-third, four twenty-three pm and out
on the shelves the following morning, eight sixteen am.'

Cullen checked the printout. 'Good. This phone was activated
on the twenty-fifth. Just after two pm. We know it was sold that day
between eight sixteen and then.' He looked at the big year planner
on the wall and tried to think. 'Is there any way you can check
when that particular phone was sold?'

Weston nodded. 'I can have a look at the transactions database
for the barcode for those units.' He pulled up another system,

typed through a few screens. 'Here you go. Found one. Sold at eleven thirty-two am.'

Cullen scribbled the reference numbers down from the screen. 'Any credit card or Clubcard information?'

Weston's finger traced along the screen. 'Sorry, no. Paid by cash.'

'Bollocks.' Cullen clicked his pen a couple of times. He'd had high hopes for this.

'We've got the time and till, though,' said Angela. 'You can surely cross-reference that to the CCTV cameras.'

Weston nodded. 'Don't see why not.'

'Don't you overwrite the recordings?' said Angela.

'Not for the last ten years or so,' said Weston. 'It's all DVDs and hard drives these days.'

'Can you get us the footage?' said Cullen.

Weston beamed his white smile. 'Sure thing.'

AN HOUR LATER, Cullen and Angela were back in the Leith Walk station car park, heading to the stairwell. Angela carried a Tesco *Bag for Life* filled with printouts of the transaction and stock systems and a DVD with the CCTV footage from all store cameras covering an hour either side of the transaction.

'The amount of information they keep is frightening,' she said. 'From a serial number, he managed to take it through to a transaction to all that CCTV footage. I shop there every other week — how many times have I been caught on their system?'

'Doesn't bear thinking about, does it?' said Cullen.

As they started up the stairs, Cullen's mobile rang. Charlie Kidd.

'Cullen, you're a hard guy to get a hold of.'

'What is it?'

'You're not going to believe this,' said Kidd. 'I've found Martin Webb.'

33

'Show me.' Cullen was out of breath from running up the stairs.

Kidd wiggled his finger at the screen. 'Look at this.' He fiddled around in his browsing history, clicked on a link and a page popped up. 'There.' He pressed the screen so hard it discoloured, as if bruised.

Cullen squinted at the image. 'What is it?' His mouth was dry. Then it hit him. The image was Martin Webb, the picture on his Schoolbook profile. 'Where did you find this?'

'That search I told you about,' said Kidd, 'it came back pretty quick.' He pointed his finger at the screen again. 'That's your boy there.'

Cullen's eyes darted around the screen. 'What is this site?'

'Digby Models dot com,' said Kidd.

'Martin Webb's a model?' said Cullen.

Kidd laughed. 'Kind of.'

Cullen was always frustrated with that sort of response from people. 'Either he is or he isn't.'

'That's just it,' said Kidd. 'I think he both is and isn't.'

'Explain.'

'Fine,' said Kidd. 'Don't interrupt, okay?' He paused to compose himself. 'This is a photographic model site, right? This page is in their stock library, so it's just full of photos people can pay for and use in design or whatever, like adverts. Martin Webb has nicked a photo off this site, cropped it and pretended it was him.' He pointed at the screen. 'Here, watch this.'

He pressed a few keys to open Photoshop, a program Cullen was vaguely familiar with from a brief flirtation with photography. Kidd pasted the image from the website into the application. There was a logo at the left hand side, obscuring part of the image, which he cropped out. He double-clicked, and created an almost exact replica of the image on Schoolbook.

'Jesus,' said Cullen. 'So how does this work? How did you find it?'

Kidd shrugged. 'No idea. I just press the buttons.'

Cullen laughed.

'Seriously, though,' said Kidd, 'I think it's something to do with just a string-matching search. An image is just a series of ones and zeroes in a set format. It's a case of matching your ones and zeroes with any other in that format. Get enough groupings of matches and you've got something.' He grinned. 'It just matches chunks of data. Pretty smart, eh?'

'This is good,' said Cullen.

Kidd held up a sheet of paper. 'Here you go. Something else for Bain's file.'

'Cheers.'

Cullen raced off towards the Incident Room and found Bain and Miller at their desks, Bain looking as pissed off as usual and Miller on the defensive.

'Ah, Sundance, there you are,' said Bain. 'Nice of you to pitch up.'

The Tesco bag was on Cullen's desk. He held it up. 'Got something for you.'

'I hope it's custard creams,' said Bain.

Cullen ignored him and took the DVD out. 'It's CCTV footage from Tesco. We might be able to see who bought that mobile phone.'

Bain looked disinterested. 'Great.'

'Try to sound a little bit impressed,' said Cullen.

Bain grunted. 'Have you watched it?'

'A bit.' Cullen ran his hand through his hair.

'And?'

'Inconclusive at best,' said Cullen.

Bain snarled a smile. 'And I'm supposed to be *impressed*?'

Cullen ignored him. 'Charlie Kidd's found something. The image on Martin Webb's profile came from a photographic model site on the internet.'

Bain frowned. 'Come again?'

Cullen handed him the sheet of paper Kidd had given him then explained the process in sufficiently simple language Bain would understand.

'So this profile's a total fabrication then?' said Bain. 'Someone's created Martin Webb?'

'Looks that way,' said Cullen.

'I'm thinking that someone is Rob Thomson,' said Bain.

Cullen frowned. 'I'd say we need a bit more evidence before we can definitively say it's him.'

Bain turned round to Miller and tossed the DVD at him. 'Right, Monkey Boy, I want you to look through this CCTV, see if it shows Rob Thomson buying Martin Webb's phone.'

'We've not got proof it's Martin Webb's mobile,' said Cullen. 'We only know it was used to call Caroline just before she disappeared.'

'That's a matter for the PF,' said Bain. 'We need to overload her with evidence.' He rubbed his moustache. 'We've got to prove Rob Thomson is Martin Webb, that's the only way to nail him.'

'Did you get any more resource for me?' said Cullen.

'Holdsworth's going to get back to me by five with a name for you.'

'I'll need more than one,' said Cullen.

'Cullen, just quit moaning and get on with it.' Bain walked off, muttering to himself.

'So, Scott, what do I do with this DVD then?' said Miller.

'Just watch it, Keith,' said Cullen. 'There's a guy buying a mobile phone, we want to know who it is.'

'That it?' Miller's face lit up. 'Happy days.' He put the DVD in his laptop with a big smile on his face.

CULLEN SPENT the next hour and a half calling through the friends list, soul-destroying work.

He could have done with another coffee, but he decided it was a carrot he needed to keep in front of his nose. There was the sound of a phone dropping to the desk. He looked over at Angela — her face was several shades paler than normal. 'Are you okay?'

She looked up at him, eyes barely focusing. 'Somebody just told me Rob Thomson made death threats to Caroline.'

34

The new Edinburgh city morgue was situated in the basement of Leith Walk station. Cullen sat in the reception area, set aside for grieving relatives waiting to identify a body — sombre colours, well furnished, a metal box of tissues on the oak coffee table.

Debi Curtis' autopsy was just finishing according to Jimmy Deeley's assistant.

Cullen looked up on hearing Bain's voice — he seemed less than happy. He recognised the Procurator Fiscal as she marched off, thinking it unusual to see her at a post mortem, but then this was turning into an unusual case.

'Sundance.' Bain didn't stop. Cullen had to hurry to catch up. 'To what do I owe the pleasure?'

'I need to speak to you,' said Cullen.

'Well, we're having a briefing,' said Bain, 'so you can wait.'

'I need to speak to you *now*.'

'Not now.' Bain turned to face Cullen. 'Whatever it is, Sundance, it can wait.'

Cullen spun around and stopped in front of Bain, blocking his progress down the corridor. 'It's about Rob Thomson. Evidence.'

Bain huffed when he couldn't get past Cullen. 'Go on,' he said, with a great deal of reluctance.

'Angela's just found out Rob Thomson threatened to kill Caroline after their divorce.'

Bain eyed him suspiciously. 'Aye?'

'It was to do with the custody of their son, apparently,' said Cullen. 'It's common knowledge in Carnoustie.'

'Bloody hell.' Bain rubbed at his moustache, almost tugging at the hairs. 'How tight is this?'

Cullen shrugged. 'We'll get it backed up with a statement.'

Bain checked his watch. 'Right, it's time to bring him in.'

35

Cullen went back upstairs to see Kidd.

'Whoever this Martin Webb guy is,' said Cullen, 'that's who's killed these two women.'

Kidd scuttled his trackball out of frustration, sending it tumbling across his desk. 'I know that.'

'Well, how are you getting on?' said Cullen.

Kidd tossed his ponytail nervously, not speaking for what felt like an age. 'I'm not getting on as well as I thought. I made a good breakthrough with that stuff last night, but that's the easy part. What I want to look at is the log files and that sort of thing.'

'And why can't you?'

'It's like what we were talking about yesterday,' said Kidd, 'they haven't given us the header data for those tables.'

'I thought they were giving us it,' said Cullen.

'Aye well, so did I,' said Kidd. 'But they haven't.'

'Who have you been dealing with?'

'That Duncan Wilson boy.'

'Right, I'm calling him.' Cullen flicked through his notebook and found a phone number.

'This is Duncan.'

'Mr Wilson, this is DC Cullen. We met yesterday at your office.'

Wilson sigh echoed down the line. 'What is it this time? Why do you lot keep chasing me?'

'If you'd given us what you promised on that database extract,' said Cullen, 'then we wouldn't have to keep calling you up like this.'

'Oh, okay,' said Wilson. 'This is Charlie Kidd's stuff, right?'

'It is.' Cullen wondered what else it could be. 'And if you want me to come back over there with uniformed officers to confiscate some of your servers, then you're going the right way about it.'

'Do you want me to go to the press with this?' said Wilson. 'I'm not sure how they'd view the police trying to strong arm a social network.'

'And I'd be asking myself how they'd view someone using your social network to perpetrate two murders due to your lack of adequate security.'

Wilson paused. 'Okay, okay, fine. I'll need to run this by Gregor Aitchison first.'

'I've already spoken to him,' said Cullen, a barefaced lie. 'Just send Mr Kidd what he needs and I won't have to pay you a visit.'

'I'll be a few hours,' said Wilson.

'Listen, if it's not here by five pm,' said Cullen, 'I'm turning up with some uniformed officers and crowbars.'

'Okay, okay, okay.'

'I don't want to hear anything about this again.' Cullen ended the call.

'Think he'll play ball?' said Kidd.

Cullen gave a shrug. 'I hope for his sake that he does.'

36

Half an hour later Cullen sat in the Incident Room finishing a large beaker of strong coffee, a filter with two extra shots of espresso. He had only managed to get back to one person on the list so far and they'd not heard about the death threats. He checked his watch — five pm. It seemed to him their earlier luck had run out.

He looked through his list of Caroline's friends, ready to get back to calling people to check on the threats.

'Sundance.' Bain had a wide grin on his face. He loomed over Miller, staring at a laptop screen a few desks over. 'Come here. Have a look at this.'

Cullen slowly wandered round. There was a video player open, black and white footage of the inside of the Hermiston Gait Tesco. 'We watched this at the Tesco.'

'Aye, but not on equipment like this.' Bain tapped Miller on the shoulder.

Miller rewound the video until the display showed 11.24am then let it run. Cullen could just make out a large figure wearing a baseball cap walk across the screen towards the mobile phone area. He picked up a package from the GoMobile section of the display. Miller froze the frame.

Bain grabbed Cullen's shoulder, his face like a kid on Christmas morning. 'It's him.'

Cullen looked more closely at the image. 'Who?'

Bain's nostrils flared. 'Rob Thomson.'

Cullen squinted at the display. 'You think?'

Bain sighed. 'Not you as well.' He leaned into the screen, pointing at the figure and pressing so hard it deformed the display. 'It *is* him.'

Cullen leaned forward even closer, tried to see it, but just couldn't. 'I think you're reaching.'

'Christ's sake.' Bain drew a box around the figure with his finger. 'Here, Miller, enhance that bit.'

'Eh?'

'Come on, what's the matter with you?' said Bain. 'Make it clearer.'

'That sort of stuff only happens in films,' said Cullen.

Bain's grey skin flared purple at the cheeks. 'Right.' He cleared his throat.

As far as Cullen knew, only he and Miller had actually met Rob Thomson. 'Have you even seen him in person?'

'Aye,' said Bain. 'He's downstairs.'

'You've spoken to him?' said Cullen.

'Aye,' said Bain. 'I went in and had a wee chat then I left him to stew in his own juice, waiting for his lawyer to turn up. Wait till I show him this.'

Cullen shook his head. 'I can't see this being admissible as evidence.'

Bain glared at Cullen. 'Miller, show him the other bit.'

Miller skipped forward to 11.30am. The view switched to a self-service till, people looking bored, one middle-aged woman getting progressively angry with the machine. Cullen's limited experience of the machines made him sympathise.

'If he's using self-service,' said Cullen, 'you won't get a witness statement from a checkout operator.'

Bain growled at Miller. 'Next bit.'

Miller skipped forward again — the screen now showed 11.32am. The same man they'd seen earlier was now waiting in the queue. Gradually, he moved through, scanned the phone then paid with cash. Miller paused the video.

'That's certainly the time it was bought,' said Cullen.

'Right.' Bain leaned in. 'And it *is* him.'

'Is there any more?' said Cullen.

Miller pressed play. The man walked away from the till towards the front of the shop. Again, the display switched showing the same man walking across the car park.

All the while, Bain stayed silent until the clip finished. 'That's our man.'

'Yes,' said Cullen.

'Rob Thomson,' said Bain.

Cullen looked at the screen. 'You can't see him clearly enough.'

Bain glared at him.

Cullen took a big gulp of his coffee.

McNeill joined them, tapping Cullen's cup. 'Could have got me one.'

'Here, Butch,' said Bain, 'have a look at this.'

Miller repeated the playback. Bain watched her reaction throughout.

'And?' she said, hand on hip.

'Oh, for Christ sake,' said Bain. 'I need to speak to Jim about getting some proper bloody coppers in, you pair are useless.'

'What am I supposed to see here?' said McNeill. 'Big man in baseball cap buys mobile phone.'

Bain held his hands out. 'It's Rob Thomson.'

She shrugged her shoulders. 'I wouldn't know, I've never met him.'

Bain cracked open another can of Red Bull. 'So, what have you been up to, Butch?'

'Apart from wasting another half tank of fuel getting stuck in traffic on a Sunday, Chantal and I have been out interviewing people who knew both Caroline and Debi.'

'And not Rob Thomson?' said Bain.

'No, I left that to you,' said McNeill. 'I need to get a whole load of witness statements taken.'

She looked at Miller, who swore.

'Anything else?' said Bain.

'I've got another suspect for you,' said McNeill.

Bain scowled. 'Who?'

'Alistair Cruikshank. He used to work with Caroline and Debi in the Linguistics Department. Chantal ferreted it out of them. I gather he's now training as a minister in some sect up north. Bit of a religious nut by all accounts and he made some comments to Caroline Adamson when she was getting divorced from Rob.'

'And when was this?' said Bain.

'Last March,' said McNeill. 'Cruikshank was in his third year of a divinity degree, mature student. He needed the cash and his job mainly involved sending prospectuses out. He kept going on about how it was unlawful in the eyes of God to get divorced. He went on and on about it to anyone who'd listen. Caroline eventually made a formal complaint, backed up by Debi. He got the push.'

'And who told you this?' said Bain.

'Margaret Armstrong,' said McNeill.

'Caroline's boss, right?' Bain downed the rest of the can then looked at Cullen. 'Did she mention any of this when you went round, Sundance?'

'I would've told you if she had.'

Bain nodded. 'Did anything else happen? Any threats? This seems pretty shaky stuff.'

'He dropped out of his course, I believe,' said McNeill. 'Then he joined this sect.'

'So this guy joined a cult?' said Bain. 'That's your evidence?'

McNeill smiled. 'He has previous. Control gave me his record. An ex-girlfriend had a restraining order taken out on him. He also made some phone calls to a girl on his course.'

Bain closed his eyes. 'For Christ's sake.'

'He has a clear grievance against Caroline and Debi,' said McNeill. 'He's a strong suspect.'

Bain nodded slowly. 'Maybe. Any idea where he is now?'

'Up north somewhere,' said McNeill. 'Inverness, Forres, Nairn, someplace like that. Armstrong couldn't remember.'

'Get Chantal on this,' said Bain. 'I don't care what Wilko or Irvine say, this is the highest priority. We need to discredit him as a suspect pretty quickly.'

'You what?' said Cullen.

'Well, now we've got two suspects,' said Bain. 'And this punter looks like he's got something against the two victims. Our man is clearly Rob Thomson, so we need to eliminate this second guy.'

'Why's Sharon finding another suspect a problem?' said Cullen. 'This could be your AN Other.'

Bain gritted his teeth. 'It's a problem because I've got this video footage against Rob Thomson and I'm away downstairs to give him a doing about it.'

He stood up, buttoned up his suit jacket and tightened his tie.

'Sundance, you can see how this is done.'

They walked down to the ground floor in silence.

Bain held the stair door open. 'Right, Sundance, I'm going to lead this, okay?'

Cullen nodded — he had no intention of trying to lead over a DI.

They turned the corner to the interview suites. Bain stopped in his tracks. 'Oh, for Christ's sake.'

'Hello, Inspector.'

Outside the interview suite was Campbell McLintock, Edinburgh criminal defence lawyer and notorious pain in the arse. He was a thin man, wearing a purple suit, black shirt and matching purple tie. He was eye-catching, if nothing else.

'Mr McLintock,' said Bain.

'I hope you don't mind me sitting in on my client's interview, Inspector?'

Bain's eyes narrowed to a slit. 'Rob Thomson?'

'The same,' said McLintock.

'Since when has he been your client?' said Bain.

McLintock gestured at Cullen. 'Since about three o'clock on Friday when your gorilla here started prodding around at my client's workplace.'

Bain sighed. 'And if I refuse to let you sit in?'

McLintock raised an eyebrow. 'I shall remind you of the Cadder case, Inspector.'

Cullen knew it well. The case had changed everything in criminal law in Scotland. Previously, the police had six hours grace with a suspect before a lawyer got involved. Now, they had to be in from the start of the first interview, like in England. Since October, Cullen had seen outright obstruction in some interviews, with every answer 'no comment'. McLintock was already a specialist.

'Even if you get a judge and jury favourable to whichever distorted view of the world you're peddling this time, Inspector, I seriously doubt you'll get a conviction.'

Bain just pushed past him into the interview room.

37

Bain and Cullen faced Rob Thomson whose hands gripped the wood of the tabletop tightly. McLintock sat next to him. The digital recorder had silently recorded the interview for more than twenty minutes.

Bain sneered. 'Mr Thomson, I'll ask you one more time. Did you, as several witnesses have informed us, threaten to kill your late ex-wife, Caroline Adamson?'

Thomson slammed his hand on the table.

'For the purposes of the tape,' said Bain, 'that was the interviewee's hand hitting the table.'

'I refer you to my client's previous response.' McLintock had used that trick all along, referring back to an initial 'no comment'. It probably looked marginally better on a transcript, Cullen figured. They had nothing out of Thomson so far.

'What's wrong with you?' said Thomson. 'I've not done anything.'

'Mr Thomson,' said McLintock, 'please remain calm.'

Bain ignored the lawyer. 'You not doing anything wouldn't appear to be the case, Mr Thomson. We've heard you made death threats.'

'I was at work when Caroline went missing. I've got alibis for the rest of the time. And I know you've checked them out.'

'Mr McLintock, I hope your client hasn't been monitoring an active police investigation,' said Bain. 'As you know, the courts take a very dim view of that.'

McLintock glared at his client. 'Mr Thomson, can I remind you not to be goaded by the aggression shown by these police officers?'

'Okay, let's change tack shall we?' said Bain. 'Where were you on Saturday evening?'

McLintock raised his hands.

'As I already told you,' said Thomson, 'me and Kim watched some telly, had a takeaway then went to bed early. Just ask her.'

'At what point did you sneak out and kill Debi Curtis?' said Bain.

'That is not appropriate and I insist you strike this entire conversation from the record,' said McLintock.

'Did you leave your flat on Saturday evening?' said Bain.

'No, I was watching TV,' said Thomson. 'I know Kim will back me up on this.'

Bain stroked his moustache. 'Back to the monitoring.'

'I didn't kill Caroline or Debi,' said Thomson.

'But you did threaten to kill Caroline?' said Bain.

'Inspector,' said McLintock.

'I didn't,' said Thomson.

'Then why would people tell us you threatened her?' said Bain.

'Inspector.'

Thomson jumped to his feet and roared at them. 'Why would I? Eh? Ask yourself that. I wanted out of our marriage. We both did. It was dead. When the divorce came through, I got shot of Caroline and Jack. I wanted to be with Kim. I'm *sorry* about what happened. I can't believe she's gone.'

He slumped over the table, his head cradled in his arms, his shoulders heaving with sobs.

Bain rolled his eyes at Cullen. 'Stop with the histrionics, pal. You're the number one suspect in this case.'

Thomson looked up, his face damp. 'This isn't right.' He stabbed his finger in the air, punctuating each word. 'I didn't kill her.' He rubbed his nose on the back of his hand, sniffing deeply. 'You're wasting your time speaking to me. You should be out there finding the bastard that did this.'

'Seems to me we've found the bastard,' said Bain.

'Inspector.'

Mucus dripped from Thomson's nose. 'I told you. I was with Kim both times.'

'According to you,' said Bain, 'and according to your bird. But for now, I'd really like to know what happened *after* you divorced your wife.'

McLintock's face was almost as purple as his suit jacket. 'This has absolutely nothing to do with this current investigation.'

'Nothing?' said Bain. 'I think it's got everything to do with it.'

'I told you,' said Thomson. '*Nothing* happened.' He smacked his fist off the tabletop again. 'Who said I did?'

Bain had a relaxed smile on his face. 'Mr Thomson, you know I can't tell you that.'

Thomson got his feet again. 'Who told you? Eh? It's a pack of lies. All lies.'

'Mr Thomson, could you sit down please?' said McLintock.

Thomson glared at Bain then did as he was told.

'Like I've already said, we have it on very good authority you made a succession of death threats against Ms Adamson,' said Bain. 'Apparently it's common knowledge in your home town.'

Thomson ground his teeth, but didn't speak.

McLintock looked rattled. 'My client would like to make no further statement on this matter.'

Bain ignored the solicitor again. 'How did you access Schoolbook?'

Thomson screwed his face up. 'What?'

Cullen glared at Bain — what was he playing at?

'Come on, tell me,' said Bain. 'This account you've got on there.'

'My client has no wish to comment on any accounts he has on any website,' said McLintock.

'Do you use the website Schoolbook?' said Bain.

Thomson nodded slowly. 'I'm on Schoolbook, aye.'

'And were you friends with Ms Adamson on the site?' said Bain.

Thomson sighed, the despair and tears echoed in his breath. 'I think she added me. Maybe it was the other way round, I can't remember.'

'Now we're getting somewhere,' said Bain. 'Why did you choose the name Martin Webb?'

Thomson frowned. '*Sorry?*'

'Inspector Bain,' said McLintock in a low tone, 'can you please desist from these blatant accusations against my client.'

'Mr McLintock,' said Bain, 'I'll ask the questions that I, the Senior Investigating Officer, deem relevant to the case. It's up to you to decide how you and your client respond to them.'

McLintock glared at Bain and folded his arms.

'Martin Webb's the name you adopted on Schoolbook,' said Bain. 'The name you used while hunting down Caroline and Debi.'

'Nonsense. I'm Rob Thomson on Schoolbook.'

Bain raised his eyebrows. 'So you say. You can have two profiles quite easily, though, I believe?'

'My client refers you to his previous answer, Inspector,' said McLintock. 'He has one account and one account only, in his own name.'

'Can you tell us your movements on the twenty-fifth of July between eleven am and twelve noon,' said Bain.

'What?'

'Answer the question,' said Bain.

'I'll need my Blackberry back,' said Thomson.

'Why?'

'I'll need to have a look at the calendar, won't I?'

Bain looked at Cullen. 'DC Cullen, can you give Mr Thomson evidence item A, please?'

Cullen reached across and handed the bagged Blackberry over. Thomson tried opening it.

'Type through the bag, please,' said Bain.

Thomson swore under his breath. Cullen watched him opening the calendar app and scrolling to the date. 'Twenty-fifth of July, I was at the Alba Bank Mortgage Centre most of the morning, went back to HQ for a meeting at half twelve.'

Cullen retrieved the Blackberry.

'And where's the Mortgage Centre?' said Bain.

Thomson sighed. 'Edinburgh Park, just across from the train station.'

Bain nodded. 'Thank you.'

Cullen realised Bain's game as he sat back down. Hermiston Gait Tesco was right beside the Alba Bank mortgage centre. If Thomson had popped in to buy a mobile phone, then he wouldn't have an alibi at work.

Bain leaned forward into the microphone, grinning like a demon. 'Interview terminated at sixteen forty-nine.'

38

Bain sat at his desk, having been deathly silent all the way up the stairs. 'He's a big bloke, isn't he?'

Cullen shrugged. 'Suppose so.'

'Looks bigger in the flesh than on the CCTV.' Bain put Thomson's bagged Blackberry and iPhone on his desk. 'We've just about got him. Should be able to get something on Thomson off these. I'll get Miller onto it.' He reached into his pocket and retrieved a folded piece of paper. He brandished a RIPSA form, obviously proud of himself. 'Take a look at this.'

Cullen scanned through the form. Bain had scrawled something entirely illegible in the section requesting an explanation of why the information required couldn't be obtained by less intrusive methods. Cullen wondered if it was intentional. It was signed and dated at the bottom, counter-signed by Wilkinson.

'How come you can get a RIPSA for a guy you've got a grudge against, but when I ask for one for the murder victim it takes forever?' said Cullen.

'Politics, Sundance.'

'There's no politics with what you've done but there are with mine?' said Cullen.

'Right, Sundance. You were asking to snoop on a big company with clout. This is just one guy who's looking guiltier and guiltier by the minute.'

Cullen gestured at the Blackberry. 'That must have Alba Bank emails on it? Isn't that snooping on a big company?'

'We'll not be looking at any commercial stuff, just having a wee look at emails between Rob Thomson and Kim Milne and whatever else incriminates him.'

Cullen handed it back. 'What about the explanation on the form?'

Bain smirked. 'I'll make something up once I've charged him.'

McNeill had been listening in. 'This is a risky game you're playing.'

'No pain, no gain, Butch.'

'What else have you got up your sleeve?' said McNeill.

'Just letting him stew for now,' said Bain. 'Sundance, can you get back to those bloody phone calls. I want this story about death threats corroborated by at least two people.'

CULLEN WAS GOING through the notes Angela had typed up, not particularly taking anything in, his mind focusing on the supposed death threats and how he could corroborate them.

McNeill grabbed his shoulder. 'Scott, come with me.'

'Huh?'

'Outside. Press conference.'

She turned and sped off. He got up and followed, catching her up at the stairwell.

'Who's giving it?'

'Campbell McLintock,' said McNeill.

'Jesus.'

They raced down the stairs and through the security doors, hoping to catch some of the lawyer's play-acting.

McNeill pushed through the front door to the station. A large crowd had assembled outside McDonald Road Library next door. McNeill barged her way through, Cullen following in her wake. There were several TV cameras.

Campbell McLintock stood in the centre of the large semi-circle, his arms gesticulating as he gave his oration. 'Now, someone once said libraries gave us power.' He pointed over his shoulder — Cullen recognised it as a song lyric from somewhere.

'Today, tremendous power has been given to those who are supposed to protect us — the police. As I have said, my client, Robert Thomson, is a fine upstanding citizen. He has strong alibis for both periods when the crimes in question were committed. And yet, the powers of Lothian & Borders Police are being used to conduct a vendetta against Robert. This is unacceptable. I'm sure you'll join with me in insisting the police desist from this reprehensible behaviour. Thank you.'

McLintock smiled as he posed for photographs.

McNeill's mouth was pursed in a slight smile. 'He's got some style.'

39

Bain's evening briefing was even more strained than his lunchtime diatribe. There was a discernible tension between Bain, Wilkinson and Irvine on one side, and Cullen and McNeill on the other.

Cullen had outlined the progress — or lack thereof — made in corroborating the death threats.

'Thanks for that, Sundance. I'm sure you'll solve the case for us all.'

Cullen glared at him.

'Priorities for tomorrow are the street team and the phones,' said Bain. 'We've still got six flats to visit in Debi's street. Plus we need to interview the other people staying at the Jackson Hotel on the night of Caroline's death. We've got another press release going out tonight, looking for people who were at the supermarket or at the hotel at the times in question.'

Bain neglected to mention that Cullen had discovered their only two leads. He knew Bain had a lot on his plate, particularly after being publicly humiliated by McLintock, but still.

'I know you'll have heard that bastard McLintock's spiel outside,' said Bain. 'We've almost got Thomson nailed on buying that phone. He definitely had the opportunity and was in the vicinity at the time. I've got him coming back in tomorrow to give a detailed statement.'

'You've let him go?' said McNeill.

Bain rubbed his ear. 'Aye. Just at the back of six there.' He nodded, taking a deep breath. 'Right, dismissed.'

McNeill was first to leave the room, closely followed by Cullen. 'He's a prick.'

'You were the one defending him this morning,' said Cullen.

'Yeah, well, a girl can change her mind.'

Cullen checked his watch — it was far too late to be calling friends of Caroline. 'I'm going to head off now. What about you?'

'Yeah, I think I'll make a night of it too. I'm shattered.'

'Tell me about it,' said Cullen. 'It's just like being back on the beat. The number of times I got a call half an hour before the end of my shift and I'd have to stay in to process it.'

They collected their coats from the deserted Incident Room, their colleagues no doubt all still trawling round the various search areas. They walked towards the stairwell.

'You heading home?' said McNeill.

'Aye. Curry and some music. Try to clear my head of all this crap for a bit.'

'Where do you stay?'

'Portobello,' said Cullen. 'You?'

'World's End Close.'

'Just off the Royal Mile?'

McNeill grinned. 'I prefer to call it the High Street but yes, there.'

'Isn't it a bastard for parking?'

'I've got a permit,' said McNeill.

'And you drive in here?' said Cullen. 'It's a ten minute walk.'

She shrugged. 'I'm always in the car in this job.'

They were at the bottom of the stairs.

'You up to anything tonight?' said Cullen.

'Think I'm going to get a Chinese and watch some really bad TV.'

'Sounds good.'

McNeill bit her lip. 'How about a drink first?'

It didn't take Cullen long to reply. 'Not the Elm.'

40

They cut out of the station's back entrance and headed through the outer reaches of the New Town, settling on the Basement Bar on Broughton Street, close enough for McNeill to walk home and for Cullen to walk back to the station for his car. They sat in a corner of the bar, the music loud enough that no one could hear their conversation, quiet enough to hear each other.

Cullen took another sip of Staropramen, the beer already going to his head. Just the one, he'd said — he had the car and he was knackered.

'Do you think it's Rob Thomson?' said McNeill.

'I'm struggling to see it,' said Cullen, 'I really am. I mean, what's his motivation?'

'Bitter at the divorce?'

'But why? He caused it by sleeping around.'

'Child support payments?'

'Well, you tell me,' said Cullen. 'You looked at his bank accounts.'

'Yeah, Bain wasn't best pleased at that.'

'This is the first I've heard of it,' said Cullen.

'Yeah, funny that. Bain didn't want it broadcast.' She paused. 'Thomson earns a *lot*.'

'How much is a lot?'

'About sixty grand a year after tax.'

'Jesus.'

McNeill nodded. 'Yeah. He's only shelling out about three hundred quid a month for Jack.'

'Drop in the ocean,' said Cullen.

'Precisely.'

'Why's Bain so set on him?' said Cullen.

McNeill took a sip of her wine. 'Easy collar, I presume. He's pushing for DCI, so getting a fast result would improve his stats a lot. Rumour is Turnbull is getting a promotion soon, which leaves the door open for Bain or another DI to step up.'

'Christ, they're like sharks,' said Cullen.

'Oh yes.' McNeill took another sip of wine.

'Bain's got nothing concrete on Thomson,' said Cullen.

McNeill ran her finger round the top of her glass. 'I notice he got his own RIPSA approved pretty quickly.'

'Yeah, by Wilkinson,' said Cullen.

'What does he actually have on this guy? Any evidence?'

Cullen thought it through. 'Just a flimsy motive, those supposed death threats, the CCTV footage and Thomson being at the Alba Mortgage Centre when the phone was bought at the Tesco nearby.'

'It's not a lot, is it?'

'No.' Cullen took a drink of his pint. 'Could he get it to court with so little, do you think?'

'I've seen it happen.'

'That Tesco footage,' said Cullen. 'It's just some guy buying the mobile used to call Caroline. It's a big man in a hoodie. It could be anyone.'

She nodded, taking another sip. 'What's the story with Amy Cousens?'

'Amy Cousens?' said Cullen. 'What about her?'

McNeill stared right at him. 'Bain and Miller are calling her your girlfriend.'

He shook his head. 'They are, are they? Funny bastards.'

She picked up her glass, took a drink and looked at him through the clear liquid. 'Do you have one? A girlfriend, I mean.'

'I wish. I can feel my virginity growing back.'

She laughed so hard wine came out of her nose.

He smiled to himself and finished his pint, wondering if he should get off home.

She pointed at the glass. 'Another?'

He stared at it for a moment — he was right at the tipping point between getting hammered and going home. 'Aye, go on.'

41

Cullen pushed the flat door open. Tom looked up from the table, the Sunday papers scattered all over it, a couple of empty beer cans beside him.

Tom playfully checked his watch. 'What time's this?'

Cullen giggled. 'Half eleven, Dad.'

'Aren't you back on at seven?'

Cullen collapsed on a chair and shrugged his suit jacket off. 'Aye. Where's Johnny?'

'At Dawn's.' Tom's nostrils twitched. 'Have you been on the piss *again*?'

'Aye, a couple of jars. Well, four. Got the bus home.'

'So this new squad of yours are a bunch of piss artists, then?'

Cullen belched. 'No, just my DS tonight.'

'What's his name?'

'Sharon.'

Tom shook his head. 'Scott, you really are some swordsman. Shagging your boss. After that bird on Friday.'

Cullen held up two fingers. 'First thing, I didn't shag DS McNeill tonight. We just had a few pints and some food. Second, Alison was just a one night stand.'

Tom laughed. 'Aye, right. Yet you're meeting her for a date tomorrow night.'

Cullen looked away. 'There's that, I suppose.' He'd totally forgotten about meeting Alison. Was it too late to get out of it?

'How's this case you're on then?' said Tom.

'It's pretty brutal,' said Cullen. 'A double murder.'

Tom held up the *Scotland on Sunday*, a family photo of Caroline splashed all over the cover, released before they'd announced Debi's death. 'This is what you're working on?'

'Aye, only now it's two victims.' Cullen exhaled. 'I almost caught the killer yesterday but he gave me the slip.'

Tom grinned. 'Getting slow in your old age?'

Cullen couldn't help but laugh along. 'Never was much of a runner.'

'It says here she was tortured,' said Tom. 'That right?'

Cullen took the paper off Tom and scanned through the article. 'It is.' He realised the press interest had been light until now. The only direct contact he'd had with the media was at Campbell McLintock's ad hoc press conference outside the library. He looked up at Tom and pointed at Caroline. 'Her ex-husband works at Alba Bank. Guy called Rob Thomson. Don't suppose you know him?'

Tom leaned back in his chair, tapping the table rhythmically. 'Vaguely rings a bell. Where does he work?'

'IT, I think.'

'Nope,' said Tom. 'I know a Rob Thomas, works in Corporate. I'm in Retail Sales, Scott. I never speak to IT unless it's about my laptop.'

'Worth a shot.' Cullen got up and stretched. 'Right, I'm off to bed. Early start tomorrow.'

DAY 5

Monday
1st August

42

Cullen stood in the queue for coffee, half-asleep. It was ten past seven and the other side of the shortest, angriest Bain tirade he'd yet seen, rage at the lack of progress, particularly from the press releases. Cullen was given a grilling over the death threats and the desperate need to validate and verify them.

McNeill barged in beside him in the queue, a series of loud tuts coming from behind. 'Morning, Scott.'

'Sharon.'

'Good curry last night?'

'Yeah, not bad.' He smiled. 'How was your Chinese?'

She winked. 'Passable.'

He laughed.

They queued in silence for a few moments, moving forward a few paces.

'Now he knows Campbell McLintock is Thomson's lawyer, Bain will be trying even harder,' said McNeill.

'I kind of guessed that,' said Cullen.

'Aside from the professional differences, Bain can't stand the fact McLintock's always in the papers with stuff for Amnesty or whatever.'

'Is Bain a fascist or something?'

McNeill laughed. 'DC Cullen, you've only been working for him for a few months and you've worked that out already. No, but he does think McLintock uses it to influence juries.'

'That's quite an accusation.'

'Bain's quite a guy.'

'What are you up to today?' said Cullen.

'Still trying to track down people who were in that hotel last week. Needle in a bloody haystack.'

They were at the front of the queue. McNeill ordered a latte, Cullen a filter.

'How's the investigation into Debi Curtis going?' he said.

'Bloody Irvine's leading it. Doubt they'll get anything.'

They collected their coffees and started to head back.

Bain was at the back of the queue, a can of Red Bull and a bacon roll on his tray. 'Look who it bloody isn't.'

'Morning,' said McNeill.

'Aye, morning Butch.' Bain's eyes were focused on Cullen. 'Sundance, just got a delivery from the High Street. A load of CCTV tapes from Saturday night, from the cameras near Debi's flat. I want you to look through them. Has to be some shots of Thomson's face on there from when you chased him.'

CULLEN PLAYED the video file for the fifth time, desperate to find anything that could help identify the man who killed Debi Curtis. He was in the video review room on the first floor of Leith Walk station. He would have used his desktop PC, like Miller had for the Tesco footage, but the CCTV office had sent a load of VHS tapes. The room was similar to the one he'd used in St Leonard's from time to time, but this had PCs with large monitors instead of the TVs and VCRs installed at the older station. Fortunately for Cullen, they also had a few VHS machines.

Cullen slowed the footage right down using a jog wheel. The traffic camera showed a line of cars up Angle Park Terrace, waiting for the traffic lights. The figure of the killer — Rob Thomson to Bain's eyes — ran across the road.

Cullen froze the image — there was something under his arm,

a bag. It figured — he had a knife and a rope, so it made sense he had something to carry them in. He took screen grabs of several individual frames and sent them to the printer, but there was nothing conclusive.

He peered at the prints — the figure could be Rob Thomson, but it could also be anybody of a similar height and build. It just wasn't definitive. He was reluctant to go to Bain with what he had. It would just be more fuel to the Rob Thomson fire and Cullen was already feeling uncomfortable about it. He copied the screen grabs to a USB stick and leaned back in the chair.

He was alone in the room and he used the time to think. The only lead he had outstanding was the cell site search. He picked up his phone and dialled.

'Tommy Smith.'

'It's DC Cullen. I'm just checking in to see how we're getting on with the cell search.'

'Checking up on me, eh?' said Smith, humour in his voice.

'Nature of the job,' said Cullen. 'I'm sure you understand.'

'Yeah, yeah. I actually got your cell site trace back overnight. You're on my list to call today.'

'Go on.'

'There was one call made from that mobile number you found on Caroline's phone, as you know,' said Smith. 'According to the trace, the call was relayed by the mast on top of the Dick Vet.'

'By the university?'

'Aye.'

Cullen quickly found a map and located the Dick Veterinary School on the corner of the Meadows. Some of the guys in his Halls of Residence in first year had studied there, all thick-necked, rugby-playing idiots. It was a few hundred metres from the Jackson Hotel. This was better. It could be used to show the killer was near the hotel when the call was made. And he used that phone.

'You still there?' said Smith.

'Oh, sorry,' said Cullen, 'just lost in thought.'

'Aye, I could hear the gears crunching away there, buddy.'

'Did you get anything else off the phone or that number?'

'Sorry, buddy, that's your lot,' said Smith.

'Okay, cheers.' Cullen hung up.

He should tell Bain, but he doubted he'd be interested. Besides, he'd get his nuts chewed over the cost he'd incurred for a dead end. He nibbled away at the end of his pen, thinking.

It was time to pay Charlie Kidd another visit.

43

Charlie Kidd was on the phone when Cullen got there, so he leaned against the edge of the desk and waited.

The office was pretty busy for so early in the morning — Cullen wouldn't have put the techies down as early birds, but then they were answerable to animals like Bain.

'Aye, go for it,' said Kidd in an enthusiastic tone, earnestly nodding his head. 'I'll have to clear it with the guys who pay the bills but it sounds like it could really help us out here. Aye, I'll call back this afternoon. Cheers.' He put the phone down and glared up at Cullen. 'He's sent *you* up now, has he?'

'Eh?'

'Bain.' Kidd rolled his eyes. 'I've had DS Irvine up here every half an hour checking up on progress.'

'I see,' said Cullen. 'And have you made any?'

'Do you cocks downstairs not talk?' Kidd shook his head then took a deep breath. 'Aye. I'm doing well. Now just let me get on with it.'

Cullen held up his hands. 'Bain hasn't sent me. I'm after a friendly update from you.'

Kidd almost stopped scowling. 'So, what do you want to know?'

'Did you get that new extract from Schoolbook?'

'Aye, I did.' Kidd sighed. 'That's why Irvine's been on at me all day. I thought I had your man, but he slipped away.'

Cullen's pulse was racing. 'How?'

'The record we got from Schoolbook had an IP address attached to the audit records,' said Kidd.

The IT courses Cullen had been on in the last eighteen months told him an IP Address was the unique number assigned to a computer when it went online. 'What audit records?'

'For God's sake, man,' said Kidd. 'I'm having to explain this shite to absolute tubes here. I've told Irvine this five bloody times already.'

'Charlie, your job is to explain it to us in a way us tubes understand, okay?' said Cullen.

Kidd shook his head slowly. 'I have to when I speak to that twat Irvine. Many times over.' He took a long deep breath. 'Okay. Every time the database gets updated, whether it's a status update, sending a message, posting on a message board, whatever, a record gets created, which tags the change with who made it. So if you go in and post an update, it logs a few things like your username, IP address and so on.'

'Okay, I get that,' said Cullen, sort of getting it.

'I'm glad somebody does.'

'So, this IP address you got off the audit record, then?' said Cullen, trying to get Kidd back on track.

'Every update to Martin Webb uses the same IP address, which you'd kind of expect. Some Internet Service Providers cycle them around live users, but this seems to be a stable IP that's been used over time. I traced the IP address, tried to find out who was using it.'

'And?'

'It's a dummy IP address,' said Kidd.

'Eh?'

'Aye, exactly,' said Kidd in a slow drawl. 'A dummy IP address has been logging changes to the Schoolbook database. Doesn't make sense. That's what that call was about. I was speaking to a mate who works for a private security firm. I tried some boys in the Met and in Strathclyde, but they've just not got the capacity to deal with it. So we've got some private firms we can bring in. Turnbull's used them in the past on other cases. Just need to get approval from him and Bain.'

'Good luck with that,' said Cullen. 'What will they give us?'

'We don't know if it's accessed using a dummy IP or some sort of masking or what. Hopefully these guys can come in and audit the database and work out how it's happening.'

'Have you spoken to Schoolbook about it?'

Kidd laughed. 'Aye. They were useless. We should be able to charge them for the cost of having to get these boys in. Lazy bastards.'

'Aren't you getting any help from them?'

'This Duncan Wilson guy is doing my head in,' said Kidd. 'He's the most obstructive twat I've ever met.'

'You obviously haven't met Campbell McLintock,' said Cullen. 'How's he being obstructive?'

'There's always stuff missing, things the extracts should have included but don't.'

'And do you get them in the end?'

'Aye,' said Kidd, 'but it's just a pain in the arse and it's bloody slow.'

'Do you think it's malicious?'

Kidd shrugged. 'It's more like incompetence.'

'Do you want me to give him another call?' said Cullen. 'I could call his boss.'

Kidd played with his ponytail. 'Already been down that road. Got nowhere fast.'

Cullen folded his arms and leaned back slightly on the desk. 'Is there anything else that could help?'

'The laptop Caroline or Debi used to access Schoolbook would be good,' said Kidd. 'If they've been chatting, some log files might have been created on their PCs. That could be useful. That's my strength, forensic analysis of computers, not data mining like I'm having to do here.'

Cullen nodded. 'I'll see what I can dig up.'

44

The Scene of Crime unit was based on the ground floor of Leith Walk station. The floor was split in two by a corridor the length of the building. The community policing section on the side fronting Leith Walk was a mixture of windowed rooms for victims and enclosed interview rooms for suspects. The Scene of Crime team occupied the other half, facing into the lane at the rear of the station.

Due to the nature of the work, the SOC section was protected by a locked security door and Cullen had to wait almost a minute before a weaselly man let him in. 'Hey, Jimmy,' he said to a colleague. 'It's the boaker.'

Anderson looked up. He laughed at Cullen as he approached. 'Puked all over any other crime scenes lately?'

Cullen smiled, trying to humour him. 'Not yet, anyway.'

'Lucky for you, you didn't bugger up my search too badly.'

Cullen had only been fed scraps by Bain and didn't know the full results of the investigation. 'I take it there was nothing?'

'Clean as a bloody whistle,' said Anderson. 'We're either dealing with a pro or a spawny bastard.'

Cullen rubbed his neck. 'Did you do Caroline's flat as well?'

'Aye, fat lot of good that was,' said Anderson. 'We know you were there. What were you up to?'

'Having a look around,' said Cullen.

Anderson smoothed down his goatee. 'Having a good look in her knicker drawer, you dirty bastard.'

'I was checking to see if she'd done a runner.' Cullen was aware his face had reddened. 'Look, can we not get into this? I'm just here to take a look at her laptop.'

Anderson frowned. 'Laptop?'

'Aye, an Apple one,' said Cullen. 'It was in the bedroom.'

Anderson picked up a pile of paper from his desk and leafed through, before shaking his head. 'No laptop, pal.'

'There was a laptop in her flat,' said Cullen. 'It was on the bed.'

Anderson looked up. 'Nope, no laptop.'

'I saw it,' said Cullen. 'Are you sure it's not listed?'

'If there was one it would've been upstairs with Dave Watson or Charlie Kidd, one of those boys. They deal with all the computers we get in. They all come through us first, mind.'

'Could someone have nicked it?' said Cullen.

'Me and Dave went round,' said Anderson. 'I did the bedroom.'

'And you didn't nick it?' said Cullen.

Anderson scowled. 'No, I didn't.' He put the papers on the table. The top sheet looked like an inventory of Caroline's flat.

Cullen picked up the list, scanning through it as Anderson huffed. 'There's a BT Wi-Fi box on this, don't you think that's enough of a clue there would be a laptop there?'

Anderson stared at him for a few seconds then grabbed the sheet off him. 'Shite.'

45

Cullen showed Bain the printout from Anderson's inventory system. They were at the meeting table in the Incident Room, McNeill sitting opposite him.

'Big wow,' said Bain.

'Why's he stealing laptops?' said Cullen.

'I don't bloody know, do I?' said Bain. 'Maybe he's a thief.'

'Caroline's laptop was on her bed when I went round there on Friday,' said Cullen. 'Someone's been in the flat between me going round there and Caroline's body being found.'

'You serious?' said Bain.

McNeill looked up.

'Yes. I saw that laptop with my own eyes.' Cullen held up his phone, showing an image he'd found on the internet. 'A MacBook. Not a particularly new one, either. It's not on the SOC manifest. I checked Debi's manifest and hers is gone as well. It's what he was carrying when I chased him.'

'For Christ's sake,' said Bain.

DCI Turnbull appeared, making a beeline for Bain.

'Here's trouble.' Bain moved to his own seat.

McNeill wheeled her chair over to Cullen's desk.

Cullen flicked through his notebook to the latest page. 'I looked at Caroline's laptop just after half twelve on Friday. The SOCOs got to her flat at half eleven on Saturday morning.'

'So there's a twenty-three hour window where someone got into Caroline's flat and stole her laptop,' said McNeill. 'It's got to be the killer.'

'The other thing the SOCOs told me was Caroline's keys were missing from her possessions at the hotel.'

'We can link the two, then,' said McNeill. 'He took her keys to get into the flat, so no break-in. Why did he take her laptop?'

'The reason I found out the laptops were missing was Charlie Kidd reckoned he might be able to track the other user from the chats if he had them.'

McNeill looked mystified.

Cullen sighed then explained IP addresses to her — she clearly hadn't been on the same courses he had. 'He found an IP address for Martin Webb, but it was fake. He reckoned there might be some useful data on Caroline's or Debi's laptops from when they'd chatted with Martin Webb. That's why I was trying to get one or other back from the SOCOs.'

'So our killer had the same thoughts and he's covering his tracks?'

'Aye, it's another dead end.' Cullen stroked the back of his neck, thinking. 'There might be another way. They could have been chatting from their work computers.'

McNeill nodded. 'Good idea. I'll get Charlie or Dave on to it. We'll need a RIPSA.' She returned to her machine and found the form. They were now experts at filling them in and it took only a couple of minutes before they printed it out. 'Let's see if we can get it approved.'

They looked over at Bain and Turnbull.

'Right, Jim, I'll get someone onto that,' said Bain, arms folded tight.

'Please do, Brian,' said Turnbull, 'I'm sure there are synergies we can leverage here.' He nodded at them and walked off at a pace.

'Leveraging bloody synergies.' Bain looked up at Cullen and McNeill then got to his feet. 'Right, where were we?'

McNeill explained the situation.

'Right, Butch,' said Bain, 'I want you and a few big ugly bastards in uniforms going round the doors in Caroline's street, see if anybody saw anything when he was swiping her laptop. I'll get Miller to do the usual checks for stolen goods and go through some CCTV.'

'Kidd can do some searches on the victims' work PCs,' said McNeill.

'Get him on it,' said Bain.

McNeill handed him the RIPSA form. 'Sign this.'

Bain didn't look at the content as he scrawled his signature on the form. 'Right, Sundance, what's happened to this stem cell search?'

'Cell site,' said Cullen, correcting him. 'I got the results back. The call was made from the area around where the body turned up, just before she left the bar in the hotel and went to the room.'

'Like I said earlier, big wow,' said Bain. 'Do you know how much this has cost?'

Cullen shrugged. 'No idea.'

'Three grand,' said Bain.

'You know how much the PF loves a clear timeline,' said McNeill. 'This will help with that.'

Bain took a kick at the bin beside him, sending it flying. 'Don't talk to me like that. For Christ's sake, Cullen's just spunked a few grand on a waste of time here.'

'If you'd let us get on with our jobs,' said McNeill, 'we might—'

Bain's glare stopped her in her tracks. 'Sergeant, you do as I say on this case, all right? If I say wash my car, you wash my bloody car, okay?'

McNeill's head bowed.

'I want you to head over to Smith's Place,' said Bain, 'get those officers going round doors. I want to find out how he got this laptop.'

'Fine.'

'What about me?' said Cullen, aware he was in grave danger of deflecting Bain's ire onto him.

'Well, Sundance, seeing as how you did such a good job in finding Caroline Adamson before she was killed, I've got another missing person for you to look into.'

46

Cullen's Golf crawled towards the traffic lights in Portobello, the ageing engine rattling slightly. All the squad cars were out, presumably on this particular case, so he'd taken his own car, having left it in the station car park before the previous night's impromptu drinking.

Bain had assigned this investigation to him out of spite. He honestly thought he'd been doing his best — he'd done everything by the book and he'd found leads left, right and centre — and yet he was being side-lined, shunted out to Musselburgh. He wasn't even fit to phone through Caroline Adamson's friends list any more.

He headed along Harry Lauder Road, powering past the train yards and the low-rent industrial units. He struck lucky at the other end, managing to get on to the A1 with only a single cycle of the new lights. He pulled off at Old Craighall and headed into Musselburgh from the south.

The address Bain had given him was near the railway station, across from the new Queen Margaret's University campus. He drove down streets of post-war terraces before turning into a modern brick-built estate and spotting a panda car parked outside the house.

A stern-faced female PC answered the door.

He showed his warrant card. 'DC Cullen.'

'PC Campbell.'

'I've been asked to take over the case for CID,' said Cullen. 'Can you bring me up to speed?'

'We got the call from the station,' said Campbell. 'The lassie's a Gail McBride — her husband called in to report her missing. She was just out for a few drinks with her pal up the town, was supposed to be back on the last train.'

'And when did he call it in?'

'Couple of hours ago,' said Campbell.

'And she's been missing since last night?'

'Aye.'

'MisPer report filed?' said Cullen.

'Aye.' Campbell reached into a bag and handed him a copy.

Cullen had a look through. The photo was good — the missing woman was an intense-looking redhead, reasonably attractive. He flicked through the report. It didn't add much to what she'd just told him or to Bain's briefing. 'Any other officers here?'

'Just Jimmy McKay,' said Campbell. 'He's making some tea the now, if you want some?'

'I'm fine.'

'They've not wasted much time in getting CID in,' said Campbell. 'Must be that Caroline Adamson case that's all over the papers.'

'And Debi Curtis,' said Cullen, unable to help himself.

'Are they linked?'

'Definitely the same killer.' Cullen nodded slowly, then exhaled. 'Let's go inside.'

Campbell led through to the living room. The house was decorated in vibrant colours — strong yellows, oranges, lime greens. The sitting room was a light purple — a pair of orange settees sat to either side of a large LCD TV, mounted on the wall.

'Mr McBride,' said Campbell in a patronising tone. 'This is DC Cullen from CID. He'll help us search for your wife.'

Simon McBride sat on one of the sofas, his eyes red. He was a big man, his head shaved, ginger stubble showing through. He was sharply dressed.

Cullen smiled politely as he sat. 'Do you have any idea where your wife might have gone?'

McBride just shrugged.

'Could she maybe have gone to her parents, or visited any friends?' said Cullen.

McBride shrugged again. 'Don't think so.'

'Who have you tried contacting?' said Cullen.

'Well, her parents,' said McBride. 'Her brother's in Ayr, but she hadn't heard from him in months.'

'Any friends?'

'Not really, no,' said McBride. 'Just Sian, I suppose. That's who Gail was meeting last night. They often go out on a Friday, usually to one of the pubs in town, but Sian couldn't make it this week so they went out last night instead.'

'By town,' said Cullen, 'do you mean Edinburgh or Musselburgh?'

'Edinburgh.'

Cullen jotted it all down. 'What's Sian's surname?'

'Saunders. They work together. As I say, they were going out in town. They work out at the Gyle, so it's halfway home, they just get off the train at Waverley. She was in work yesterday on overtime, supposed to be off today.'

'What time did they arrange to meet?'

'I can't remember,' said McBride. 'I think it was the back of six.'

'What time did you start to get concerned?' said Cullen.

'I don't know, really.' McBride exhaled. 'I was watching the game last night, had a couple of cans. When I turned the telly off it was about half ten, so I just went to bed.'

'Does your wife often come back after you've gone to bed?'

McBride looked away. 'She does, aye.'

'So it was only this morning you first noticed she hadn't come home?'

McBride shrugged again. 'Aye. About seven. I started calling her mates from work, starting with Sian.'

'Have any of her clothes gone?' said Cullen.

'Not that I've noticed.'

'What did Sian say happened?'

'She said they got the train back together,' said McBride. 'Sian stays in the Pans, so she saw her off the train at Musselburgh.'

'And that's the last she saw of her?'

'Aye,' said McBride. 'I spoke to her this morning. She hadn't seen Gail on the train to work, so she was a bit worried. She's managed to swing a half day, see if she could help me find Gail.'

Cullen jotted a few more notes. 'How have you tried contacting your wife?'

McBride frowned. 'I sent her a text.'

'A *text?*' said Cullen. 'You didn't try to phone her?'

McBride looked away. 'Well, aye, I did after. No answer.'

This guy's a tube, thought Cullen. 'Did you go out to look for your wife?'

'Well, I had a wee look out on the street,' said McBride, 'but I didn't want to venture too far in case she came back.'

Cullen pinched the bridge of his nose. 'So you haven't bothered to look for her?'

A tear appeared on McBride's cheek. 'Things haven't been great between us. She... She might have left me.'

'Do you have an address for Ms Saunders?'

47

Sian Saunders lived in part of an ex-council block just off the top road in Prestonpans, a short walk to the railway station, two stops down the line from Musselburgh. Cullen parked in the station car park and walked over. He rang the buzzer and waited.

'Hello?' The voice through the intercom system was heavily distorted.

'Ms Saunders? It's DC Cullen of Lothian & Borders police. Can you let me in?'

The door clunked open. The dark hallway was painted red on the lower half, then cream above — Cullen could never understand why they did that. He went upstairs, passing a large window, and was astonished by the change. There were plants on the balcony and the walls were painted a fresh cream shade. Cullen figured the downstairs flats were probably still council-owned, but the upstairs were now private.

Sian Saunders was standing in the doorway, tall and thin with bright ginger hair tied back in a long ponytail, an intense look in her eyes. 'Come in. I've just got back.' She turned around and went into the flat.

The inside was roasting — it felt like the heating was on full blast, despite it being the middle of summer.

'I'm through here,' said Sian.

Cullen followed the voice through to the kitchen.

She was distractedly mashing a teabag against the side of the cup. There was a half-empty bottle of red wine on the counter, beside a takeaway pizza box. 'I'm just back from work. Simon told me Gail's disappeared, so I've taken a half day. I was just going to head over to their house after I've had a cup of tea. Can I get you anything?'

'Tea,' said Cullen. 'Just milk, thanks.'

Sian made him a cup of tea, tipping in milk from a carton sitting on the counter. She put their cups on a tray and led the way through to the living room. She sat in the armchair, folding her legs up under her, Cullen sitting on the settee opposite. There was a good view out of the window, across the railway line looking up to Tranent perched on the hill the other side of the dual carriageway.

Cullen took out his notebook. 'Can you tell me about your movements last night? You and Mrs McBride.'

'We were at a bar in town,' said Sian.

'Which bar was this?'

'The one on the corner of George Street, at the St Andrews Square end,' said Sian. 'Grape, I think it's called.'

'Is this a regular meeting on a Sunday?' said Cullen.

'No,' said Sian. 'I was away at the weekend, so we didn't go out on Friday. We were both in work yesterday, so we went out last night instead.'

'And you left the bar together?'

'Aye, we got the last train home. We'd only meant to have a couple of glasses, but ended up getting sloshed.'

'What time was the last train?'

'Just after eleven,' said Sian. 'Five past, I think.'

'So the last time you saw Mrs McBride was when she got off the train?'

Sian blew on her tea. 'I watched her walk up the path to the road, but aye.'

'Did you see anyone suspicious get off the train?' said Cullen. 'Anyone lurking at the station?'

'No,' said Sian, quickly. 'I wasn't looking, mind.'

Cullen took a mouthful of tea, far too weak for him. 'Did Simon McBride call you this morning?'

'Aye, back of eight.' She sat back and folded her arms. 'I was just getting to work. He said she'd not come home. He didn't seem too bothered. Things haven't been great between them.'

From the way Simon McBride seemed earlier, Cullen could understand why. 'How do you mean, not great?'

'Well, she was pretty fed up with him,' said Sian.

'Had she talked about leaving him?'

'A couple of times,' said Sian. 'She was talking about it last night.'

'Do you have any reason to suspect her husband of foul play?'

'No.' Sian shook her head. 'Simon's not the sharpest card in the deck.'

'How do you mean?'

'Well, he's good at his job,' said Sian. 'He sells pensions, but all he's into is football and rugby. He's not got a bad bone in his body, really. I know him fairly well, he'd never harm her.'

'I see,' said Cullen. 'Do you think he had any suspicions Gail was thinking of leaving him?'

'I doubt it,' said Sian. 'They barely talked.'

'How do you think he would react if she did?'

'Gail's his life,' said Sian. 'He'd just fall to pieces. He'd struggle to cope. She practically babies him, does all the cooking, washing and cleaning and that. He loves her to bits, but she's... Well.'

Cullen handed her his card. 'I'll be in touch.'

48

Cullen leaned against the side of his car and called Bain.
'Hello there, Sundance,' said Bain. 'How's sunny Musselburgh?'

'I'm in Prestonpans now,' said Cullen.

'Okay, how's sunny Prestonpans then?'

'Yeah, great,' said Cullen. 'I'm pretty much done here. I've just been speaking to the friend she was out with.'

'Oh aye?'

'Gail McBride was out in Edinburgh with a friend last night,' said Cullen. 'The friend says she saw her off the North Berwick train at Musselburgh. She's gone missing in the three hundred metres between the train station and her house. Her husband went to bed after the football last night. She didn't come back.'

'I see.' Bain sounded disinterested. 'And you believe him?'

'I've no reason not to.'

'And this pal said she saw her off the train and that's it?' said Bain.

'That's what she just told me,' said Cullen. 'I'll maybe re-interview her later.'

'Take it you've confirmed all this, aye?'

'With the friend anyway,' said Cullen. 'We could probably do with checking a few other sources.'

'What do you think happened?'

Cullen stood up and started pacing along the pavement. 'I think there are probably three possibilities. One, she was attacked on the way home from the station. Two, she's run away. Three, the husband's killed her when she got home.'

'Go on.'

'The friend confirmed there have been problems between Gail and the husband,' said Cullen. 'Gail's talked about leaving him. I'd say it's most likely she's run away. The husband seems like he's a bit dim and I'm not sure it's an act. I'm struggling to imagine him planning to kill her, or anything like that. Could have been a spur of the moment thing, I suppose, but it's not like there's a dismembered body in a ditch. If he did kill her, he's done a good job of covering up and he just doesn't seem capable.'

'Right. So basically, any one of your three could have happened?'

Cullen took a deep breath and thought it through. 'I suppose so.'

Bain paused. 'Do you think it could be linked to Caroline and Debi?'

Cullen thought about it for a few seconds. 'Doesn't look likely, but there are a few things I'd like to look into.'

'And if you were a gambling man?'

'I am one,' said Cullen. 'If I had to put money on it, I would say she left him. It's the likeliest scenario, I'd say.'

Bain sighed with relief. 'Jim's shitting himself we've got another one. Good work. I'll get some officers on to it. I've palmed this off onto Wilko. I've got my plate full with this case as it is and he's doing bugger all other than get in my way.'

'What about me?'

'Wilko's on his way out,' said Bain. 'Get back over to Musselburgh. He'll meet you at this boy's house.'

'So I'm one of his officers then?' said Cullen.

'Try not to use your initiative till Wilko gets there, Sundance.'

49

Cullen spotted Wilkinson sitting in a panda car around the corner from Musselburgh train station. He parked along the road and went over. The window in the car was wound down, Wilkinson smoking an untipped cigarette, TalkSport blaring out, a Scouser railing against Liverpool's pre-season form. Cullen slid into the passenger seat.

Wilkinson ignored him, taking a long drag on his cigarette then laughing at what the caller was saying. 'There's no way they'll finish top four this season. They've had their time.'

'Thought you'd be more a Rugby League guy,' said Cullen.

'What, you mean cos I'm a fat bastard?' Wilkinson laughed. 'Can't stand either flavour of bloody rugby. I'm Leeds United through and through.'

'Bain asked me to report to you,' said Cullen.

Wilkinson laughed. 'So he did.' He took another drag, taking his time exhaling. He held up the *Evening News*, the still of Martin Webb at the supermarket beneath the headline *Caroline Killer: Photo*. 'She's still the main story. Poor Debi's not getting the coverage she deserves. And Caroline's a single mother, too.' He tutted.

'What do you want me to do?' said Cullen.

'Need another body to go door-to-door,' said Wilkinson. 'And Bain sent you.'

As Cullen was formulating an objection, Wilkinson reached over and picked up an Airwave, the latest generation police radio, and called for PC Campbell. 'I want you to pair up with Vicky Campbell. She's a good cop and no mistaking.'

Cullen wasn't too chuffed by being paired up with her.

Wilkinson gestured round the crescent. 'You pair are to do the houses leading away from the McBrides' on that side.'

'Anything specific you want to know?' said Cullen.

'Just use the initiative DI Bain praises you for.' Wilkinson turned up the radio. 'Now, out you get.'

Cullen got out and walked back to his car. He reached in and retrieved the roll he'd bought from a petrol station on the way back over. He leaned against the side of his car and ate it as he waited, pissed off at Bain, Wilkinson and pretty much everyone else.

∿

IT WAS JUST after one and they'd managed to visit eighteen houses. Campbell agreed she would make some return visits that evening, then went back inside Simon McBride's house to check on any updates at that end.

Cullen got in the squad car and informed Wilkinson of the lack of progress they'd made, having no idea what he had been doing all that time, other than sitting on his arse.

'So that's it?' said Wilkinson. 'Nothing at all?'

'Afraid so,' said Cullen. 'I'm going to head back to the station. I don't think you need a DC for this, not when I've got other actions Bain wants me to close down.'

Wilkinson grunted. 'Go and see McAllister before you leave.'

Cullen deflated. 'McAllister?'

'Aye, lad,' said Wilkinson. 'I've had him looking for anyone who was on the last train yesterday. He's on the platform, bottom of the hill.'

'What's he doing down there?'

'Speaking to people getting off the train, what do you think?'

'And what do you want me to do?'

Wilkinson looked at him for a few seconds. 'See what he's found, then tell me.'

'Can't you do that?'

'No,' said Wilkinson. 'I'm supervising everything.'

Cullen reluctantly headed off for the train station, checking out the new Queen Margaret's University campus sprawled on the other side of the tracks. Looking down he saw a train pulling off, a group of about twenty people starting the march up the hill. He moved out of the way at the top to let them past.

As he waited he spotted McAllister with a young PC, standing in the middle of the path up from the platform. They were talking to a woman who looked mid-thirties, but dressed mid-twenties. Cullen started down towards them, the woman walking off as he approached.

'DC Cullen,' said McAllister. 'Heard you'd be sniffing around.'

McAllister's protégé moved away towards the platform.

'Wilkinson's asked me to see how you were doing,' said Cullen.

McAllister got into Cullen's face. 'Snooping around, are you? Going to grass me up to Bain again?'

Cullen stepped back and sighed. 'Not unless you've been messing about again. I'm just doing DI Wilkinson's job for him.'

McAllister actually laughed. 'He's like that.'

'Well? Have you made any progress?'

McAllister shrugged. 'Spoken to five people now who were on the last train. That lassie I was just speaking to was one of them. None of them saw anything. A couple actually recognised this Gail lassie, mainly by her face, not her name. They didn't see her on the train last night.'

Cullen frowned. 'Really? So it doesn't look like she was on it?'

McAllister raised his hands in the air. 'Christ knows. I'm wasting my bloody time here. Most of them would've been pissed, wouldn't remember if their husband or wife was sitting next to them on that train. I mean this is bloody Musselburgh, hardly the smartest bit of the Lothians.' He yawned. 'I doubt I'll get anything until later on when the commuter crowd start heading home.'

'I guess you're right,' said Cullen. 'Have you told Wilkinson?'

'What's the point? He's just listening to the radio.'

Cullen grudgingly smiled at the PC before climbing back up the hill and pacing over to the patrol car. Wilkinson snapped the radio off as Cullen got back in. The car stank of stale cigarette smoke, so Cullen wound down the window on his side. A gentle breeze started to flow between the two windows.

'Did you get anything, Curran?'

Cullen took a deep breath and decided not to correct him. 'McAllister's found a few people who were on the train. None of them saw Gail.'

'Did any of them know her, like?'

'Yeah,' said Cullen. 'Two of them knew her by sight. They didn't see her.'

'That's interesting,' said Wilkinson.

'This doesn't feel right.'

'How come?'

'Well, Sian Saunders told me Gail got off the train at Mussel-burgh,' said Cullen. 'Now, McAllister has found five people who were on that train. Two of them knew her, but nobody saw her getting off.'

'Were they in different carriages?'

'Don't know,' said Cullen. 'Wouldn't have thought it's an issue, though, there's only one way out, up that hill. It's not exactly a big station.'

Wilkinson looked out of the window, distracted. 'Aye, it's a bit funny, Curran.'

Cullen tried to avoid getting irritated by Wilkinson's continual mispronunciation of his name. 'I don't imagine there'd be a lot of folk on the train at that time of night, maybe twenty at most getting off at Musselburgh.'

Wilkinson looked around. 'So what?'

'I think there's something going on here,' said Cullen. 'We've got people going door-to-door and nobody's seen or heard anything.'

'There's still a fair amount left to check, though,' said Wilkinson.

'Do you think she was on the train or not?'

'I've no idea. Hopefully McAllister will unearth something.'

'I think you need to look into this a bit harder,' said Cullen.

Wilkinson glared at him. 'Yeah, well, I'm the Senior Investigating Officer here and I'm not far off handing this back to uniform. Wild goose chase.' He checked his watch. 'I've got a date

with a pint of lager in a couple of hours, so can you piss off back to
Bain?'

50

Cullen was on the phone to Colin Green, friend thirty-four of Caroline's. Green knew her from school in Carnoustie and had already been called by Angela on Saturday afternoon.

Contacting people was much slower the second time around — they were either less available than on a Saturday and Sunday, or were now irritated at being called again. They had selected a subset of people, but it appeared to contain all of the harder-to-contact friends.

Green gave Cullen a rambling story about how he had returned to live in the area and still kept in touch with people from school. In Cullen's mind, he should have been a good source to validate the death threats.

'So you're saying you never heard of any threats made by Rob Thomson against Caroline Adamson?' said Cullen.

'I am. More than happy to put it in a statement.'

Cullen was tempted, becoming irritated by the singular lack of confirmation. He thanked him and hung up.

This whole death threat story wasn't stacking up. Bain had Rob Thomson in his sights with the main piece of evidence being the death threats. Everything else wasn't even circumstantial — sightings of a man who loosely fitted his description.

He looked over at Angela, just wrapping up a call. His phone rang.

'DC Cullen? This is Margaret Armstrong. We spoke the other day about Caroline.'

Cullen sat forward on his seat — he couldn't work out why she'd called, other than Dave Watson or Charlie Kidd blundering in there to have a look at Caroline's work PC. 'Is this about my Technical Support colleagues?'

'I'm sorry?' said Armstrong.

'They were going to have a look at Caroline's work computer. There may be some important information left on it.'

'No, no, they left an hour ago with Caroline's machine.' Armstrong paused for a moment. 'The reason I'm calling is... Well, I had a visit from your Asian colleague yesterday at home. I can't recall her name, but I found your business card, and well... I'm sorry, I'm not handling this as well as I should.'

'It's okay,' said Cullen, 'take your time.'

'Thank you,' said Armstrong. 'Your colleague was asking me some questions about Alistair Cruikshank.'

Cullen recalled the name from the previous afternoon — McNeill and Chantal Jain had uncovered someone from Caroline's past, the man who'd been objectionable about her divorce on religious grounds and who Caroline got sacked. 'Have you remembered something?'

'No, Mr Cullen, he was here at the office. He's just left.'

51

McNeill came back into Armstrong's office with a cup of water and handed it to her. 'There you go.'

Armstrong took the most delicate of sips. 'Thank you.' She was sitting at her desk when Cullen and McNeill arrived, face flushed and struggling to speak.

'Can you tell us what happened with Mr Cruikshank?' said McNeill.

Armstrong's hands were fiddling with the St Christopher at her neck. 'I'm sorry, I just can't help but think he killed Caroline and Debi and now he's been here.'

Cullen nodded. 'We don't know whether Mr Cruikshank was even in the city at the time of either attack. Can you tell us about your encounter from the start?'

'Okay.' Armstrong took a deep breath. 'I was just going through some paperwork when there was a knock on my door.'

She pushed the glass of water away. 'It was Alistair. He stood there smiling, as if to say 'Look who it is'. I nearly fainted, I can tell you.' She gulped down some more water, a trickle slipping down the side of the cup. 'I just thought he was here for me. We had to get rid of him after all that business with Caroline, I found it very hard. I struggled with the guilt. Just seeing him there like that absolutely terrified me.'

'Did Mr Cruikshank say anything to you?' said Cullen.

'Why yes.' Armstrong regained some of her composure. 'He was most effusive. He was talking about atoning for his sins, that he'd resolved what had happened between him and Caroline and a few other things.'

'Did he say what he was doing in Edinburgh?' said Cullen.

'Yes, he's here for some sort of divinity conference,' said Armstrong. 'You know he's studying to be a minister in whatever church he's in. He studied divinity here before at the university. I think he said the conference was on 'redemption'.'

Cullen shared a look with McNeill — she raised an eyebrow. 'Do you have any idea where he might be staying?'

'He mentioned something about staying at the Minto Hotel,' said Armstrong.

It was Cullen's turn to raise an eyebrow — it was right next door to the Jackson Hotel, where Caroline was found.

MCNEILL PARKED OUTSIDE THE MINTO. What would once have been the front garden of a Victorian house was now the car park of a heavily extended hotel. Cullen noticed the police markings were still up at the Jackson Hotel, a few doors down.

'You lead,' said Cullen, as they got out of the car.

'You're such a gentleman, Scott.'

'I just can't figure out who would choose to stay here,' said Cullen.

'Parents of students at the university halls round the corner?' said McNeill.

'Maybe,' said Cullen. 'It's nowhere near any big businesses, though, and it's not particularly cheap.'

'It'll be rammed during the festival.'

'Yeah, but that's only one month of the year.'

McNeill shrugged and entered the hotel. She showed the receptionist her warrant card. 'Do you have an Alistair Cruikshank staying here?'

The receptionist nodded. 'We do indeed.'

'Do you know if he's in?' said McNeill.

'I don't believe so. He's been out all day.' The receptionist gestured behind her at the rack of keys. 'He left his key this morning.'

'Okay,' said McNeill. 'Would we be able to have a look around his room?'

The receptionist frowned. 'I'm not sure that's allowed.'

McNeill glared at her. 'This is related to what happened just down the road.' She didn't have to mention the name of the Jackson.

'I see.' The receptionist bit her lip. 'Okay, but please don't touch anything. This is just a look around.'

McNeill held her hands up. 'That's perfect.'

The receptionist led them to a room at the back of the hotel on the ground floor. Cullen's heart was in his mouth — he had a sudden vision of Gail McBride naked and dead in the room, that he and Wilkinson were wrong, that Cruikshank was the killer and had struck again.

The receptionist opened the door.

The room was empty.

Cullen felt a flutter of relief. There was a suitcase on the stand at the end of the bed, a tweed jacket on the back of a chair and a copy of the Bible sitting on the desk. The room looked out onto what was left of the garden at the rear.

'Mind if I look in the bathroom?' said Cullen.

The receptionist's eyes kept flicking back to the door. 'Just a check, okay?'

'Sure thing,' said Cullen.

He wandered into the small enclave in the rear of the room, one of the smallest bathrooms he'd ever seen. A green leather wash bag was on the sink, a toothbrush placed behind the taps. He touched the bristles, bone dry. He went back through.

'Have you pair seen enough?' said the receptionist.

McNeill left her card, instructing her to call if Cruikshank returned.

52

'Can't you just stick to one task, Cullen?' said Bain.

Cullen and McNeill were back in the Incident Room, standing by the whiteboard with Bain.

'If you actually gave me a task you'd let me finish,' said Cullen.

'You what?' said Bain.

Cullen tried and failed to bite his tongue. 'On this case, you've given me task after task after task, each time throwing me on to something new before I'm even half way through.'

Bain glared at him. 'If you'd just found Caroline Adamson when I assigned you that case.'

'She was already dead a day and a half when you assigned me it,' said Cullen.

Bain didn't have a response. He glared at McNeill instead. 'So you're telling me we now have two valid suspects in this case.'

'I'd say your other suspect is a bit flimsy,' said Cullen.

Bain pointed at him. 'Shut your mouth, Sundance, all right? What's got into you?'

Cullen said nothing, just looked away. Most of the officers in the room were staring at them and listening in. He was fed up with Bain. He was busting a gut on this case and getting no thanks for it.

'I'd say Alistair Cruikshank's a valid suspect,' said McNeill. 'He definitely has a motive, I suppose, and Margaret Armstrong was seriously shaken up by his visit.'

Bain rubbed his temple. 'I want you and Chantal to get to the bottom of this, okay? Bring this guy in and we'll batter the truth out of him.'

'Do you want me to help?' said Cullen.

'No, Sundance, I don't,' said Bain. 'I want you to finish something for once. Get back to those phone calls. As far as I'm aware, nobody's corroborated these death threats yet.'

When Cullen returned to their desks, he found Angela in an even worse mood than Bain. She was taking a break from the calls, trying to catch up on the documentation.

'There must be something better than this,' said Angela.

'Tell me about it,' said Cullen.

'We've been at this solid since yesterday and we've got nothing.'

'Well,' said Cullen, 'we've got the rumour about the death threats.'

'But we still haven't managed to back that up.'

'Don't I know it,' said Cullen.

'Heard you got another doing off Bain.'

Cullen shrugged. 'I reckon I gave as good as I got this time.'

'Not what I heard,' said Angela.

'Who from?'

'Miller.'

Cullen laughed. 'He wasn't even there. Little bastard.'

'What was it about?'

'He was having a go at me for not sticking to tasks.' Cullen sighed. 'I pointed out I wasn't the one who was preventing me from sticking to them.'

'Brave boy,' said Angela.

'No doubt I'll be cleaning the whiteboard next.' Cullen checked his watch. He was due to meet Alison in twenty minutes. 'Sod it. I can't see us getting any more joy today with these calls. See you tomorrow.'

53

Cullen parked around the corner on Thistle Street, managing to sneak into a space just vacated and he fed the meter for an hour. Having the car might be a good move — it meant he could only have the one, though his complete lack of willpower probably meant a late bus home and a parking fine.

It wasn't until Alison waved at him that Cullen recognised her.

On Friday, her hair was pulled back with a hair-clip, but tonight it hung loose. She was wearing natural looking make-up today and a work suit. She looked a lot older than he remembered.

Cullen sat opposite her. There was a seat next to her, but he didn't want to send out the wrong message. 'Sorry I'm late.'

'Don't worry about it.' She took a sip of wine. 'Thanks for turning up.'

Cullen decided maybe she had a nice smile. 'I always had every intention of doing so.'

Alison put both hands around her glass of wine. 'Do you want to get yourself a drink?'

'Can I get you anything? Another glass of wine?'

'Yeah, the Pinot Grigio is nice.'

'Large or small?'

She giggled. 'Oh, large.'

Cullen went up to the bar and stood in the queue. While the

barman poured his pint Cullen had a deep conversation with himself — what the hell was he doing? He needed to grow up. On Saturday morning he'd worked the old Cullen magic yet again with her.

Idiot.

He only needed a slight opening and he was off, charming away. In his heart he knew he wanted another steady girlfriend, another Katie, but one who didn't mess him around, that didn't mind about his job and the hours he kept. He knew how thin on the ground they were.

He looked over at Alison as the barman went to the till. He seriously doubted anything could come of this — she shared a flat with his ex, for a start. They'd had a one-night stand, just a bit of fun — there was no commitment to anything else. Everybody knew the rules. He doubted if there was anything they had in common, apart from music, maybe. She was at a techno club on Friday as part of the wider group and they had some techno and house playing at the party afterwards.

He carried the drinks to the table. 'So.'

'So.'

They sat in an uncomfortable silence for a moment.

Cullen took a drink of lager. 'How's Katie?'

CULLEN WAS STARTING to think about making his excuses when his mobile rang.

'Sorry,' said Cullen. 'It's probably work. Do you mind?'

Alison looked irritated. 'No.'

Cullen looked at the display — McNeill. He reddened slightly. He swiped his finger across the screen and answered, playing innocent. 'Scott Cullen.'

'Scott, it's DS McNeill.'

He turned away from Alison. Why was McNeill being formal with him?

'Have you left for the evening?' said McNeill.

'Yeah,' said Cullen. 'I'm just having a drink with a friend.'

'I see.' McNeill paused for a moment. 'Listen, Bain's told me to get your arse over to Edinburgh Park. His words.'

'What's the hurry?' said Cullen. 'I'm off duty.'

'He said you'd say that,' said McNeill. 'He said you're to get back on duty.'

'What's up?'

'Gail McBride's body has been found.'

54

Edinburgh Park train station was across from Hermiston Gait, recently opened to service Edinburgh Park, a ramshackle grouping of corporate offices a few hundred metres away — banks, insurance firms and technology companies. All three Edinburgh banks had offices here — nearest to the train station sat Alba Bank's Edinburgh Park House, the most recently built and Gail McBride's workplace.

Cullen followed the road round, passing underneath the flyover for the tram system, his warrant card getting him through security barriers designed to prevent access to the bypass. He passed a tunnel on his left that led under the dual carriageway, a suspended platform above a heavy-flowing river. The SOCO lights were in another cordoned-off tunnel filled with construction equipment, a JCB and stacks of concrete blocks. On the other side of the road was a set of Portacabins, site offices for the tram works.

Cullen parked and hurried over, looking for McNeill or Bain. He quickly found Bain flapping around, barking orders to whoever would listen.

Bain shouted at some uniformed officers. 'I want someone round all of those offices in Edinburgh Park, now. I want CCTV from all the shops in Hermiston Gate and I want some bastard making a nuisance of themselves in the tram office. Somebody must've seen something and I want them here now.' His eyes were struggling to focus as they settled on Cullen. He looked deranged. 'Thank Christ you're here, Sundance.'

'DS McNeill told me you were looking for me,' said Cullen. 'What happened?'

'That idiot Wilko's buggered off somewhere and turned his mobile off,' said Bain. 'I've been landed with this case on top of nailing Rob Thomson for the other murders.'

'What can I do?' said Cullen.

'McNeill's taking a statement from the cyclist who found the body,' said Bain. 'You'd best listen in. Turns out this bloody tunnel is a cycle shortcut to that RBS monstrosity over there.' He gestured behind him with his thumb — RBS Gogarburn lit up the surrounding trees, a mile or so distant. 'Goes through a field. They're supposed to use the proper path through another tunnel just up the way, mind. Anyway, this poor sod found the body just before six on his way to the train.'

Bain marched away, shouting for Jimmy Deeley.

Cullen headed into the tunnel, surrounded by stacks of concrete blocks on pavements on either side of a giant puddle in the middle. Bodies in protection suits milled around. He stepped in the puddle and got mud right up his ankle. His leather brogues could barely cope with a splash let alone full immersion.

'Keep your stomach contents to yourself today,' said a passing SOCO, voice suspiciously similar to Anderson.

'Check for laptops,' said Cullen.

Anderson pulled his mask down and rubbed his goatee. 'Aye, well.'

'Seen McNeill?' said Cullen.

Anderson pointed down the tunnel. 'Through there.'

Cullen walked on. At the end was a field of wheat, a SOCO tent poking up above the crop. He could see a track through the field, grooves worn into the soil by bike tyres, running off towards a copse of trees in the distance. There was a turkey farm at the far end and he could certainly smell it.

McNeill was near the tunnel entrance speaking to a heavyset man dressed in black cycling gear underneath a fluorescent yellow and orange bib. An expensive-looking mountain bike lay on its side, a green rucksack beside it on the ground. Angela was helping with the note taking.

McNeill nodded at Cullen as he approached, before looking back at her notebook. 'I'll just read your statement back to you. You were cycling away from work heading to the station, aiming for the quarter to six train. You were running late, so you cut across the fields rather than going round the cycle path.'

She paused, waited for him to nod. 'You were unable to stick to the usual path due to someone overtaking you and forcing you to diverge across the field. You corrected your course back towards the tunnel and you came across the body.'

The cyclist was visibly shaking. 'Yes.'

'Okay, you can get away on home,' said McNeill, 'but we'll need to get in touch again. Do you need a lift?'

'I should be fine.' He picked his bike up and slowly cycled off through the tunnel.

'Is he going to be okay?' said Cullen.

McNeill looked sideways at him. 'He's just discovered a dead body.'

'Shouldn't he be getting taken home?' said Cullen.

'That was the fifth time I asked,' said McNeill, 'but he refused each time.'

'Is he under any suspicion?' said Cullen.

'Doubt it,' said McNeill. 'He's got an alibi. He was away for the weekend with his girlfriend, would still have been driving back when Gail McBride was getting the train to Musselburgh.' She nodded at Angela, who smiled at Cullen. 'Caldwell will check out his alibi but I don't think he's in the frame.'

'What else do we have?' said Cullen. 'Bain wasn't making much sense.'

'Tell me about it.' McNeill put her notebook away. 'He's been nipping my head since we got the call out here.'

'It's definitely Gail?' said Cullen.

McNeill grimaced. 'We've got her husband in a panda car over there. Uniform brought him over. He confirmed it's definitely her.'

'Rough,' said Cullen. 'That's not exactly standard procedure, is it?'

McNeill raised her eyebrows. 'Bain's not exactly going by the rulebook on this, is he?'

'What's Deeley saying about it?' said Cullen. 'Bain was screaming for him.'

'He's not saying much,' said McNeill. 'I don't know what the story is. Now I think about it, Bain went off the deep end after he spoke to Deeley — he was fine before that. Well, fine for him.'

'So what do you know then?' said Cullen.

McNeill bit her lip. 'It's pretty grim. Throat cut.'

'Jesus.' Cullen's stomach felt queasy. 'How did she end up here? She got off the train in Musselburgh last night and now she turns up, what, twenty miles away?'

McNeill shrugged her shoulders. 'That's our job to find out, I suppose.'

Cullen looked up at the dual carriageway above the tunnel he'd walked through, rush-hour traffic streaming past. He pointed up. 'Someone must have seen something, surely?'

'This is Edinburgh,' said McNeill. 'Nobody sees anything.'

Bain appeared from the tunnel and headed straight for them. 'Got a rough time of death. Between nine o'clock and midnight last night.'

Cullen almost laughed. 'Nobody noticed a dead body until six pm?'

Bain stroked his moustache. 'To be fair, the body is in a ditch in a crop of wheat. Irvine's spoken to the farmer — they were supposed to be harvesting it in a couple of weeks.'

'What about drivers on the bypass?' said Cullen.

'Nobody sees anything, do they?' Bain sighed. 'To be fair, you're more interested in the road in front of you and what that idiot in the Corsa's up to or why that BMW's up your arse.' He took a breather. 'I'll get a press release out. Another one. Jesus Christ.'

Cullen pointed up at the road. 'The part of the field she was in is shielded by the trees. You wouldn't see anything.'

'What I really want to know is how she ended up here and not in Musselburgh,' said Bain.

'That's what I've been asking,' said Cullen.

'Well, I'm asking you to get the answer, Sundance.' Bain glared at Cullen, then McNeill. 'Butch, you and the Sundance Kid are going to find out what the hell's happened here.'

55

Thirty minutes later, Cullen pulled into Prestonpans and parked outside Sian Saunders' flat.

'I can't get my head around this,' said McNeill.

Cullen took a deep breath — the lager burned in his gut and he could have done with a bottle of water. 'Sian Saunders was the last person to see Gail alive. According to her, Gail got off the train at the back of eleven in Musselburgh. It's a two minute walk to her house.'

'Her body turns up in a ditch just by her work.' McNeill took her notebook out and started fiddling with her pen, a silver ballpoint. 'And this Sian Saunders told you they'd been at the pub in town and got the last train home.'

'Aye,' said Cullen. 'No corroboration I'm aware of.'

'What about what Wilko's been up to in Musselburgh?' said McNeill.

Cullen smiled. 'What, smoking and listening to TalkSport?'

McNeill laughed. 'Apart from that.'

'Well, I spoke to Willie McAllister at the train station this afternoon,' said Cullen. 'He'd been questioning people getting off, asking if anyone was on the last train. He'd found a couple who knew her by sight. They hadn't noticed her on the train.'

'That's odd.'

Cullen looked up Sian's flat and saw the lights were on. 'Come on, then.'

The front door to the building was open, so they went up and knocked on the flat door. After a while, Sian Saunders answered it. She looked at Cullen, eyes wide. 'Has she turned up?'

'I'm afraid she has,' said Cullen. 'Her body was found this evening.'

Sian looked at McNeill, then back at Cullen, tears welling in her eyes. 'Her body? Oh, Jesus.' She ran away from them into the flat, her hands covering her face.

McNeill looked at him. 'I don't think we're going to get much out of her.'

'Me neither,' said Cullen.

'You go have a mooch around,' said McNeill, 'I'll see if she's okay.'

Inside, it was as warm as it had been in the afternoon, absolutely baking. McNeill followed Sian through to the living room, while Cullen searched around the flat. He didn't find anything suspicious or out of place. He did find Sian's train season ticket, tucked in a white ScotRail wallet, meaning there would be no trace of her travel the previous night.

In the kitchen, Sian stood in front of the sink facing the window, tears running down her face, McNeill stroking her arm gently. Sian sniffed again.

'Would you like something to drink?' said Cullen.

Sian turned and looked at him. Her lip trembled. She nodded towards a bottle of red wine on the counter, a cork jammed in the top. Cullen reached into the cupboard and took out a wine glass. He opened the bottle, a reasonable Italian red. He recognised it from earlier so he sniffed it — it still seemed okay. He poured a generous measure, almost draining the bottle.

Sian downed half the glass. 'Thanks.'

'Ms Saunders, you said you saw Gail McBride leave the train last night?' said McNeill.

Sian nodded her head, looking at Cullen. 'I went through all this earlier with him.'

'What time was this?' said McNeill.

'Would be about quarter past eleven,' said Sian.

'And what time did you get off the train at Prestonpans?' said McNeill.

'I wasn't keeping an eye on my watch.' Sian folded her arms. 'Twenty past probably.'

'Gail's body was found at Edinburgh Park,' said Cullen. 'We think it's a bit odd she's been transported twenty miles, close to where she works.'

Sian shrugged. 'So?'

'Can you outline your movements since I last saw you?' said Cullen.

Sian frowned. 'Is that necessary?'

'Yes,' said Cullen.

Sian shook her head slowly. 'I've been out looking for Gail. I went to Musselburgh and spoke to Simon. Then I just wandered the streets round the station, trying to see if I could spot anything.'

She broke down in tears, her entire body racked with sobs.

BACK IN THE car outside the flat, Cullen held up his phone. 'Do you want me to call Bain or do you want that pleasure?'

'Be my guest,' said McNeill, which Cullen took to be an instruction not to involve her.

He called Bain.

'It's Cullen.'

'I know who it is, Sundance, these mobile things tell you.' Bain snorted down the line. 'You got anywhere yet?'

'No,' said Cullen. 'We're not going to get much out of her tonight. Tomorrow maybe.'

'Christ's sake,' said Bain. 'This is a murder.'

'She's just lost her best friend,' said Cullen.

'I know that,' said Bain. 'Doesn't she want to find who did it?'

'I suppose so,' said Cullen, 'but she's a bit upset right now.'

'McNeill's with you, isn't she?' said Bain.

'Aye.'

'Drop her off at the station,' said Bain. 'I want you to work your magic up at the CCTV suite on the Royal Mile. Boy named Naismith is already allocated.'

'What for?'

'Someone's driven her from Musselburgh to Edinburgh Park,' said Bain, 'I want you to find out who.'

56

The CCTV Monitoring Centre on the Royal Mile was a dark room in a dimly lit basement beneath the City Chambers. It housed feeds from the city's entire CCTV network, from the Musselburgh outskirts in the east to Ratho and the Newbridge road network in the west and everything inside the City Bypass.

Cullen found Giles Naismith, just finishing off some work on what looked like footage of the Shore in Leith. He didn't even stand up, just huffily acknowledged Cullen's presence.

'Can you please stop doing that?' said Cullen. 'DI Bain has sent me.'

Naismith tugged his glasses off and rubbed at his eyes. 'What is it?'

Cullen explained what he needed.

Naismith burst into activity, giving no commentary or explanation as to what he was up to.

After twenty minutes, Cullen checked his watch again, wondering how long this was going to drag on. 'How are we getting on?'

'Getting there. Won't be long.'

'Any chance you could hurry this up?'

Naismith swivelled round. 'You've got to remember your request is somewhat complex.'

That was the third or fourth time he'd used that sort of line.

'I thought the AI and the bypass would be automatic?' said Cullen.

Naismith sighed. 'They are, but that's only half of the job. You want to know which cars drove from Musselburgh to Edinburgh Park. There's an ANPR camera at either end of the bypass, but that's a massive volume of traffic plus there's a few other routes I'd need to include. It's going to take a lot of work.'

Cullen was introduced to the Automatic Number Plate Recognition system on a training course the previous summer. It recorded every single vehicle passing through the sensors at either end of the City Bypass, plus all exits between. 'I understand it's complex. All I want to know is how long it's going to take.'

'I can leave it running overnight.'

Cullen pinched his nose. 'All night?'

'I've got to get home at some point,' said Naismith.

'So, what, seven am, say?' said Cullen.

Naismith turned to glare at him. 'This is highly irregular.'

'I know it is, but we've got three murder cases here, none of which are going to go away. I just need you to give me some help then I'll not bother you again, okay?'

Naismith looked around the room. 'Okay, just this once, I'll try and come in early to get your results.'

57

'Doesn't he know this is a murder case?' said Bain.

'It's half nine now and he's coming back in at seven,' said Cullen. 'And he's a civilian, not a police officer. In fact, he's a council employee so we're bloody lucky.'

'You think?' said Bain, practically snarling. 'I could still have his knackers for this shite he's pulling.'

'What do you want me to do now?' said Cullen.

Bain flattened his moustache down. 'You've still not finished checking those death threats, have you?'

'If anyone's still up,' said Cullen.

'Remember that conversation we had earlier. I want you completing tasks.' Bain clapped his hands together. 'Right, I'm off to put the boot into those SOCO bastards downstairs.'

For once, Cullen almost felt sorry for Anderson. He headed back to his desk. Angela was still around, chatting to Miller.

Cullen felt guilty about leaving earlier. 'You're still here?'

'Aye,' said Angela. 'We're still nowhere near finished.'

Cullen frowned. 'Who's we?'

'Keith's been helping,' said Angela.

Miller grinned. 'Cushy little racket you've got here, Sundance.'

'Don't call me that,' said Cullen.

Miller grinned. 'How come the gaffer gets away with it?'

Cullen snapped. 'Because he's the gaffer.' He looked at Angela. 'How are we getting on?'

'Still no confirmations,' said Angela. 'Must be about halfway through, but I keep getting shoved on to other things. Had to check the alibi from that cyclist.'

'Better get used to it,' said Cullen. 'CID is like that. Isn't that right, Keith?'

Miller laughed. 'Only if you get landed with working for Bain.'

Cullen sighed as he sat down. 'Give me some numbers to call.'

∽

AT THE BACK of eleven people were starting to move from being irritated into threatening complaints territory.

'That's it, I'm not making any more calls,' said Cullen. 'You two either switch to typing up notes, or clear off home.'

Miller got up, grinning. 'I'm off.' He marched towards the stairwell.

Cullen pointed after Miller. 'How's he doing?'

'Okay, actually,' said Angela. 'Better than McAllister.'

'Who isn't?' Cullen stood. 'I need you bright and breezy tomorrow, so go and get some shut-eye.'

Angela grinned. 'Shut-eye?'

Cullen tried to laugh it off. 'Okay, sleep.'

'Just finishing these notes,' said Angela. 'I'll be off in about five minutes.'

Cullen looked at her for a moment, admiring her dedication and still feeling guilty for heading off earlier. He sauntered over to the stairwell. He bumped into McNeill at the door, her face distorted by a scowl. 'What's up with you?'

'Been wasting my time,' said McNeill. 'Interviewing hotel residents in the Novotel just across from Edinburgh Park. Bain has a bee in his bonnet about it. He could have used Miller, doesn't need a DS doing it. Now I've got to type all my notes up. Bloody hell.'

'What's he had you doing?'

'I've interviewed everyone who stayed last night,' said McNeill. 'There weren't many given it was a Sunday. I've got a load of follow-up to do on the people who were there last night then left today. Waste of time. Nobody's seen anything.'

'I'm just heading off,' said Cullen.

McNeill sighed. 'I really should head, too. Do you fancy going for a drink? The Elm will still be serving.'

Cullen's gut was still aching from the pint earlier — he needed his bed, not another drink. 'Another time,' he said, somewhat reluctantly.

'Another time.' She nodded slowly. 'Glass of wine at home on my own, then.'

Cullen didn't know what to say, so said nothing.

Downstairs, he got into his car and fished out his mobile. There were a few personal messages he'd not had time to check. There was one from Tom. *Did you get your hole?* It took him a while to remember about his date with Alison.

No, he hadn't.

He had a couple of emails from Schoolbook. There was a message from a mate from home, Richard McAlpine, who was thinking of moving back up to Edinburgh from London. Cullen suggested he move in when Johnny moved out, but he'd have to speak to Tom about it.

The other was a friend request from Alison. He took a few seconds before accepting it. It loaded up her profile in the app. Her status update read *'Early days with a new man called Scott.'*

He pocketed the phone and drove off.

DAY 6

Tuesday
2nd August

58

Bain stood at the front of the Incident Room addressing the assembled troops, a giant Starbucks beaker of coffee in his hand, dark rings around his eyes.

Cullen sat on the edge of a desk, absolutely shattered. He'd had less than six hours sleep and even then he'd struggled. On top of the case and half a bottle of red wine when he'd got home, the message from Alison had set his mind whirring. He'd fought against his caffeine-fuelled brain all night, trying to figure out how badly he'd led her on. Nothing he'd done could have made her think they were an item. Well, nothing except for shagging her and then meeting her for a drink a couple of days later. If only he had the time to put her straight.

DCI Turnbull wandered in halfway through the briefing and sat off to the side.

Cullen leaned over to Angela. 'What's he doing here?'

'Probably trouble for Bain or Wilko,' said Angela.

Cullen nodded. 'The smart money's got to be on Wilkinson, what with him buggering off early last night.'

'He looks like he's drunk a bottle of whisky.'

'Shame,' said Cullen. 'I was hoping Bain would get a rocket up his arse.'

Bain continued with his briefing, it all washing over Cullen.

'One last thing,' said Bain. 'We have now ascertained Caroline's keys were missing from her person in the hotel and her laptop was stolen from her flat. DC Cullen used that computer on Friday afternoon. We put out a press release yesterday looking for anyone who'd seen anything suspicious in or around Smith's Place on Friday or the early hours of Saturday.' He held up *The Scotsman*, open at a picture of the press conference given by Bain and Turnbull. 'We're currently just dealing with the usual weirdos phoning in, but we're keeping a close eye out for anything useful.'

'We're getting there.' Bain looked over at Turnbull. 'Finally, the chief inspector would like a word.'

Turnbull spoke in his usual smooth tones. 'I want you to know you are all working on the highest priority investigation now ongoing in the Lothian & Borders Police Service. The Chief Constable is closely following the hunt for the killer of both Debi and Caroline. I've been tasked with keeping the entire Senior Control Group informed with your progress.

'I want you all to know the pressure sits squarely with myself and my leadership team. You are an excellent collection of officers and we have implicit faith in the ability of every single one of you.'

He paused and looked around the room. 'We've also been allocated the investigation of the Gail McBride murder. This should take just as high a priority in your minds. In Lothian & Borders we don't have to deal with a large volume of murders, unlike in Strathclyde or the Met for example, but the expertise we do have is squarely in this room.'

He furrowed his brow. 'I know from bitter experience these can be trying and difficult times, but we need to stand firm and stand together. Our priorities must only be these murders and the families who have been torn apart by these deaths. These killers must be brought to justice. I know we can do it.'

Turnbull gave a final smile around the room then left, Bain and Wilkinson following him like a pair of dogs at their master's heels.

Cullen found McNeill standing with Chantal Jain. 'Any idea why they've got the big guns out?'

Jain tapped her nose and winked. 'Bain and Turnbull had a six am with ACC Duffin and were hauled over the coals, by all accounts.'

'So they're getting pressure from above?' said Cullen.

'I heard a rumour Strathclyde are sniffing about. They've got a dedicated murder squad.' Jain checked her watch. 'I've got to dash. Bain's got me and Alan out at Edinburgh Park, trying to stop uniform making a mess of everything.'

'See you later,' said McNeill.

Jain walked off towards the stairs, her car keys jangling in her hand.

'Is that true what she was saying?' said Cullen.

McNeill shrugged her shoulders. 'Probably. It's funny. A couple of days ago Bain and Wilkinson were fighting each other for the case so they could boost their stats. Now they're trying to ditch it to save their jobs.'

'There might be an opening for you.'

McNeill laughed. 'Wouldn't say no, but I wouldn't be surprised if Turnbull brings someone in from outside.'

'Back to the phone calls, then,' said Cullen.

'What about those number plates?' said McNeill.

Cullen yawned. 'Still not got them through. I've been chasing, but Naismith isn't in. Why do you ask?'

'Bain's asked me to supervise you,' said McNeill. 'Let me know when they're in.'

'Will do.'

59

An hour later and Cullen was wading through more calls, getting nowhere. He looked at Angela sitting next to him. 'This isn't right,' said Cullen. 'That's three people I've managed to get a hold of so far and none of them heard anything about these death threats.'

'I've had nothing, either,' said Angela.

Cullen frowned. 'How many so far have confirmed the death threats?'

'None.'

'*None?*' said Cullen. 'I'm going to get this sorted.'

His phone rang. He answered it.

'It's Mr Naismith, returning your call.'

'Finally,' said Cullen.

'Have you been chasing me?'

'This is a multiple murder investigation, Mr Naismith. Are you surprised?'

Naismith sighed. 'I suppose not.'

'Okay, so have you got the results in yet?' said Cullen.

'I've just got them back now,' said Naismith. 'Six cars.'

'Thank you,' said Cullen. 'Can you send me the details through?' He hung up the phone and shook his head. 'What sort of person calls themselves Mr?'

'Don't you do it?' said Angela. 'You say DC Cullen all the time.'

'That's my rank, though.'

'Same difference.'

Cullen closed his notebook. 'Can you and Miller try and find out who gave you the lead on these death threats? I've got to go looking for cars with DS McNeill.'

~

CULLEN PHONED AHEAD and agreed to meet the first car owner at his workplace, a council office on Gorgie Road. He stood with McNeill by her Punto in the car park waiting for him to arrive.

'That wind can piss off,' said McNeill.

'You're in a cracking mood,' said Cullen.

McNeill sniffed. 'Can't believe I'm reduced to this.'

An overweight man in his mid-twenties walked across the car park towards them. 'DC Cullen?'

Cullen nodded his head sharply.

'Alan Gregor.' He held out his hand. 'How can I help?'

McNeill introduced them and explained about the case. 'Mr Gregor, your car was spotted travelling between Musselburgh and the Edinburgh Park, South Gyle area on Sunday night. Can you tell us the reason for your journey?'

Gregor frowned. 'I was at my bird's in Musselburgh.'

'Can you confirm your address?' said McNeill.

Gregor rattled off an address in a block of flats not far from the South Gyle station, roughly a mile from Edinburgh Park.

'Bit strange you stay in South Gyle and work in Gorgie,' said McNeill.

'Used to work at RBS,' said Gregor. 'Used to be able to walk in to work. Got punted at Christmas time, though. I should really move, but the market's bad just now.'

McNeill nodded. 'Can we have the address in Musselburgh?'

Gregor gave an address down by the harbour.

'Thanks for your time, Mr Gregor,' said McNeill.

Gregor walked off back towards the office.

'Where next?' said McNeill, her voice despairing.

~

CULLEN AND MCNEILL watched Bill McKay wander off towards his car.

Last on the list, he did overnight security at the Younger Building, one of the RBS offices at Edinburgh Park. He seemed like a typical security guard to Cullen — ex-Forces, definitely a Rangers supporter. He lived in Wallyford in East Lothian, just past Musselburgh, and his commute took him via the A1 onto the City Bypass, hence being picked up by their search as he drove to work on Sunday evening.

McNeill leaned back against the car, her arms folded. 'This is getting us absolutely nowhere.'

'It's not even getting us that far,' said Cullen.

He looked around the area, quite leafy despite the offices. There was a Paolozzi sculpture just up the road on the corner, a giant steel robot standing guard over the corporate offices. He thought it wouldn't be the worst place in the world to work, but then remembered the level of tedium those inside would be subjected to, based on his experience in Financial Services.

'How was the wine?' he said.

McNeill frowned. 'Wine?'

Cullen grinned. 'After I spurned you last night, you said you were going to have some wine?'

McNeill raised her eyebrows, a pouting smile on her lips. 'Don't worry, DC Cullen, you *will* be taking me out for that drink.' She left a pause, holding his gaze until he looked away. 'It was fine, a nice South African Merlot. I only had a couple of glasses. I'll need to finish it tonight — it doesn't keep in this weather and I hate to chuck out good wine.'

'I had a Rioja myself,' said Cullen.

Something began nagging at his brain as he watched a group of people get off an RBS-branded minibus, most of them wearing navy suits and staring at their Blackberries.

Wine.

The glass of wine he'd poured for Sian Saunders. It had smelled fine, yet it was roasting in her flat and she'd been away at the weekend.

'Scott.'

He looked up.

'You weren't listening to me again,' said McNeill. 'I said we should share a bottle some time.'

'Yeah, we should.' Cullen bit his lip. 'I was just thinking. How long do you think a bottle of Chianti would keep for?'

McNeill screwed her eyes up. 'What?'

'In this weather,' said Cullen, 'how long before a bottle of Italian red went off?'

McNeill shrugged. 'A day at best. It would start tasting a bit funny after two, definitely. Why?'

'Sian Saunders might have been lying.'

60

Cullen and McNeill sat in Sian Saunders living room. She looked washed out.

'Can I ask how long a bottle of wine usually lasts you?' said Cullen.

Sian glared at him. 'What's that got to do with anything? My best friend's just been murdered and you're asking about how much I drink?'

'Ms Saunders, please answer the question,' said Cullen.

'Are you saying I'm a piss head?'

'Answer the question,' said McNeill.

'Two days,' said Sian, finally.

'Do you mean two sessions?' said Cullen.

'Sorry, I don't understand,' said Sian.

'Do you always finish a bottle the next day if you open one?' said Cullen.

'Yes.' Sian looked at both of them, eyes blinking.

'Do you ever leave it longer than a day?' said Cullen.

Sian shook her head vigorously. 'Never. It goes off. I chuck it out.'

'Can you tell us why there was a half-empty bottle on the counter yesterday?' said Cullen.

'Well, I'd had a couple of glasses on Sunday night after work,' said Sian.

'So you weren't out with Gail McBride then?'

Sian gripped the arms of the sofa. 'Shite.'

'We spoke to the bar manager in the Grape on the way over here,' said Cullen. 'He was working on Sunday. You weren't there, were you?'

'Why have you been lying to us?' said McNeill.

Sian looked at the carpet. 'Gail asked me not to say anything.' She took a deep breath. 'I wasn't out with Gail. I came home from work, drank some wine, watched some telly, read my book then went to bed.'

'Why did you tell us you were with Gail?' said McNeill.

Sian looked up, her eyes moist. 'She asked me to cover for her.'

'You've got a lot of explaining to do,' said McNeill.

'You've got to understand,' said Sian. 'Gail had been unhappy with Simon for a long time. She wanted to work in publishing. She had a job at a company on the Royal Mile, but Simon forced her to move to a bank, wanted her to get a "proper job".'

She rubbed her hands up and down her skirt as she spoke. 'Gail's not been happy there for a while. I mean she could be quite strong, at least on the surface, but inside she wasn't a banker. It's a shit job working for a bank, you know? You've got idiots full of ego telling you what to do every day. Gail was smart. She should never have worked there. She was too good for it.'

'So what was Gail up to on Sunday night?' said Cullen.

Sian bit her lip. 'She was supposed to be meeting a man. As I say, her marriage was dead in the water. She'd been looking around, looking for a nice guy to take her away from it all, and she'd found him recently. Some guy called Jeremy Turner. He was in Edinburgh on business this week and she was going to meet him outside work.'

'And that's why you lied?' said McNeill.

'Yeah,' said Sian. 'She didn't want Simon finding out until things had progressed a bit. She asked me to lie for her. If anyone asked, we were at Grape in town.'

'And why didn't you tell us this when the body turned up?' said McNeill.

Sian didn't reply for a few seconds. 'I was worried I'd get into trouble.'

'I see,' said McNeill, voice stern.

'Are you going to press charges against me?' said Sian.

McNeill looked at Cullen, who just shrugged. 'I don't know yet.'

'Where did Gail meet him?' said Cullen.

'You know Schoolbook?'

61

B ain was on speakerphone as McNeill drove them back to the station.

'You're kidding me,' said Bain.

'Wish I was,' said Cullen.

'So, Gail met this guy on Schoolbook,' said Bain.

'It sounded more like *he* met her, from what I can gather,' said McNeill. 'He started messaging her, swept her off her feet and so on.'

'Shite, shite, shite,' said Bain. 'So does this look anything like the same pattern as the other two?'

That morning, Cullen had noticed the wall at the side of the whiteboard now had several sheets of A3 paper taped together, showing the flow of messages on a clear pattern terminating with the deaths of Caroline and Debi. He didn't know who'd drawn the diagram, but Bain had continually talked about patterns at the morning briefing.

'It certainly looks that way,' said Cullen.

'I take it her getting the train was a load of shite?' said Bain.

'Aye,' said Cullen.

'What happened on Sunday night, then?' said Bain.

'As far as we know,' said Cullen, 'they had a project implementing on Sunday, so they had to work all day.'

'I know the feeling,' said Bain.

'According to Sian,' said Cullen, 'Gail was supposed to meet someone called Jeremy Turner afterwards. He'd told her he was in Edinburgh on business.'

'So this Sian's been lying to us?' said Bain.

'That's right,' said McNeill. 'We've got some Musselburgh plod getting a statement from her. I'll let you decide if you want to charge her.'

'I think I will,' said Bain. 'Wasting our time like that.' He paused for a few seconds. 'Sundance, I thought you told me yesterday this was a different killer.'

'I said it didn't look like the same one,' said Cullen.

'You should've been sharper,' said Bain.

'Look,' said Cullen, trying to keep his voice level, 'I was the one who worked this all out. I was the one who spotted her lie and got her to admit it.'

'Well done there, Sundance,' said Bain, 'thank the Lord we've got your powers of deduction to help us through this case. Does it look like it could be different killers?'

McNeill answered. 'We need to look into it further. I'd say it's highly likely it's the same killer, but we need to establish the links and hear back from forensics.'

Bain sighed. 'I really need this to be another killer.' There was a pause, then the sound of a desk being hit. 'Oh, you beauty.'

'What?' said Cullen.

'I let Rob Thomson go at the back of six on Sunday,' said Bain. 'Bastard could easily have got over to Edinburgh Park, couldn't he?'

'I suppose so,' said Cullen.

Bain ignored him. 'Magic.'

'All three arranged to meet a man on Schoolbook,' said Cullen, 'that's all we know. Same account for the first two. I'll see if I can get Kidd to link this latest account to the original one.'

'Get on it,' said Bain.

'Have they found anything on those office PCs?' said Cullen.

'I've not heard anything,' said Bain. 'Actually, we need to get them to have a look at this Gail's computer as well. I take it that wasn't stolen?'

'No idea,' said Cullen. 'I'd go down to speak to Anderson if I were you.'

'I'll get Miller onto it,' said Bain. 'The abduction methods are similar. They all arranged to meet in private or secluded places. He attacked Caroline Adamson at a hotel. Debi Curtis was attacked at her flat. Gail McBride's body was found in a field. Where was she meeting this punter again?'

'Outside her work, according to Sian Saunders,' said Cullen. 'The Alba Bank Mortgage Centre at Edinburgh Park.'

'So he meets her there,' said Bain, 'kills her and dumps her body just off that cycle path. Pretty handy.'

'This fake name thing,' said Cullen. 'At the moment, we don't actually know whether Jeremy Turner exists.'

'You'd better check into that, Sundance,' said Bain.

Cullen sighed. 'Will do.'

'Has Gail's PM been done yet?' said McNeill.

Bain paused. 'Aye. Strangled, throat slit.'

'So the same MO then?' said McNeill.

'Similar,' said Bain. 'Need to prove it is. I've got twenty officers looking into that proof as we speak.'

'Gail and Caroline were both dead when we found them,' said Cullen. 'Caroline had been subjected to a lot of torture. Gail's looked more like a gangland hit. The only reason Debi wasn't dead was because we got there before he could finish her off.'

'Not your finest hour there,' said Bain.

McNeill scowled. 'What's your problem? Because of Scott, we almost managed to catch this killer.'

They heard another thump down the line from Bain. 'Listen, Butch, I need to be able to link Rob Thomson to this Gail lassie.'

'These murders might not have been down to him.' McNeill made a face at the phone that almost made Cullen burst out laughing.

'Butch, I know for a fact Caroline was done by him,' said Bain. 'Therefore Debi was.'

'But we don't know that,' said McNeill.

'I've almost got enough to send him away,' said Bain. 'I just need you lot to tie off the loose ends.'

Cullen frowned. 'Why are you so focused on him?'

'It's obvious,' said Bain. 'He's a big nasty bastard. Had a grudge against his ex-wife and a grudge against her mate.'

'What about Alistair Cruikshank?' said Cullen. 'He also had a definite grudge against both Caroline and Debi.'

'What about Gail, though?' said Bain. 'How does that fit in there?'

'What's the link between Rob and Gail then?' said Cullen.

'Where did she work?' said Bain.

'Alba Bank,' said Cullen.

Bain laughed. 'Where Rob Thomson works.'

Cullen could practically hear the size of the grin down the phone. He shared a look with McNeill. Neither spoke — Cullen knew where this was heading.

'Right, so I need to find a more solid link between Gail and that bastard,' said Bain, 'but once we get that we've nailed him.'

'I still think we should be looking for this Cruikshank guy,' said Cullen.

'Chantal Jain is,' said Bain. 'You aren't, all right? We'll see what fun he brings to the party when we find him.'

'So what's the plan of attack?' said McNeill.

'I'm going to get Irvine looking at linking Thomson to this woman,' said Bain. 'Get him going round her work and stuff like that. He's a proper copper I can trust. I'll also get him looking at the CCTV at Edinburgh Park, see if this boy drove there. As for you pair...' He exhaled down the line. 'I need you to concentrate on Schoolbook and this Jeremy Turner boy.'

'How many bodies can we have?' said Cullen.

'I can only spare you pair,' said Bain, 'plus maybe Angela.'

'We'll need more than that if you want it done this week,' said McNeill. 'We're struggling with Debi and Caroline as it is.'

'Right.' Bain sounded irritated. 'I can give you Keith Miller full-time once Wilko's finished with him.'

'Oh, fantastic,' said McNeill.

They heard Bain's mobile ring. 'Ah, shite, I need to take this. Butch, I want an update at two, okay?'

'Okay,' said McNeill.

The line clicked dead.

Cullen sat for a moment, letting McNeill gather her thoughts as she drove past Duddingston Golf Club. She shook her head.

'Was Bain for real there?' said Cullen.

'Well, it's his neck on the line here,' said McNeill, 'not ours.'

'Fair enough,' said Cullen, 'but someone else could get killed while he's pissing about, lost in his stupid vendetta. What's he actually planning on doing?'

'Who knows?'

n hour later, Cullen was back at his desk looking through Gail's Schoolbook Friends list feeling like he was going round in circles.

'This just isn't efficient,' he said to Angela.

'It's tedious,' she said. 'I'm getting nowhere fast. There's hundreds of them.'

Cullen got up, deciding to see Kidd. He'd tried contacting him earlier but he'd got no reply. 'That's it, I'm off upstairs.'

He pounded up and saw Kidd with a telephone headset on, avoiding his gaze.

'Are you on a call?' said Cullen.

Kidd pressed the secrecy button. 'Aye, I'm on with Schoolbook.'

'What about?'

'Trying to get a better pipe to their database,' said Kidd. 'Getting more progress cos that Duncan boy is off today.'

'How did that private company go?' said Cullen.

'They're the ones setting the pipe up for us.'

Cullen handed him a sheet of paper with Gail McBride and Jeremy Turner's details on it. 'I need you to get me all messages between these two users.'

'Are we cleared for it?' said Kidd.

'It's the same case, so aye.'

'I'll get it back to you by two,' said Kidd. 'I'm tied up till then and that's come straight from Bain.'

'Fine.' Cullen was tempted to try and play with Bain but decided against it. He thanked Kidd then bounded back downstairs.

McNeill was chatting to Angela. She nodded when Cullen appeared. 'How's it going?'

'Not great,' said Cullen. 'We're just spinning our wheels here.'

'What have you looked at?' said McNeill.

'Been calling through the friends list,' said Cullen. 'It's much bigger than Caroline's but so far we're getting nothing. I've got Kidd extracting all the messages between Gail and this Jeremy Turner.'

'The good news, I suppose, is I've managed to get some more resource to ring through the list,' said McNeill.

'Aye, and what's the bad?' said Cullen.

'McAllister is one of them.'

Cullen shook his head. 'We don't need him.'

'Well, if it can free you up for a couple of hours to do something else,' said McNeill, 'then I'd look on it favourably.'

Cullen was already worrying about how much time would be lost to managing McAllister. 'What sort of thing?'

'There might be some other avenue of investigation that's being screwed up under Wilkinson which might help what you're doing here,' said McNeill.

'You're not clutching at straws, are you?' said Cullen.

McNeill laughed. 'I haven't drawn the short one yet.'

Cullen had a thought. 'Give me a minute.' He got up.

Wilkinson was standing by the Incident Room whiteboard, scrawling some information about Gail McBride, copying the techniques Bain had been using on Saturday morning.

'Sir,' said Cullen.

Wilkinson's face contorted into a sneer. 'Curran, what can I do you for?'

'Gail McBride's phone logs,' said Cullen. 'Did anyone look over them?'

Wilkinson frowned. 'Irvine did it.'

Cullen grimaced. McNeill was right — there was no doubt he'd have messed it up. 'Any idea where he is?'

'Back at our old desks,' said Wilkinson. 'Trying to get some peace and quiet.'

'Thanks.' Cullen moved off.

Wilkinson grabbed his shoulder. 'Nice of you to drop me in it, by the way.'

'How do you mean?' said Cullen.

Wilkinson folded his arms. 'Somebody told Turnbull I was off on the lash last night.'

'Well, it wasn't me.'

Wilkinson eyed him suspiciously. 'I don't believe you, but I'll let it pass for now.'

Cullen left the Incident Room and followed the maze of corridors back to their old office space. Irvine was sitting at Cullen's old desk, his feet up on the table, reading a sheaf of documentation.

'Alan,' said Cullen.

Irvine looked up. 'What do *you* want?'

Alan Irvine was a fat, prematurely balding DS, much in the image of Wilkinson. Cullen had heard he was once a high-flyer in the force, shooting up rapidly from PC to DS in a matter of years, before his career stalled. He was notorious for being one of the laziest officers in Lothian & Borders, though he was good at managing up the way.

'Have you been looking through Gail McBride's phone records?' said Cullen.

Irvine held up the sheet of paper. 'Just going through it now.' He got to his feet and stretched. 'Actually, you know what, can you do it for me? Wilkinson wants me down in the CCTV suite.' He handed the papers to Cullen, spat a wad of chewing gum into the bin and headed off.

TWENTY MINUTES LATER, Cullen had cross-referenced Gail's phone records against the numbers in his notebook. Gail appeared to be much more of a communicator online than by telephone. Once he'd removed her home number, Sian Saunders and Simon McBride's mobile, he had the list down to five numbers.

He looked through the remainder of the list. The first two he'd traced to addresses in Ayr. Gail's maiden name — McGuire —

matched the surnames of the two account holders, most likely parents and brother.

The next two numbers were addresses in Glasgow, again members of the McGuire clan.

The last number was a mystery. It was a mobile number. He dialled it but it was dead.

He picked up the desk phone and called Tommy Smith in the Phone Squad.

'Smith, Forensic Investigation.'

'Tommy, it's Scott Cullen.'

Smith sighed down the line. 'I got back to you as promised didn't I?'

'You did.'

'Thank Christ for that,' said Smith. 'Got a to-do list longer than a gorilla's arm.'

'I need you to trace a phone number for me,' said Cullen.

'Another one?'

'Different case,' said Cullen.

'You sure get about, buddy.'

Cullen read out the number.

'Just want me to do a cell search?' said Smith.

'What else can you do?' said Cullen.

'Unblock drains,' said Smith.

'Very funny.'

'Seriously, though, we can do a lot of things,' said Smith. 'We can get a list of calls, trace to cell sites, logistic analysis.'

'What's that?' said Cullen.

'We can look at the supply chain for getting the phone from the manufacturer to the network to the shop to the user,' said Smith.

'Are you serious?'

'Aye,' said Smith. 'Don't you believe me?'

'So I didn't have to do all that for the other number?'

'If you'd come to me in the first place,' said Smith, 'you could have saved the force a lot of petrol.'

'How long will that take?' said Cullen.

'Overnight,' said Smith, 'if I put it to the top of my to-do list.'

'Where is it, then?'

'It's second from top, buddy.'

63

An hour later, Cullen sat with Miller having paired him with McAllister to search through the databases for Jeremy Turner, just as he'd done for Martin Webb.

'At the end of the day, though, I just can't find him,' said Miller, 'and neither can Willie.'

Cullen rubbed his hand over his face. He didn't trust their conclusion. He could get Angela to verify it. 'So it looks like Jeremy Turner doesn't exist then?'

'I'm not saying anything,' said Miller. 'Drawing conclusions is your responsibility.' He pulled out a pair of dark green tickets. 'Here we go, though, Scotty. See, I can find some things.'

'What's this?'

'Hibs tickets for tonight, man,' said Miller. 'We're going to watch the Leith boys murder Barca.' He laughed. 'Sky were saying Messi's made the trip. Makes it well worth it. Him, Villa, Xavi and Iniesta all travelled.'

Cullen had forgotten all about it. 'We need to see how the case is going before we decide if we can go.'

'We?' Miller screwed his face up. 'I'm going.'

'Have you cleared it with Bain?' said Cullen.

Miller pocketed the tickets. 'Just let me know. One of my pals might want to go instead.'

'Go and help Caldwell making phone calls now,' said Cullen.

'Wish I could, Scotty, wish I could.' Miller sniffed. 'Got to chum Wilko through to Ayr to see this lassie's parents.'

Cullen felt a slight relief — at least there was no imminent threat of Miller messing up their investigation. That and the fact he'd escaped the parent visit this time. 'Thought you'd already been?'

'Nobody's been able to get hold of them till now,' said Miller. 'Been away on their holibags.'

Cullen hated the way people called it 'holibags' — it didn't mean anything. 'You'd better be back in time for the game, then.'

'Eh?'

Cullen grinned. 'It'll be a good five or six hour round trip to Ayr once you factor in speaking to her folks.' He made a show of checking his watch. 'It's almost two now.'

'Shite.' Miller ran for the door.

Back at his desk, Cullen found the printed sheets of Gail's friends and contacts still sitting there, goading him.

Angela finished a call just as he sat. 'This is so slow.' She picked up her sheets, pointing to the last name on the last page. 'Tom Rowlands.'

'That rings a bell.' Cullen logged onto Schoolbook and clicked through to the profile. It was one of the Chemical Brothers, the one with the blonde hair. He'd seen them at T in the Park as a teenager and had a few of their albums. 'So there are celebrities in the list.'

'Well, I don't think she's been setting up dates with one of the Chemical Brothers.' Angela ran her finger down the page. 'I've got John Terry. And Fatboy Slim. And Robbie Williams. Takes the number down, I suppose.'

'We can't eliminate a Robbie Williams from Armadale.' Cullen looked at the next name on the list. The profile mercifully had a mobile number. He'd just dialled the first four digits, when he felt a tap on the shoulder.

It was Chantal Jain, out of breath. 'Scott, have you seen Sharon?'

'Think she's out at Edinburgh Park at the Alba Bank office,' said Cullen.

'Shite.'

'Why do you need her?'

'Alistair Cruikshank has turned up at his hotel.'

64

Cullen and Jain stood outside Cruikshank's hotel room at the Minto.

'Ladies first,' said Cullen.

'You big jessie.' Jain rapped on the door. 'Mr Cruikshank, it's the police. Open up.'

Nothing.

'Mr Cruikshank,' said Jain, louder this time. 'Please open the door. We need to speak to you.'

'Do you have a warrant?'

Jain rolled her eyes at Cullen. 'Mr Cruikshank, we just want to talk to you.'

There was a dull thud from inside the room, like a sash window being raised.

They shared a look.

'He's made a run for it,' said Jain.

Cullen ran back down the corridor, looking through the window to the car park. A heavyset man ran towards the wall at the back, almost at the garden area. 'I'll follow him. You get round to Blacket Place. And get some back-up.'

He wrestled with the window and eventually toppled out through it. He got up and sprinted across the lawn as Cruikshank's leg disappeared over the top. Cullen had a flashback to Saturday night in Fountainbridge, the killer escaping from him.

There was a wooden picnic table leaning against the wall. He used his momentum to climb up it. He almost winded himself as he landed, stomach across the top of the wall.

Cullen was above a large garden overgrown with weeds, a Victorian villa at the far end. Cruikshank was limping up the path at the side of the house, looking like he'd similarly injured himself.

Cullen carefully lowered himself down but slipped at the bottom, almost falling over. He got to his feet and ran as fast as he could up the side of the house towards the street.

He emerged onto Blacket Place, a rabbit warren. He couldn't see Cruikshank anywhere. If he didn't find him quickly, he'd lose him, limp or not.

He heard footsteps from the left, round the bend. He ran towards the sound and quickly spotted Cruikshank making a vain attempt to continue running. He followed, heading straight for the main road. He was gaining speed — if Cullen didn't catch him soon then he might lose him in the foot traffic on Minto Street.

Cullen pushed himself on. He was closing, but maybe not quickly enough.

Cruikshank made it through the archway at the end of the street, heading through to freedom.

Jain came from nowhere and rugby tackled Cruikshank to the ground, just yards from the road.

'You. Are. Under. Arrest.'

65

Cullen opened the double doors set in the jutting diagonal entrance to St Leonards station, allowing Jain to push a handcuffed Cruikshank through the door. They'd agreed to keep Cruikshank clear of Bain for now, until they knew his story.

The desk sergeant nodded at Cullen as he approached. Barry Smith — Fat Barry. His eyes were darting between Cruikshank and Jain. 'DC Cullen, how you doing?'

Cullen smiled in response. 'I'm doing all right, Barry.' He pointed at Cruikshank. 'Got a spare interview room available?'

'Aye.' Smith grinned inanely at them. 'What's wrong with Leith Walk?'

Cullen cleared his throat. 'We're full up down there. That big case that's on, you know how it is.'

'Yeah, okay.' Smith chuckled. 'I can give you room three.'

Cullen signed them in and they set off down the lightless corridor through the building. They stopped outside the room and Cullen pushed against the scarred wood of the door.

Jain took Cruikshank into the interview room, while Cullen stopped outside to recover. He'd jarred something in his foot when he jumped down from the wall and his legs were still aching from the chase.

Cruikshank had certainly used his right to silence — there

hadn't been a word from the man. Cullen's mind struggled to match him to the figure he chased on Saturday. He could sort of see it, but he wouldn't stand up in court and say it.

Jain came out of the room and shut the door behind her. 'He's still not said anything.'

'Well, this is our one chance to get to him before Bain does.' Cullen rubbed the muscles in the backs of his legs. 'That was a good tackle you made back there.'

'My dad made me play rugby when I was wee,' said Jain. 'I thought I'd lost the pair of you. I'd been up and down the street a couple of times. I'm glad I hung around.'

'Not half as much as I am,' said Cullen. 'Losing three suspects in the same week wouldn't be good.'

'One of them was the same one twice,' said Jain.

Cullen grinned. 'Maybe.'

'So what's the plan here?' said Jain. 'Why are we hiding this guy from Bain?'

'I'm not hiding him. I just want to get a statement out of him quickly.'

'This is supposed to be my collar.'

'I know,' said Cullen. 'I'll take the blame for it, okay? Me or DS McNeill anyway.'

Jain nodded. 'Do you think he's our man?'

'Don't know,' said Cullen. 'He's just as likely a suspect as Rob Thomson.'

Jain raised an eyebrow. 'Let's see what he has to say, then.'

She pushed through the door and Cullen followed.

Alistair Cruikshank was mid-thirties and well turned out. He fitted the profile of the man in the CCTV footage as much as Rob Thomson did. He was a big guy, probably with some farming stock in him, with huge hands and the traces of a ginger beard in his stubble.

Jain opened her notebook, looked at Cruikshank and spoke into the tape recorder, going through the formalities. They hadn't upgraded the facilities to digital recorders at St Leonard's yet. 'Why were you running away from us?'

Cruikshank's eyes darted between them. 'No comment.'

'If you have nothing to hide, then why did you run away from us?' said Jain.

Cruikshank swallowed hard. 'As I said, no comment.'

'Okay, if that's how you want to play it,' said Jain, 'can you tell us about your movements over the last couple of days?'

'Certainly.' Cruikshank smiled. 'When would you like me to start?'

'When did you arrive in Edinburgh?' said Jain.

'I came down on Sunday afternoon.'

'And that's down from?' said Jain.

'Elgin. Had to change at Inverness. I got into Edinburgh early evening.'

'At roughly what time?'

'Back of nine,' said Cruikshank. 'Five past I think.'

'And you went directly to the hotel?' said Jain.

'By taxi.' Cruikshank's eyes shot over to Cullen then back to Jain. 'And I spent the rest of the evening studying in my room.'

'What were you studying?' said Jain.

'The Bible,' said Cruikshank. 'I'm training to be a minister. I would have come down on Saturday, but I was giving the early morning service. I also had a Bible class on Saturday evening.'

Cullen noted it all down — Cruikshank had a few potential alibis for the murder of Debi Curtis and CCTV would surely place him getting off the train at the time Gail McBride was murdered, not to mention the taxi receipt.

'What brings you to Edinburgh?' said Cullen.

'There's a conference at New College I'm attending as part of my studies,' said Cruikshank.

'That's the old university buildings on the Mound overlooking Princes Street?' said Cullen.

Cruikshank nodded.

'Okay, Mr Cruikshank, can I now ask you to outline your movements last Thursday night?' said Jain.

'Well, I was in Inverness all day, at college,' said Cruikshank. 'Thursday night was the church choir.'

Jain gestured to the door. She paused the interview and they left the room. 'Well?'

'How many alibis can one man have?' said Cullen. 'According to him, he was with a choir when Caroline was killed, at a Bible class when Debi was attacked and on a train when Gail was killed.'

Jain nodded. 'He's not our killer.'

'Not likely.' Part of Cullen felt disappointed as Cruikshank had plausible motives against Debi and Caroline.

'I think it's safe to hand him over to Bain now,' said Jain.

'We could probably charge him with resisting arrest,' said Cullen. 'Maybe for wasting police time or something. Just wonder why he legged it like he did.'

'No idea,' said Jain. 'I'll maybe ask him after I get all those alibis checked out.'

'Not even Bain would touch him with that many,' said Cullen.

Jain laughed.

Cullen's mobile rang — McNeill. 'I've been looking for you.'

'I'm helping Chantal up at St Leonards,' said Cullen.

'I'll pick you up from there. I assume Chantal can get back here?'

'Yeah, we've got a pool car,' said Cullen. 'What do you want me to help with?'

'We've got a potential witness for the person stealing Caroline's laptop.'

66

M cNeill pulled up in front of a rundown house on a grim street deep into Gracemount, a notoriously feral estate on the city's south side.

'Who are we going to see?' said Cullen.

'A guy called Jonny Soutar,' said McNeill.

'And what's his tale?'

McNeill pulled the handbrake on. 'The story goes he left a flat on Friday night in the street where Caroline lived. His mum called it in. She reckons he saw something.'

'Why didn't he call it in?' said Cullen.

'This is Gracemount,' was all McNeill said.

They got out of the car and walked up the path. The harled exterior walls would originally have been white, but had greyed with time and lack of upkeep. The garden had long since gone past the point of neglect — it wasn't even a forest of overgrown grass, just a patch of rubbish-strewn dirt with bits of old cars and motorbikes, decaying clothes and discarded shopping bags.

McNeill rang the doorbell and they waited.

Cullen looked down the street. In front of the neglected housing were several brand new Fords, Toyotas and Vauxhalls. 'They've got their priorities right on this street.'

'What?' said McNeill.

'Shite houses, brand new cars.'

She laughed.

Cullen pointed at the door. 'Think there's anybody in?'

McNeill rang the bell again. 'I don't know. His mum said he would be.'

Cullen could make out a thumping noise from inside, someone coming down the stairs. The door opened slightly on the chain and an eye appeared.

'Police,' said McNeill. 'We're looking for Johnny Soutar.'

The eye looked them up and down then disappeared from the gap. The door opened. A young guy stood there wearing only boxer shorts. He was late teens, maybe early twenties. His skinny white body was hairless with a slight paunch.

'I'm Johnny Soutar. In you come.'

Cullen followed McNeill into the living room. It was a state — an ironing board sat in the middle, heaped up with junk over-flowing from the coffee table.

Soutar sprawled on the sofa. He had dark spiky hair in a mullet, a dyed blonde rat-tail hanging at the back, which he stroked like it was a pet.

McNeill perched on an armchair across from the sofa. 'Put some clothes on, please.'

The youth picked up a green and white striped dressing gown and tied it loosely around himself.

McNeill flashed her warrant card. 'Johnny Soutar?'

'Aye.' Soutar had an arrogant leer on his face.

'Your mother called the helpline regarding the Caroline Adamson case,' said McNeill.

'Aye, so she did,' said Soutar. 'She's off out.'

'Could you go over your story?' said McNeill.

'Suppose I'd better.' Soutar scratched his stomach. 'I was shagging this bird—'

'Could you go from the start, please?' said McNeill.

Soutar sighed. 'Aye, okay. I was up town with my mates Stevie and Darren. We were in that bar in the Omni Centre for a few jars then we went to that club in there. I got fired into Darren's cousin who we met in there but she told us to piss off, so I went for anything I could find.'

McNeill nodded along, though her body language had become

aggressive, sitting further forward with her hands clenched on her trouser legs.

'I found some bird, can't even remember her name.' Soutar frowned. 'Gemma or something. Took her back to her flat and slipped her a length.'

McNeill scowled. 'And her flat was on Smith's Place in Leith?'

'Think that's the street, aye,' said Soutar. 'It was right at the end, in the corner just by that chippy, *The Mermaid*?'

'Can you describe what you saw that night?' said McNeill.

'Well, after I'd boned the bird,' said Soutar, 'I was in no mood to stay, so I waited till she was asleep then I snuck out.'

Cullen was stunned at Soutar, as much at the casualness with which he described his conquest, as the ease he seemed to feel in front of the police. Not that Cullen was much better, given his antics on Friday night. 'Did you wake her?'

Soutar gave a chuckle. 'I'm an expert at sneaking out.' He scratched himself again. 'So, aye, I saw some boy leaving the flats in the corner, just as I came out the stair door.'

'Do you know what time this was?' said McNeill.

Soutar shrugged. 'Would've been about five in the morning, something like that.' He sniffed and tugged at the back of his ear. 'Hang on, I texted Darren on the way out of the street, telling him what I'd done.' He picked his mobile up from the sofa beside him, then fiddled with it for a few seconds. 'Five eleven am. I got a text from Stevie saying Darren had shagged his cousin in the bogs. Dirty bastard.'

McNeill sat back in the armchair. 'What did you do after you left Smith's Place?'

'I got a taxi home,' said Soutar. 'Managed to get one at the corner of the Walk.'

'And what did the man from the flat do?' said McNeill.

'Punter just sauntered away along the street,' said Soutar. 'Turned right at the end.'

Cullen tried to work it out. Right would have taken him further into Leith, maybe into Lochend, the opposite way from the direction Rob Thomson would have gone, assuming he was going directly home.

'Did you get a good look at the person you saw in the street?' said McNeill.

'Aye, I did,' said Soutar. 'I just wanted to get the hell out of there, you know? But I do remember the boy, though. He was a big bastard. Wearing a hooded top.'

'Was he carrying anything?' said Cullen.

'He had a bag with him, I think.' Soutar mimed picking something up. 'And he had one of them Apple computers they have in John Lewis.'

Cullen looked up — this was definitely moving into witness territory. The last thing they needed was for some defence lawyer to tear his evidence apart on the grounds of being too drunk. 'How sober were you?'

Soutar frowned. 'I'd had a skinful but I'd been dancing with this bird for hours and we'd got chips on the way to her flat. By the time I left I was pretty sober.'

Cullen wanted to check the witness statement would hold up and also to see if they could get verification from the taxi driver. 'What were you wearing at the time?'

'My posh trousers and my Ralph Lauren shirt,' said Soutar. 'Got sauce from my chips on it. Mum says it's ruined.'

Cullen showed him a print of the CCTV footage from Saturday night near Debi's flat. 'Was this the man?'

Soutar nodded immediately. 'Aye, pal, that's him.'

67

They got back to the Incident Room to find Chantal Jain updating Bain on Alistair Cruikshank.

'So where's this Cruikshank lad now?' Bain's tie was loosened — no doubt the tidiness of his appearance had lapsed since the press conference.

'In the cells downstairs,' said Jain.

Bain grinned. 'And he's in the clear?'

'It looks that way,' said Jain. 'As long as those alibis check out.'

'I'll get some big uniform bastards in to grill him,' said Bain. 'You just make sure you nail those alibis.'

'Did you find out why he was running away from us?' said Cullen.

Jain grimaced. 'Would you believe Margaret Armstrong threatened to call the police when he visited?'

'I can quite easily believe it,' said Cullen. 'Still doesn't explain why he ran.'

'She threatened to get him done with all that stuff about Caroline years ago,' said Jain.

Cullen frowned. 'I thought he was just going on about her divorce?'

'Turns out he was hoax calling her as well,' said Jain.

Cullen rolled his eyes. 'Jesus Christ. Are you doing anything about it?'

Jain shrugged. 'There's nobody to press charges.'

'We'll get him with a fine,' said Bain. 'Good work, DC Jain.'

'Thanks.' Jain marched off towards her desk.

Bain stared at Cullen. 'Sundance, how do I find you in every little nook and cranny on this case?'

Cullen held his hands up. 'Jain asked me to help, all right? That's all.'

'I gather you actually managed to catch the bastard this time?' said Bain. 'Would've been better if you could've done that on Saturday night, though. Gail McBride would still be alive.'

Cullen was speechless. He felt anger burn in the pit of his stomach.

McNeill cleared her throat. 'We've got some good news for you. That guy in Gracemount, Johnny Soutar, reckons he saw a big man in a hooded top carrying a laptop out of Caroline's stairwell door about five on Saturday morning.'

Bain folded his arms. 'Are you on the level here, Butch?'

'He's spilling his guts downstairs to one of the Torphichen Street DCs,' said McNeill. 'We'll get a statement pretty soon.'

Bain nodded slowly. 'I'm liking this. Can we get a line-up in front of him?'

McNeill shrugged. 'That's your call.'

'Right,' said Bain, 'let's you and me go and show this guy some pictures.'

Cullen produced the CCTV photo. 'He's confirmed it's him.'

Bain grabbed it off Cullen. 'What's this?'

'It's a screen grab from that CCTV footage you had me looking at yesterday,' said Cullen.

'Are you holding back on me?' said Bain. 'This is the same punter who bought the phone.'

'I know,' said Cullen.

Bain closed his eyes and took a deep breath. 'Cullen, can you get back to whatever task you're currently not bothering your arse to complete.' He looked at McNeill. 'Butch, I want a quick word with you.'

McNeill and Bain walked off towards the corner of the Incident Room.

Cullen sat at his desk, way past the point of having had enough.

Angela looked just about as fed up as he was.

Cullen gestured at the desk. 'Is it still just you? I thought McNeill said she'd secured a couple of officers?'

'She got rid of McAllister pretty quickly,' said Angela. 'And Steve Thomas has a court appearance.'

'Is that the truth?' said Cullen.

Angela shrugged. 'Probably.'

'I didn't even know we had him.' Cullen sighed. 'How are you getting on?'

Angela counted up her sheets. 'I've got through three and a half pages of these. You?'

'Halfway through my second.' Cullen tossed them on the desk. 'There's got to be a smarter way of doing this.'

'Wish there was,' said Angela. 'It's just good old-fashioned shoe leather work. Except instead of sore feet, I'm getting earache from the phone.'

Cullen picked up the sheets of paper of Gail's friends and looked through them, trying to figure out if there were other ways to approach the problem. He saw names he recognised, famous names — the guy out of Wet Wet Wet, the gay comedian who wears a leather kilt, a footballer who once played for Aberdeen who was going out with some Scottish pop star.

He looked down the sixth sheet and stopped in his tracks.

He'd found a name he recognised that wasn't famous. 'Jesus Christ.' He logged into Schoolbook and checked it out — he wasn't wrong.

'What is it?' said Angela.

Cullen raced around the room looking for McNeill and Bain, but they'd disappeared after their quick chat. He checked the meeting rooms, no sign.

DS Holdsworth was speaking to Wilkinson near the entrance, arguing about some point of pedantry on Holdsworth's part.

They both looked up.

'Have either of you seen Bain or McNeill?' said Cullen.

'Think she went upstairs for a coffee,' said Holdsworth. 'Bain's gone off to interview that guy you brought in.'

Cullen ran up the stairs taking them three at a time, clutching the papers in his fist. He burst through into the canteen.

McNeill was in the queue.

'Sharon,' said Cullen, out of breath.

McNeill looked back at him. 'What is it?'

'I've got something,' said Cullen. 'The friends lists. There's someone who's on all three of them.'

He handed her the sheet of paper, the name circled.

McNeill gasped. 'Rob Thomson.'

68

B ain looked disgustingly happy. 'Sundance, I could kiss you.'

They'd tracked him and Irvine down to the CCTV suite, the screen filled with the image of the mobile phone buyer at Tesco.

'Wondered when you'd make your move on Scott,' said McNeill.

Bain glared at her. 'This is really good work.' He took a slurp of Red Bull Cola. 'At last, there's some solid irrefutable evidence that's pointing to Rob Thomson. Those bloody alibis were a pack of lies.'

'It isn't solid evidence,' said Cullen. 'It's a lead, an avenue of investigation.'

'It bloody is evidence,' said Bain.

'Rob was a friend of Gail's,' said Cullen, 'that's all.'

Bain scowled.

Cullen looked at Irvine. 'How did it go with the CCTV footage from Edinburgh Park?'

'Nothing so far,' said Irvine. 'Keith Miller's doing a search into it.'

Cullen nodded — he leaned forward and tapped the screen. 'Have you shown any of this to that Jonny Soutar guy we brought in?' He looked at Bain. 'You need some witness statements to back this up.'

Bain's left nostril twitched as he stared at Cullen. 'I can do what I bloody like, I'm the Senior Investigating Officer here.'

'So you haven't shown it to him yet?' said Cullen. 'The only thing he's seen is the photo I showed him?'

'Aye.'

'He's confirmed it's the person he saw,' said Cullen. 'He hasn't confirmed it's Rob Thomson.'

Bain evaded his gaze. 'I've been down prepping him. DS Irvine's just printing off some of these shots for him to peruse.' He took another swig of cola. 'It could be Rob Thomson.'

'It could be anyone, though.' Cullen hit the back of the chair Irvine was in. 'It could be DI Wilkinson, could be Keith Miller in a padded jacket. It's a tall, well-built man, that's all. You've got nothing to prove it's Rob Thomson.'

Bain practically snarled. 'Listen, Cullen, it is him.'

Cullen folded his arms. 'There's no way you can say that for definite.'

'Butch, back me up here,' said Bain.

McNeill shook her head. 'I'm not saying anything.'

Bain glared at Cullen. 'How about those death threats? You were supposed to verify them for me.'

Cullen rubbed his ear. 'I'll give you an update by seven o'clock.'

Bain's nostrils flared again. 'Cullen, this is the last straw. Can you stop buggering about and do what I ask you for once? All you've done today is assault a member of the public instead of corroborating these death threats.'

Cullen didn't say anything, deliberately restraining himself from reminding Bain it was he who linked Gail McBride to the other murders just that morning.

Bain squared up to him. 'You're buggering about here, Constable. Every single task you've been set you've not completed. I've found you away with other officers on random trips at least three times today and I still don't have corroboration of the death threats.'

Cullen stepped back. He couldn't even look at Bain for fear of punching him.

Bain pointed at Cullen. 'I need you to go back to your desk, pick up the phone, dial some numbers, speak to some people and verify those death threats.'

Cullen took a deep breath and tried to work out whether to punch or head butt.

'Now, Cullen,' said Bain. 'Those are the witnesses I want at the trial. I'm away to speak to the Procurator Fiscal, see if I can pull Thomson back in.' He took a step back, shaking his head. 'Verify those death threats.'

69

Cullen turned the key in the ignition, his pulse still racing from the confrontation, his hands still shaking.

There was a rap on the passenger side window. McNeill.

Cullen took a deep breath and turned the engine off. He reached over and opened the door to let her in.

'Are you on your way home?' said McNeill.

Cullen nodded and looked away. 'I just can't take any more of this nonsense from him.'

'It was uncalled for,' said McNeill. 'I don't know what the hell he's playing at.'

'I know exactly what he's playing at,' said Cullen. 'It's like you've been saying, they're all playing for Turnbull's job. If Bain can get a quick conviction here then he's a shoo-in for it.'

'It's that or the pressure of this case,' said McNeill. 'His swearing is getting worse. I wouldn't be at all surprised if Strathclyde murder squad pitches up here soon because we've made such a mess of it.'

They sat in silence for a while. Cullen's pulse gradually slowed. 'Am I out of order here? I seem to be the only one challenging him.'

'I am as well,' said McNeill.

'Are you?' said Cullen. 'It feels like it's just me. Bain's giving me a total kicking for it.'

'That's just Bain being Bain.'

'Yeah, well, if it wasn't just me shouting about it,' said Cullen, 'he'd maybe listen to some sense. I need you to back me up.'

McNeill glared at him. 'Scott, you're lashing out.'

'I'm not,' said Cullen. 'I'm in at the deep end here.'

McNeill closed her eyes and took a deep breath. 'Do you have an alternative suspect?'

Cullen thought it through for a few seconds and realised he didn't. 'Do I have to? Bain's going after Rob Thomson with very little evidence.'

'He's under pressure to get someone,' said McNeill. 'I'm not defending his behaviour but unless we've got a credible alternative, Bain won't listen to you.'

Cullen looked out of the driver's window across the car park, past the rows of cars, to the ramp up to street level at the end. He thought about what she said — much as he hated to admit it, he really didn't have an alternative. She was right.

'Are you still going home?' said McNeill.

'I'm not exactly doing much good here, am I?' said Cullen. 'And I'm certainly getting no thanks for it.'

'Just because Bain doesn't appreciate your efforts, doesn't mean you're not helping,' said McNeill. 'You're probably the only one finding leads.'

'Thanks.'

'Why do you think it's not Rob Thomson?'

Cullen drummed his fingers on the steering wheel. 'I don't know whether he did it or not, but I do know we don't have any solid evidence against him. Everything we have is just circumstantial, hypothetical supposition. Bain needs a collar and Thomson looks like he fits the bill. That CCTV footage is the clincher for me. It's totally inconclusive. All he can say definitively is it's a big man in a hoodie. And those death threats are just hearsay as far as I can tell. We've got nobody backing it up. No corroboration at all.'

'Has anyone denied them, though?' said McNeill.

Cullen frowned. 'Just Rob Thomson, I suppose.'

'And who else have you tried?' said McNeill.

'Caroline's friends on Schoolbook.' Cullen thought it through

— Angela had contacted more people than he had, but neither of them had found anyone who'd heard of the threats. He punched the steering wheel. 'I've been a total idiot.'

'Eh?'

'You've just given me a good idea.'

ullen knocked on the door. After a few seconds, it was answered.

Amy Cousens looked awful, her eyes circled with dark rings. This was the first time Cullen had seen her since Caroline's body was found. 'What do you want?'

'I need to speak to you about a couple of things,' said Cullen.

'Come in, then,' said Amy, somewhat reluctantly.

Cullen followed her inside. Jack was sitting playing with his Doctor Who dolls, though he appeared quieter than before. He was surprised the boy was still there. He wondered if Jack knew what had happened to his mother.

Amy collapsed into the armchair. 'I take it there's been nothing?'

Cullen grimaced. 'Not yet, I'm afraid.'

'Jesus.' Amy had a hanky in her hand and she clenched it tighter. 'I hope they catch him.'

'How are you doing?' said Cullen.

Amy sniffed back a tear. 'It's hard. I'm not coping too well. I can't believe she's dead. Looking after Jack is keeping my mind off it.'

It was the opposite reaction to that of Caroline's parents the other day — no stoic Calvinist 'get on with it', just a tidal wave of emotion. He gestured towards Jack. 'How's he doing?'

'Not great,' said Amy. 'He keeps asking where his mummy is. Caz's dad came through this morning. He's clearing out her flat. He's taking Jack back to Carnoustie this evening.'

'How's Rob taking that?'

Amy sighed. 'From what I hear he's fine with it. So long as he can see him every so often, he said he doesn't mind. Besides, he's got a few things on his plate.'

Cullen noted it down.

'Why are you here?' said Amy. 'I don't need you to babysit me, you know?'

'I'm not attempting to,' said Cullen. 'Did Caroline ever say anything about Rob making death threats against her?'

Amy sat forward in the chair, like she'd been jolted. '*Death threats*?'

'Yes,' said Cullen. 'After they divorced. Someone who knew Caroline told us it was common knowledge in Carnoustie.'

Amy shrugged. 'Caroline didn't have much to do with that place after she left university. Obviously she still saw her parents, but she didn't go back to see her pals or anything. I'm not surprised there were rumours like that going round, though.'

'Not surprised?'

'Well, you must know what small towns are like,' said Amy. 'People make shite up and, before you know, it's spread all around the place.'

'Do you know if Rob kept in touch with people there?' said Cullen.

'Don't think so.'

'Okay.' Cullen figured the rumours had to come from Caroline's friends if there was any truth to them — Thomson wasn't likely to go around bragging about them. 'Can you give me a little bit more about the sort of relationship Caroline and Rob had after the divorce?'

Amy stared at the coffee table. 'From what I remember, Rob really backed off, just let the divorce go through. I don't think he even saw Jack till the divorce papers were signed.'

'How long would that have been?' said Cullen.

'Couple of months.'

'And after the divorce, how often did he see him?'

'Afterwards, it was just Rob picking Jack up for his paternal visits,' said Amy. 'And not every time he was supposed to, either. Rob and Caroline didn't speak about anything other than Rob's access.'

'You mention he wasn't reliable,' said Cullen. 'Did Caroline give him a hard time about it? Did she make anything of it?'

'Hardly,' said Amy. 'She figured they were better off without him in their lives. She didn't push it. She'd bitch to me about it, but it was more about having to change her plans last minute when he didn't show up.'

'And you never heard of any death threats?'

'No way,' said Amy. 'Caroline would've told me.'

71

Cullen talked as he walked onto Leith Walk, clutching his mobile to his ear.

'Mr Allen, it's DC Cullen again. We spoke on Friday about Caroline Adamson.'

'I remember.' Steve Allen sounded torn up about her death.

'Are you okay?' said Cullen.

'No, I'm not doing too good. I suppose I'll cope. Eventually. Have you got anywhere?'

'We're making good progress,' said Cullen. 'I wanted to ask you some more questions, if that's okay?'

'Fine,' said Allen.

'Okay,' said Cullen. 'You'd been friends with Caroline from your Carnoustie days, that's correct, isn't it?'

'It is.'

'We recently received some information from an acquaintance of Caroline's that Rob Thomson had made death threats to her after their divorce,' said Cullen. 'I wondered if you'd heard the same story.'

'Who told you that?'

'I'm not at liberty to divulge that,' said Cullen.

Allen exhaled down the line. 'I was one of Caroline's closest friends. She never told me anything like that and, believe me, she would have. We shared things with each other that we wouldn't with other people and neither of us would blab, certainly not to anyone from Carnoustie.' He almost spat out the name of the town.

'So just to confirm, you've never heard anything about death threats?' said Cullen.

'That's correct.'

'Thank you for your time,' said Cullen. 'I'll be in touch if I need to.'

He ended the call. He was outside Caroline's flat. He pressed the buzzer.

∿

DAVID ADAMSON CLUTCHED the cup of tea in his hand. 'So you've heard we're taking the boy up to Carnoustie today?'

Cullen nodded as he put his empty mug on the window sill of Caroline's living room. Most of the furniture had gone, the flat an empty shell. The room was piled high with boxes and bin bags, most of her possessions now stowed away.

'It's for the best,' said Adamson. 'He's a lovely wee laddie. He doesn't deserve what's happened to him. None of us do.' He took another sip of tea. 'Are you any closer to finding this animal?'

'I can assure you we're doing all we can,' said Cullen. 'We're still progressing a few leads. We're confident we'll find whoever killed your daughter.'

'I hear he did this to other girls,' said Adamson. 'Is that right?'

Cullen nodded slowly. 'There have been some other murders in the city over the last couple of days and we're investigating any links, as we are with any murders over the last few years.'

Adamson gripped the cup in his hand. 'Why haven't you got him yet?'

'There's nothing I can confirm yet, Mr Adamson, but I can assure you this case has the highest priority in Lothian & Borders just now.'

Adamson put his cup onto the coffee table.

'We received a report your son-in-law made some death threats against Caroline,' said Cullen.

Adamson frowned at him.

'I take it you weren't aware of this?'

'No,' said Adamson. 'No, I wasn't.'

'Is it likely you wouldn't have heard?'

Adamson paused for a few seconds. 'My daughter could be very headstrong. She didn't want to share much with either myself or my wife.'

His eyes welled up — Cullen thought about how his own parents didn't know much about his private life either.

Adamson cleared his throat. 'No, I'm sure there was nothing like that, understand? I know his father very well and I still play golf with him. We were both very disappointed with what happened between Caroline and Rob, you know? But it happened.'

'How would you describe their relationship after the divorce?' said Cullen.

'After the divorce?' Adamson took a deep breath then sat forward on the sofa, leaning in towards Cullen. 'I don't know. Things seemed to improve between them. It was fairly amicable. And believe you me, if I'd had wind of anything like these threats, I would've battered him, regardless of how big he is.'

72

Half an hour later, Cullen sat in the station canteen at a table in the corner, keeping away from everyone. In truth, he was hiding from another confrontation with Bain. The information he'd just gained was bound to kick off another fight, especially if Bain was trying to get the PF to charge Rob Thomson.

He took the final bite of his chicken salad sandwich and crumpled the bag into a ball, before drinking the last of the Dr Pepper.

It was after half six in the evening and he was messing about with his iPhone, checking the Aberdeen football news on the BBC. There were rumours they were signing some guy who had played for Hearts a few years previously. He didn't have great expectations for the coming season. When Craig Brown became Aberdeen manager, Cullen's flatmate Tom reckoned he would make them hard to beat — in Cullen's eyes, all he'd done was make them unable to win.

A notification pinged up from the Schoolbook app — another message from Alison. *'Looking forward to meeting tonight. See you at eight.'*

He couldn't remember arranging to meet her. It must have been something he said the previous evening as he rushed off.

His reply read *'Not likely to get away tonight. Will call.'*

He had no intention of calling.

He sighed then ran a search for Martin Webb again, to see if anything had changed with the account. Schoolbook hadn't removed the profile yet, the same chiselled model face beaming out of the page.

After a moment's hesitation, he tapped on the button to add Martin Webb as a friend.

He immediately regretted it. He put his phone down, feeling like an idiot. That's something I can't undo, he thought.

The phone pinged again. He picked it up — another message from Alison — *'I understand, but you need to make some time for me.'* He had no idea what she thought their relationship status was, but it wasn't what it said on her Schoolbook page.

Another message pinged up on the screen — he and Martin Webb were now friends. He sat and stared at the handset for a few minutes, thinking it through. The account was not only active but Martin Webb was still using it. Cullen wondered if it was automatic or a manual action on the part of whoever was behind the account. Rob Thomson wasn't in police custody at the moment, so it played right into Bain's vendetta.

Eventually, Cullen replied to the message from Martin Webb. *'Please call me.'* He put his mobile number in and sent the message.

73

C ullen walked through the Technical Support Unit floor, heading towards Kidd's desk.

'How are you getting on with that new pipe, or whatever you called it?' said Cullen.

'I'm getting there.'

Cullen grabbed a chair from an adjacent desk. 'Good.'

After a few seconds, Kidd sighed. 'What are you after? I'm busy here. I could do with either you asking me something or pissing off.'

'I might have done something stupid,' said Cullen. 'I added Martin Webb as a friend.'

Kidd glared at Cullen for a few seconds. 'Why on earth did you think that was a good idea?'

'I don't know,' said Cullen, 'I wasn't thinking. I just did it.'

'You're an absolute idiot.'

'I know I am,' said Cullen. 'But he accepted me.'

Kidd frowned. 'You're pulling my leg.'

'No,' said Cullen. 'Do they have automatic acceptance on that site?'

'Nope,' said Kidd. 'It's all active. Was chatting to the new guy at Schoolbook this morning about that. They're trying to be like the anti-Facebook. They don't do anything to your data you haven't explicitly agreed.'

'Other than give it to the police,' said Cullen.

Kidd chuckled.

'Can you look at the IP address?' said Cullen. 'He's still on there.'

'I can't just now,' said Kidd. 'I'm not getting another extract until ten this evening.'

'I'll see you first thing tomorrow then.'

'I don't doubt it,' said Kidd. 'You're a total cowboy.'

Cullen got up to leave. He had a thought and sat down again, gesturing at the machine corpse on Kidd's desk. 'How's it going with the PCs from Caroline and Debi's offices?'

Kidd slumped back in his chair. 'I've had six voicemails from Bain asking me the same thing.'

'Have you replied to him?'

Kidd laughed. 'No. We've been flat out since we got them this morning.' He pointed at the contents of his desk. 'I'm just about finished going through Debi's work PC just now.'

'And?'

'Nothing,' said Kidd. 'Not a sausage. She wasn't using the chat app on it, so there's no dice, I'm afraid.'

'Did you look at anything from Gail?' said Cullen.

'That prick Irvine brought her netbook up which I'll do next,' said Kidd.

Cullen nodded. 'Okay, I'll come back and see you tomorrow.'

Kidd slowly exhaled. 'Fine. Can you piss off now?'

McNEILL WAS SITTING at her desk when Cullen got back to the Incident Room. 'How did your idea turn out?'

'Not bad.' Cullen sat down, thinking about telling her he'd added Martin Webb as a friend. 'I managed to speak to Amy Cousens, Steve Allen and Caroline's father. None of them know about the death threats. We've now got four people actively denying them, though one of them is Rob Thomson.'

'We need to get to the bottom of this,' said McNeill. 'Who gave us this information in the first place?'

Cullen stopped. 'No idea. Angela made the call.'

They looked over at her desk and walked over.

Angela looked up at them. 'I get worried when it's both of you.'

'How many people have corroborated the death threats story?' said Cullen.

Angela looked down her list. 'None.'

'And Miller?' said Cullen.

Angela shrugged. 'No idea.'

'Where is he?' said Cullen.

'Not got back from Ayr, I suppose.' Angela picked up a sheet of paper. 'Nope, doesn't look like he's had any either.'

'Who was it told you about these death threats?' said McNeill.

'Hang on.' Angela flicked through her own notebook. 'There you go — some guy called Duncan Wilson.'

74

Cullen froze. 'Did you say Duncan Wilson?'

McNeill was frowning as well.

'Who's he?' said Angela.

'He's the DBA at Schoolbook,' said Cullen. 'The techy Kidd's been dealing with.'

'Are you sure it's the same one?' said McNeill.

Angela woke up her computer and navigated to Schoolbook. She tapped a few keys then pointed at the screen. 'Here's his profile. He's a friend of Caroline's.'

Cullen looked at a moody photograph of the same man they'd met at Schoolbook. 'That's him. When was the last time you spoke to him?'

'First thing this morning,' said Angela. 'He was going to try and remember who told him about the threats and call me back.'

'And has he?' said Cullen.

'No,' said Angela. 'I was going to chase him, but I've been busy.'

'Do you think there actually is anyone?' said McNeill.

'Seems unlikely,' said Angela.

'Call him back,' said McNeill.

Angela picked up her phone and dialled. 'Voicemail.'

McNeill played with her notebook for a few seconds. 'Have you got his home address?'

Angela ran her finger down the screen. 'Portobello, by the look of things.'

McNeill got up. 'We're going to go and see this guy. I'm fed up being pissed about. Scott, you're coming with me.'

'What about me?' said Angela.

'Finish checking through her friends list,' said McNeill. 'We need to keep Bain happy.'

Angela looked disappointed.

Miller arrived, a smirk on his face. His tie was loosened at the collar and he carried his suit jacket over his shoulder.

'Where the hell have you been?' said McNeill.

'Me and Wilko were over at Gail's folks in Ayr,' said Miller. 'Just got back now. I was wondering, can't find the gaffer. Do you mind if I slope off early to go to the football?'

McNeill looked him up and down, then grinned mischievously as she shook her head. 'Grab your coat, we've got a job for you.'

75

McNeill got out of Miller's silver Saxo just as Cullen parked alongside. Wilson's flat was just off King's Road roundabout in Portobello, not far from Cullen's flat.

'This is your neck of the woods, isn't it?' said McNeill.

'Aye,' said Cullen. 'I stay just along the high street.'

Cullen looked up at the block of flats, a red sandstone building called College House. He knew a little of the history of the place. It had been a chocolate factory then became a technical institute in the fifties — WM Ramsay Technical Institute was still emblazoned on the front in brass lettering — before being redeveloped into flats in the early nineties.

McNeill nodded at Miller. 'Keith, stay here and keep an eye out.'

'Aw, man.' Miller looked over towards Easter Road, a couple of miles distant. 'They'll be kicking off soon.'

'Forget about the football.' McNeill led Cullen round to the door at the front of the building. 'Buzz it.'

Cullen pressed the intercom labelled Wilson for a few seconds. No answer.

'Give it ten seconds,' said McNeill, 'then try again.'

They waited in silence, looking at each other nervously. Ten seconds up, he buzzed again, pressing for longer this time. Still no answer.

McNeill pushed the adjacent buzzer, which had the name Gillespie in pencil. The door clicked open, no questions asked.

Cullen held the door open for McNeill. 'Very chivalrous,' she said as she stepped through.

They set off up the stairs. Cullen looked up at the elaborate glass ceiling, the shadow from the chimneys cast across it. The door to the first flat on the second floor was ajar, fairly unimaginative dance music booming out accompanied by an unmistakable sweet smell.

'Hash,' said Cullen.

McNeill gestured for Cullen to lead. He got out his warrant card and moved inside. McNeill closed the door behind them.

'Through here, Jim,' said a voice from the living room. Male, Glaswegian.

'It's the police.' Cullen was struggling to be heard over the music.

'Aye, like hell it is, Jimmy.' A cackle followed.

Cullen entered the living room. A man in his late twenties sat in a dressing gown, looking away from them, through the front window down King's Road towards the promenade and the beach. He held a joint in his hand and took a hefty toke. 'Sit down, Jimmy.'

Cullen crossed the room and held his warrant card in front of the man's face.

Gillespie's head whipped round and he did a double take. He jumped to his feet.

'Jesus— Who the— GET OUT!'

'Mr Gillespie,' said Cullen, his voice steady, 'we're from Lothian & Borders Police.'

'It's for personal use,' said Gillespie.

'You might want to turn the music down a bit,' said Cullen.

Gillespie fumbled for a remote control and turned the stereo off.

'We're not interested in your drugs,' said McNeill. Gillespie seemed to relax. 'Not today anyway. We're looking for your neighbour, Duncan Wilson.'

'He's out of town,' said Gillespie.

'Where?' said Cullen.

'Working in Glasgow for a couple of days, I think,' said Gillespie.

Cullen frowned. 'I thought he worked in Livingston?'

'No idea.' Gillespie shrugged. 'He told us he was away through west for a few days.'

'Do you know when he'll be back?' said McNeill.

'No idea,' said Gillespie. 'He's coming round for the football after work on Friday.'

'Do you have a contact number for him?' said Cullen.

'No, I don't.' Gillespie laughed. 'Don't really need to phone him given he just lives next door.'

'Do you know where he's working?' said Cullen.

Gillespie shrugged again. 'No, just that it's Glasgow.'

'In future,' said McNeill, 'you should make sure you know who you're letting in.'

'And keep the music down,' said Cullen.

'Aye, I will do,' said Gillespie.

They left the flat. McNeill crossed to Wilson's door and peered through the letterbox. 'Definitely nobody in.'

'What next?' said Cullen.

'Keep trying his mobile, I suppose,' said McNeill. 'If we don't get anything back tonight, we'll put out a call for him.'

They walked to the car in silence. Miller was nowhere to be seen.

Before he opened his door, Cullen thought of something. 'This fits perfectly for Caroline's murder, doesn't it?'

'How do you mean?' said McNeill.

'Well, you know,' said Cullen. 'It's all back roads from here up to Minto Street, through the park. No one's going to see a thing. He could have walked home just as easily as Rob Thomson.'

'You could be right,' said McNeill.

Miller wandered over. 'Nothing round the back.'

'Thanks.' McNeill smiled. 'Keith, I want you to stake out the building.'

Miller looked crestfallen. 'But I've got tickets for the game.'

'And we've got a triple murder investigation,' said McNeill, her voice hard.

'Fine,' said Miller. 'What am I supposed to be doing?'

'You're training to be a detective, Keith, show us some of your detection skills. If Duncan Wilson turns up, I want to know.'

~

CULLEN DROVE THEM BOTH BACK, leaving Miller and his car at Wilson's flat. 'So what do we do?'

'I don't know,' said McNeill. 'Do you think Wilson is a suspect?'

'He's definitely someone we need to speak to.'

'I don't think we should go to Bain with this yet,' said McNeill.

'Why not?'

'He's running around trying to pin this on Rob Thomson,' said McNeill. 'The last thing we want is to point him at another innocent person.'

'Agreed,' said Cullen. 'I'm going to get to the bottom of these death threats. Tonight.'

'Do it,' said McNeill. 'And try and get hold of Wilson.'

Cullen rubbed the back of his neck. 'I can't believe I've been so sloppy.'

'How?'

'If it's him, I can't help but think Gail McBride might still be alive,' said Cullen.

'You can't allow yourself to think like that,' said McNeill. 'You're exhausted. You were supposed to be off on Saturday and Sunday, instead you've been putting in fourteen-hour shifts. And you've been pulled from pillar to post by Bain.'

'I guess you're right.' Cullen sighed. 'Doesn't make it feel much easier.'

'I don't think you putting two and two together earlier would've swayed Bain anyway,' said McNeill. 'In his world, he's looking for a five not a four from a pair of twos.'

'And we don't know Wilson is the man we want, either,' said Cullen. 'Back to your point — we don't want another innocent man in the frame here.'

76

Cullen sat back in his chair and looked around the Incident Room. There was still a large number of officers in the room, with at least the same again off doing the rounds in the various channels of investigation Bain was running.

He'd been trying to contact Wilson for an hour, in amongst attacking his portion of the list, which now felt like pointless admin. He picked up his phone and dialled the number for Gregor Aitchison — Wilson's boss — figuring he might know where he was.

'Hi, this is Gregor.' There was pub noise in the background.

'Mr Aitchison, it's DC Cullen of Lothian & Borders.'

'What do you want?' The sound was getting quieter in the background — he was clearly going outside.

'I want to speak to Duncan Wilson,' said Cullen.

'He's not been in today.'

'That's what I was calling you about,' said Cullen. 'I believe he's through in Glasgow.'

'I wouldn't know.'

'Isn't he full time at Schoolbook, then?'

'No, he just does three days a week,' said Aitchison. 'He's been in for the last seven days solid, mind, but he's normally only part time. He's self-employed. He gets a decent rate, I can tell you, but we just pay him by the day. I know he's got other clients, but it's usually last minute work he picks up online when he's not working for us. It can be quite lucrative, too. The banks are big on it. Keeps people off the payroll.'

'Is Mr Wilson due in tomorrow?'

'No.'

'I see,' said Cullen. 'I've got his mobile number and his flat address. Do you have any other contact details?'

Aitchison yawned down the line. 'Sorry, that's all I've got as well. Don't even have an email address for the guy.'

'How's he been recently?'

'Busy,' said Aitchison. 'I mean, that Kidd boy of yours has been keeping him on his toes for the last couple of days.'

'And before that?'

'He's always been one to throw himself into his work,' said Aitchison. 'He's always looking into the security protocols we've got and adjusting them if needs be.'

'How's his mood been over the last few days?' said Cullen.

'Look, what is this?'

'Mr Wilson supplied some additional information that may prove crucial to the case,' said Cullen. 'I just wanted to get some background to his character.'

'Right, well, he's been quite upbeat over the last few days. Walking round like he owns the place.'

'Okay,' said Cullen, 'thanks for your time. I'll be in touch.'

ANOTHER HOUR LATER, Cullen had just about finished his portion of the list. It was proving difficult to track down the last couple of friends. He was almost ready to go out and visit their homes.

He tried Wilson again, the fourth time since they'd got back. It rang and rang. He was about to give up when it was finally answered. 'This is Duncan.' It sounded like he was driving.

'Mr Wilson, this is DC Scott Cullen of Lothian & Borders.'

'And?'

'You've been dealing with a colleague of mine, PC Caldwell, about some alleged death threats made by a suspect in our murder inquiry. Have you managed to remember who told you about those death threats yet?'

'Hasn't anybody else told you yet?'

'No,' said Cullen. 'We need you to try and remember who it was told you.'

Wilson gave a deep sigh. 'Okay. I've been thinking this through, trying to remember. I was just about to give your colleague a call.' There was a lengthy pause. 'It was Kim Milne who told me.'

Cullen noted it down. 'Kim Milne?'

'Yes,' said Wilson. 'I think she's Rob Thomson's girlfriend.'

'And how do you know her?'

There was another pause. 'We worked together a few years ago,' said Wilson. 'We were good friends.'

'Where was this?'

'At Alba Bank.'

Cullen was confused. 'You worked at Alba Bank?'

'Yeah, till May last year,' said Wilson. 'That was before I went contracting.'

'I see,' said Cullen. 'And you're sure this came from Kim.'

'Yes, I'd stake my life on it.'

'Is there anyone else who may have told you?'

Another pause. 'Now you mention it, there was someone else. Can't quite think who.'

If they were in the same room, someone would have to hold Cullen back. 'Mr Wilson, I want you to report to Leith Walk station at eight am tomorrow to give a formal statement, otherwise I'll be bringing you in for questioning regarding wasting police time.'

'Okay, okay,' said Wilson. 'I'll be there.'

Cullen ended the call. He was in half a mind to get him in that evening but wanted him to fester overnight, figuring a sleepless night could work wonders.

He picked up his phone and called Miller to tell him he could come back in or go home. No answer.

He leaned back in his chair and stared up at the air conditioning units dotting the ceiling at irregular intervals. He needed to speak to Kim Milne. She might have been covering for Thomson when they interviewed her. It threw the validity of her alibis into doubt. Maybe Bain was right.

He felt a hand grip his shoulder.

'Sundance, Sundance, Sundance.' Bain had a shit-eating grin on his face.

'What?'

'Case closed,' said Bain. 'Caught Rob Thomson red-handed. He's killed again.'

'Who?'

Bain's grin widened. 'Kim Milne.'

77

Cullen walked up the stairs ahead of Bain's entourage, finding McNeill on the second floor landing. The flat door was smashed in and loosely propped up against the wall. There were already SOCOs milling around.

'What happened?' said Cullen.

McNeill nodded recognition at him. 'Anonymous 999 call. Someone heard banging and shouting from the flat and called it in. Some uniform from Gayfield Square ran round, burst open the door and caught him in the bedroom with the body. She had her throat cut with a knife, just like the others. She was already dead.'

'Holy shit.' Cullen entered the flat and signed into the outer locus on the clipboard and put on a SOCO suit. 'So Thomson did it?'

'Certainly looks that way,' said McNeill.

'Bain seemed pleased,' said Cullen.

'Of course he is. He's just solved four murders. Better get used to calling him DCI Bain. Where is he?'

'He's speaking to Wilkinson and Irvine downstairs,' said Cullen.

They heard a call from behind — they turned to face Bain, with the other two following in his wake. 'Butch, Sundance, come with me. Wilko, have a peek in the bedroom.'

Cullen and McNeill followed Bain through to the living room, while Wilkinson and Irvine followed their orders. An officer in full jumpsuit stood outside the bedroom holding a clipboard.

Thomson was on the red leather sofa, his head in his hands, wearing the same business suit as when Cullen met him the previous Friday. A uniformed officer sat on either side of him, both wearing full protective uniform under their jumpsuits.

Bain snorted. 'Care to bring me up to speed?'

One of them got up — his hair was dark brown and cut in the same style Paul Weller and Johnny Marr had adhered to since the eighties. 'DI Bain, is it?' He had a London accent. 'PC Simon Buxton.' He held out his hand.

Bain shook his hand. 'Hall.' He thumbed behind him. 'Cullen, with me. McNeill, keep an eye on the suspect.'

They went back out into the hall and slipped into the recess just outside the box room, out of the way of the officers milling around.

'So then, PC Buxton,' said Bain, 'tell me what happened here?'

'We got a call into the station of a domestic in progress at this address,' said Buxton. 'It was flagged on HOLMES in a murder inquiry.'

Cullen thought of Miller keying all the information into the system, everyone else treating it as a frivolity, a piece of procedure to be delegated to a junior officer.

'We're based in Gayfield Square, so this is just round the corner,' said Buxton. 'Me and Tommy ran round. The first floor tenant let us in. We came up to the flat, tried the door. Nobody answered so we broke it down. We found the suspect in the bedroom, bent over the body with a knife in his hands.'

'He was just standing there?' said Bain.

'Yeah,' said Buxton.

'Was she dead?'

'She was by that point, yeah.'

'Did he put up much of a fight?' said Cullen.

'Not at all,' said Buxton. 'I was surprised. Tommy grabbed him and I disarmed him. He just let us. He was crying.'

'Guilt.' Bain grinned. 'Did you get your prints on the knife?'

'No, I was careful,' said Buxton. 'It's with Jimmy Anderson now. He'll get the prints done quick smart, I'd expect.'

'Was there anything else?' said Cullen.

'There was a blue rope round her throat,' said Buxton. 'Like you'd use camping, you know? Jimmy's sent it off to the lab as well.'

Bain nodded at Cullen. 'Same as the others. Oh ye of little faith.'

'Did Thomson say anything when you grabbed him?' said Cullen.

'Nothing,' said Buxton.

'A sure sign,' said Bain.

Cullen looked around the flat at the busy crime scene, thinking hard. Something nagged at his brain. 'You said you came up to the flat. Did the 999 specify which flat it was?'

Buxton frowned. 'Think so, yeah. I mean I didn't take it. Someone out in Bilston got it from the OAC in Inverness. They'd flagged it with your murder inquiry on HOLMES but it got put through to us as well, being the nearest station.'

'They specified the flat?' said Cullen.

'Yeah,' said Buxton.

'Have you been round the flats here?' said Cullen.

'Not yet,' said Buxton, 'we wanted to secure the suspect and wait for you guys to arrive.'

'Good work.'

Buxton headed back through.

Cullen thought it was odd the call identified the specific flat, but wasn't going to press it with Bain just yet.

'Guess who's going to be doing the flats,' said Bain.

Cullen rubbed his face. 'Will do.'

'Right, let's get in and about Mr Thomson then, shall we?' Bain led through to the living room. He pulled over a chair from the other side of the room — checking the nearest SOCO was finished with it — and sat right in front of Thomson.

Cullen hovered beside him. Buxton returned to his position beside Thomson on the sofa and McNeill was now leaning against the wall with her arms folded.

'Mr Thomson,' said Bain. 'Can you hear me?'

Thomson looked up. 'Yes, I can.' His voice was deep and staccato, but he appeared lucid enough.

'Can you explain what happened here?' said Bain.

'I've no idea.'

'Come on, Mr Thomson, you need to try harder than that,' said Bain. 'Your bird's dead, you've got her blood all over you and your prints are all over the knife. It's not looking good for you, is it?'

'She was dead when I found her,' said Thomson.

'Oh, you *found* her, did you?' said Bain.

'Came back from work,' said Thomson. 'When I got in, I couldn't find Kim. She was in the bedroom. Dead.'

'Can you tell me why you didn't phone the police when you found her?' said Bain.

'I don't know,' said Thomson. 'I was going to. They just turned up, didn't they?'

Bain leaned forward, right into Thomson's face. 'You're not getting away with this. That's you proper buggered now. Four murders — that makes you a serial killer. You'll be away for a long, long time. They'll write books about you.'

He got up, looked at Buxton. 'Constable, can you read him his rights then take him to Leith Walk for questioning, please?'

He looked at Cullen and McNeill and pointed out of the room. 'You two, come with me.' He led them from the room, back into the alcove in the hall by the box room door. 'I think we've finally cracked it.'

McNeill shrugged. 'Looks that way.'

'It does, it does,' said Bain. 'Butch — can you go to his work and find out when this bastard left this evening.'

'And me?' said Cullen.

'Like I said, Sundance, visit the other flats in this stairwell. I want to speak to whoever called this in.'

78

Cullen walked into a packed Incident Room an hour and a half later. He stood at the back and leaned against the wall.

Bain was at the front, leading the briefing with the same grin he wore earlier. He pointed at Cullen. 'So, just to recap for DC Cullen's benefit, we've charged Rob Thomson with the murders of Caroline Adamson, Debi Curtis and Kim Milne. DS McNeill has managed to ascertain that Mr Thomson left the Alba Bank office at the back of seven, which fits with the timeline we've established. The initial round of questioning by DI Wilkinson and DS Irvine has yielded no further information, as you would expect.'

Cullen couldn't tell if the comment referred to Thomson's reticence or Wilkinson's incompetence.

'Jimmy Deeley's initial findings show the murder of Kim Milne follows a similar pattern to the others, but this is still to be fully confirmed. We haven't charged Thomson with Gail McBride's murder yet but that's a mere formality I'll iron out with the Procurator Fiscal tomorrow morning.'

In Cullen's mind, Gail was the most tenuous connection. The others were definitely linked to each other — Caroline and Debi by the Schoolbook identity of Martin Webb, Kim to Rob's presence. They were all apparently linked by the method of execution.

But the only connection between Rob and Gail was they both worked at Alba Bank.

Bain held up an envelope. 'I've just got the forensic report on the threads found in the wounds of both Caroline and Debi. They were from the very same rope. The strands from Debi's body had traces of Caroline's blood on them.'

He paused for a moment then grinned. 'At the scene, we found the actual rope around Kim Milne's neck along with the knife that killed her. Forensics should confirm the same knife was used in all four murders.' He took a sip from a mug of coffee. 'Now, Cullen, can you give us an update on the 999 call?'

Every officer in the room turned to face Cullen. He felt himself redden slightly. He moved away from the wall and cleared his throat. 'I visited every flat in the stairwell and the two adjacent stairs. Where there was no-one present, I managed to get a contact number from neighbours, or I crossed them off if they were away on holiday. I've not found anyone who'll own up to making the call.'

Bain scowled. 'Typical.'

'It's allowed to be anonymous,' said Cullen.

Bain laughed. 'Looks like it was a passer-by then.'

'How could a passer-by point us to a specific flat?' said Cullen.

Bain shook his head. 'Anyway, DCI Turnbull has offered to buy everyone a drink across the road. We've agreed to a late start tomorrow — turn up at nine rather than the usual. We're not finished with this case, but we're on the home straight.' He clapped his hands together. 'Right, off you go to the pub.'

The room emptied, accompanied by a bustle of chatter.

Cullen made a beeline for Bain.

'So you found nothing then, Sundance?' Bain stroked his moustache. 'Still leaves a hole in this bloody case.'

'Just the one?'

'Leave it out, Sundance,' said Bain. 'How's it going with the guy who told us about the death threats? We need that nailed down soon.'

'He was through in Glasgow when the murder happened tonight, according to him and his neighbour,' said Cullen.

'See, there you go,' said Bain, 'he's got an alibi. Stop looking.'

'Nobody's actually confirmed the death threats yet,' said

Cullen.

Bain shrugged. 'Doesn't matter now. We've nailed Thomson to these murders.'

'I'm not one hundred per cent convinced,' said Cullen.

Bain raised his arms. 'You need to lighten up, Sundance. This is a big moment. This'll look good on your record, you know, playing a key role in solving a multiple murder.'

'Do you honestly think this will get a conviction?' said Cullen. 'Our evidence linking the crimes together is circumstantial at best.'

'I'm confident.' Bain slowly nodded his head. 'The Fiscal is as well. And this was before we caught him red-handed. We've got plenty of time to consolidate the other evidence we need before it gets anywhere near a jury.'

'Fine, whatever.' Cullen sighed. 'I'm just sceptical, that's all. I think we're putting all of our eggs in one basket.'

'No,' said Bain. 'We've *found* four eggs in one basket. There's a world of difference.'

Cullen just shrugged his shoulders.

'Are you going to come for a pint?' said Bain.

'Aye, I'll see you over there. I just want to write up my door-to-door.'

Bain raised an eyebrow. 'If you're not desperate to get fired into the lager, could you do me a favour?'

'Depends what it is.'

'I've had to put Wilkinson and Irvine in with Rob Thomson at Turnbull's insistence to ensure independence or some such shite,' said Bain. 'I want you to sit in, as I could do with Wilkinson over at the boozer.'

'Why?'

Bain looked away from Cullen. 'Need the superior officers to show a proper thank you to the junior officers.'

Cullen clocked it immediately — Bain didn't want Wilkinson gaining any ground on him in the promotion stakes, so he was using some sort of solidarity with the junior officers as a ruse to prevent him uncovering anything before Bain. 'Fine.'

Bain patted him on the shoulder. 'That's my boy.'

Anyway, Cullen wanted the opportunity to ask Rob Thomson some questions about Gail McBride.

79

Thomson slouched in his chair across the table from Cullen and Irvine. He looked terrible, his white shirt soaked through with sweat and dark rings under his eyes. A brown leather jacket was draped over the back of his chair. Campbell McLintock once again sat in and had done all of the talking since Cullen entered.

'I'll ask you again.' Irvine's mouth was pounding on the contents of a pack of chewing gum when he wasn't speaking. 'Where did the knife come from?'

Thomson continued to stare at the table. He and McLintock had obviously practiced their hand-offs since the earlier interview. Thomson was mute throughout, deferring to the lawyer.

'I will refer you to my client's previous comment,' said McLintock.

Irvine glowered — he'd made no progress with the case since Cullen had arrived, only eliciting a stream of 'no comment' responses. The only thing he was in danger of doing was getting a punch in the face from McLintock. Bain's fears were obviously unfounded — Cullen couldn't imagine Wilkinson had somehow raised the bar before being relieved.

'Mr Thomson,' said Cullen, 'can you please explain how you know Gail McBride.'

Thomson frowned — it was obviously the first time they had used her name. 'Gail?'

'Please refrain from any further comment,' said McLintock.

'Wait a minute,' said Thomson. 'Why are you asking me about *Gail*?'

'Can you confirm you know a Gail McBride?' said Cullen.

'No further comment,' said McLintock.

Cullen sighed. 'I'll take it from your response you know Gail. She was murdered on Sunday night.'

Thomson snapped forward in his chair. 'Gail's dead?'

'Yes,' said Cullen.

Thomson closed his eyes. 'Fine, yes, I know Gail. *Knew* her. Christ.'

McLintock slapped his fountain pen on the desk.

'Thank you, Mr Thomson,' said Cullen. 'Can you elaborate on your relationship with Mrs McBride?'

'I worked with her for a while,' said Thomson. 'She works at Alba Bank too. I'm running the project to integrate Eire Finance with our systems. Gail worked in operations and used the system all the time. She was on the project as a subject matter expert on the first phase. I was in Dublin for about nine months. Gail was there for two or three.'

'I imagine being away must have been pretty hard on your marriage,' said Cullen.

'Of course it was,' said Thomson. 'I was over there, flying back every weekend. Sometimes we had stuff going in at the weekends as well, so I had to stay there.'

'And during this period your marriage fell apart, am I right?' said Cullen.

'Yes,' said Thomson. 'Caroline was nipping my head all the time — Jack this, Jack that.'

'And this was when you started seeing Kim Milne?'

'Aye. I didn't mean for anything to happen. The three of us were out — me, Gail and Kim — along with a big group of us. We had an expensive meal, few bottles of nice wine, all on expenses. Then we went on to a club.'

'I thought you were supposed to be *working* out there?' said Irvine.

Thomson shrugged his shoulders. 'Not all the time.'

'This night out,' said Cullen, 'this was when you got together with Kim Milne?'

'Aye,' said Thomson. 'I can't remember the name of the club. Kim was dancing on the tables and we almost got chucked out. Gail was embarrassed, kept telling her to stop it, but...' He broke down in tears, muttering 'Kim'.

'I must insist we terminate this interview until my client is in a more receptive frame of mind,' said McLintock.

'Okay,' said Cullen. 'Interview terminated at twenty-two twenty-six hours.

Cullen didn't know how Bain would interpret this new connection.

80

As Cullen pushed open the Elm's front door, his phone rang — Alison. He let it ring out. He couldn't be bothered with that just now.

The Elm was absolutely rammed. Cullen recognised a few faces at various tables, but his attention was drawn to the bar. Bain was holding court — Irvine, Wilkinson and Holdsworth all hanging on his every word, along with an irritated-looking McNeill. Miller was at a table with McAllister.

Cullen's phone buzzed with a new text — Alison left a voicemail.

'Sundance.' Bain was already three sheets to the wind — he held up his glass in toast. 'Well done, Scott Cullen, you cracked the case.'

Wilkinson looked bemused as he raised his glass.

Bain turned round to the barman and ordered a pint of Stella.

'How have I cracked the case?' said Cullen.

'You just linked him to Gail McBride,' said Bain. 'That's good work.'

'How did you find out?' said Cullen.

'Irvine just told me,' said Bain. 'Really good effort there, Sundance. Think I can charge Thomson with killing Gail McBride as well.'

'You know my thoughts on that,' said Cullen.

'None of that, Sundance,' said Bain. 'We're celebrating. It's not often we catch the bastard in the act and this time we have.'

Bain handed him his pint.

'Where's DCI Turnbull?' said McNeill.

'Updating the Chief Constable just now,' said Bain. 'Should be over here soon. It's his card behind the bar and Miller's already been taking liberties.'

McNeill took a sip of wine. 'I take it you're pleased, then?'

Bain grinned. 'Oh, God aye.' He turned round and started chatting to Irvine about the Rangers match.

Cullen backed away from the bar and started on his pint, sinking half of it in two quick gulps.

McNeill moved over to join him. 'You've done well.'

Cullen shrugged. 'I don't think I have.'

'If Jim's on a conference call with the Chief Constable, you'll be getting credit at that level. There's not many of us get that sort of attention.'

She was close to him, her eyes locked on his. Cullen wasn't sure what to do.

'Come on, Sharon, I've just made sure the wrong man is tried for this. Well, maybe not even the wrong man. Someone's going to be tried for the murders without real evidence. And I'm the one that's given Bain most of the stuff he's using. That he's misusing, even abusing.'

'He was caught red handed,' said McNeill.

'Have we got any witnesses to him stabbing her?' said Cullen. 'No. He left work at the back of seven, right?'

'Aye. Got it on CCTV backed up with his security pass.'

'We arrived at the flat at eight o'clock,' said Cullen. 'That's a hell of a lot of activity for one hour. He walked home from work, killed his girlfriend, then we get a 999, our boys pop round, catch him.'

McNeill closed her eyes. 'I don't have the energy for this, Scott. If you're right, the best we can hope for is it gets thrown out of court.'

Cullen took a sip of beer. Maybe she was right. Maybe he was pushing this too hard. Maybe he needed a break. He sighed. 'I'm not happy about it.'

'Me neither. Just try and enjoy the limelight for now. We'll sort something out tomorrow.'

'I finally got hold of Duncan Wilson,' said Cullen. 'He told me he heard about the death threats from Kim Milne.'

'Seriously?'

'Yeah, he used to work with her at Alba Bank.'

McNeill stared into space. 'The plot thickens.'

Cullen held up his glass and clinked it with hers. 'Well, here's cheers.'

McNeill raised an eyebrow. 'This doesn't get you off that drink, by the way.'

'I'd hoped it hadn't,' said Cullen. 'Let's set a date and time.'

'Tomorrow after work?' said McNeill. 'Whenever that is.'

'Fine by me,' said Cullen.

'Good.' McNeill drank, all the while keeping her eyes locked on his.

Cullen spotted Turnbull enter the pub. The DCI clocked Bain's group and headed over. McNeill hustled Cullen into the centre.

Turnbull beamed at him. 'DC Cullen, I gather you're responsible for a lot of the progress in the case?'

'I noticed a few links along the way,' said Cullen. 'I can't take all of the credit.'

'Nonsense,' said Turnbull. 'Brian, get this man another drink. I'll have a pint of IPA.'

Bain went to the bar and ordered.

Turnbull patted McNeill on the back. 'You're doing a great job of coaching young Cullen here, Sharon.'

McNeill grinned. 'Thanks.'

'I was just saying to Bill Duffin we need more young officers like the pair of you, especially detective sergeants who are looking to better the police service, rather than merely their own careers — those who take a long view of things.'

Bain and company slipped back to the bar, leaving Cullen with McNeill and Turnbull.

Cullen thought McNeill was flirting with Turnbull even more blatantly than she had with him.

'You should think about going for a DI job, Sharon,' said Turnbull, 'you've clearly got the skills.'

'I'll bear it in mind,' said McNeill. 'I've only been a DS for a year.'

'We've got ways and means of promoting people who demonstrate key behaviours, Sharon. Officers who deliver on our targets, you know that.'

Cullen went to the bar to fetch their pints.

Bain leaned over and spoke to him. 'Keep an eye on that one, Sundance. She'll shag anything to get ahead. Just you watch.' He turned away before Cullen could reply.

Cullen slowly shook his head before he went back. He handed Turnbull his pint, who took it without looking, totally engrossed in the world of Sharon McNeill.

Cullen noticed McAllister had left Miller on his own. He moved over, neither McNeill nor Turnbull noticing his departure. Sitting next to Miller, Cullen sipped his pint and tried to figure out what was going on. He was getting tied in to Bain's vendetta in a way he didn't like. In the upper echelons of Lothian & Borders, his name was being bandied about as the officer who'd pulled everything together. The real clincher was Thomson being caught with Kim's blood on his hands, but not from anything Cullen had done. Was Bain trying to spread the blame should the collar go pear-shaped?

'All right, Scotty,' said Miller, his voice slurred, 'didn't notice you there, my man.'

'Aye, I've only been sitting here for about five minutes, Keith.'

Miller looked broken already. If Bain was three sheets to the wind, Miller was the whole ream. He'd taken the free bar as an opportunity to consume as much as possible, as quickly and as stupidly as possible. The table was covered in empty beer and whisky glasses.

'You're a good copper, you know that?' said Miller. 'That's what everyone is saying.'

'Thanks.'

Miller rummaged around on the table looking for something else to drink. There was a glass of white wine on the far edge, the last remnants of some ice cubes floating on the top.

'Seen Caldwell?' said Cullen.

'She just left.' Miller held up the glass. He burped. 'Spoke to Jim Turnbull earlier, by the way, did I tell you?'

'No?'

'Aye, he's making me a proper DC.'

'When?'

'Early September,' said Miller.

Cullen couldn't believe it — he'd worked with Miller for a while now and had come to realise he was completely useless. There were a significant number of competent officers who were miles better than him, but who were in the wrong roles. Angela was a shining example. He held his glass up. 'Congratulations,' he said, not exactly meaning it.

Miller tried to clink glasses but missed. 'We got tonked tonight, by the way. Five nil. Aw, man.' He threw back some wine. 'Messi was superb. Best player I've ever seen in the flesh.' He leaned in close to Cullen, laughing conspiratorially. 'Don't tell the gaffer, right, but I went to the match.'

Cullen rolled his eyes. 'Keith, for Christ's sake, you were supposed to be watching that house for us.'

'Aye, I was, but there wasn't anybody there.'

Cullen wondered if he should tell Bain. 'You shouldn't do stuff like that, Keith. Turnbull could rescind his offer.'

'What does that mean?'

'Take it back.'

'Nothing bad happened,' said Miller.

Cullen knew there was no telling him. He might have to tell Turnbull himself.

'Look who it is.' McAllister was clutching two pints of lager. 'It's Robocop.' He sat and handed one to Miller. 'You're the hero of the hour, pal, everyone loves you. No idea why you're sitting here with us plebs. That DCI of yours is over there. Why don't you go lick his arse, get yourself a nice promotion out of it?'

Cullen gripped the pint glass tightly, barely controlling his anger. He put his half-empty glass on the table and got to his feet. 'Catch you later, Keith.'

He left the pub, his mind thinking of two things — a curry and a bottle of wine.

81

Cullen carried the plastic bag up the stairs, the smell wafting out. He was starving — the beer hadn't exactly helped. He'd had a few handfuls of Bombay mix in the Prince's Balti as he waited, but it only made him hungrier. As he unlocked the door to the flat, he noticed the lights were on. He checked his watch — quarter to eleven. Dawn was sitting at the table talking to someone. A girl. She turned around.

'Alison,' said Cullen.

She got up. 'Scott.'

'Where have you been?' said Dawn.

'At work. You know how it is.' He couldn't look Alison in the eye. He took off his jacket, put the bag on the table. He turned his gaze to Dawn. 'Are Johnny and Tom in?'

'They were at the Hibs match. I'm off to bed.' Dawn smiled at Alison. 'Nice meeting you.'

Dawn went into Johnny's room, leaving Cullen with Alison. She walked over to him.

Standing there, just the two of them, Cullen realised there was an opportunity. 'Listen, I'm sorry about having to dash off like that the other night. I've been really busy with work.'

'I understand.'

'It's genuine, believe me. I'm working on this murder case that's in the papers. I wish I could tell you about it.'

'It must be hard. Katie gave me your address, suggested I might as well come over.'

Cullen sighed. 'She did, did she?'

Alison bit her lip. 'Scott, I really like you. I understand about your job and... Well, I'm here.'

Shite, thought Cullen. Shite, shite, shite. What should he do? She looked good. She was here, throwing herself at him. He could get into something with her. He made a snap decision. 'Alison, thanks for coming over. I appreciate it.' He paused. 'But I'm just not looking to get involved with anyone just now.'

Alison's glare almost cut him in two. 'What?'

'I'm sorry, I'm really not,' said Cullen. 'It's the truth.'

Her eyes were full of fury. 'Then why the hell did your friend there talk to me for the last hour and a half about how sweet you are and how you're looking to settle down?'

Cullen closed his eyes. 'That's just Dawn, all right? She means well, but I'm just too busy for a relationship just now.'

Alison held his gaze for a few moments then shook her head. 'Katie was right about you.'

'I wouldn't listen to her. She was shagging that accountant behind my back.'

'Maybe if she'd seen your front more often she wouldn't have had to.'

'What was all that stuff on Schoolbook?' said Cullen. 'Saying you're in a relationship with me?'

Alison slapped his face. 'Scott, we slept together and went on a date. That's pretty close.'

'Not to me.'

Alison snatched up her jacket and made for the door, tears flowing down her face. 'You don't know what you're missing, Scott.'

As the door slam echoed through the flat, Cullen sat and put his head in his hands. He knew all too well what he was missing and that, well, he didn't want it.

He wouldn't miss it one bit.

'CULLEN, YOU ARE A STUPID BASTARD,' said Bain.

Cullen had just told him about making friends with Martin Webb on Schoolbook, expecting praise.

'You've probably jeopardised any chance of getting a conviction,' said Bain. 'A police officer doesn't get involved in a case in this manner. You've been like this all along, doing stupid shite for the last three months.'

'But I can—'

'But nothing.' Spittle covered Bain's chin. 'This is the sort of thing I'd expect from Monkey Boy Miller, not from you. I know you've put in for a DS position. I'll make sure you don't get it. You'll stay a DC forever, son, that's if they don't chuck you off the force.'

Cullen woke up with a start.

It was just a nightmare.

He sat up, relieved but with a deep ache in his gut and a throbbing head. He picked up a glass of water from the bedside table and took a sip. He couldn't get it out of his head. The Bain in his dream was right — he was a stupid bastard. What had he been thinking?

Christ knew what the consequences of his idiocy would be.

DAY 7

Wednesday
3rd August

82

C ullen sat at his desk at ten to nine and tore the lid off the double-strength coffee he'd bought from the canteen. The Incident Room was deserted — no doubt the result of fifty-odd hangovers.

He'd spent the rest of the night tossing and turning, continually waking up with the recurring vision of Bain taking any hope of a promotion away from him. Ironic, he thought, given he had no great ambitions, not for a few years at least — it must be all the talk of Bain chasing a higher rank. The dream sometimes had a Glaswegian taking his job away, which he figured was Strathclyde coming in and stealing the case from Bain — sometimes it was a cockney, meaning the Met.

He took a big gulp of the burnt-tasting coffee and noticed a piece of paper on his keyboard. It was a note from one of the desk sergeants downstairs. *'DC Cullen - A Duncan Wilson came in for a meeting at 7.45. I let him go at 8.30. Sgt Mullen. 8.35'.* Scribbled in the corner was another note. *'Call Tommy Smith'.*

Cullen crumpled it up. He was past caring now. Bain had his collar — maybe McNeill was right. He'd done some good work, tied things together, chased down some key leads and contributed to the arrest. One conviction for four counts of murder was what they wanted at the top.

'Morning, Scotty.' Miller looked totally destroyed.

'Late night I take it.'

'Aye. We ended up in the Liquid Lounge till two.'

'Was Bain still with you?'

Miller shrugged. 'No idea.' He looked at Cullen's coffee. 'Jesus, that smells bad.'

'Filter with two extra shots. They call it a red eye.'

'Smells like they burnt it.' Miller took out a four pack of Lucozade Sport and two cans of Red Bull. 'Magic tonic this — the gaffer told me about it.'

'I'm not surprised.' Cullen stared at the bottles. He had an idea. 'When you've had your tonic, can you get a statement from Duncan Wilson about these death threats? He said it was Kim Milne who told him. I want you to check. You'll need to head to his flat.'

Miller slouched in his chair, his eyes shut. 'Aye, okay.'

Cullen checked his watch. 'Bain time.'

~

BAIN STOOD at the front of the Incident Room. He took a sip from a mug — Cullen wondered if it was the same potion Miller was drinking. 'Okay, I'll keep it brief this morning as we're all feeling a bit tender.'

Cullen was leaning against the side wall by the large window. He looked around the room and all he saw was hungover cops, none quite as bad as Miller, but nobody looking particularly fresh. That said, he didn't feel on top form with his dire lack of sleep. Hopefully, his indiscretion with Martin Webb wouldn't come to light.

'First, DC Cullen has managed to dig up a connection between Rob Thomson and Gail McBride. I've spoken to the Procurator Fiscal and she's happy to add Gail's murder to the list of charges. Well done, Constable.'

Cullen felt the room looking at him again, wondering if anyone had noticed his early exit the previous evening.

'Second, Jimmy Deeley pulled a late shift last night and completed Kim Milne's post mortem. We had already proved Caroline and Debi were killed by the same person, who also killed Kim Milne. The post mortem uncovered our key piece of evidence

— traces of the same murder weapon — linking him to the rest of the murders. Good work to all involved in securing this.'

Cullen could see a game plan forming. There was a wealth of circumstantial evidence that could be deemed to connect Thomson to the killings but, using the similarity of the murders, they could add what appeared to be hard evidence and make the case against him much stronger and seemingly backed up by facts.

Bain wasn't mentioning the links to Schoolbook, about how the killer had used the same method to lure his victims online.

'Jimmy Anderson's submitted a draft report of their search of Thomson and Milne's flat. The only thing of note is there's damage to the wallpaper by the flat's front door, probably caused by fingernails. This shows there must have been a struggle. We can make the assumption Rob Thomson pushed her inside the flat, she fell and scratched the wall — we found paint under her nails.'

He took another sip.

'We can also assume she would've screamed or made a noise. If she did, a neighbour could have heard and made the 999 call. Cullen couldn't find any of the neighbours who would take responsibility for the call, but I'm not too concerned about this.'

He cleared his throat and looked at a sheet of paper.

'One of the key challenges we face is raising the awareness of domestic incidents and anonymity is a part of that. Therefore, nobody owning up to making the call isn't unexpected.'

Cullen would have liked to speak to the caller. He still felt there was something not quite right with it.

'Finally, today's evidence day. I want you all to check your statements and notebooks, make sure everything is consistent and supports the case. We've done a great job here, four murders solved. You'll all be aware of the pressure we're under due to rising crime figures in Lothian & Borders. This result helps to ensure the public has faith in the ability of the police to bring killers to justice.'

He took a long drink from the mug. 'Dismissed.'

Cullen remained leaning against the wall, realising how much pressure Turnbull and Bain were under from on high to get convictions for the murders. This was four in one, an easy statistic.

Bain wandered over. 'Sloped off a bit early last night, didn't you?'

'Wasn't in the mood.'

'You need to be more of a team player, Sundance.'

'I thought I was,' said Cullen.

'You need to accept the plaudits and celebrate a decent collar.'

Cullen sighed. 'What do you want me to do now?'

'I won't pretend I understand what you found on Schoolbook,' said Bain, 'but I want you to tidy all that up and get it linked to Rob Thomson properly.'

'Fine.'

Bain almost smiled. 'And cheer up, you miserable bugger.'

'Cullen, you really are a stupid bastard,' said Kidd.

'I know, I know, I know,' said Cullen. 'You don't need to keep reminding me.'

They sat at Kidd's PC investigating the effects of Cullen making friends with Martin Webb on Schoolbook. There was a big audit trail, like giant neon lights pointing at Scott Cullen.

Data danced across the screen. Cullen struggled to concentrate. His vision was blurry from the lack of sleep.

'Here we go,' said Kidd.

Cullen leaned in close, trying to focus on the screen. 'What?'

'See this?' Kidd pointed to a row of data. 'This is the audit trail of him accepting your message. It's all blank values on his side, but the record is still there. He can't delete it, so when the database writes a new record when he does something, he has to overwrite it immediately.'

'How difficult is that to do?'

'If you had admin access it would be easy.'

Cullen stared at the wall. 'So if you were a DBA there?'

Kidd laughed. 'Not so fast, cowboy. Their security's a bit shit. They've had some big hacks this year, passwords leaking all over the place. If you had access to the server remotely it would work. Anyone could have set this up.'

Cullen tapped his pen rhythmically against the desk. 'And their data's stored on servers at Alba Bank, right?'

'Think so, aye. That's what they said.'

'So Rob Thomson could have had access to it?' said Cullen.

'Maybe,' said Kidd. 'I'm sure there would be some sort of audit on it at their end.'

'Can you look into it?'

Kidd sighed. 'I suppose I'd better, aye.'

'Does this mean we've worked out how he's been doing it?'

'Aye.'

'So, I'm not such an idiot, then?'

Kidd tossed his ponytail. 'I wouldn't go that far. This is probably inadmissible as evidence, given you've gone in two footed and ripped your own kneecap off.'

He started tapping again, leaving Cullen to feel slightly positive about the potential blunder. Still, he just knew Bain would give him a proper doing when he came clean.

'What can you tell about my actual message?' said Cullen.

'The 'call me' one?' said Kidd.

'Aye.'

Kidd pulled it up on the screen. 'Well, he's read it.' He ran his finger along the line. 'Hang on. This is a different access record.'

'What?'

'Every time he accesses the account, it logs it on a table.' Kidd went into another screen. 'Here we go. This is a list of all the times the Martin Webb account's been accessed.'

'Is this the first time you've looked at it?'

'It's the first time I've been able to,' said Kidd. 'I only got this extract sorted out last night. That security firm's given me access to a backup at the Schoolbook end, so I'm dialling in to their server rather than having them send stuff here.' He searched along the line. 'Got it. He's using the same values to default the record.'

'Eh?'

Kidd sighed. 'Keep up, Cullen. As I told you earlier, every time he accesses the site it generates a new record. The database doesn't allow a permanent delete, so what he does is alter all the values in the record to blanks.'

'Any way we can see what it was before?'

'Only if a copy was taken at the exact millisecond the record was created.' Kidd tapped the screen. 'This wiping activity is pretty much immediately after the creation of the record, so we'd have to be really fluky. It'd be like winning the lottery.'

'So you were saying this is the same pattern for both records.'

'Aye. Must be a program he's got that just resets the values to blanks after the record's created.'

'Can you check if Jeremy Turner and Martin Webb use the same pattern?'

'Will do.' Kidd's fingers tapped away. 'I've searched for all matching records. Here he is, Jeremy Turner. Exactly the same values on the records.'

'So the Jeremy Turner and Martin Webb accounts are accessed using the same method?' Cullen looked down the screen, his eyes stopping at a line that looked different. He pointed at it. 'What about that one?'

Kidd frowned. 'Looks a bit funny. Let's have a wee look at it.' He tapped at the keyboard, his fingers a blur.

'Don't you use a mouse?'

'Just slows me down. Keyboard shortcuts are where it's at.' Kidd brought up another screen. 'Here we are. The account name is under Jenny Scott.'

Cullen looked up. 'What did you say?'

'Lassie called Jenny Scott.'

The name rang a bell with Cullen. 'Bring up her profile for me.'

Jenny Scott's profile filled the screen. Cullen looked at the photograph — he recognised her. Where from? He looked at the message board on her page.

There was a message from Kim Milne.

'Who is she?' said Kidd.

'A friend of Kim Milne's.'

'That lassie who got killed yesterday?'

'Aye, her.' Cullen flicked through his notebook, stopping at Friday afternoon. He'd gone to Rob Thomson's flat to check his alibi with Kim Milne. Jenny Scott was there. She was flying to Thailand on Friday evening. He looked back at Kidd. 'Any idea what he was up to with this account?'

Kidd scrolled through a few screens. 'Sending messages by the looks of things.'

'Can I have a look?'

'Aye.' Kidd pulled up a series of five messages, all sent from Jenny Scott's account to Kim Milne.

Cullen read through them quickly. The first and the last were the most important.

The first message on Sunday read —

'Hey Kimmy. Had a fight with Tom. Heading home. Going to need somewhere to stay while I sort this shit out. Jenny x'

The last read —

'Thanks! I'll get the bus in and walk down, think I'll be there by half six. Don't meet me at the airport — I'll be fine on the bus, it's quicker. Could do with seeing Edinburgh. Jenny x'

'You've gone all quiet for once,' said Kidd. 'What does this mean?'

Cullen tapped his pen against the edge of the desk and thought it through. 'One of two things. Either Jenny really did arrange to meet Kim at her flat last night or whoever's behind this is trying to frame Rob Thomson.'

'Or Rob Thomson's trying to throw you off the trail.'

Cullen glared at him. 'This is messed up enough without that sort of crap.' He scribbled it all in his notebook regardless. 'Don't even begin to think about mentioning that little chestnut to Bain, by the way.'

Cullen noticed he'd taken Jenny Scott's number, at the time thinking they might need to check the alibis or get further character references for Kim Milne. That, or his latent prowling nature Miller had accused him of earlier. He hadn't known it would lead to this. He called the number but it just rang and rang, eventually going to voicemail. He left a message and ended the call.

'No joy?'

'Nope.' Cullen put his phone on the desk. 'Typical of this bloody case.'

'Tell me about it.'

'How did it go with Gail's netbook?'

Kidd nostrils flared. 'Even worse than you trying to befriend murderers on Schoolbook. I got an IP address.'

'Isn't that good?'

'Hold your horses, cowboy. The IP address traces to a server in Iraq.'

'Iraq?' said Cullen. 'Do they have computers there?'

'I expected more of you,' said Kidd. 'Of course they do. Loads of dodgy ones. I've got no chance of getting any further. It's all blocked. It's virtually lawless. They can do whatever they like to block searches and checks.'

Cullen slumped back in his chair. 'So what do we know about what's happened to Jenny Scott's account? Bain wants me to tie the Schoolbook stuff together and this just seems to be making it messier.'

Kidd shrugged then tapped at the computer.

'Whoever's doing this hacked into Jenny Scott's account and arranged to meet Kim Milne at her flat.' Cullen had a sudden insight. 'At a specific time.'

Kidd turned around. 'Eh?'

'It wasn't just 'I'll see you at any time', it was, 'I'll be there at half six'.'

'And that means?'

'Well, whoever's doing this is planning the whole thing out in detail, in advance. He knew when Rob Thomson would usually be leaving work.'

Kidd grinned. 'Or it was Rob Thomson?'

Cullen almost laughed. 'Indeed.'

Kidd pointed to the screen. 'I've found another while you were on the phone there.'

'You're joking.'

'I'm serious.' Kidd scrolled through the messages on the screen. 'Some couple arranged to meet at the Travelodge at Haymarket last night.'

Cullen felt sick. Another killing?

84

M c Neill got her warrant card out. 'We need into room two one seven. Now.'

The Polish receptionist stood wide-eyed. 'I can't.'

Cullen and McNeill had gone inside, leaving Miller out in the car park just in case the killer made a run for it again. Angela was similarly stationed outside the front entrance. Buxton and another uniform were in a car outside, the engine running.

'We have reason to believe a murder may have been committed in that room.'

'Okay,' said the receptionist.

'Can you get me a key?' said McNeill.

'Yes.' The receptionist fiddled with the key card machine, eventually producing a card coded to the room. She handed it to McNeill with a trembling hand.

McNeill looked at Cullen. 'Come on.'

They ran to the lifts. Cullen hammered the call button. The door on the right opened immediately.

McNeill got in and pressed the button for the second floor. 'This better be right.'

'Part of me really hopes it's not,' said Cullen.

They burst out onto the corridor, Cullen leading. The brass plaque on the wall indicated rooms 210 to 220 were to the left. 'This way.'

They ran along the corridor. 217 was on the left, just before the turn. A *Do Not Disturb* sign hung from the door handle.

McNeill pulled the key card from her pocket. 'Better knock first.' She rapped on the door. No answer. She knocked again. They both extended their batons. 'On three. One. Two. Three.'

She slid the card down. The light turned green and the door clicked. She pushed it open.

There was a door immediately to the left, presumably the bathroom. The bed was round the corner.

There were sounds of a struggle.

Cullen rushed forward.

A man shouted. 'What the—?' He was on top of a woman.

Cullen grabbed him, jamming the baton over his throat and pulling him to his feet. He was naked, hairy and overweight. His penis was erect and encased in a condom.

The woman sat up in the bed, pulling the covers up over her. 'What are you doing?'

'Police,' said Cullen. 'We're investigating a murder.'

The man was trying to resist him, so he tightened his hold.

'There's no murder going on in here,' she said.

Cullen loosened his grip.

'What's going on?' said McNeill.

The woman looked at her, enraged. 'What's it look like, you cow? We were having consensual sex when you pair barged in.'

~

'NICE TRY, SCOTT,' said McNeill.

They were outside in the car park with Miller and Angela, who couldn't stop giggling.

Cullen shook his head at her. 'Can you stop that, please?'

'Aye, aye, all right.' Angela was struggling to keep her mouth and face straight. 'So what was their story then?'

'Having an affair,' said McNeill. 'The bloke works at School-book. He had been changing the logs to cover their tracks. They were worried about the woman's husband guessing the two of them were at it, so he created a fake account.'

Angela's laughter had finally subsided. 'There's easier ways of having a fling, surely? Pay As You Go mobiles, sneaky email accounts. Christ.'

'You seem knowledgeable on the subject,' said McNeill.

'I've got a suspicious mind,' said Angela.

Miller scowled. 'So they weren't the killers?'

Cullen was about to abuse him when his mobile went. He didn't recognise the number but answered it anyway — it could be any number of snouts, both new and old, maybe with a nice juicy bit of information. He moved away from the group and answered it.

'Scott?'

Cullen struggled to place the voice. 'Who is this?'

'Jesus, Scott, we lived together for three years. It's Katie.'

'What do you want?'

'Can I speak to Alison?'

Cullen frowned. 'Why would I know where she is?'

Katie paused. 'Aren't you two an item?'

'No,' said Cullen. 'What makes you think we are?'

'Just what Ally's been saying. The pair of you have been getting close.'

'Well, we haven't.'

'So you haven't seen her then?' said Katie.

'I saw her last night. We had a bit of an argument.'

'Are you sure?' said Katie.

'Of course I'm sure,' said Cullen. 'She came round to my flat and I brushed her off.'

'You brushed her off. Some things never change.'

'When you see her,' said Cullen, 'can you make sure she's got the message that we're not an item?'

'I'll try, but I'll need to speak to her first,' said Katie. 'Her boss just called me. She's not turned up for work.'

'She's probably just upset with me telling her the truth.'

'Scott, you really are a callous bastard.' Katie hung up.

Cullen wandered back over, hoping nobody had noticed. Angela and Miller were getting into the back of the squad car.

'Who was that?' said McNeill.

'Nobody,' said Cullen.

85

Bain hit his desk. 'Have you tried calling Jenny Scott again?'
'Of course I have,' said Cullen. 'She's not answered. Yet.'

'Have you tried going round to her flat?' said Bain.

'I don't know if she's even in the country,' said Cullen. 'I very much doubt she is.'

'Christ's sake, Cullen,' said Bain, 'this is a massive part of this bloody case. This could definitely prove to Rob Thomson we've got him.'

'We don't know it's him that's in Schoolbook,' said Cullen. 'I mean, we don't know it's not, but we've got no direct evidence.'

Bain smacked the table again. 'Cullen, you're supposed to be linking Rob Thomson to these murders, not blowing the whole case wide open. I've got Wilkinson interviewing Thomson again and I've enough spanners being shoved in by that wanker McLintock without more from one of my own bloody officers. I heard about you and your bloody girlfriend bursting in on some couple rutting away in a hotel. I want you to focus exclusively on linking Rob Thomson to Schoolbook.'

Cullen sat back. 'I don't know how many times I've told you this, but I don't think we'll find anything to link him. Whoever it is — and I'll even assume it's Rob Thomson if it'll make you happy

— they're not leaving a breadcrumb trail in there. Everything's covered over. It would be virtually impossible to catch them at it.'

Bain sat and glowered for a minute. 'In that case, I need you to bury this.'

Cullen scowled. 'What do you mean, 'bury it'?'

'I mean get rid of any evidence pointing to Schoolbook,' said Bain. 'We don't use it in the case.'

Cullen folded his arms. 'I can't do that.'

'Yes, you can.' Bain leaned forward. 'I've got enough without it.'

'Are you sure?' Cullen sat up straight. 'You've already committed yourself on tape asking Rob why he was using the name Martin Webb. McLintock will tear you to shreds.'

'The Fiscal will just have to deal with it,' said Bain. 'I want to get this all covered up and passed on to her.'

'Fine,' said Cullen.

'Last warning, Sundance,' said Bain. 'If you're not going to help collar this bastard, then keep yourself out of my hair.'

86

'Don't you think you're being just a little bit mental?' said McNeill.

'Mental?' Cullen took a drink of coffee. 'You think I'm the one that's being mental?'

They'd both realised they now had very little work to do, so headed for a sit-down lunch in the canteen, Cullen opting for a chicken pie and chips, McNeill a baked potato with coronation chicken.

'You're going against what Bain and all the superior officers are saying,' said McNeill. 'To them, Bain's pretty close to an air-tight conviction and you're running around picking holes in it.'

'Yeah, you said it, air-tight to them.' Cullen dropped his fork on the plate. 'He needs to see the holes and deal with them. If it's not me doing it, it'll be McLintock in front of a jury. Does he want a failed conviction?' He drank the last of the coffee. 'Besides, you started this the other night.'

'Yeah, well, I've given up. I can't fight him any longer. That hotel room this morning was the last straw for me.'

'Are you blaming me for that?'

McNeill put down her cutlery. 'I'm not, but I just don't have the energy for this.'

'Oh, come on,' said Cullen, 'that could've been useful. It still can.'

'How?'

Cullen was aware he was clutching at straws. 'Well, for starters, it shows using that method to link the murders together isn't one hundred per cent reliable. It's not unique to the killer. The killer used it, but so did the guy we burst in on this morning. Assuming he's not the killer.'

McNeill smiled. 'You're something else.'

There was an uncomfortable silence between them. McNeill scraped away at her lunch, while Cullen played with his empty coffee cup. He'd found it difficult to think of the previous night, the way she'd been with Turnbull. Bearing in mind Bain's comments, he wondered if she had shagged Turnbull. His stomach lurched every time he thought of it, feeling sick. 'Did you have a good night last night?'

McNeill looked up. 'Wasn't bad, as these things go. I bailed out not long after you.'

'Did you?'

'Of course,' said McNeill. 'I was knackered and there's only so much brown-nosing I can do with Turnbull before he starts getting creepy. Besides, you're supposed to be buying me a drink tonight.'

She looked into his eyes. His heart pounded.

She broke off and finished eating the last piece of charred potato skin. 'Okay, Scott, I'll tell you what, you go through your deduction about how this guy used Schoolbook, and I'll tell you if you're mad or not.'

'Fine.' Cullen sat back and collected his thoughts. 'First, we know it's someone with behind the scenes access to Schoolbook, someone with access to the audit records who can hack in and change them. Now, Charlie Kidd told me it doesn't have to be someone actually at Schoolbook.' He paused for a moment. 'How does he do it? First, he finds a victim, then creates a dummy account and uses it to send messages to them.'

'Isn't it a bit convenient just to pick those particular people and get one hundred per cent success?'

'I've thought about that,' said Cullen. 'All those messages are just bits of data on a database. I've seen how they look on Charlie Kidd's PC. Somebody can have a look round those private messages if they've got the right access. So they get access to the whole set of intimate, private messages. These sites are like email nowadays, loads of people communicate through them. Our killer could look through the messages and see what makes these women tick, what their desires and needs are and so on. It makes it easier to lure them in if he's already got the answers.'

McNeill tossed her head from side to side. 'Okay, I can buy that so far. What about with Kim Milne? Those messages you found with Charlie this morning weren't from some made up character like Martin Webb or Jeremy Turner, were they? They were from a real person. Jenny Scott is a living, breathing person who you've met.'

'Agreed.' Cullen sat and thought for a moment. 'Holy shit.'

'What is it?'

'I just remembered something.' Cullen tapped at the side of his head. 'What I was just saying there, this killer accessed their messages to read up on them. Well, what if he didn't have to dig for Kim, what if he already knew her pretty well? He used his access to the messages to keep tabs on what's going on in her life, but he's also in there looking for an opportunity to frame Rob Thomson.'

'Right, that's it, you have gone mental.'

Cullen laughed. 'Maybe I have.'

'What about motive?' McNeill put both hands around her mug of tea. 'Why does he want to trap Rob Thomson?'

Cullen picked up a sugar sachet from the dispenser on the table. He tore it open and started grinding the grains of sugar between his fingers. He thought it through — they were after somebody who badly wanted to frame Rob. One of the things Bain focused on, as a motive for Rob to kill Caroline, was the affair that ended their marriage. In that scenario, there were two people cheated on — Caroline Adamson and Kim Milne's boyfriend at the time. Cullen remembered Amy Cousens saying something about having met him. He got up. 'I need to go speak to Amy Cousens.'

'Your girlfriend.'

'You know I don't have one.' Cullen felt a pang of guilt about Alison. 'If a certain lady wants to play her cards right...' He winked at her and walked off to the stairwell, leaving her with her tea.

Back in the Incident Room, he got his mobile out and called

Jenny Scott's number again. He picked his jacket up from the back of his chair, the phone clamped to his ear.

'This is Jenny, I'm not in the country just now so I might not have reception. Please leave a message and I'll try and get back to you.'

Cullen left his umpteenth message. Where the hell was she?

He figured he had one last shot. Maybe McNeill was right and he was mental. After this, he would give in, let Bain get thrown out of court. Or worse, convict someone with scant evidence.

Miller wandered over. 'That potion did the trick, by the way. I feel reborn.'

'Glad to hear it,' said Cullen. 'How did you get on with that statement?'

Miller shrugged. 'That Duncan boy's not got back to me yet.'

Cullen nodded. 'Can I borrow you for an hour? I need to go speak to somebody, and I might need corroboration.'

87

'I need you to tell me everything you can about Kim Milne's boyfriend at the time,' said Cullen.

Amy Cousens frowned and sat forward on the armchair. 'I don't remember much. I met him just the once. I think he worked at Alba Bank with Kim and Rob. Can't remember his name.'

'What did he look like?'

Amy exhaled deeply. 'This was a couple of years ago.'

'Did he look like me?'

'Not really, no. He was much bigger.'

Cullen pointed at Miller. 'What like ADC Miller, was he big like him?'

'He's not big,' said Amy, 'he's just tall.'

Miller raised his eyebrows and looked upset.

'I mean *big*,' said Amy, 'the same way that Rob's big. I think Kim maybe has a type.'

'Thanks.' Cullen nodded, thinking that could explain Bain seeing what he wanted to see on the CCTV footage. 'Do you know what happened to him after Rob and Kim got found out?'

'I heard some stuff,' said Amy. 'He went off the rails a bit.'

'How so?'

'He was stalking Kim for a bit, following her home, that sort of thing. Eventually he went back to his parents' house out in West Lothian somewhere.'

'How do you remember that but not his name?' said Cullen.

'I'm bad with names.' Amy shrugged. 'We talked about West Lothian. My boyfriend at the time was from Linlithgow, near where he came from, and they were talking about it the night we went out for dinner.'

'Do you know anything else about him?' said Cullen.

'I think Rob got him sacked from the bank.'

Cullen frowned. 'Are you sure?'

'Yes,' said Amy. 'Some guy they both knew told Caroline a few months ago. She told me when we were pissed once.'

Cullen's mobile rang. 'Keith, can you take a statement?'

Miller tried to act professional. 'Aye, will do.'

Cullen went into the kitchen.

'Will you accept the charges for the call?'

'Yes.' Cullen hoped he didn't regret it.

'Connecting you now.'

After a moment, he was through. 'Hi, it's Jenny Scott.'

Cullen leaned back against the kitchen wall. Finally.

'Sorry, I was out of reception area,' said Jenny. 'Then I moved on and got like fifteen voicemails from you. Thanks for accepting the charges.'

'Okay, thanks for calling me back,' said Cullen. 'Are you still in Thailand?'

'I am.'

Cullen felt relieved — it looked unlikely she had sent the messages to Kim.

'I assume it's important?' said Jenny.

Cullen realised she wouldn't know about Kim's death. 'There are a couple of things. Are you with someone just now?'

'There's my boyfriend.'

'Okay,' said Cullen, 'you might want to sit down.'

'Go on.'

'I'm sorry to have to tell you this,' said Cullen, 'but Kim Milne was found dead yesterday evening.'

'Oh my God.' Jenny started crying. 'Is this some sort of wind-up?'

'No, Ms Scott, this isn't a wind-up. She was found dead at roughly seven thirty last night.'

Pained gasps came down the line. 'How did she die?'

'She was murdered.'

'Have they got the bastard that did it?'

'Our investigations are ongoing.'

Jenny paused for a few seconds. 'How's Rob coping?'

'He's helping us with the investigations.' Cullen waited a moment to let her start to process things. 'There are a couple of things I'd like to ask you.'

'Go ahead.' Her voice was thick with tears.

'First, have you been sending messages to Kim on Schoolbook in the last couple of days?'

'Schoolbook? I've not been on the internet since I got out here.'

'So you didn't send the messages?'

'Absolutely not.'

'Someone's hacked into your account and sent some messages to Kim,' said Cullen.

'Oh my God.'

Cullen switched his phone to the other ear. 'Did Kim have a boyfriend before she started seeing Rob?'

'Aye, she did,' said Jenny. 'He was an absolute prick. I never liked him.'

'What was his name?'

'Duncan Wilson.'

88

Cullen pulled the street door open and they headed out to the car. As they walked, Cullen tried to call the superior officers — Bain's mobile was engaged, McNeill wasn't picking up, Irvine the same. He was even considering calling Wilkinson.

He tried to piece it together in his mind.

Duncan Wilson was Kim's boyfriend.

He'd lost Kim to Thomson.

He was sacked by Thomson.

It was a bit extreme to go on a killing spree, but Cullen had heard of lesser grievances being settled the same way. This would show Bain. This was the silver bullet to tear the case apart.

They got in the car and Miller drove them towards the station.

Cullen's phone rang — Kidd.

'Finally.'

'What do you mean?' said Cullen.

'I've been trying you for the last quarter of an hour.'

'Sorry, but I've been trying to nail this case down. Is it important? I need to speak to Bain.'

'You bet your life it's important,' said Kidd. 'I've been looking into Jenny Scott's account. There's some metadata he's not blocking. And I've managed to find another account that's been hacked into, same as Jenny's.'

'Go on.'

There was a pause. 'It's yours.'

Cullen couldn't speak.

'Scott, this guy's hacked into your account and has been sending messages to some girl,' said Kidd.

'*My* account?'

'Aye,' said Kidd. 'He's been sending messages to someone called Alison Carnegie. Is that your bird?'

'No, it's not,' said Cullen. 'What do the messages say?'

'Stuff about meeting up last night.'

Cullen swallowed. He felt sick to the stomach. That was why Alison thought there was more going on between them than he did. That explained her pitching up at his flat and all the confusion. Why him, though? Why pick on him?

He ended the call.

'Who was that?' Miller pulled in at the lights on Leith Walk, indicating left for the station.

'Charlie Kidd.' Cullen opened the Schoolbook app and went to the messages from Alison Carnegie. There they were — a chain between him and Alison, messages he'd never sent. Soppy, cloying stuff, nothing like him.

Katie had called earlier, looking for Alison. Cullen started to worry about what had happened to her.

He called her phone. Nothing.

He called Katie.

'Katie Lawson.' Her phone voice still sparkled.

'Katie, it's Scott. Has Alison been in touch yet?'

'No, I was just about to call you again. She's still not turned up. I went home and she's not there. Her phone's not even ringing.'

Cullen felt queasy — he was being set up for a murder. 'I'll find her.'

He hung up, fervently hoping when he found her she was still alive.

He desperately needed to see Duncan Wilson.

They were still sat in the middle of the road, indicating left, still hadn't got through the lights.

'Head to Portobello,' said Cullen.

'Come on, man, I'm not giving you a lift home.'

'Keith, just do it. This is serious. We're going to visit Duncan Wilson.'

89

They stood outside the entrance to the block of flats. Cullen pressed the button for Duncan Wilson.

'Who is it?'

'It's the police,' said Cullen.

'In you come.'

The door buzzed open. Cullen led the way, taking the steps two at a time, right up to Wilson's flat. He hammered at the door. The stairwell was a lot brighter during the day. He looked up at the glass ceiling — there was a ladder leading up to the roof.

Finally, Wilson's front door opened. He stood there in jeans and a t-shirt. 'How can I help?'

'I need to ask you a few questions,' said Cullen. 'We can do it here or down the station.'

Wilson frowned. 'I went in this morning at your insistence, but I'm more than happy to come back in.'

Cullen pushed past him into the flat. 'Here will be fine. We've been unable to corroborate the story about death threats you gave to my colleague.'

Wilson led them through to his living room at the far end of the flat. He sat on an armchair, leaving Cullen and Miller to the sofa.

'Nice place,' said Cullen.

'I bought it a few years ago,' said Wilson. 'It didn't cost that much at the time, but its value has soared.'

Cullen nodded slowly. 'Not working today?'

'I don't work nine to five at Schoolbook. It's a twenty-four seven thing. Got a few days off just now, then I'm in nights. I'm sure a policeman would understand that.'

Cullen leaned forward on the sofa. 'Can you describe your relationship with a Kimberly Milne.'

'I told you on the phone last night.' Wilson sighed. 'We briefly worked together.'

'You didn't mention you were in a relationship with Ms Milne for six years.'

Wilson frowned. 'Who told you this?'

'A friend of Ms Milne's,' said Cullen.

'Sorry, the wounds are still a bit raw, you know? We only broke up last year.'

'So I gather,' said Cullen. 'Was it Rob Thomson who moved in on your territory?'

'Aye, it was.' Wilson looked out of the window, avoiding Cullen's gaze. He turned back, his eyes locking on. 'What's this about? I've given you my source.'

'I'm afraid we need a further source of corroboration,' said Cullen, 'now Ms Milne is deceased.'

Wilson swallowed. 'What?'

'She was found murdered at her flat last night,' said Cullen.

There was a crash from another room. Wilson looked at the sitting room door.

'What was that?' said Cullen.

'Think it was outside,' said Wilson.

The crash sounded again. Then a cry. 'Scott!'

'Miller, keep an eye on him.' Cullen left the room and went into the hall. 'Hello?'

There was another noise from behind a door to the right, away from the flat entrance.

Cullen dashed for the door and tore it open. A bedroom. Alison lay tied up on the bed.

90

Cullen rushed forward. Alison had silver duct tape partially covering her mouth, like it was done in a hurry. He pulled the remaining tape off and started untying the rope.

'Scott, oh my God.' She sucked in air.

Cullen held her. 'It's going to be okay.'

A scream came from the living room.

'Wait here.' Cullen went back into the hall, just as a figure disappeared into the stairwell. He ran into the living room.

Miller lay on the floor, his white shirt slowly turning red. His eyes rolled, struggling to focus. 'Aw, man...' He clutched at his chest.

Cullen kneeled and pulled his mobile out. He struggled to control his fingers, as he dialled Bain.

'Sundance, what—'

'Get over here. Bring an ambulance.' Cullen killed the call.

Miller tried to sit up. 'Go get him, Scotty, I'll be fine.'

Cullen hesitated for a moment, then ran out of the flat. He looked down the stairwell. An old man was slowly climbing up, carrying a bag of shopping.

'Did anyone come down the stairs?' said Cullen.

'No, son.'

'Call the police.'

Cullen looked up — the ceiling hatch was open. Wilson was going to cut across the roof and descend another stairwell. Cullen didn't have time to work out which one, he'd have to go after him. If Cullen waited outside, Wilson could hide in any of the flats. He pulled himself up the ladder, hanging precariously over the centre of the stairwell, and climbed up onto the roof. He couldn't see Wilson.

The blow sent him sprawling.

Cullen tumbled and slid to the edge of the roof. He stopped himself just in time, his fingers clawing at the roof felt and eventually grabbing hold of the gutter pipe. His face hung over the edge, nothing between him and the car park below.

He pushed himself away, reaching round to feel the back of his head. It was wet. His hand was covered in blood.

Wilson was coming towards him, carrying a broken slate dripping with blood.

Cullen tried to pull himself to his feet, but his legs failed to respond.

'Thought you were pretty smart, didn't you?' said Wilson. 'Finally caught up with me? Well, after I've finished with you, I'll go back and finish my work downstairs. Your friend down there can't have much time left. And as for your bird, well, I'll take my time with this one.'

Cullen's feet slipped on the moss, preventing him from getting up.

Wilson was almost on him. 'Should have brought my knife with me, but it's hanging out of your mate's guts. Had to buy a new one, can you believe it? This slate will do just fine.'

'Why did you do it?' Cullen was desperately trying to buy time. His feet slipped again.

'Why does anyone do anything?' said Wilson. 'Because they can. And because they can get away with it.'

From this angle, Wilson seemed gigantic. Cullen could never beat him in an even fight.

'You won't get away with it. You'll have killed two police officers. They'll hunt you all over the world.'

'Yeah?' Wilson smiled. 'Oh well.'

He raised the slate over his head, ready to bring it down on Cullen. He kicked out wildly, his left foot connecting to Wilson's knee with a satisfying crunch.

Wilson screamed, then staggered forward. He landed on Cullen. Wilson's fists started pounding into him — fire burned in his chest, head and arms. He couldn't breathe. He felt something snap in his chest. His whole body seared with pain.

Wilson straddled him and picked up the slate, ready to smash it down on Cullen's head.

Cullen brought his left knee up as hard as he could, sending a jolt of pain through his own body. It connected with something soft.

Cullen brought his knee up again. Wilson squealed and slumped forward, a dead weight. Cullen struggled to roll him off, his ears ringing from Wilson's yells. Ignoring the pain in his chest, he struggled to his feet.

Wilson rolled over and tried to get up. Cullen stumbled towards the ladder, sliding on the slippery roof.

Cullen heard Wilson behind him. He turned — Wilson had picked up the slate again. He staggered towards Cullen and swung the slate at his head. He lurched back, just avoiding the blow. He lost his footing and slid towards the edge of the roof again. He managed to stop himself and scrambled to his feet. He looked around. Wilson was limping towards him slowly, almost casually.

It had all come to this one moment. Wilson had killed four people. Miller lay dying, Cullen was next, then Alison.

Cullen edged up the slope. Wilson circled, holding the slate out in front of him like a knife. Cullen slid forward on the moss and kicked out. He connected solidly with Wilson's damaged knee. The knee buckled and Wilson pitched forward.

Cullen leapt onto Wilson and grabbed him in a half Nelson hold, arm locked tight behind his neck, his knee hard into the small of Wilson's back, immobilising him.

Cullen reached into his jacket pocket and pulled out his mobile. He called Bain with one hand, the other gripping Wilson tight.

'Where the hell are you?'

'Not far away,' said Bain. 'Two minutes.'

'I've got him on the roof.' Cullen ended the call. 'Duncan Wilson, I'm arresting you for the murder of Caroline Adamson. You are not obliged to say anything but anything you do say will be noted down and may be used in evidence. Do you understand?'

91

They were back at the station, standing outside the interview room with McNeill. DS Holdsworth, in his remit as First Aid officer, patched up Cullen's head. His ribs burned but he didn't want to go to hospital until he'd spoken to Wilson.

Keith Miller had been rushed off to the Royal infirmary — it was touch and go at best.

'I want to be in there,' said Cullen.

'Sundance, you're in no fit state to be interviewing anyone.'

'I don't care,' said Cullen. 'I need to hear his words. I'll sit at the back.'

Bain raised his arms in the air. 'Come on, then.'

Cullen smiled. 'Thank you. How's Alison?'

'Your bird?' said Bain. 'She'll pull through.'

A frown passed over McNeill's face.

'Did they find anything in his flat?' said Cullen. 'Any evidence? There are two missing laptops.'

Bain shared a long look with McNeill then slowly nodded. 'Aye, we found something. Not the laptops, though.'

'What then?'

'We *think* we've found Caroline's flat keys,' said Bain. 'Irvine's around there now, checking they fit the locks.'

Cullen breathed a sigh of relief. 'Aren't you going to say anything?'

'Eh?'

'Aren't you going to apologise to me?' said Cullen.

Bain put his hands on his hips. 'Don't push it, Sundance. I'll say you did some good work there. I do need to give you a doing about something, though.'

Cullen sighed. 'What?'

'Doing more unauthorised phone checks,' said Bain.

'Gail's number, right?'

'Right.'

'Did anything come back?' said Cullen.

'A huge bill.' Bain gave a deep breath. 'Tommy traced it to a phone from the same consignment as that one for Caroline.'

'You're kidding me.'

'No, it was in the next transaction at that till,' said Bain. 'You missed that one. Our killer bought two phones in separate transactions.'

Cullen ran his hand through his hair. His head throbbed when he touched the bandage. 'So that links the killer to Gail and Caroline.'

'Got it in one,' said Bain.

'And Rob Thomson?'

'I've let him go.' Bain laughed bitterly. He thumbed towards the interview room. 'We may have to use him as a witness against this chump.'

'Just hope he doesn't sue,' said Cullen.

'Aye.' Bain rubbed his moustache. 'The reason I was on the phone to Tommy Smith was to get a trace on that 999 call.'

'And?'

'Untraceable,' said Bain. 'He did ask me where I wanted the bill sent, which pissed me right off, so I got him talking.'

'Well, some good came of it,' said Cullen.

'Aye, I suppose,' said Bain. 'Right, let's get in there and interview him.'

92

Bain and McNeill were leading the interview. Cullen sat at the back of the room behind Bain, with PC Buxton by the door.

'I will refer you to the point about police brutality, Inspector Bain.' McLintock wore a more sober outfit than when he'd defended Rob Thomson. 'Your officer gave chase to my client and then assaulted him.'

'And I'll remind *you* that your client had just stuck a knife in another of my officers,' said Bain. 'The incident you're referring to was actually your client clattering an officer on the head with a slate as the officer popped his head out of a roof hatch.'

'Inspector, my client has suffered a severe injury to his knee and his shoulder as a result of the attentions of one of your men,' said McLintock.

'Your client had the victim of a kidnapping in his bedroom with the probable intention of murdering her,' said Bain. 'And that's in addition to the four murders we intend charging him with. So let's cut out all of this rubbish, shall we?'

Bain looked over at Wilson. He sat there expressionless. Cullen hoped there was no last minute surprise in store to get him off.

'Mr Wilson, I'm going to charge you with the murders of Caroline Adamson, Deborah Curtis, Gail McBride and Kimberly Milne. I hope to God I don't have to add Keith James Miller to that list. I'm also going to charge you with the abduction of Alison Carnegie and the assault on DC Cullen here. Have you got anything to say in your defence?'

Wilson shrugged. 'Nothing.'

There was a knock at the door. Buxton opened it and took a paper message from the uniform on the other side. He moved over and spoke a few words into Bain's ear, but Cullen didn't catch it.

'You do know we've found keys in your flat?' said Bain. 'We've just confirmed they're for the door to the flat belonging to Caroline Adamson.'

McLintock exchanged a look with Wilson. 'Inspector, I'd like to confer with my client in private.'

Bain slowly got to his feet and spoke into the recorder, pausing the interview. He pointed at Buxton by the door. 'He's staying.' He led Cullen and McNeill out. Cullen shut the door behind them.

'What's he doing?' said McNeill.

'I don't think it's good news, Butch' Bain rubbed his moustache. 'He's going to try and whitewash us. This is classic McLintock — he'll try and discredit us, suggest or infer a plant. We've got him with those keys. Any jury's going to convict on those grounds alone.'

'Can't believe he's representing both of them,' said Cullen.

Bain nodded. 'He doesn't give a shite about ethics. He's just after the cash.' He looked at McNeill. 'I want to get a line-up in front of that boy who saw him in the street ASAP, but with this Wilson boy in it instead of Rob Thomson.'

'Will do.'

'All of the circumstantial evidence you've got for Rob backs it up, though,' said Cullen. 'They're dead ringers, especially at a distance.'

'You might be right,' said Bain.

'How do you want to play it?' said McNeill.

'See what he says, I suppose,' said Bain. 'We've got him by the bollocks here.'

Buxton opened the door and nodded at Bain. 'They're ready for you.'

Bain led them back into the room and restarted the interview. 'So Mr Wilson, do you have anything to say?'

'My client would like to say a few words,' said McLintock.

Wilson looked between Bain and McNeill, directly at Cullen. 'I'll admit to the abduction.'

'I'm not accepting that,' said Bain. 'We're throwing the whole book at you.'

Wilson looked at the table. When he looked up, it was at Cullen. 'I'd like to hear what DC Cullen's got to say about all of this. He caught me, after all.'

Bain looked round at Cullen and nodded.

Cullen didn't know what was going on — did Wilson think he was Moriarty and Cullen was Holmes? He took a few seconds to put his thoughts in order. 'You made a couple of mistakes.'

Wilson tilted his head at him. 'I did, did I?'

'The death threats,' said Cullen. 'That was your big mistake. You told us Rob had threatened Caroline. You hoped that would push us towards charging him. It almost worked. But nobody backed you up, though. You made another mistake — you said on the phone Kim Milne told you about the death threats when you'd just killed her.'

'Anything else?' said Wilson.

'The keys we found in your flat,' said Cullen. 'They linked you to all of the murders. But if you hadn't made up the story about the death threats, we'd never have found them. Shame we didn't find the laptops you stole.'

Wilson smirked. 'So why did I do it all, then?'

Cullen took his time, framing his words carefully. 'I think you killed these women to get your revenge on Rob Thomson. He took Kim away from you. You lost your job because of him. And that messed you up.'

He took a deep breath.

'You stalked Caroline on the Schoolbook site, read her private messages. You contacted her posing as Martin Webb and eventually persuaded her to meet you. You used an image from a male model website as the profile photo. You set up a false paper trail that led us nowhere. You bought a Pay As You Go mobile phone, which we traced from CCTV footage. You dressed in clothing that made you look like Rob Thomson if you were spotted.'

He took another deep breath and fiddled with his bandage. 'I'll admit I'm struggling to understand why you killed Gail and Debi.

But you killed Kim Milne to frame it all on Rob Thomson. You wanted him caught red-handed.'

'Very good,' said Wilson. 'Carry on, I'm enjoying this.'

'You could have done a much better job of framing Rob Thomson, though. You didn't leave any DNA evidence linking him to the crimes and you didn't leave a breadcrumb trail on Schoolbook. That would have been the clincher. I wouldn't have doubted your trail if it had led straight to one of Rob's computers. And I wouldn't have doubted the stupid death threats story you'd put out there.'

Wilson burst out laughing. 'I'll remember that for next time I kill someone's girlfriend.'

'Mr Wilson, these allegations are unsubstantiated,' said McLintock. 'You do not have to respond to them until they are laid before you in court, in front of a judge and jury.'

Wilson shrugged. 'I think they've probably got enough on me now.' He stared at Cullen. 'Okay, I did it. I killed them all.' He looked at McLintock. 'I'll save the taxpayer a load of money by not having some long, drawn out court case. Besides, I think Rob's suffering enough now and that was always the main thing. His beloved is dead. I really, really don't care. I can take prison.'

Bain and McNeill shared a look.

'How did you do it?' said McNeill.

'Like Cullen said there, I used Schoolbook,' said Wilson. 'It was actually pretty easy. They were all on there. Everyone I needed, everything I needed. All of this led from Rob.'

'Was this all about revenge?' said Bain.

'Yes.' Wilson twitched slightly. 'Rob took everything I had. My girlfriend, my job, my whole life. And for what? He just wanted to screw Kim, that's all. I was really happy with her, you know? Then Rob Thomson comes swooping in, steals her from me and sacks me.' He took a deep breath.

'How did he sack you?' said McNeill.

'I was on long-term sick from the bank, struggling with what happened.' Wilson rubbed the stubble on his head. 'I had built up a future with her in my head and this bastard steals it all away. One day, I was called in for my catch-up interview — which should have been done at my house — and it turned out it was with Rob. That was totally out of order. I lost it with him. There was another guy there and he had to drag us apart. They had me on a disciplinary by the end of the day. Gave me a month's notice and that was it.'

'Tell me about Caroline,' said McNeill.

'Caroline was the first and the hardest.' Wilson took a sip from the glass of water on the table. Cullen had no doubt Bain would have the glass kept for forensics. 'She was very cagey on Schoolbook. I knew her pretty well — we used to double date a lot, you know. It seems funny now, doesn't it? I set up the Martin Webb profile to snare her. Took a few months but I got to her in the end. The messages got quite racy. I managed to skip a few stages from a traditional relationship. We went straight to meeting in a hotel.'

'And this was to frame Rob?' said Bain.

'Yes' Wilson took another sip. 'Kim was the second easiest. I knew Jenny was going away, so I set that up pretty well. I was hiding in the stairwell, upstairs from their flat, when Rob came in. The police came in just after that. That 999 call was a good effort.'

'Who was the easiest?' said Bain.

Wilson folded his arms. 'That'll be Debi Curtis. She just walked right into it. She actually started it off by flirting with Martin Webb. Caroline and I had the message thing going on and she got involved. She started messaging me. It got pretty intense. I was tempted to let her go, but I thought I should get some practice in.'

'So that was you running away?' said Bain.

Wilson laughed. 'Yeah. Almost got caught there.'

'What about Gail?' said Bain.

Wilson crushed the cup in his fist. 'Gail should have stopped those two getting together. I was disappointed with her. She had always struck me as being someone with morals. She should have stopped Rob and Kim. And she didn't.'

'So you killed her?' said Cullen.

Wilson smirked. 'Yes.'

'And you knew her?' said Cullen.

Wilson laughed. 'No. I never met her in my life until I killed her. But the way Kim talked about her, it felt like I knew her.'

'Why did you go after Alison?' said Cullen.

'She was an insurance policy,' said Wilson. 'You were getting too close. I knew I could get at you through her if things started to go the wrong way.'

'Were you going to kill her?' said Cullen.

'I think so,' said Wilson. 'Probably this evening. Disposing of the body would've been a challenge, but I would have found a way.'

'One thing I don't get,' said Bain, 'is how you managed to do all that stuff on Schoolbook.'

Wilson looked down his nose at Bain. 'That was the easy part. You just run a daemon that tweaks the audit records. The Schoolbook boys do it themselves all the time, usually as practical jokes, or to cover tracks of some illicit activity.'

'What about the CCTV?' said Cullen.

Wilson looked at the ceiling and smiled. 'CCTV. You cops love it. I suggested Gail get Sian to cover for her. I'd seen their messages. You know, they were on there all day at work, chatting when they should have been working. She suggested the cover story about the train. That way I got you looking in entirely the wrong place for a while.'

'That's not what I meant,' said Cullen.

Wilson frowned. 'Well, what did you mean?'

'The CCTV in Tesco,' said Cullen. 'We thought it showed Thomson buying the mobile phone — how did you know he was at Alba Bank Mortgage Centre, not far from the Tesco?'

Wilson nodded. 'Oh, yes. *Very* simple. I called his PA, pretended I worked at the Mortgage Centre, and she told me his itinerary. She didn't even check.'

'So your entire plan was to frame Rob Thomson for all of this?' said Bain.

'It almost worked,' said Wilson.

'Why not just kill him?' said Bain.

'Where's the suffering in that?' Wilson's eyes were on fire as he spoke. 'If I killed him it would've been too quick. If I'd tortured him, it would still be too quick. I lost *everything*. I wanted him to lose everything and have to endure his life without those things.'

93

C ullen sat in the A&E ward, a few hours later. He'd just had another x-ray. Assuming the results were clear he could go home.

McNeill had accompanied him to the hospital. She came over with two cups of coffee from the machine and handed him one. 'I got a call from Bain.'

'And?'

McNeill bit her lip. 'Keith Miller didn't make it.'

Cullen looked at the floor and felt a tear in his eye. 'Stupid bastard.'

McNeill rubbed his shoulder. 'He wasn't the brightest.'

Cullen looked up at her. 'I meant me.'

'It's not your fault,' said McNeill.

'Feels like it is. I'm responsible for his death. I took him there. I should have stayed with Wilson in the living room.'

'Scott, you can't think like that.' She blew on her coffee. 'You caught the bad guy and rescued a damsel in distress. You saved an innocent man from prison. Who knows how many others Wilson might have killed before he got caught?'

'I got a colleague killed in the line of duty,' said Cullen.

McNeill shook her head at him. 'I know it's hard but, really, it's not your fault.'

'I ordered him to come with me.' Cullen rubbed at his forehead. 'I was running around like Billy Big Balls, off on my mental hunt for the real killer.'

'And you got him.'

'I upped the body count by one. Almost by two.'

'Keith was just doing his duty, though,' said McNeill. 'He died being a proper copper for once, you know that. Most of Keith Miller's career, he just pissed about and got away with it. That was the first real piece of police work he'd done.'

'I guess.' It was all he could think of to say. He tasted the coffee. 'I drank this brand when I worked in life insurance, all those years ago. They'd installed a machine upstairs and a few of us would go and get a coffee. I used to get totally wired, but nowadays I drink so much coffee it barely touched the sides.'

She smiled and rubbed at his shoulder.

He looked at her, a tear slicking down his cheek. 'Keith worked in financial services, too. If he'd stuck at it, he'd still be alive.'

'You can't think like that.'

'Can't I?'

'What's the story with this Alison girl?' said McNeill.

Cullen evaded her look. 'There is no story.'

'Come on, there must be. She put on her Schoolbook account she's going out with you.'

'That was Wilson's doing,' said Cullen.

'She must have got the idea from somewhere.'

He looked her in the eye. 'I pulled her on Friday night, okay? A one night stand.'

'I see.'

'She meant less than nothing to me,' said Cullen.

They sat looking at each other for a while, Cullen trying to think of things to say that didn't revolve around Alison Carnegie or Keith Miller.

In the end, it was McNeill who broke the silence. 'Well, this is some drink.'

Cullen frowned. 'Eh?'

'We were supposed to go for a drink after work tonight,' said McNeill.

'Well, once I've got my x-ray back, we could...'

NEXT BOOK

The next Police Scotland book is out now!

"DEVIL IN THE DETAIL"

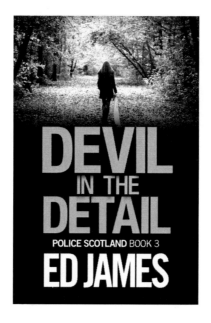

Get it now!

If you would like to be kept up to date with new releases from Ed James and access free novellas, please join the Ed James Readers' Club.

AFTERWORD

Thanks for reading this. I hope you enjoyed it.

Many of the settings in the book are entirely fictional. There is no Alba Bank — the head office is still a derelict sixties monstrosity and the mortgage centre now has a Premier Inn on the site. Leith Walk Station doesn't exist and is still wasteland. Most of the pubs and clubs don't exist either. Most of the websites don't exist either, especially Schoolbook.

The behaviours of the police are entirely fictional.

I published this in April 2012 and it exploded, with over 400,000 downloads. Since going full-time as an author, I decided to redraft it.

Why?

In the first scene, there's a reference to a band called New Order. They're fascinating for so many reasons, but one of the key ones is their repeated remastering and reworking of their back catalogue.

Take *Temptation* for example — one of the two songs in the opening scene to this novel. They recorded it in 1982, when they were just finding their sound after the resurrection of the band in the wake of Ian Curtis' tragic suicide. They reworked it in 1984 (I think), starting again from scratch and that's the version that features on the *Trainspotting* soundtrack that Caroline hears before her death. The second version is astonishing — the flaws of the previous version had been eradicated and the songwriting and technological prowess they'd developed over a few albums allowed the pop genius to come out. They did it again — most notably with the 1994 reworkings of True Faith, Bizarre Love Triangle and 1963, the latter of which had the most interesting genesis, by moving from a b-side to a top twenty single.

Again, why did I do it?

The important thing is that the new world of eBooks allows and enables this reworking — this evening I'll upload this file to Amazon and this remastered version will be the canonical GHOST IN THE MACHINE.

My style has crystalised over the last two years — some of the text in this goes back to 2007 and 2009 when I started writing it. I hired a professional editor for Cullen 4, DYED IN THE WOOL, and I developed my style a lot, even more so since completing BOTTLENECK, Cullen 5.

Fixing GHOST has been itching at the back of my skull. It's a major redraft, losing 15,000 extraneous words in the process and really tightening up the flow. There's a new start to the book but, really, it's nothing drastic.

Reading it back, I'm pretty proud of the novel — my memories of the book had been confused by the twelve or so drafts I'd done over five years and now I've got my head straight with it.

One final thing, if you liked this, then please leave a review on Amazon — it really helps aspiring indie authors like me.

— Ed James
East Lothian, March 2014

ABOUT THE AUTHOR

Ed James is the author of the bestselling DI Simon Fenchurch novels, Seattle-based FBI thrillers starring Max Carter, and the self-published Detective Scott Cullen series and its Craig Hunter spin-off books.

During his time in IT project management, Ed spent every moment he could writing and has now traded in his weekly commute to London in order to write full-time. He lives in the Scottish Borders with far too many rescued animals.

If you would like to be kept up to date with new releases from Ed James, please join the Ed James Readers Club.

Connect with Ed online:

Amazon Author page

Website

OTHER BOOKS BY ED JAMES

DI ROB MARSHALL

Ed's first new police procedural series in six years, focusing on DI Rob Marshall, a criminal profiler turned detective. London-based, an old case brings him back home to the Scottish Borders and the dark past he fled as a teenager.

Also available is FALSE START, a prequel novella starring DS Rakesh Siyal, is available for **free** to subscribers of Ed's newsletter or on Amazon. Sign up at https://geni.us/EJLCFS

POLICE SCOTLAND

Precinct novels featuring detectives covering Edinburgh and its surrounding counties, and further across Scotland: Scott Cullen, eager to climb the career ladder; Craig Hunter, an ex-squaddie struggling with PTSD; Brian Bain, the centre of his own universe and everyone else's. Previously published as SCOTT CULLEN MYSTERIES, CRAIG HUNTER POLICE THRILLERS and CULLEN & BAIN SERIES.

14. THE DEAD END

DS VICKY DODDS

Gritty crime novels set in Dundee and Tayside, featuring a DS juggling being a cop and a single mother.

1. BLOOD & GUTS
2. TOOTH & CLAW
3. FLESH & BLOOD
4. SKIN & BONE
5. GUILT TRIP

DI SIMON FENCHURCH

Set in East London, will Fenchurch ever find what happened to his daughter, missing for the last ten years?

1. THE HOPE THAT KILLS
2. WORTH KILLING FOR
3. WHAT DOESN'T KILL YOU
4. IN FOR THE KILL
5. KILL WITH KINDNESS
6. KILL THE MESSENGER
7. DEAD MAN'S SHOES
8. A HILL TO DIE ON
9. THE LAST THING TO DIE

Other Books

Other crime novels, with Lost Cause set in Scotland and Senseless set in southern England, and the other three set in Seattle, Washington.

- LOST CAUSE
- SENSELESS
- TELL ME LIES
- GONE IN SECONDS
- BEFORE SHE WAKES

DEVIL IN THE DETAIL

PROLOGUE

Four slices of toast smoothly emerged from the polished steel Dualit toaster and Elaine Gibson tossed them into the clean, white ceramic toast rack. She put another four slices on then put the rack on the dining table. She sat down with her mug of coffee and set about spreading crunchy peanut butter on the wholemeal toast.

She yelled upstairs. 'Thomas! Mandy! Can you hurry up?'

She took a bite of toast and sat looking out of the kitchen window, across the lawn at the Hopetoun Monument perched on one of the hills overlooking Garleton, ominous rainclouds looming in the west.

Her husband, Charles, came into the room, tying his necktie. 'Morning,' he said.

'There's coffee in the pot,' she said.

'Ah, toast today. Good. I'm starving.'

He poured a cup of coffee and started whistling. He sat down and buttered the toast, reaching for the jar of Marmite. The second batch of toast slowly emerged from the guts of the machine.

'Kids not up yet?' he said.

Elaine shook her head. 'It's your turn today.'

'I'll have my breakfast then I'll get on to them.'

'Fine.'

She finished her toast then added the new slices to the rack. She refilled her mug with coffee.

Thomas wandered in, mumbling something that might have been 'Morning.' He immediately set about the toast, gulping through two thickly buttered slices. Elaine almost castigated him again for not chewing but decided it would just fall on deaf ears.

'Have you seen your sister?' she said.

'No,' said Thomas, through a mouthful of slice three.

'Charles...'

Gibson raised his hands as he stood up. 'Fine, I'll get her.' He left the room, heading upstairs.

'Won't be back till seven tonight,' said Thomas. 'Got ATC.'

'Okay.' Air Training Corps was Charles's idea to get some discipline into the boy. They, like many of their friends, had decided to send their children to the local comprehensive, the best in the area and at least equivalent to the private schools in Edinburgh, but they were determined he would get the same standard of extra-curricular activity.

'Any more toast?' said Thomas.

She reached over and put another two slices into the machine.

Gibson burst into the room. She turned to face him.

'She's gone,' said Gibson, locking eyes with her.

'You're sure?' she said.

Thomas looked up at them.

'Yes,' said Gibson. 'I checked all the rooms upstairs. Nothing. And the front door's locked.' He went over to the back door and tried it.

'I'll look in the conservatory,' she said.

She rushed into the hall then into the conservatory, pulling her dressing gown tighter as the bitterly cold air hit her arms. She tried the French doors. Locked.

She checked the large cupboards in the hall, stuffed with shoes and coats but not hiding her daughter. She went back into the kitchen.

'It's locked,' she said.

'Same with the back door,' said Gibson. 'The utility room is empty, too.'

She let out a deep sigh. 'Not again,' she said, her voice a murmur.

Gibson held her shoulder. 'Don't worry, I'm sure she'll be fine.'
'Do you think she's gone to Susan's again?' she said.
Gibson nodded. 'I'll check.'

~

Morag Tattersall opened the gate beside the gatehouse at
Balgone Ponds and walked through as though she owned the
place. She led her greyhounds, Meg and Mindy, along what she
still considered a public footpath.

The owners of the place — the *new* owners — had unilaterally
taken the decision to block off the path and turn it into their
garden. This irritated Morag and her neighbours in the cottages
around the corner.

Every day she used the path to walk a series of dogs around the
ponds, until *they* moved in. The only other way was through the
hedge behind the gatehouse but she didn't want to cut her jacket
or the dogs' paws on the hawthorn.

She thought about leaving the gate open but decided against
such pettiness. Besides, it looked like they were away. She closed it
and marched on.

She breathed in the fresh early morning air and powered on
down the path. The dogs were pulling on their leads — she tugged
them to the side and they obeyed. The sun was just beginning to
rise from its winter slumber, appearing over the slight hills in the
middle distance. The trees were bare and the path damp under-
foot as it led down to the ponds.

She came to the downward slope and let the dogs off, putting
their leather leads in her jacket pocket. They set off slowly — tails
raised, heads combing the ground for trails, their muscular thighs
bouncing along like they were shadowboxing before a fight, occasionally stopping and sniffing at a patch of ground.

As she overtook them, her thoughts turned to her itinerary —
a yoga class in North Berwick in an hour and a half, then meeting
Liz for lunch afterwards. She was looking forward to both.

Morag continued down the path descending to the level of the
ponds. She walked on for a minute or so, lost in thoughts of
getting around to Andrew's laundry and taking Meg to the vet for
her boosters.

She couldn't see the dogs. 'Meg! Mindy!'

She looked back the way she'd come. There was no sign of them. They'd no doubt seen a rabbit and run off after it. They'd only caught one once — she'd had to pull Mindy away from the squealing animal — but they'd given chase countless times. She turned back and retraced her steps.

She climbed the rise back to where she let them off. To the left, away from the pond, another path ran along the higher ground. She could see movement through the trees, grey like Mindy.

'Mindy!'

There was a rustling. Mindy raced through, coming right up to Morag. She grabbed her collar and put her back on the lead.

'Meg!'

Morag marched through the trees in the direction Mindy had come. She spotted Meg sniffing at a spot between two trees a few metres apart, in front of a row of rhododendrons.

'Meg, stop that.'

Meg turned around, looked at Morag then went back to her sniffing.

Morag paced over to her and grabbed her collar. 'Bad girl.'

Mindy started pulling on her lead while Morag fiddled with Meg's collar.

Mindy lurched forward, almost pulling Morag's arm out of the socket, digging with her front paws at a patch of loose earth.

'Stop!'

The dog ignored her.

Morag saw some pink cloth. She gasped, letting go of the leads. Kneeling down, she joined in digging.

She scraped around the cloth, revealing an arm.

Morag rocked back on her heels, reaching into her pocket and fumbling with her mobile phone.

～

DEVIL IN THE DETAIL is out now. You can get a copy at Amazon. I hope you enjoy it!

Manufactured by Amazon.ca
Acheson, AB